# eleanor

Jason Gurley is the author of *Greatfall*, *The Man Who Ended the World* and the fiction collection *Deep Breath Hold Tight*, among other works. His stories have appeared in Lightspeed Magazine and the anthologies *Loosed Upon the World* and *Help Fund My Robot Army!!!*. He was raised in Alaska and Texas, and now lives and writes in Portland, Oregon.

# eleanor

## JASON GURLEY

**HARPER**
Voyager

HarperVoyager
An imprint of HarperCollinsPublishers
1 London Bridge Street
London SE1 9GF

www.harpervoyagerbooks.co.uk

This paperback edition 2017
1

First published in Great Britain by HarperVoyager 2016

Copyright © Jason Gurley 2014, 2016

Jason Gurley asserts the moral right to
be identified as the author of this work

Originally self-published as a paperback and ebook
in a slightly different form in 2014

A catalogue record for this book
is available from the British Library

ISBN: 978-0-00-813294-1

Printed and bound in Australia by Griffin Press

Find out more about HarperCollins and the environment at
**www.harpercollins.co.uk/green**

*For Felicia and Emma—all the muches*

*Time is a river, and it flows in a circle.*

—UNKNOWN

*prologue*

1962

# eleanor

S he sits in the breakfast nook and watches the rain. It falls with purpose, as if it has a consciousness, as if it intends to eradicate the earth, layer by layer. The front lawn is hard to make out in the downpour, but Eleanor can already see that the topsoil has been churned into mud. Her flowers bend sideways, petals yanked off by the storm. By afternoon only the thorny rose stems will remain.

"A little rough out there," Hob says, sliding into the nook, across the table from her.

Eleanor loves Sunday mornings, but particularly rainy ones like this. It's why Hob built the nook for her last year, one of the few things he'd crafted for her during their marriage that was truly useful. He had made other attempts with less success: the rotating spice rack that wouldn't rotate; the bookshelves in the den, which were lovely but intimidatingly large and which remain embarrassingly empty. The nook, however, gives Eleanor a sense of place. It isn't much to look at, merely a slim table jutting from the wall, flanked by short benches just wide enough for a single person on each side. At first Eleanor thought it presumptuous that Hob had made two benches—she was possessive of her mornings, of the quiet before her day became a thing owned by her five-year-old daughter—but Hob rarely joined her, somehow understanding that he wasn't building a table for their little family but a one-person submersible, a vessel for a woman who would happily sink to the bottom of the ocean and reside there, alone, for the rest of her days, content with the view.

Eleanor watches the rain fall outside and agrees. "Indeed."

"Rougher than usual," Hob adds. He sips his tea with the faintest slurp.

Eleanor cringes, just a bit, but Hob notices.

"Sorry," he says. "Habit."

She knows. It's what he says each time. She searches immediately for something to say next. If she doesn't, he'll take her silence as an invitation to explain the habit, and he'll tell her again of his years during the Korean War, the food he'd developed a fondness for (though he knew he shouldn't have), the customs he'd observed and, in some cases, unconsciously adopted, such as the practice of slurping audibly to indicate one's pleasure or appreciation for a dish.

"Do you think it will clear?" she asks, cupping her tea in her hands to warm them. Her fingers are reedy and slim and envelop the mug. Her mother had wished her to play the piano, citing her fingers as the sole reason, but Eleanor had never felt music in her bones. She had tried, for a time, to please her mother. No—she had tried for *years* to please her mother. But after a few weeks of plinks and clanks on the old upright piano in the hallway, Eleanor had admitted defeat. Her mother had left the keys exposed, the wooden cover open, for the rest of her life, the dust gathering on the ivory a sort of tribute to her disappointment in Eleanor. Years later, when her mother had died unexpectedly, she came home to find Hob sitting proudly in their own living room, tinkering with the piano.

Even in death, Eleanor wasn't free of her mother's criticisms.

"News report says three days of this. Maybe we should stay in this afternoon," Hob adds.

Almost hopefully, Eleanor notices.

She shakes her head. "No," she says. "We don't—"

"We don't stay in," Hob says, completing her familiar sentiment. "I know."

She lifts her tea but stops short of drinking it. She can feel her shoulders drawing tight, the way they do when an attack comes on. She flexes her fingers, her knuckles crackling like wax paper.

It had been such a nice morning.

"Ellie," Hob says, but already she can barely hear him. He's gentle, attuned to the signs. "Ellie, look at me, please."

He repeats himself three times before Eleanor finds the strength to lift her eyes. She meets his only for a moment, then looks away. She wasn't always this way. It isn't that she worries Hob will grow tired of these small breakdowns, or of her, and take Agnes and leave Eleanor to her unhappiness; it's that she doesn't like the protective instinct that her attacks bring out in him. His voice changes, his eyes soften, and he takes her hand and cradles it, as if he could somehow save her . . .

"We don't stay in," Hob repeats.

She nods and takes a deep breath, her first in a long moment. It comes in a gasp, and her tears spill over with the force of it. Embarrassed, Eleanor turns away from her husband, willing herself to evaporate.

"Ellie," Hob whispers. He takes her cup of tea, puts it aside, and slides his hands over her own. They are warm and unyielding, as if his skin sheathes bones of iron. His thumbs find the soft skin between her own thumbs and index fingers, and he rubs lightly, waiting for her to relax in his grasp.

He has, of course, tried to convince her to see someone. Eleanor did, once, and Hob had offered to join her. She'd refused, but she sat in the doctor's leathery office, aware of Hob's presence in the waiting room beyond the oak door. Of course he wouldn't press his ear to that door and eavesdrop. If their positions were reversed, she would have, however, and what would she have heard Hob say to this doctor, this stranger?

"Shortness of breath?" the doctor had asked her. "Muscle tension? Mental distraction?"

She looked down at her hands and nodded. Yes, to each of those things. Hearing them described so simply should have robbed them of their power, she thought; they were only words. But instead, she felt as if she should defend them. *No,* she should say. *It's so much more. They're so much bigger than just those words.*

"Can you describe what you're feeling? Not medically," the doctor clarified. "Just . . . tell me as if you're telling a child. Close your eyes. What do you feel when it happens?"

What had she answered? She couldn't remember. And would it have mattered what she said to a man who did not, could not, have possibly understood what she felt?

Sunday afternoons were everything to Eleanor. Without them, she thought she might die.

Hob strokes her hands now, reminding her to breathe, and she does, taking the air in until she stabilizes. He says again, "We don't stay in," and it has the desired effect. She gives all her attention to her breathing now; each long, slow, outward breath restores her just a little more. She feels a flush of shame, as she always does, and takes her hands away from him. She doesn't want to look at him, but she does, and he is staring kindly, warmly back at her.

Eleanor pushes the tears away with the heels of her palms, as if they're evidence of a crime she is embarrassed to have committed. She glances at her husband again, wondering at this man who loves her so, who so patiently endures her ridiculousness.

"I'm sorry," she says. Her voice is thick and hardly sounds like her own. "I'm sorry, it's—"

"Hush," Hob says. "You've nothing to apologize for."

This man, she thinks. She finds him handsome, almost impossibly, ruggedly so, and she feels a fresh rise of guilt at her own appearance. She's put on weight in the last few months—not enough to change how he looks at her, not yet, but enough that she feels it. She feels larger on the outside than on the inside, as if her body is trying to permanently fasten her to the earth. She wonders now and again if Hob understands why they don't sleep together as much as they once did. Instead, she makes excuses to stay up late, and sometimes he wakes her, having crept downstairs to find her tucked into a ball on the sofa, awash in the light of the television's off-the-air program card, the national anthem warbling quietly in the dark.

"I bet you wish you knew how to fix me," Eleanor says. It's supposed to be a joke, but Hob looks offended.

"I *adore* you," he insists.

She starts to tell him that she loves him, but from the doorway comes the sound of small feet. Hob lights up and turns and beams at the little girl standing there, dark hair in need of a brush, too-large nightgown floating around her like a halo. She crosses the kitchen and clambers up onto the bench beside her mother, just small enough to squeeze in.

"Sit on your father's side, Agnes," Eleanor says. "Please."

Agnes protests but falls quiet when she sees her mother's face. She slides down from the bench, then climbs up onto the opposite one. Hob bundles her into his arms.

"Breakfast, Ags?" Hob says. "What would the little lady like?"

"Cinnamon toast!" Agnes says, patting her palms on the tabletop.

"Oh, Hob, I'll take care of it," Eleanor says, but he shakes his head and waves her off—as Eleanor knew he would—and goes to the bread box and the stuck-fast spice rack and stands there, assembling his daughter's breakfast, turned away from them both. The three of them settle back into Hob's stage play, everybody back on script, a family happily gathered together in the cozy, bright kitchen while the storm rumbles outside.

Eleanor wishes she were out there.

"Mama," Agnes says, tapping on the table with her little fingers. "I've made up my mind. I'm going swimming with you today."

"Oh? And what about *that*?" Eleanor asks, pointing at the rain. "And stop drumming on the table."

"Oh," Agnes says, crestfallen. Then she brightens. "Well, I'll just swim under the water instead."

"There you go," Hob says over his shoulder. "It's all just water."

"It's all just water, all just water," Agnes repeats, singing the words. "But, really, I want to come!"

"I know you do," Eleanor says. "Tell you what: Maybe we'll go to the city pool after. It's indoors, out of the storm. Maybe Marjorie will be there. What do you say?"

"No, no, no," Agnes says. "The ocean!"

"No," Eleanor says. "And don't ask again."

Agnes's smile fades, and her eyes glisten darkly.

"Ocean's too dangerous for little girls," Hob says, turning to show Agnes a plate with three slices of bread prepared for toasting. "How's this?"

Agnes inspects the buttered bread and the fine layer of cinnamon and sugar sprinkled on top. She points at one of the slices. "This one is sad," she says. "It only has a little cinnamon."

Eleanor watches Hob swirl back to the kitchen. With a flourish he dashes more cinnamon onto the impoverished piece of bread, and then Agnes leaps up to help him arrange the slices on the baking pan and slide it under the broiler.

Eleanor watches Agnes, a tiny knot of energy beside Hob. One day, of course, in Agnes's future, Hob and Eleanor will be gone. Hob, the gentle giant of a man who taught her how to navigate the world with confidence, who was always a source of strength, a wellspring of love: That's almost certainly how Agnes will remember her father.

How will Agnes remember Eleanor?

She thinks about this for a moment, but the rain is a messenger with news of the sea. Eleanor closes her eyes and imagines she is there.

DESPITE THE STEADY rain, the ocean is warmer in the early afternoon. This is a relative term; *warmer* does not mean that the water is warm, only a few degrees less cold than it is in the morning. Eleanor stands in the shallows, impatient to begin, wearing the thermal wet suit that Hob ordered for her. She always feels restricted in the suit, at least until she's submerged and it begins to flex with her movements.

Each Sunday afternoon, at two o'clock, Eleanor and Hob drive down to the shore. The Pacific spreads wide and gray before them like a rippling, dark parachute. Behind them, their little town of Anchor Bend goes about its own routines. The first wave of fishing trawlers returns at this time, chugging into port a few miles up the coast, trailing inky belches of oily black smoke. The fishing lanes are crowded, and the patchwork sound of collision horns becomes nearly constant.

It is Eleanor's favorite time of the week. Hob leaves Agnes at Marjorie's house and accompanies Eleanor for her afternoon swim, rain or shine. It's the only day he's free from work, and he's always been uncomfortable with the idea of Eleanor swimming alone.

Hob says, "Hold up a second, there," as if Eleanor is about to plunge into the sea without him. She looks over her shoulder, shielding her eyes from the glare of the bright gray sky, and watches him cross the gravelly beach to the pier. He is fully dressed and carries a waterproof duffel bag, inside which are Eleanor's clothes and a short stack of fat, fluffy towels. Hob's boots echo on the short pier, heavy and hollow. She loves the sound, although she privately wishes he would permit her to swim alone, even just now and then.

Eleanor crouches and inspects the water at her feet. It's clearer than usual, even with the rain dancing on the surface. She watches a tiny crab pick its way over the pebbles, its delicate shell wobbling upon its back. It passes her toes, almost touching her, and then moves along into deeper water.

Eleanor flexes her toes, digging deeply into the cool sand beneath the layer of smooth stones. She's ready to go.

"Come on now, Hob," she calls.

"All right, already," comes his faint reply.

She squints and watches as he pulls at the lashes that keep the old rowboat moored to the dock. It isn't their boat, but it's been there for as long as either of them can remember. It belongs to the town now, which means that sometimes when the two of them come to the beach, the boat isn't there, and on those days Hob cancels the afternoon swim altogether. She argues with him, but he's resolute: Without the boat, he can't be there to assist her, and to Hob, that's a risk too great to accept. "I won't have Aggie grow up without her mother," he said to Eleanor in the beginning, after watching her battle her way back to shore against an unexpectedly strong undertow.

She had begged him to buy a small boat, then, so that Sunday afternoons at the beach weren't at the mercy of some community-use vessel. He'd refused that as well, explaining that it wasn't practical to buy a boat that would only be used once a week. Or maybe he thought she might abscond with it and drift away forever, contentedly lost at sea.

"Come on!" she shouts again.

But he's got it now. He throws the duffel down into the boat, then steps aboard himself. By the time he settles in and grips the oars, Eleanor is already away, fifty yards offshore, stroking hard against the current.

IN HER YOUNGER days, Eleanor was a competitive swimmer. As the star member of the high school swim team, she set district and state records in freestyle events. She'd attended Oregon State on an athletic scholarship, where her coach talked about entering her in an Olympics qualifying event, but Eleanor never made it that far. At nineteen, she had already met and fallen in love with Hob, despite their nearly twenty-year age difference. She began to miss practices, then swim meets. She married Hob between freshman and sophomore year, and then Agnes arrived, a slow and steady swell that began small and built into a wave that crashed over Eleanor's academic career.

For a time, Eleanor hardly noticed what she had lost. Hob was charming and older and wise. He had cheered at her events and even liked to come to her practices. He would sit high in the bleachers and watch as she carved through the pool, the water collapsing into her wake. Afterward he would take her to dinner, and then they would go to his place—a real house, not a dorm. That first year was almost magical.

When Agnes was born, Eleanor transformed before Hob's eyes, from just a girl herself into a mother. Her body changed, responding well to the pregnancy and the early months of breast-feeding and healing. For Hob, nothing could be better. Eleanor knew that he was the happiest he would ever be, the conquering soldier returned home, finally able to build a family from such promising raw materials.

Eleanor didn't feel the water's quiet tug again until Agnes was nearly two. By then, Eleanor had given up her own dreams and settled contentedly into this new chapter of her life. Agnes was a lovely child. She picked up words quickly. She furrowed her brow like a small, grumpy old man, reducing Eleanor and Hob to laughter. Theirs was a happy home, and Eleanor was proud to be a better mother than her own.

One evening they went to Hob's sister's house for dinner and returned along the winding, dark Highway 101, high along the coastal cliffs. The sea sparkled under a fat moon, and Eleanor fell into a trance as the waves rolled lazily below. Lying in bed that night, Agnes finally snoring softly in the corner crib, Eleanor nudged Hob and said, "I want to swim again."

The college pool had been closed for repairs, the municipal pool was stuffed with children and teenagers, and Hob had been ready to throw in the towel when Eleanor suggested Splinter Beach. He resisted at first, muttering about sharks and frigid water and such, but Eleanor pooh-poohed all these excuses. That day, Hob stood on the shore, watching, as Eleanor swam parallel to the land, reveling in the slow suck of the tide at her belly, the taste of salt upon her lips. *This* was swimming. The sea took her in like a surrogate parent.

Hob thought that she should return to competition. "You're only twenty-three," he said after taking her home that day. "Twenty-three isn't too old for the Olympics. You could still try."

"I'm not sure," Eleanor said. "It was nice just to be in the water. And I've lost years of training already. Nobody's going to remember me. They're all years ahead of me now. They've been swimming and winning medals while—" She had stopped short of finishing her thought: *while I've been mashing up bananas for a two-year-old*.

But Hob persisted, and one afternoon they left Agnes with Marjorie and drove to Oregon State. Eleanor met with her former coach, who echoed her own arguments: "Motherhood weakens a woman," he said to her. "It isn't the woman's fault. Women have babies, and the world moves on without them. It's a shame, too, Els. You were really good."

"She can do it," Hob said. He'd been so committed to the idea that Eleanor tried—for his sake—to make a go of it. She swam at a local event, in a fifty-meter freestyle, and placed dead last. Hob encouraged her not to give up—"It's just your first event back, you'll get back into the swing of it"—but Eleanor had already had enough. The battle wasn't in her blood anymore.

The sea was.

Driving back from that swim meet, Hob said, "Summer Games are two years away. You can practice hard, but that's too soon. So—what? You train for the next one, in sixty-eight. Yeah?"

"I'll be almost thirty," Eleanor said. "Nobody medals at thirty, Hob."

"So you're too old to swim," Hob said. "Are you too old to dive?"

ELEANOR LEANS INTO each stroke. The waves diminish as she puts distance between herself and the mainland. She can't hear the horns bellowing in the port lanes anymore. The sound of the waves in her ears is too close, too loud. She loves the sound. It's almost a part of her, her momentum stripping molecules of water from the ocean. The water clings to her skin. Her arms break the surface.

She turns her head, sucks in a breath, drops her face into the sea again.

Hob rows a safe distance away, giving the oars a long, lazy pull now and then, matching Eleanor's pace.

He loves her. She knows that he's different. She can't think of a single man in her life who ever demonstrated an interest in a woman's dreams. In her cooking, yes. In her figure, of course. But what man would insert himself into a woman's heart and embrace the things that moved her most deeply? Hob is unique, and she supposes this is why she loves him, even if the dreams he took an interest in were dreams she'd already given up.

But here, in the ocean, the water sluicing over her face, the briny tang of the sea filling her nose, she imagines what it might be like to return to a distant time, to the days before she met Hob. Knowing what she knows now—knowing his love and the sparkle of her daughter's eyes—would Eleanor make the same decisions? Would she allow herself to fall in love?

As she swims, she glances in Hob's direction. He's a good man: quiet and patient and gentle.

She dives beneath the surface for a few strokes, kicking to a depth at which she knows she cannot be seen from above. And only there, where the light begins to dim and the warmer surface water turns abruptly cold, does she permit herself to answer the question.

ELEANOR IS NOT a natural diver. She learned this early, standing atop the island cliff for the first time. The fifty-foot drop was significantly higher than any competitive diving platform. The island, called Huffnagle, was, on all sides but one, a disaster zone, its shallows a minefield of broken rock. But if a girl was to go ashore, and if she was to discover the gnarled path that led to the top of the island, she might find that the side of the island that faced the Pacific horizon also overlooked a deep blue cove mostly free of skull-shattering rocks.

That first day, Hob had rowed the little boat into the cove and drawn close to the cliff, where he waited, craning his neck to see her high above. It had taken her forever to gather her courage and actually dive, and when she did, her dive was formless, like a crumpled origami pattern. Despite weeks of practice on the high boards at the municipal pool, she had hit the water like a child pushed down a flight of stairs.

"You were never a gymnast," her coach had cautioned when Eleanor told him that Hob was encouraging her to explore diving. "Swimmers don't make good divers. Gymnasts and ballerinas, surprisingly enough, *do*. And you have a swimmer's build, Eleanor. Do not get your hopes up. Please."

Now, a full season later, her dives are fluid, clean. Hob believes she has promise, but she knows she will never be a competitive diver. She is good out here, on the cliff, but in a regulation pool, with professionally trained athletes vaulting from the limber boards, she would be outmatched. So while Hob encourages her, praising her form and her grace, Eleanor simply learns to enjoy the sensation of flight, that moment of weightlessness before gravity snatches her out of the sky. After each dive, she swims around the island to the beach, then goes ashore, climbs the path, and repeats the routine. On a good afternoon, when it isn't too cold, when the water isn't too hard, she might dive a dozen times.

But on a great afternoon, she lingers in the water between dives, swimming the long way around the island. On those days she might dive four times, maybe as many as six, which is never enough for Hob but is more than enough for her.

SHE EVENTUALLY TOLD Hob that he had to stop hoping, that she would never be a competitive diver. To his credit, he adjusted his expectations and stopped trying to coax greatness from her. "We don't have to go to the island anymore at all," he said. "You can just swim." So, most times, that's what they did. But on other days,

Eleanor herself suggested they go out to Huffnagle again, and she would dive a time or two, just to relive those fleeting moments when she almost floated above the entire world, untouchable.

Instead of commenting on Eleanor's form, Hob just waits in the boat, reading a book or his newspaper, like a parent waiting patiently for his child to wear herself out on the playground equipment. He has found the right spot to hover in the boat, where the slow ocean swells keep him pinned to the cliff wall. He can turn his pages without worrying that he'll drift away.

This day the rain has made reading difficult, so Hob sits beneath his umbrella, watching Eleanor's dives more carefully than usual. Her first dive is graceful—maybe the best yet. But he doesn't say so; he just watches her swim back to the beach. If he is honest, he might admit to himself that he prefers this to coaching her: huddling in the boat in his raincoat, enjoying the damp smell of the cliff beside him, watching the occasional fish break the surface. A quarter mile out, seven or eight seagulls bob on the water, unconcerned about the rain.

Eleanor dives again, then smiles at him before swimming around the rocks. It usually takes about seven or eight minutes for her to go ashore and reach the top of the cliff, so this time, when more than ten minutes go by, he tilts his head back and looks up at the cliff. She isn't there. He calls her name, and she answers—but her voice is smaller than it should be.

Hob grabs the oars and begins to row.

1963

# eleanor

Eleanor sits in the breakfast nook and watches the rain fall. The tree that Hob and Agnes planted two summers ago bends sideways with the wind. Even from here Eleanor can see the earth around its base beginning to pucker. If the storm gets much worse, the tree won't survive.

She can hear the rain lashing the house with each gust of wind. Up above, the attic moans like a Coke bottle as the wind whistles through the rafters.

"No swimming today," Eleanor says aloud.

She's surprised to have spoken the words but more surprised that they crossed her mind at all. She and Hob haven't gone to the ocean since the accident, which was minor enough. A misstep on the island path, a twisted ankle. Normally that sort of thing would have kept her out of the water for a couple of days, no more.

But Eleanor had turned up pregnant again. And that, according to her doctor, made swimming in the ocean a no-no.

"And no throwing yourself off cliffs, either," he advised upon learning why Eleanor was at Huffnagle in the first place. "I'm surprised you're *still* pregnant, to be quite honest. That kind of pounding can terminate a pregnancy in a heartbeat."

Hob had babbled on the way home about having a son, but Eleanor barely heard him.

Pregnant.

*Again.*

Sometimes Eleanor swore her life was being written by someone else's hand. Certainly it wasn't Eleanor's. Maybe Hob's. Maybe Agnes's, even—she'd asked not six weeks earlier for a little brother or sister.

"And we can call her Patricia," Agnes had pronounced. "Or Patrick!"

Eleanor sips her tea now and sighs. She does this an awful lot now, the air pushed worriedly out of her lungs by the weight of her thoughts. Dark, awful, guilty thoughts. A few nights before, she dreamed about a man who had bothered her at the grocery store. He had been holding a clipboard and a pen, and instinctively she had tried to step past him. He'd said, "I'll see you on the way out," and let her pass, and she had forgotten about him. But he was there when she finished shopping, and this time as she tried to slide by, he said, "Vote for Eleanor," and she stopped.

"Excuse me?"

"Eleanor," the man repeated. "The town is voting on her issue."

"What issue?" Eleanor asked.

"It's simple," the man said, folding back one of the pages on the clipboard and holding it up for her to see. There were two big words on the page: *Yes* and *No*. Below each word was a list of names, some scrawled illegibly, some in neat cursive. "Either Eleanor can start over, or Eleanor can stay in prison."

"Prison?"

"Right," the man said without explaining further.

"But—but *I'm* Eleanor."

"Oh!" the man said. "Well, then, you definitely should consider voting. Right now it's a tie. You'll be the tiebreaker!"

"Isn't voting a private affair? This looks like a petition to me."

"Not at all," the man said. "But bananas eat for free on Thursday afternoons."

"What?" Eleanor asked.

"I said, you'd better hurry and vote, because I think you're about to wake up."

But she had woken from the dream before she'd had time to cast her ballot. The dream has remained with her since, her brain working on the question of her vote—while she makes dinner for Hob and Agnes, while she washes dishes, while she sits in the bathtub, the deepest water she's been in for months.

She mourns the sea. At night, when Hob sleeps, Eleanor listens and can almost hear the sound of the surf, small and distant.

Prison.

She tells Hob that her hormones are all over the place, and that's why he catches her crying so often these days. He believes her, she thinks. She can't remember if she was this way when she carried Agnes.

Eleanor rubs her belly idly as the storm worsens. She's showing now—not much, but enough that strangers have begun complimenting her when she goes to town. She and Hob haven't made love since they found out. She hasn't been in the mood, and he's been worried about hurting the baby—something she thought he'd figured out during her first pregnancy.

She's grateful that preparations for the new baby seem to have distracted Hob and Agnes. She worries that those terrible, guilty thoughts are readable on her face. Her attacks come all the time now, but she finds quiet, dark places—such as the closet floor, behind Hob's hanging shirts and sweaters—and cries there, where nobody can see her.

She hears Agnes upstairs, asking her father if the baby can sleep in her bed when it comes.

At least someone is excited.

SHE SLIPS OUT of the house, furtively, before Hob or Agnes wake. The sky is dim and growing darker. She sits behind the wheel of the Ford and stares up at the clouds, leaning forward to see them through the windshield. They're ominous and dark, almost black. She wonders what the view from above the clouds is like. She thinks that it's probably all blue skies and sunshine up there, unlike life down here in Anchor Bend.

The rain bangs on the Ford like a bag of rocks in a tumble dryer. Eleanor drives slowly, both hands tight on the wheel, the only thing moving for miles. None of the shops is yet open. There are no pedestrians on the sidewalks. Days like this feel a bit like the end of the world. Everything is still and murky and slow.

Like a magnet, she is drawn to the ocean. She parks the truck in the small lot beside the beach and kills the engine and turns off the wipers. Rain courses down the windshield in waves. In the distance she can see the shape of Huffnagle, blurred by the rain until it's only a cottony shadow.

Eleanor closes her eyes and quiets herself. The world is made of water. It falls upon the Ford, the asphalt lot, the beach stones, comforting her. The ocean has some life today, every wave a low roar as it breaks on the beach. Chaos up here, but below the water, she knows, there is only quiet. Peace. Like the sky above the clouds. Like a moment of weightlessness.

When Eleanor opens her eyes again, she has made up her mind. She leaves the keys in the ignition, opens the door, and steps out into the rain. In an instant she is soaking wet, her nightgown and housecoat clinging to her swollen body.

Another pickup truck is parked at the opposite end of the small lot. The only other person in the world arrived at the beach while Eleanor's eyes were closed. She can see the shape of the driver inside, perhaps enjoying the weather.

The beach stones are black and wet and shiny. Eleanor crosses them slowly, though she isn't worried about slipping and falling down. Two sandpipers putter around, dipping their beaks into the sand after each receding wave. The distant clouds pull apart like taffeta, feathery black tendrils separating from their bodies.

Eleanor walks to the edge of the beach and stands there for a moment in her heavy, wet housecoat. The waves are needle-sharp, crisp and hard against her ankles and feet. She closes her eyes again, hands deep in her pockets, and thinks of Hob and his pleasant smile and his broad shoulders and secrets and his carefully parted slick hair and his deep, true eyes. She thinks of Agnes and her knotted hair and the premature wrinkle lines around her own sad, dark eyes.

Eleanor knows those eyes. They're her own.

Agnes will be better off. Hob will see to that.

Eleanor pulls her housecoat off, sleeve by sleeve. It grabs at her skin, resisting, but she casts it onto the beach. She bends over and grasps the hem of her nightgown, the wet flannel squishy between her fingers. She gathers it into her fists, lifts it up and over her head, then casts it aside and faces the ocean, naked. The rain is bitingly cold, the wind worse. She can barely swallow. It's hard to breathe. Her shoulders and hands are tight, her head pounding. This is the moment when Hob would reach for her, would soothe her.

Behind her she hears the muffled *snick* of the other truck's door opening. A distant male voice shouts something unintelligible.

Eleanor doesn't answer, doesn't look back.

She steps into the ocean and strides forward, the water reaching her knees, then her hips. Her panic dissolves the deeper she goes. The sea beckons her, as if it alone knows her.

She's home.

When she's waded in waist deep, she spreads her arms wide and lunges forward into the water, and she begins to swim and swim and swim.

*part one*

1985

# agnes

The twins are six years old—just weeks away from their shared birthday—when it happens.

Agnes rushes about the house, looking for her rain boots.

"Esme," she huffs as she climbs the stairs. "Ellie—have either of you seen my galoshes?"

"They're called rain boots, Mom!" Esmerelda shouts. "Galoshes are the things you wear over your shoes."

"Those are called overshoes," Agnes says.

"No, they're—"

"Just—" Agnes pauses on the landing, breathing hard. "Stop. Just stop."

Esmerelda stands in the doorway of the girls' bedroom. She shrugs, then squeezes past her mother and walks to the bathroom.

"Where's your sister?" Agnes asks.

"Attic," Esmerelda says, as if it should be obvious, and she shuts the bathroom door.

Agnes raps on the door with her knuckles. "Make it fast in there. Your father's going to be waiting at the airport for us."

"Whatever," Esmerelda says, her voice muffled by the door.

Agnes pounds the door sharply with her fist. "Young lady, you're too young for 'whatever.' Save it until you're thirteen. What are you doing in there?"

Esmerelda doesn't answer. Agnes turns and leans against the wall and presses her fists against her eyes and drops her mouth open in a hushed scream. Then she straightens up, pushes off the wall, and unclenches her hands slowly, stretching her narrow fingers wide until they tingle slightly. She takes a deep breath, then exhales.

"One thing at a time," she says softly. "One thing, one thing."

She stands there for a moment, almost swaying on her feet, eyes still closed. Then she takes a deep, calming breath, opens her eyes, and goes to the attic door.

"Ellie!" she shouts up the stairs. "You'd better be ready!"

# eleanor

Eleanor sits alone in her father's workshop, studying the unfinished model house. It's dim in the attic. The rain has turned the outside world a pleasant gray. She prefers days like this to any other kind—no sunshine, just rain. At age six, her favorite word is *inclement*. She uses it whenever she can, having learned it from her first school closure of the year. Today can certainly be described as inclement.

But the light spilling through the circular window at the far end of the attic is too pale, too far removed from the workbench, and Eleanor cannot see the details of her father's latest project. Reluctantly she reaches up to the lamp and switches it on. A warm orange glow floods the work space, and the small house before her casts a long brown shadow across the table.

She can see the house clearly now and can almost pick out the last part her father painted: a hardened dollop of blue paint lurks beneath one tiny windowsill. She can picture his careful, deliberate brushstroke. He would have realized that he had too much paint on the brush. Under ordinary circumstances, he would have dabbed the excess paint on the mouth of the small bottle, but he had probably been in a hurry, in which case she could imagine him stroking the exterior of the house this way, then that way, and working the extra blob of paint into the narrow crevice beneath the windowsill, where it would be mostly hidden from view, a secret that only she can share with him.

The rest of the house is well constructed. She thinks it's probably her father's best work yet. The floor plan is creative, different from the simpler houses that she draws during art hour at school. Her houses are single-room blocks with leaning doors and lumpy rooftops. Her father's are split-level constructions, sometimes with elaborate windows that reach all the way from the floor to the ceiling of a room.

Her favorite days are spent in the attic with him, perched on the stool on the other side of the table. She would be careful to stay out of his light. He would pull the lamp closer and peer through its magnifying lens at the house, delicately pressing the skeletal bones of the structure into the Styrofoam foundation with tweezers.

"Why do you make little houses?" she had asked him once.

"Well," he answered slowly, drawing the word out as he fit a miniature chimney into place, "because I'm not a very good architect."

"What's an architect?"

He smiled at her without looking up. "Someone who designs buildings. They say where everything goes and what it looks like."

"Why aren't you a good one?"

"I'm not a very good student," he confessed. "You have to be a good student to be a good architect."

"Oh," Eleanor replied. Then she said, "But you make pretty houses."

"Well, thank you, sweetheart."

She watched him a little longer, then asked, "What's your work instead?"

"You know the answer to that," he said. "What does Daddy do for a job?"

Eleanor bit her lip. "Real cheese."

"Realty," he corrected.

"I know," she said, then laughed. "'Real cheese' is funnier."

She studies the unfinished house on the table now and marvels at the microscopic detail: the insect-size stairs leading to the front door, the little brass knocker on the door itself. Her favorite parts are the lawn and trees, something her father's houses didn't always include but which this one does. The lawn spreads wide around the roofless home, rolling with little hills and crunchy vegetation. The driveway is empty, but a perfect mailbox stands at the end of it.

Down the attic stairs, the second-floor door bangs open. Eleanor jumps, jostling the diminutive house in her hands.

Her mother calls upstairs. "Ellie! You'd better be ready!"

"I'm ready, Mom!" she shouts back.

"Good."

Eleanor hears the door creak as Agnes begins to close it again, but then the sound stops.

"You shouldn't be up there without your father," her mother adds. "Come on down now."

"Yes, ma'am."

Eleanor jumps down from the stool. It rocks under her bottom, and she takes a moment to steady it before heading downstairs.

That's when she notices the mailbox, its post snapped clean in half.

## agnes

The attic door opens a little more, and Eleanor comes out, looking sheepish.

"You know your dad wouldn't like you being up there alone," Agnes says.

Eleanor nods meekly and stares at the floor. "Yes, ma'am."

"No time for moping," Agnes says. "I can't find my galoshes."

"Your rain boots?" Eleanor asks. "They're by the back door."

Agnes shifts her jaw and goes into her thoughts, then snaps her fingers. "That's right—I was covering the petunias."

Eleanor turns toward her room, but Agnes puts a hand on her shoulder.

"No goofing off," she says to her daughter. "I need you both downstairs. We're late."

Paul will return from Boca Raton in just under two hours. He had complained to Agnes on the phone last night that he'd seen only the inside of a Holiday Inn—his room and the banquet hall where the realty seminar was being held—for six days straight. He had put postcards in the mail—quaint photographs of gulls on the sterns of sailboats, funny pictures of elderly women in bathing suits—but none had yet arrived.

"I don't want to hear it," Agnes had said. "You're in Florida. It's your own damn fault if you can't find the beach."

She knew the strain in her voice was obvious. Paul had to have known she was approaching her limit—he had traveled three times last month, and then there were his regular nights drinking with the other realtors, plus a few late showings in the new beachfront development—but he went, anyway. Maybe he didn't know how little patience Agnes had to start with. Maybe he couldn't see that it was running out.

"How are things going?" he'd asked.

But her problems wouldn't matter much to him. The walls of his hotel room were so close that he couldn't see past them. Agnes and her problems weren't real until he got home again and they were something he had to confront and solve.

"When you get home," Agnes answered, "I'm driving to Portland, and I might spend all your money on wine and a suite of my own. And I might not ever come back."

"Agnes—"

But she had hung up on him, and her frustration hadn't diminished overnight.

She scurries downstairs now. On the landing behind her she can hear the bathroom door open, and Eleanor and Esmerelda murmuring together. Agnes misses the bottom step and almost falls down. The red runner that covers the hardwood floor bunches up under her feet, and she slides and grabs at the banister.

She steadies herself and kicks the runner flat again.

Her boots are exactly where Eleanor had said they were, like small sentries beside the sliding glass door. It's one thing off her back, and she exhales slowly. The glass is cool, and she rests her forehead against it and watches the rain falling in the backyard. Her breath fogs the glass, and then the fog quickly retreats when she inhales. Then it comes back with the next breath.

The backyard was supposed to be her place—her version of Paul's attic. The petunias are lined up carefully beneath the plastic cover she put out the night before, safe from the rain, but now she doesn't care. They're only flowers. If they'd been destroyed by the rain, Paul would only tell her to get some more from the nursery. He wouldn't consider the care she'd put into them, teasing them out of the ground, transforming them from hard bulbs into delicate, lovely paintings.

She's serious about the hotel room in Portland.

Upstairs, the twins are fighting. She can hear the sound of their voices filter through the ceiling.

She should go up and pull them apart, but the glass feels nice against her skin, and her hair hangs around her face, separating her from the world outside, creating a small space that is all her own. She can feel the chill radiating off the glass, and each breath she lets out is warm and slow. The contrast between the temperatures is delightful.

Agnes closes her eyes. A lifetime of rainy mornings like this one. They are beautiful in their own cold way, but they burrow into her and turn her into somebody else. An angry parent, a lost child. Every one reminds her of her mother.

What little she remembers of her.

"It's all water," she mutters to herself. "Fucking water."

Agnes pushes away from the glass door. She slips her feet into her boots. They slide in comfortably. The rubber creaks. Her shoulders are tight. Her head has begun to pound. She reminds herself to breathe—in, out, slowly, slowly—but the migraine will come along, anyway, and there is nothing to be done about it.

She goes to the foot of the stairs and calls again for the girls.

They appear at the top, disheveled, elbowing each other for standing too close.

"Get your coats," she tells them. "We're late."

She presses her thumbs against her temples gently and moves them in circles. The girls reappear and thunder down the stairs. Agnes winces. This is not the time for one of her headaches.

The telephone chirps in the kitchen.

"I'll get it!" Esmerelda crows.

"No, Esme—," Agnes starts, but the girl moves in record time, and, given the choice now between her exasperated mother and her sister's sudden important task, Eleanor also darts from the hall into the kitchen.

"It's Aunt Gerry," Esmerelda calls.

Agnes says, "Tell her we're out the door, and get your bottoms over here and into your coats."

"She says you have to talk to her," Eleanor says, reappearing in the hallway.

"Jesus," Agnes grumbles. "Fine."

Gerry offers to drive to Portland for her. "I closed the office because of the storm," she says. "You might as well keep the girls home. Let me go get the big guy for you."

But that isn't part of the plan, and though Agnes does not look forward to the long round-trip, she declines the offer. "We're running late. I've got to get the girls into the car. Come for dinner later, if you want."

She takes her own raincoat from the peg beside the front door and puts it on. She leaves it open, because it's a stiff coat, and getting into the car is difficult when it's zipped up. Her purse hangs on another peg, and she grabs it, too, then reaches instinctively for the small foyer table. Her fingers meet its empty surface, and she glances down.

"Keys," she says, looking around.

The girls are waiting beside her in their coats: purple for Esmerelda, blue for Eleanor. The different colors were Paul's idea. "So we can tell them apart," he said. It wasn't his brightest idea.

Agnes points at the coats. "Switch," she says. "We don't have time."

Eleanor frowns and shrugs out of the purple coat. "You're not supposed to be able to tell," she complains.

Agnes pats the pockets of her coat, ignoring her daughter.

*Jingle.*

Esmerelda is holding the ring of keys on one finger.

Agnes exhales in a rush. "Thank you," she says. "Are we ready?"

She looks again at her daughters. Esmerelda has a book in one pocket of her coat. Eleanor has a spiral notebook and a pencil case. Given time, the girls often retreat into their own worlds in exactly this way. Esmerelda reads books that she has sneaked from her parents' stash, tired of her Nancy Drew mysteries, and Eleanor draws elaborate maps—underground tunnels full of misdirection and booby traps.

"What book did you take?" Agnes asks.

Esmerelda looks away. "Oh, just a book. It's nothing."

Agnes lets it go. She'd discovered a copy of *The Shining* under Esmerelda's pillow a few weeks earlier and had interrogated the girl. As it turned out, Esmerelda didn't understand most of what she was reading, but she understood the Danny parts of the story. To her, *The Shining* seemed to be the story of a boy who got to play all day in an empty hotel. It sounded like an adventure.

She opens the door. In the short time it has taken them to get ready, the rain has become a torrent, thundering down onto the lawn and driveway as if it might shatter the pavement. She ushers the girls onto the front porch with her, beneath the eaves, and locks the door.

"Count of three?" Eleanor asks, looking up at Agnes.

"Go now," Agnes says, putting a hand on each girl's back and nudging them down the porch steps.

The three of them run squealing into the rain. It pounds on their thin coats. Their boots splash in new lakes on the driveway. The blue Subaru glistens in the pale light. Eleanor and Esmerelda wrestle for control of the front door, jostling each other.

"*In, in, in!*" Agnes shouts over the rain.

But the doors are locked.

They scream and run back to the safety of the porch, breathing hard, their faces slick and wet. Eleanor stomps in place, shaking like a puppy.

"Front seat," Esmerelda declares.

"It's *my* turn," Eleanor argues.

"*Mom!*" Esmerelda howls. "*I called* the front seat—"

"We don't have time for you to fight over stupid things," Agnes says. "This is a stupid thing. *Figure it out.* Okay? Now, count to five, then come after me."

Agnes turns and darts to the car. Her hood falls away, and her hair is immediately soaked. She jams the key into the lock and yanks the door open and heaves herself into the driver's seat. She slams the door behind her and sits, mildly dazed. The girls appear at the windows a moment later, yelling and pounding on the glass. Agnes snaps out of her momentary haze and throws the locks.

Esmerelda reaches for the front-door handle, but Eleanor throws a hip and beats her to it, scrambling into the front seat.

"*Mom,*" Esmerelda complains, standing beside the car in the downpour.

"Inside! Now!" Agnes barks.

Esmerelda stomps furiously in a puddle, then climbs into the backseat and slams the door as hard as she can.

Eleanor turns and looks at her sister triumphantly.

Esmerelda sticks her tongue out.

"Buckle," Agnes says.

She starts the car and slides the heater toggle all the way up in one motion. The engine thrums to life, and cold air blasts from the vents. Eleanor pushes them toward the ceiling.

"Are we late?" Esmerelda asks, wiping the rain from her eyes.

Agnes starts to answer, then flinches, interrupted by a drop of water that smacks her in the eye. She inspects the ceiling. The cloth lining is dark, soaked through. Water collects slowly into a fresh, fat bead, then falls onto her upturned cheek.

"Oh, fuck me," Agnes complains.

"Mom!" Eleanor gasps.

"Yes, all right," Agnes says, a little more angrily than she intends. "Don't be a prude, dear." She yanks the stick into reverse, then turns, snaking one arm over the back of Eleanor's seat. She pushes the gas, and the Subaru rattles down the drive and into the street. "We're very, very late."

"And the rain doesn't help," Eleanor adds.

"Right," Agnes says. "The rain doesn't help."

"I like the rain," Esmerelda says.

"Don't be difficult, *Esmerelda*," Eleanor says, glaring at her twin.

"What?" Esmerelda asks defiantly. "It's only water."

Agnes stares at her daughter in the mirror.

"What?" Esmerelda asks.


AGNES DRIVES AS fast as she dares through the neighborhood, then wrenches the car onto the avenue that will carry them through town to the highway. Eleanor folds open her notebook and continues drawing a map that looks like a cross section of a militarized anthill. In the backseat, Esmerelda unbuckles and slides closer to the window, then buckles herself in again. She watches the passing cars, then focuses on the steam on the window. With one fingernail, in very tiny print, she writes her mother's swear word in the steam: F-U-C-K. Then she quickly erases it. She takes out her book; this time it's *Jaws*. She turns to the part of the book where Hooper and Chief Brody's wife begin their affair, curious at the words there and what they mean.

The road hisses under the car, and every passing vehicle sends up a fan of water that rat-a-tats on the Subaru's metal hide. The girls, accustomed to these sorts of storms, don't look up.

Agnes follows the coast road to the highway. She only takes this road when they head inland to Portland. She tries not to look at the view when the rows of houses and scruffy fields of pine fall away and the rocky beaches spread out beside the ocean, but it isn't easy, and eventually she looks, anyway. Huffnagle Island slides into view, partially obscured by a heavy bank of fog. They've already driven past the pier where her father borrowed the rowboat, past the section of beach where her mother would dive into the sea for her Sunday swim. But she can still see Huffnagle looming out there on the horizon, dark and knotted, its hunched back scraping the black clouds above.

# paul

Anchor Bend sits on Oregon's coastline like a burl on a redwood, knobby and hard. It is a postcard town, nestled quietly in deep pines. Its sunsets are spectacular, its mornings gloomy and drenched with fog. The town was built to serve the sea, and during the Second World War it thrived as a small-market port. Thousands of tons of machinery left America through the tiny keyhole of Anchor Bend: engines for troop transports, windshields and doors for command vehicles, even the occasional wing structure for a bomber. Those were good years, and as the sea became an avenue to prosperity, the fisheries and canneries followed. Working families flocked to the town, and it swelled from its original population of two thousand to nearly thirty-seven thousand in just five years.

These days the docks and warehouses are still there, battered and rusted but standing, though the fisheries are gone, moved up the coast into Washington. A fire had torn through the industrial district, reducing the two largest fisheries to ash and cinder. Management opted not to rebuild, and their scorched lots stand empty even now.

Anchor Bend recalls its populous, profitable past but has very little pride left. Entire suburbs stand empty, street after street of unoccupied homes that sag and wither. The herd has thinned, and fewer than twelve thousand people remain within the town's borders. Most are simply holding on.

It's a strange town for a realtor. Nobody at Paul's annual conferences can tell him how to sell a home in a town where empty houses lie discarded on the side of the road like crushed cans.

Anchor Bend is no short distance from the Portland airport, where Paul's plane has arrived unexpectedly early. The flight knocked him around like a tennis shoe in a dryer. Putting the plane on the ground safely was a terrific feat, and when Paul bumps into the pilot in the terminal, he surprises himself by congratulating the man.

"You have no idea how close we came," the captain whispers, his white cap tucked under one arm, his collar loose. He shakes his head and grins. "Kidding, of course. Bit rough back in coach, I imagine."

Paul looks at his watch. "I've got some time to kill," he says. "Can I buy you a drink?"

They enjoy a couple of beers in an airport pub that fancies itself an old English watering hole. It's called the Peat & Pear, though there's nothing earthy or particularly fruity about the place. Its walls are covered with illustrations of biplanes turning lazy circles over black-and-white meadows. The pub is little more than a hollowed-out nook in the concourse, with a few sticky tables and a short bar lined with bolted-down stools.

The captain's name is Mark, and he regales Paul with stories of troublemaker passengers and bad-weather landings, and when the two men finish their first beer, Paul glances at the clock over the bar. It's still early yet; his flight had been scheduled to land at four, and it's now ten minutes till. Agnes and the girls should be here by four-fifteen. Time enough for a second beer.

At twenty minutes past, Paul and Captain Mark abandon their stools and walk slowly to the arrivals ramp. The sidewalk zone in front of the airport is strangely empty, and Agnes's Subaru is no-where to be seen. Paul leans out and watches the horizon, but the car doesn't materialize. Agnes is not driving in slow circles around the airport waiting for him.

"Wife late?" Captain Mark asks.

"Little bit," Paul says. He turns and looks back, spying a clock over the United desk. Four twenty-five now.

"Probably traffic," says the captain. "Saw lots of it on approach."

Outside, the world is gray and opaque. The large windows welcoming travelers into the airport have begun to fog over. He can barely make out planes on the distant runway, lining up, awaiting their turn to leave the earth.

"Yeah," Paul agrees. "You're probably right."

But his world sways a little on its axis.

# *eleanor*

C an we stop?" Esmerelda asks from the backseat.

The scenery rushes by, wet and gray and chalky, and Eleanor hardly no0tices. She bites her lip as she draws, carefully threading a single gray line down the sheet of paper, then pairing another beside it. The entry tunnel. She pauses, studying it, seeing something taking shape on the page that nobody else would see if they were to look. She erases bits of her pencil marks, making little notches in the pair of lines, unevenly spaced. Then she draws angled lines forking away from the first two, flanking each of the gaps. Secondary tunnels.

This continues for a time as she builds the spine of her underground bunker and its central nervous system. The primary tunnel is wider than the others and will carve deeply into the graphite earth around it. This tunnel will be a distraction, a red herring. It will seem to be the important corridor, will appear to lead to the secret stash she'll bury somewhere in the map, but, in truth, one of the dozen forked paths will be the truly meaningful hallway.

"Can we stop?" Esmerelda asks again.

Eleanor looks up this time and sees the fog beginning to swamp the highway ahead of them. The trees seem half-erased, the fog tangled high in their branches like some ghostly predator caught up in a green net.

"I like the fog," she says to nobody in particular.

"Nobody cares," Esmerelda retorts. "*Mo-oomm*, can we stop? I have to pee."

"We're almost through it," Agnes replies. Her knuckles are white upon the wheel. There hasn't been a moment of sunlight during the drive; this is the first respite from the rain. "Let's get to the airport, and you can go there."

"It's so *far*."

Eleanor sighs at her sister's childishness. "Grow up, Esme."

"We're the same age, dummy," Esmerelda retorts. "*You* grow up."

Eleanor turns back to her map. This is a new one, and she can't wait to share it with her father. "What if," he'd said to her, weeks ago, "the model house had a trap door . . ." He'd pointed to the entrance of her tunnel. "What if it led *here*?" His excitement had thrilled her, and now she drew atop each map a rudimentary house, hiding the world she'd designed below it. Her father had asked if she had a name for it, this world; when she'd drawn a blank, he said, "What about the Belowgrounds? Sounds magical to me."

She sketches a small, curled scroll that floats in one corner. In careful, serious lettering, she prints THE BELLOW GROWNDS. She runs out of room, and the last word arcs off the scroll and into the sky, overlapping a fluffy cloud.

There's a metallic *snick* as Esmerelda unfastens her seat belt and scoots to the middle. A moment later she pops up between the two front seats like a jack-in-the-box, clutching at her mother's sleeve.

"I really, really have to pee," she moans.

Eleanor elbows Esmerelda in the shoulder. "Get out of the way!"

"*You* get out of the way."

This infuriates Eleanor. How could *she* be in the way? *She's* the one sitting in her seat, buckled up, exactly where *she's* supposed to be. Esmerelda is the one tumbling around in the car like an escaped hedgehog.

"Sit *down*," Agnes barks, and both girls recognize the fractured timbre of her voice. This is Agnes when the world seems to be closing in around her. Eleanor doesn't know the word *stress* just yet, but if she did, she would recognize that her mother is very, very stressed out.

Esmerelda sits back, sullen. "If I pee on the seat, it's not my fault," she mutters, but such is the mood in the car now that nobody replies.

Eleanor casts a furtive glance at her mother. Agnes's jaw is clenched as tightly as her hands on the wheel, and it makes Eleanor think that driving must be very hard, because her mother looks as if she's being crushed into a tiny ball.

In the backseat, Esmerelda crosses her arms and pouts. Eleanor turns around, leaning against her own seat belt, and says, "You're gonna pee yourself."

"*You're* gonna pee yourself," Esmerelda snaps. "You pee yourself all day every day. You're peeing yourself right now."

"Both of you," Agnes says through gritted teeth. "Stop. Now."

The fog crashes in again like a wave, and Eleanor returns to her map as the Subaru becomes a spaceship in some pale cosmic ocean.

# *agnes*

Highway 26 curves inland from the Oregon coast, a narrow ribbon that winds through miles of tall trees and more miles of golden meadows that roll away toward the mountains. It is, on its best days, a beautiful, scenic route; on days like this, it is a tightrope strung into nothingness. Agnes feels like a circus performer on that rope, barely able to see the wire at her feet, two unruly monkeys perched on her shoulders.

Her hands are beginning to ache from keeping such an intense grip on the wheel, so she opens them, stretches her fingers, and steers with her palms. Her fingers crack like ice in warm water, which makes her feel a little better.

"*Seriously*, Mom," Esmerelda says.

Agnes takes a focused breath and lets it out slowly before she responds. "You really can't hold it?"

"I really, really can't."

Agnes glances up at the rearview mirror, then tilts it with one hand so she can see her daughter. Esmerelda's knees are tucked up to her chin, arms tightly cinched around her legs.

"We've already passed most of the stops," Agnes says. "Can you hold it a little longer? I'll stop at the first place at the bottom of the hill."

"Mom!" Eleanor shouts from the passenger seat, and Agnes feels a spike of fear in her heart and whips her attention back to the highway.

There's nothing worth shouting about. The cars ahead of the

Subaru are braking, a little river of red lights rising out of the fog. After a moment of deep breaths to calm back down, Agnes sees why.

The fog begins to shred, torn into floating gobs of cotton by the rain, which starts again in earnest. It's as if a dam somewhere has given way. The water comes down in heavy sheets. The Subaru's hood and roof thrum angrily beneath the downpour. Water drips steadily from the leaky roof onto Agnes's shoulder. She leans to one side to avoid the persistent *tap-tap* of it.

"Don't do that," Agnes says to Eleanor, feeling the rush of alarm and adrenaline fade. "You could make us have an accident."

The rain robs her of sight once more. It's impenetrable, and she loses the shape of the cars ahead. She can see the taillights of the one just before her but little past that.

"Mom, I really have to—"

"*Shut. Up!*" Agnes says, her voice like sheared steel, and the girls both lapse into an aching silence.

Highway 26 weaves through Hillsboro and Beaverton on its path to Portland, eventually diving down a steep, winding grade, then finally pushing its way through a mountain tunnel. The grade is often jammed with drivers who seem unnerved by the sweeping curves, possibly confused by the trifecta of exits, and cowed by the enormous yellow sign, festooned with blinking amber lights, that reads SLOW. In the lane beside the Subaru, a steady stream of vehicles courses by much too quickly. Their drivers seem oblivious to the signs that order them to remain in their designated lanes—NO PASSING FOR NEXT 1 MILE—and this drives Agnes's heart rate up considerably. She can hear the blood pounding in her ears, overtaking the sounds of the world.

Agnes guides the Subaru into the far left lane, which hugs a concrete barrier, and slows the car to almost no movement at all. She worries about the brakes on the grade—they're wet now, and they've been a little creaky lately, regardless—but finds herself distracted, a little, by the driver to her right. The woman is stunningly old, her skin a crumpled brown paper bag, her hair a pale robin's nest. She drives a twenty-year-old Volvo and rides her brakes. The Subaru's own brakes may be in bad shape, but the Volvo's sound like rusted nails on metal. The driver's chest practically hugs the steering wheel. She's so small, she might not even be in her seat anymore. Agnes can almost imagine the woman standing in front of the wheel, both feet jammed down on the brake pedal so far from her that she can barely peer over the dashboard—

"*MOM!*" Eleanor shouts.

The car directly in front of them has screwed to a stop, its rear end angled from a skid. Agnes lays into the brakes with everything she has. For the first time ever, they lock, and the Subaru glides down the steep road like a sled on packed snow.

"No," Agnes says, her voice calmer than she might have expected. "No, no, no."

She throws an arm out instinctively, pinning Eleanor to her seat. In the back of the car, Esmerelda makes a sound like a quiet owl, a long, low whistle.

Agnes has enough time to see the old woman in the Volvo notice what's happening beside her. The woman's eyes widen, and Agnes thinks, rather selfishly, that this should be happening to the Volvo, not the Subaru, to the old woman who has lived a thousand years, not to this young family of hers.

And then, like a break in a hurricane, everything is abruptly okay.

The Subaru's tires catch gravel, and that's enough to end the slide. The car grips the road again, lurching sideways. If not for this almost balletic turn, they might have rear-ended the vehicle ahead—a pickup with one of those gaudy roll bars and big spotlights—but, instead, the Subaru skids to a stop, its nose tucking tightly, almost perfectly, into the narrow space between the truck and the concrete highway divider.

"Shit!" Eleanor squeaks.

Agnes turns to look at her daughter, perhaps to correct her. She lowers her arm, releasing Eleanor. Agnes can feel her heart threatening to punch right through her chest, can taste again the sharp tang of adrenaline on her tongue. She asks, "Are you okay?" Eleanor nods slowly, and Agnes turns to the backseat to ask Esmerelda the same question, but the words catch in her throat, because she sees the U-Haul van, and there's not even time to say, "No," not even time for Esmerelda to turn and see it coming; there is only time for Agnes to *want* to do those things, and then it happens, and it cannot be undone.

THE PICKUP DRIVER is the first to respond. His door barely opens at all. The Subaru's crushed front end is only a few inches away, tilted down toward the ground. The driver is too large to squeeze through the space. He crawls over the stick shift and his briefcase and ejects himself from his truck through the passenger door and tumbles onto the asphalt. The impact of the Subaru has pushed the truck forward and sideways; its damaged bed now hangs into traffic like a broken limb.

Agnes is dimly aware of these things; she can see the man heaving himself into the bed of his pickup. He's dressed like an engineer, in khakis and a short-sleeved white shirt buttoned to the throat, but he becomes a gorilla. He steps up onto the rim of the pickup's bed, then hops onto the hood of the Subaru. The hood is mangled and covered in broken glass and bits of concrete, but the man hurries across it and drops into the tight gap between the station wagon and the broken highway divider, and then he is at Agnes's window.

The glass is splintered but intact. Agnes wants to understand why, but then the man is there shouting at her. She can't understand him—his words sound muffled and distant to her—so he repeats himself loudly, waving his hands, and she finally sees that he's trying to tell her to lean back. He scuffles with the door, but it isn't opening, and he acts without thinking, caught up in the rush of what has just happened, and he puts his elbow through the splintered window. It doesn't shatter, just sort of buckles, so he does it again, then again, and Agnes flinches with every impact. The man seems unaware that he has cut himself—his forearm is smeared with blood now—and then the glass creaks and comes apart.

"Cover your face," he says from his faraway place, and Agnes's hands feel as if they weigh hundreds of pounds, but she puts them over her face. She can hear the man striking the glass out of the door frame, and then he says, "You all right? Lady?" and Agnes takes her hands down to see that his face is *right there*, that he's leaning into the car.

She shakes her head, disoriented, and then the man's eyes focus past her, and he says, "Oh, Jesus," and Agnes is confused, but she follows the man's gaze and sees Eleanor there, leaning forward, supported by her tightly drawn seat belt. Eleanor's bright red hair has fallen over her face, and her head dangles forward, and Agnes feels something sharp chew its way through her belly and right into her heart: She has killed her child.

"Little girl!" the driver says, leaning through the window and toward Eleanor. He can't quite reach her—his fingers stop short of her shoulder, and he waves them, almost comically, in the air. "Can you hear me? Are you okay?"

A rush of heat subsumes Agnes, stirring her into action. She grabs Eleanor's hand, roughly.

"Eleanor, Eleanor," she says, shaking her daughter's arm like a rubber band.

"Careful, lady," the driver says, still wearing his look of horror. "Careful, she could be—"

"Eleanor!" Agnes shouts, her voice overpowering in the confined space. She slaps the back of her daughter's hand and then bursts into tears when Eleanor stirs.

Eleanor lifts her head, and her hair falls away from her face, and it's immediately obvious that her nose is broken. Her lips and chin are red with blood, and her eyes are glassy, but she's alive.

"Ellie!" Agnes chokes.

Eleanor just blinks at her, then leans forward and vomits on the floor. When she's finished, she coughs and heaves, then closes her eyes and relaxes against the seat belt again.

"Ezzz," Eleanor croaks.

"Eleanor, sweetie," Agnes pleads, squeezing her daughter's hand. "Come on, Ellie. Wake up. Wake up, Ellie."

"We have to get an ambulance," the pickup driver says. He extricates himself from the Subaru's window and looks around wildly. The driver of the U-Haul hasn't emerged, so there's no telling if he's okay or even alive. The rear end of the Subaru, cocked up onto the hood of the van, obscures the view. A woman suddenly peeks around the back corner of the U-Haul, like a cardboard character in a pop-up book. The pickup driver brings a hand to his ear, miming using a telephone, and shouts, "We need an ambulance! Call an ambulance!"

Agnes turns and looks at the pickup driver and tries to ask him how anybody will call for an ambulance, but the words come out funny, and she doesn't know what she has actually asked him.

"There's a call box just up the hill," he says.

So she must have made sense.

The driver leans back into the car and looks closely at Eleanor, who appears to be unconscious again. "She okay?" he asks, and Agnes turns to look at Eleanor, then back at the driver.

"I'm not sure," she says, the first clear words she's spoken since the collision. They feel strange in her mouth, oddly formal.

"A woman went to call for help," the man says, but then he trails off, distracted again.

It's getting difficult for Agnes to hold herself upright. Gravity draws her toward the steering wheel. She can't figure out why. In the rearview mirror, she sees a tilted world—the rear window, glass cracked and buckled inward, the top of the U-Haul van, dense fog beyond, the ghostly shapes of trees along the edge of the highway.

"Lady?" the pickup driver says apprehensively.

Agnes turns in her seat and looks toward the rear window. She doesn't understand the angle of things. "Tilted?" she asks. "Are we tilted?"

"Lady," the driver says again.

Agnes turns to the driver and sees him staring at the windshield, and so she looks at the windshield, too, and sees the gaping hole there, the broken safety glass scattered across the dashboard and the hood beyond, and then something moves, and she sees a matted hank of red hair snagged in the broken glass, a few errant strands fluttering wet and heavy in the breeze. Blood clogs the hair like paint in the bristles of a brush, streaks across the hood of the car, thinning in the rain.

She stares at this for a long time, and then she looks at the driver, who says, "Lady, was there someone else—" and Agnes turns and looks at the empty backseat of the Subaru and feels that chewing sensation inside her turn ravenous, chasing the terrible wail out of her mouth and into the fog, where it lingers forever and ever.

## paul

Back in the bar again, Captain Mark reluctantly declines another beer and slides off of his stool. He's flying deadhead back to Boston, he explains, and doesn't have the luxury of an overnight stay in Portland and so must get back into the sky. He shakes Paul's hand, then warmly says, "I'm sure everything will be just fine. Things usually are."

Paul raises his glass in a small gesture of thanks, but when Captain Mark disappears around the corner, he downs the last bit of now-warm beer and exhales in a rush. He climbs down from the stool, perfectly steady, and grabs his bag.

"Have a great day," the airport bartender drones, cheerless in his green vest and golden bow tie.

Paul falls into the throng of arriving passengers on the concourse. By now Agnes and the girls are more than an hour late. He's called the house and gotten the machine—"Hey, it's the Witts, leave us a message," followed by the girls singing in unison, "So we can delete it!"—and his repeated trips to the window looking out upon the arrivals ramp have been fruitless. No sign of the car, no sign of the girls. No Agnes.

He was angry at first. He's tired; it's been a long trip. There's a two-hour drive ahead. All he wants to do is fall asleep early in the bed he and Agnes share, then maybe wake up in the middle of the night, when everyone else is asleep, and nudge Agnes into a bit of sleepy sex. That won't happen, never does, so, instead, he would probably wander upstairs, into the attic, to work on his current model house. He hasn't told Eleanor yet, but he's cut a tiny square hole into the floor of the house and fashioned a miniature trap door with a hooked latch and a single brass hinge. He wasn't going to reveal his work to her until he finished the second phase of the project, which was to build a sort of diorama shell beneath the house's foundation, one in which Eleanor could install her tunnel system with modeling clay and bits of wire.

Thinking of Eleanor makes him think of Esmerelda, and he feels that twinge of guilt, of regret, that comes to him when he realizes that he and Esmerelda have no such secrets to share. He should find something, he knows, but Esmerelda has shown no interest in Paul's models. He can't think of a single thing she loves as much as Eleanor loves her maps. Books? But when they visit bookstores or libraries together, she slumps to the floor with a book from a shelf and buries her nose in it for as long as they're in the stacks. It's a private occasion, shared between her and the characters within the book's pages, and there's no room for Paul in such moments.

But he isn't angry anymore. He's worried and thinking about the hours ahead. Even if everything is fine—even if it *is* just traffic—he's too unnerved to think of relaxing.

He hails a taxi outside baggage claim, looking hopefully at the

Arrivals ramp one last time before he tosses his bag into the back-seat and climbs inside. It takes a long time to get through the city proper to Highway 26. Captain Mark was correct about the acres of traffic he'd seen, and the clotting hadn't broken up in the hour they'd spent over beers. The taxi slows to a crawl, picking its way through the snarl of vehicles like a bird tiptoeing through brambles, and Paul grows more impatient with every moment.

"Can you detour me to a phone?" he asks the driver, who works his way across three lanes to the first exit. He pulls into the parking lot of a gas station, and Paul leaps out and runs to the pay phone by the air compressor. He dials, covering his free ear to mute the sound of the compressor, which rattles loudly, as if someone plugged too many quarters into the thing, then walked away, leaving the machine to happily and uselessly thrum.

"Hey, it's the Witts, leave us a message—so we can delete it!"

He waits for the dull beep and says once more, "Aggie? Esmerelda? Girls? Pick up. Pick up!"

But nobody picks up.

He stares out the passenger window of the taxi as the driver merges onto Highway 26. The city gives way to forest, and then the forest gives way to the flash of tunnel lights, and then the forest returns again. The hill grows steeper, and as the car climbs higher, the rain gets stronger.

"Where you have been?" the driver asks Paul.

"What?" Paul asks. "Sorry."

"Where you are coming from?"

"Oh," Paul says. "Florida."

"Ah," the driver answers. "Sunshine. Swimming."

"Right," Paul says, leaning his head against the passenger window again.

"All this beauty you have missed," the driver says with a chuckle, raising one hand to indicate the rain and rising fog.

Paul doesn't answer; he just keeps staring up at the trees as they speed by. The driver is quiet until they pass a commotion on the opposite side of the freeway.

"Shameful," the driver says, his somber tone suggesting a great disappointment in humanity.

Paul doesn't pay attention, doesn't see the now-empty family Subaru crumpled like a ball of tinfoil in the rain. He doesn't see the U-Haul van wedged beneath it or the emergency technicians working to remove the dead man from its front seat. Had he looked, he would have seen a police cruiser angled sideways in the two nearest lanes, and the slow, steady march of traffic squeezing into the remaining lane. He'd have seen the flashing lights of the two ambulances and the fire engine. He'd have seen the concerned pickup driver and the woman who had gone to the call box standing in the rain, drenched, wringing their hands.

Though it's buckled by the accident, the concrete divider would have prevented Paul from seeing the worst of it: a small white sheet on the asphalt, rippling gently under the falling rain, a still, child-size lump beneath it.

"Shameful," the taxi driver repeats. By the time Paul realizes that the man is talking again, the accident has fallen away behind them, and the taxi drives on, leaving rubbernecking drivers in its wake, carrying Paul away from his family and to the coast, where his dark and empty home stands waiting.

1993

# eleanor

Eleanor wakes up from a dream that she is falling, not toward anything in particular but from some indeterminate height and without gathering much speed. In her dream she was tumbling slowly, almost gently, through a pleasant updraft. There was no earth below her, only endless blue. She doesn't wake from the dream because it frightens her—she dreams this dream all the time—but because the migraine that sent her to bed early the night before has returned, manifesting itself in a red pulse above and behind her left eye. She visualizes the pain in much the same way every time it returns: as a strong, hollow needle that slides through her eye and into her brain and then, not content with simply invading, begins to rotate like a long spoon in a cauldron. It scrambles her thoughts and puts her pain receptors on high alert, and she starts from bed so quickly that she almost tumbles to the floor—something else that is not an uncommon occurrence.

The red pulse starts as a single dot that flexes and trembles; it lies over her vision, then broadens, as it always does, until her left eye sees the world through an alarming red haze. She focuses on each breath, visualizing the air rushing through her nose, into her lungs, and out again. She imagines that the outgoing breath carries her pain away with it.

Today it doesn't help. She loses sight in her left eye a moment after waking, which sometimes happens, but she can tell that today is one of the worst days, because flickers of red encroach upon the sight in her remaining eye, like a filmstrip curling and melting on the reel.

"Mom," Eleanor calls, but her voice comes out in a whisper. Even that small sound aggravates the migraine, and the pain swells like the sea, threatening to overtake her.

Mornings like this, she wishes her father still lived at home. He knew just how to take her mind off the pain; he would sit with her and gently rub the space between her thumb and index finger while humming some soft, strange song.

But he isn't here. Hasn't been for a while now.

Eleanor turns in her bed, delicately lowering her feet to the floor. Her head pounds with every tiny movement. She needs to find her mother, who will know what to do; Agnes has battled vicious migraines for as long as Eleanor can remember.

Except this is just an errant thought, and dimly, through the searing pain, Eleanor knows this. Agnes will not be helpful. Agnes is most likely in the same place she was when Eleanor went to bed the night before: curled into a worrisome and small ball in the blue corduroy–upholstered recliner in the den. Agnes will be lost to Eleanor, lost to the whole world around her, courtesy of the slim, tall vodka bottle that will almost certainly stand, nearly empty, on the end table.

This realization swims up to Eleanor through the red sea around her, and she course-corrects. In the bathroom, in the medicine cabinet, is a plastic bottle of migraine pills. She gets to her feet, arms extended to steady herself, and walks across the carpeted bedroom floor at a ponderous pace.

In the hallway, she stands on the hardwood floor. The cool smooth wood feels like a balm on her skin, better than the painful overstimulation of the carpet, its every loop a barb in her heightened state. During the worst headaches, her every cell becomes hypersensitive, attuned to each air molecule that brushes against her. A mote of dust collides with her skin like a meteor. Everything hurts.

She can faintly hear Agnes snoring downstairs.

On an ordinary day she would wake a bit later, shower and dress, and prepare breakfast for herself, making a little extra for her mother. As the bread browned in the toaster, she would go to the den and wake Agnes and make her eat something. Agnes would pick at her breakfast with trembling hands; her eyes, red and bleary, would stare through the table. Eleanor would kiss her mother's cheek and leave her at the table, then ride her bicycle to school. Later she would return home to find her mother asleep again—sometimes in the recliner, sometimes on the couch, on very rare occasions in her bed upstairs. Sometimes Agnes wouldn't have moved from the table at all. Mostly she remains confined to the ground floor, perhaps recognizing that stairs are a dangerous gauntlet for a woman who is almost constantly drunk.

Eleanor finds the migraine pills and takes three, scooping water from the bathroom tap to wash them down. She pats her hand dry on a towel and returns to her room. The clock radio beside her bed reads 7:14, and she feels a bolt of panic. When the numbers flip to 7:15, the clock radio will come alive with the loud jangles of 97.3, the sonic shrapnel of which will almost surely drop Eleanor to the floor, where the red will overtake her entirely. So she walks as quickly as she can without sending seismic waves from her feet to her brain.

She makes it, sliding the alarm's switch to the off position and in the same movement softly flying into her bed, visualizing a feather wafting from the ceiling to the creaky mattress. She pulls the blankets over herself and lies very still on her back and pulls her extra pillow over her face and presses it down, down against her humming skin and eyes, feeling the surge of her heartbeat through her veins. After a very long while she crashes into sleep and stays home from school with her incapacitated mother.

WHEN ELEANOR WAKES, her bedroom has fallen into cool gray shadow. She blinks slowly, but the red gauze has removed itself from her eyes, and she lies still for a long moment, attuned to her body's state of being. The migraine has gone away, leaving behind only the slightest headache.

When she finally turns and looks at the clock, she is startled by what she sees: 8:22. She has slept for more than twelve hours. She lies there, still, shifting her attention to the sounds of the house. The faint ticking behind the wall means that the heat has recently shut off, and Eleanor reminds herself to adjust the thermostat later. Winter has long since become spring, and the house has felt uncomfortably warm lately.

Beyond the heating system, Eleanor hears nothing at all. She wonders if her mother has slept the entire day away as well. She dresses as though it is morning and the day lies new and glistening before her, pulling on a pair of clean shorts and a bright orange T-shirt with STÜSSY printed across the middle in aggressive script. She runs her hands through her short red hair, grateful for its abbreviated length, which means there are no painful tangles to brush out. She has kept her hair short for all the years since the accident, the memory of Esmerelda's torn-out hair and bits of scalp forever seared into her mind.

Eleanor opens the door to the hallway. She pauses on the landing but hears nothing from downstairs. The ceiling above her creaks a little, and she glances up, curious, and notices that the attic door is open. Light shines through the narrow opening.

Eleanor pulls the door open and looks up the stairs. For a moment she imagines that the doorway is a portal into the past, that if she steps through it and climbs the stairs, she will hear the thin strains of the Eagles waft down from above, will find her father perched at the workbench, his tools clicking and clacking as he secures a new roof to a miniature house.

But that is impossible. Her memory of the day her father left is blisteringly clear, as is the afternoon her mother dismantled the workbench and threw Paul's tools and materials into cardboard boxes.

"Dad," Eleanor had pleaded, following her father to the garage. The door had clattered up, and he'd explained himself, said something important, and she'd missed it in the racket. "Don't go," she'd begged. "Don't leave me with her." She remembers the pain those words had caused him, the helpless guilt that flashed in his eyes.

He'd left, anyway, promising to return for her. And he did, every other weekend for the past couple of years, relieving her of the awful burden of holding her mother together with string and duct tape and sweat.

Now she hears the creak again from the attic, slower, more pronounced. This isn't the past. That isn't her father up there. She doesn't hear "Take It Easy" or her father's weight shifting on the stool.

*Creak.*

"Agnes?" Eleanor calls.

She climbs the stairs carefully. They're caked with dust, but the dust is thinner in alternating patches on each step. Footprints, uneven, made by unsteady feet.

She reaches the top of the stairs and sees that the single bulb fixed to the ceiling is aglow, barely illuminating the gutted attic. Her mother sits cross-legged in the middle of the floor, her back to Eleanor. There is a bottle of Wild Turkey beside her but no glass.

"Mom?"

Agnes turns, surprised by Eleanor's sudden appearance. Eleanor is startled, too, by the bright bloom of red in her mother's face, the delicate latticework of broken blood vessels in her cheeks and on the slope of her nose. Agnes's brown hair has begun to lighten and turn gray—something Eleanor is surprised she hasn't noticed before. Her mother's eyes are ringed with deep, dark circles, like bruises. Her skin is oily and marked with clogged pores.

The attic floor creaks beneath Eleanor's feet as she joins her mother. There is a cardboard carton on the floor in front of Agnes, one of only a few objects left in the attic since her father cleared out years ago. Eleanor recognizes the box immediately and reaches for the lid to seal it up again.

"No," Agnes snaps, her voice thick and indistinct. "Don't."

"You shouldn't be going through her stuff," Eleanor says.

"Don't tell me what to do." Agnes takes another sip from the bottle. The bourbon glistens on her chapped lips. "Don't *you* tell me what to do."

Eleanor resists a sudden urge to grab her mother beneath her arms and drag her down the stairs and into her bedroom, to strip her and throw her into the shower, to scrub her clean, to prop her on the bed and brush her hair until it shines again, to rub cream into her face and press a tube of balm to her lips—all in a vain attempt to restore her mother to the woman she once was.

But it wouldn't fix anything. Agnes is rotting inside.

"You're just a—" Agnes can't find the word. She sputters, flecks of spittle dotting Eleanor's bare legs. "Ungrateful," she finishes. "You're *ungrateful*."

"I'm not, either," Eleanor says.

Agnes shakes her head. "*She* should be here."

"*She* has a name."

"Don't you say it," Agnes hisses.

Eleanor sinks to her knees. She touches her mother's hands. "Mom," she says quietly. "How could you blame yourself? It was an accident."

For the briefest of moments, Eleanor sees something flicker over her mother's face; Agnes's hard stare softens. But only for a moment. Eleanor tries to pull her mother close, but Agnes stiffens and leans away, peering accusingly at Eleanor through strands of unkempt hair.

"*You* chose the front seat."

Eleanor opens her mouth but cannot form a response.

"Don't want to hear *that*, do you?"

Eleanor recoils. It has never occurred to her that she is responsible for Esmerelda sitting in the backseat of the Subaru that day. "Don't say—"

"Don't say what?" Agnes interrupts. "That it was your fault? It *was*."

"Mom!" Eleanor gasps.

Agnes turns away from her, reaching again for the bottle. "Just—get out."

Tears fill Eleanor's eyes. She goes, leaving her mother in the attic with the box of Esmerelda's baby clothes and stuffed animals and the little white card from the hospital with her inky small footprints and the taped-down tiny lock of red hair and the small square packet containing her first lost tooth. She takes the stairs carefully, wondering what would happen if she should trip and break her neck and leave her mother alone. Maybe it would serve Agnes right. Would she even grieve? Or would she feel released from the awful bonds of motherhood?

"Run and hide!" her mother crows after her. "Hide from what you did!"

Eleanor is trembling as she pushes the attic door closed. She thinks that she will never have a daughter. Mothers and daughters are horrible, horrible to each other.

In the morning, Jack waits at the end of the driveway, straddling his bicycle. His skinny legs are capped with practical sneakers, the sort that the kids at school like to mock because the shoes are absent any swoosh or trio of stripes. Jack barely seems to notice this—in fact, does not notice that his classmates chuckle behind their hands at his clothing, at his jeans with the worn-out knees, his backpack that frays around the straps, even at his hair, which he demonstrates little talent for styling.

These are all things that Eleanor likes very much about him.

"I'm going," Eleanor calls over her shoulder, but, of course, there is no answer. She closes the door gently, aware that anything more than a gentle *snick* will wake her mother with a pounding hangover headache.

Jack has already retrieved Eleanor's bike from the garage. It leans against the mailbox, which used to read WITT 1881 COVE but now reads WIT 1881 CO E.

"Did you put the—"

"—key back?" Jack finishes. "Yes, I did."

He's eating a banana in giant bites, even the mushy brown parts that make Eleanor wrinkle her nose. He holds it out to her now, but she shakes her head. There isn't much left, and she isn't very hungry.

"You're supposed to eat breakfast," he says. "Most important meal of the day."

"I do eat breakfast," she says.

"You're a terrible liar."

"I'm not lying."

Jack finishes the banana and twirls its empty skin like a floppy nunchuk. "What did you have?"

"Cinnamon toast," Eleanor answers, too quickly.

Jack crosses his arms. "I don't believe you."

"You're just going to have to," she says. "We're late."

"We're not late," Jack says. He glances at his bare wrist. "Wait, what time is it?"

"It's almost eight."

"We're late," Jack says. "Do we care?"

Eleanor frowns at him. "Just because it's the last week of school doesn't mean we can get lazy."

"You sound like Mrs. Hicks," he says.

"Mrs. Hicks doesn't want you to lop your finger off with a table saw," Eleanor says. "*Lazy* means a different thing in shop class."

"I guess." Jack brightens. "Hey, want to go the back way today?"

Eleanor looks at her watch. "It's no shorter."

"I know, but it's not really much longer."

"We're late," she says again, but she knows she'll give in. The back way will carry them down Piper Road, a long, subtle grade that comes down out of the hills. It's a truck route directly into Anchor Bend, but these days it's barely traveled. The road falls away steeply into the woods on either side, and the last time Eleanor and Jack biked there, they came across a fallen tree near the bottom of the hill and skidded to an almost-disastrous stop. They climbed over the dead tree one by one, Jack passing the bicycles across to Eleanor. She wonders now if the tree has been cleared.

Jack seems to read her mind. "I was up there last weekend," he says. "Clean ride. But if you're scared . . ."

She sighs. "Okay. But we have to be fast. I don't want to be late to class."

"You said we're already late."

"I don't want to be *more* late."

"I believe it's *more later*," Jack corrects.

She takes a playful swing at him, then climbs aboard her bike and follows him up Cove Street. He weaves across the road in wide arcs. There are blue wheeled trash containers parked at the end of every driveway, and Jack swings close to one of them and somehow manages to flip the lid open and deposit his banana peel inside in a single fluid motion.

"Damn," Eleanor says. "Jack, wait."

He turns a lazy circle back to where Eleanor has stopped on the road.

"I forgot to take out the trash," Eleanor says.

"Well, hurry up," Jack says. "If we're going to take the back way."

"I didn't even gather it all up yet," she says. "It'll take too long. You should go ahead without me."

Jack looks at her sternly. "We leave no man behind," he says in a deep voice. "No pretty girls, either."

Eleanor walks her bicycle back to the driveway and rests it against the mailbox post again. "Go on," she says over her shoulder. "It's going to take at least ten minutes. It's glass day."

Jack climbs off his bike and leans it against Eleanor's. "Shit," he says. "Okay. I'll help."

"Jack—"

"No," he says. "Really. I can be quiet. I know how this part goes. Let me help."

*    *    *

ELEANOR PAUSES AT the doorway to the living room. She can feel Jack come up behind her, and, without turning, she says, "She's snoring."

Agnes rests under a blanket on the blue chair. The chair's ribbed covering has worn smooth, almost shiny, from years of use. Agnes is small, nearly invisible, beneath the blanket. It rises and falls imperceptibly with each of her breaths.

On the table beside her is an empty bottle of Smirnoff and a mostly empty bottle of Jack Daniel's.

"Glass day," Jack says. "Let me do that part."

Eleanor looks back at him. "You have to be very, very quiet," she warns.

"I know," he says; then he looks down. "I've done this for my dad for years."

Eleanor softens a bit. "There's a bin under the sink."

Jack gets to work, and Eleanor goes upstairs, taking each step quietly, moving left and right to avoid the creaky spots. She gathers the small bags from her bathroom and bedroom wastebaskets, then goes into her mother's room. Eleanor usually skips it, but today when she peeks into the connected bathroom, she sees the wastebasket overflowing onto the floor. She goes to collect the fallen bits, then stops, recognizing them as the photos and other memories that her mother had been sifting through in the attic the night before.

"Oh, Esme," Eleanor says softly.

She drops to her knees on the tile floor and starts to gather the crumpled papers. The small trash bags forgotten, Eleanor presses smooth every photograph. The wrinkles and folds are permanent, though. Esmerelda playing with her plastic pony on the fence in the front yard. Esmerelda stretched out on the floor as a little girl, her feet propped on the fireplace hearth, an encyclopedia open on her tummy. Eleanor tries her best to save the photos, but most have been crushed with such force that the thin emulsion layer flakes away at the creases, leaving white scars stitched across the image.

She presses the photographs to her chest and closes her eyes, the memories rushing in. For once, she doesn't push them back. She lets them come.

1984.

More than a year before the world would end.

They were five, almost six. Heat had stormed the coast that year, melting the clouds away, the sun an incandescent marble that never seemed to drop out of sight. The house was intolerably warm, and Eleanor remembers her mother begging for air-conditioning, and her father complaining about money. The windows stayed open, curtains fluttering in the ponderous, hot breeze. Her father propped a box fan in the front doorway and left the door ajar, claiming that this would stir the air currents inside.

It did little good. The days were long, the nights sticky. Agnes was too exhausted to cook, and it was too hot for that sort of thing, anyway. So they ate microwavable dinners or peanut butter sandwiches. Ice was a precious treat. The girls would hold a cube on their tongues to see whose melted the fastest.

In the heavy evening, ushered off to bed while their parents watched the news and then the late shows, Eleanor and Esmerelda lay on the beds in their room, blankets thrown back, arguing about who was more affected by the heat.

"I'm so hot, my tongue dried up," Esmerelda would say.

"Well, I'm so hot that I'm turning to ash," Eleanor would retort.

"I'm so hot that I just set the house on fire."

"*Pffff.* I'm so hot, I just set the whole *town* on fire."

They took cold baths together, flagged down the ice cream truck together, and ran around most of the time in nothing more than T-shirts and underpants.

Then one day Esmerelda chased Eleanor through the house, and Eleanor stopped short.

"Do you hear that?" she asked. "What's that sound?"

The twins stood still in the kitchen, heads cocked, listening.

Splashing.

Laughter.

That's what Eleanor remembers most now: the sound of her mother's laughter.

A rare thing, like a black dove.

Eleanor followed Esme through the kitchen to the patio door. In the backyard sat something marvelous.

A yellow inflatable swimming pool.

Her father sat in it, splayed out, shirtless. The girls watched as he yanked their mother onto his lap, and Agnes squealed in delight, kicking the water with her feet. She wasn't dressed for a pool. She was in a sundress, wearing her gardening hat and gloves.

Eleanor looked at Esmerelda.

"That's *our* pool," Esmerelda said.

Eleanor nodded.

The girls ran outside, shrieking, chased their parents out of the pool, and stomped and splashed like monsters towering over a tiny sea.

The memory seems to unwind, and Eleanor recalls how fleeting that moment was, how her mother quickly returned to her flowers. The absence of Eleanor's sister is a terrible burden, a great dark world that crushes her beneath its inescapable weight.

"Hey," Jack says from the doorway.

Eleanor jumps, startled, and thumps her head on the bottom of the porcelain sink. She ignores the pain and realizes that she's already crying. She can't hide her hot tears from Jack.

"Whoa," he says, crouching beside her. "You okay? What happened?"

Eleanor shakes her head, and though she doesn't want to cry in front of Jack, his simple question flushes her skin with warmth, and she remembers distantly what it's like for someone to care what she is thinking, how she is feeling. This notion lodges itself in her throat, and she suddenly finds it difficult to breathe. She puts one hand to her chest and opens her mouth, and an embarrassing honking sound comes out.

"Hey, hey," Jack says, putting his arm around her. "Hey, now."

She honks and gasps in big lungfuls of air, which only make her chest hitch more, and when she finally is able to let the air back out, she sobs on his shoulder.

She doesn't see the photos still in the wastebasket—more crushed pictures of her sister, among them a photograph of the two girls together, torn in half, Eleanor's side of the photo ripped into even smaller bits.

Eleanor lets Jack hold her for a moment, and then, certain that she has humiliated herself enough, she presses the heels of her palms into her eyes, roughly brushing away the tears, and she says, "This stuff isn't trash. I'll save it all later. We're late."

Jack regards her curiously. "Maybe you should play hooky today," he says.

Eleanor shakes her head firmly. "I want to go now. Please."

He gets to his feet, then offers her his hand, and she can feel the wiry cords of his muscles as he draws her up from the floor. She gives him a sheepish grin and wipes more of the tears from her face and says, "I still have to get the kitchen trash."

"I already got it all," he says. "Your, uh—your mother . . ."

Eleanor looks up at him and waits. "My mother what?"

Jack averts his eyes. "Those bottles . . . that's from, like, a month, right?"

"No," Eleanor says, squeezing past him. "That's from this week."

He follows, still keeping his voice low. "It's so much."

"I know."

"She shouldn't drink so much."

"I know."

"Seriously! Where does she even get—"

"I *know*," Eleanor spits. She whirls around to face him, and Jack almost collides with her. "You think I don't know? I *know*."

He works his jaw but can't find the right words, and so, instead, he says nothing at all. Eleanor stares at him, hard, and after a very long moment she turns around sharply and goes down the stairs. She no longer cares about being quiet and hits every noisy step on the way down. She glances in at her mother as she passes the living room doorway, but Agnes hasn't stirred.

Eleanor goes out the front door with a bang, and a moment later Jack follows, holding the plastic bags that Eleanor had forgotten upstairs. She climbs astride her bicycle and watches as Jack quietly puts the bags into the blue can, then wheels it out to the curb. He goes back inside, emerges a moment later with the glass-recycling crate, and carries that to the curb, as well. The dozen or so empty bottles inside clink like wind chimes.

When he's finished, Eleanor pedals away without waiting, without asking if Jack has locked the front door. He catches up with her and rides silently a few feet behind. He doesn't say anything when she bypasses the turn that would take them to Piper Road, and when they arrive at the school fifteen minutes later, not having spoken a word, Eleanor drops her bike on the front lawn and goes inside.

Jack patiently picks up her bike and pushes it to the rack. He threads his chain lock through both front tires and around the gray metal tube of the rack, and then he goes into the school too.


THE HALLWAY IS jammed with students. No one takes notice of Eleanor. She walks behind a clump of girls with frizzy, teased hair. Kids make out against the bank of lockers. She watches a couple of burnouts in sagging jeans and windbreakers escape through a side door and sees the dumpster across the lot where their friends are already milling about under a fog of cigarette smoke.

The warning bell rings, and slowly the hall empties.

She hates to ignore Jack. He won't take her behavior to heart, she knows. He's one reason she hasn't already lost her mind. But reminding herself of this does nothing to diminish her guilt.

When Eleanor was thirteen years old, her father came to the house to pick her up for the weekend, and he and Agnes got into it, as usual. Eleanor didn't even try to break up their fights anymore. She just left her bag in the hallway and went upstairs to wait them out. An hour later her parents were still trading barbs. Exhausted and feeling smaller than she liked, Eleanor pulled on her coat and shoes and sneaked out of the house. It began to rain as she pedaled away.

Jack pulled a curtain back when she tapped on his window half an hour later. He stared at her in surprise, then pointed toward the back door. He met her there and let her in.

"What's wr—," he started, and Eleanor burst into tears. She stepped forward—she almost *fell* forward—and he staggered back a step, then let his arms close around her.

He fashioned a pallet beside his bed, using cushions from the living room sofa, but Eleanor took his hand and led him to the bed. He sat down, and she sat beside him, and when she drifted off to sleep on his shoulder, he worked his way out from beneath her and guided her head to his pillow. She didn't stir as he pulled his blankets over her, then stretched out himself on the sofa cushions.

"Miss Witt."

Eleanor jerks back to the present. She's standing in the middle of the empty hallway, her backpack sliding off her shoulder. Mr. Holston, her history teacher, stands in front of her.

"Are you feeling all right?" he asks.

She just stares dumbly at him.

"Miss Witt, I'm speaking to you."

What is she supposed to say?

\*   \*   \*

THE NEXT TIME Eleanor sees Jack is during lunch. She's still angry at him. It's not entirely his fault; his words—and her mother's behavior the night before, and the bottles, and the crumpled photos—reminded her of something she tries so hard to forget: that her mother is resentful of Eleanor, would rather drink herself to death than comfort her surviving child.

*Drink herself to death.*

She stands gloomily in the cafeteria line for a few minutes, holding her plastic tray, waiting to reach the front, where the old women in the hairnets and the sauce-stained white aprons wait to spoon pasty mashed potatoes and overcooked peas onto the tray, and Eleanor's stomach turns. She leaves the line and puts her tray back on the stack.

Jack and her other friend, Stacy, have already secured their usual shared table. They have spotted Eleanor leaving the line, and she can feel them staring at her. She steers wide around their table, refusing to meet their curious stares, and heads for the double doors. Posted at the door is Mrs. McDearmon, on lunch duty for the day, and she looks at Eleanor and opens her mouth to ask a question.

"I need to visit the principal's office," Eleanor lies, feeling the same tension in her chest that she felt in her mother's bathroom earlier that morning. She wants to escape the cafeteria and the prying eyes of her friends and the suspicious gaze of the teachers before she starts to cry again.

Mrs. McDearmon says, "There and back, and hurry," and allows Eleanor to pass, because what child would willingly visit the principal's office who didn't have a reason to?

Eleanor nods gratefully and lowers her head to hide her damp eyes. She wishes that her hair were longer. She wishes a lot of things: that she was still a child, that her father had never traveled to Florida, that her mother had never loaded the girls into the car on that stupid, foggy, rainy day.

Mrs. McDearmon returns to her post, and Eleanor passes through the cafeteria doors, and everything changes, forever, just like that.

# *mea*

Her name is Mea.

This wasn't always her name, but it is the name that was given to her—after. She cannot recall her real name or remember who or what she once was.

She lives in the dark, in a world of vivid shadow that reminds her of a fishbowl filled with black water. Most of the time, Mea is deep in the center of that bowl, embraced by shadow; however, from time to time she drifts up against the glass, and the black water parts, and she can see beyond this strange new world, into others. The glass that separates her from those other worlds is warm and malleable and hums with music that she cannot hear but only feel. She forever associates it with the sight of a woman hanging sweet-smelling laundry on a line in a green yard beneath a blue sky, a woman who sings a song within her chest, wordless and soft. This was the first world that Mea peered into, beautiful and foreign and rimmed with memory.

The boundary between Mea's world and the ones beyond is not glass, of course, but a sort of fine, strong membrane. It is firm enough to support her boundlessness if she rests herself against it, and strong enough to keep her contained within her fishbowl, but it reshapes itself to her form, like a hammock distended by a sleeping body. Mea finds this interesting, because she has no idea what her *form* is. She knows that she had one, once, but it no longer hems her in. Here in the darkness, Mea has no edges. She simply breathes the dark. The dark is a part of her. In a sense, she *is* the dark, and she has grown accustomed to this sensation.

It wasn't always this way. She trembles when she recalls her first moments in this world, flung into the dark bowl like a missile, the blackness enveloping her, alien and complete. Like a beast the darkness swallowed her, and Mea felt she was being dissolved by its juices, felt as if she had been torn apart at her seams. Her senses weren't up to the task, and she flailed about in the blackness, blind, amputated from her own body.

In time, she met the other occupant of the darkness. He called himself Efah, and when he spoke to her, she realized that there was a greater dark beyond her fishbowl. Efah was on the other side of the glass, free to move about, curiously inspecting Mea.

*What are you called?* he had asked her. When she was unable to answer, he said, *From now on you are Mea, for you are mine.*

She is afraid of Efah, who flits and swarms beyond the glass like smoke in the darkness. She doesn't speak when he calls to her, and in time he teaches her what he knows while she huddles silently in the center of her confinement.

He tells her about the rift, which is the name of the great dark beyond her fishbowl. *The rift is older than anything,* Efah explains. He speaks without words, seeming to effortlessly force his way into her thoughts. She cannot build a wall that will keep him out, though she tries.

Efah tells her of his own birth and naming, of the visions that he has witnessed over the years. The rift is ancient and remembers the birth of time. It is the great river of memory and being, Efah tells Mea; all things float within the rift.

*Every birth and death,* Efah says. *Every sunset or falling leaf. Every extinction, every child's cry.*

Mea does not answer Efah, and only when he vanishes from the other side of the membrane does she relax. She cannot tell how long he is gone, for time seems to mean nothing at all in her shadowy prison, in this endless night.

In time, Mea returns to the glass of her fishbowl and presses herself against it. The membrane is not thick, and she can see through it if she chooses to, into the black rift that Efah inhabits. But if she focuses carefully, the membrane reveals its secrets. The membrane is a current within the rift. The membrane is time itself, and, as she soon discovers, time can be *directed*.

Mea can swim upstream, visiting memories that the membrane holds. They shimmer and flicker within its gauzy surface. She absorbs everything she can, feels the loves and ambitions of every living thing flow over her like water, feels them become a *part* of her, as if she carries those memories now in veins she cannot see.

In her research of the past and future, Mea stumbles upon a scene that she recognizes. She is startled by this discovery and what it means. Mea has never remembered her own name, her former self, and over the ages has come to feel as if she belongs in her glass container. She simply *is*, as Efah *is*, as the rift and the boundless current of time *are*. She is a witness to history, in a sense, observing the membrane's captured memories like films trapped in amber. Mea has watched so many of these memories that she has ceased to think of them as real events that once occurred in some other realm. A bird who falls from its nest and starves while its mother stares down at it; a planet that forms from the dust of a long-dead star and flowers in the deepest, quietest night, then one day withers away, unnoticed by the universe; a mountain that grows out of deep seismic unrest and rises powerfully into a violet sky and is then immobilized by ice. Each of them beautiful and tragic, each of them far removed from Mea's home in the darkness.

Until now.

Longing rushes through her like a toxin. Mea is not accustomed to feeling such things. She has lived like a cloud, like a vapor, for so long that when this new memory awakens her feelings, it is as if her feathery form has begun to solidify.

For the first time in a great while, Mea feels constrained.

In her fishbowl, the darkness has its own tides, and Mea is so shaken by her new discovery that she slips free from her attachment to the membrane. The dark carries her away from the trauma of the world she has peeked into, and Mea tumbles in the blackness, wondering what is happening to her. She bumps into the membrane now and again, each collision revealing some other forgotten and fragile event, memories of warm suns and symphonic stars and clouds and seedlings and oceans and fire. Each memory occupies its own frozen void within the membrane, each a tenuous bubble that strains to remain expanded, but as Mea slides by, each collapses, the membrane clouding to obscure the scenes from her view.

Time ascribes no meaning to these events; it simply presents them for Mea's observation, then swallows them again as she drifts by.

She shakes herself from her startled state now, aware that the memory that has shocked her so is now somewhere behind her. What if she can't locate it again? She claws against the black tide within her fishbowl, swimming upstream, pressing herself against the strange membrane, searching, searching.

Until she finds it. It flickers at the edge of Mea's vision, and she surges to it, pressing herself flat against the membrane as if trying to take the memory into herself, to possess it.

The strangely familiar memory expands until it is now world-size itself, and Mea lingers at its boundaries, staring obsessively into it, drinking in the things she sees. A room of child strangers, large windows, and a gray, damp neighborhood beyond them.

And a red-haired girl, darkly familiar.

Mea leans into the membrane, hungry for more, until it stretches like taffy, until it seems she will burst into the world that yawns before her. It flexes, but the membrane is unbreakable.

Mea *yearns* for the strange, red-haired girl, reaches for her.

Then something happens that Mea can't explain: a tiny vortex seems to appear in the membrane's surface, no larger than the head of a pin. It swirls, twisting rapidly. Through its eye, sound and light spill into the darkness of Mea's cell. She hears muffled voices and conversation, feels the hum of cool light like a tiny, amorphous finger that reaches into her, stirs her.

A window between Mea's world and the red-haired girl's.

Mea pulls at the vortex, trying to enlarge it, but it is not elastic, and it resists her manipulations. After a moment it snaps shut with great force, and the membrane ripples like water.

Mea stares through the membrane at the world beyond. The red-haired girl is no longer there. Mea feels frantic, then calm, for time is a river, and Mea can navigate it like a leviathan. She is hopeful: If she cannot escape her imprisonment, perhaps she can draw the red-haired girl from her own world into Mea's.

Mea retreats to the center of the fishbowl to consider this, to plan it carefully. On the opposite side of the membrane, drifting in the greater dark of the rift, Efah watches her.

# *eleanor*

There and back, and hurry," says Mrs. McDearmon.

Eleanor hides her eyes, feeling her tears spill over. She is humiliated by her breakdown in front of Jack and embarrassed by the way she has treated him since that moment. He is, after all, only concerned for her. It isn't as if Jack is inexperienced in these matters. Hasn't he told Eleanor often of his mother's departure, of his father's depression and alcoholism? Isn't it funny that their lives should be so similar now? Except in Eleanor's case, it is her father who has left, and her mother who has collapsed like a black hole.

She can hear Jack's voice through the din of the cafeteria, just one voice among the hundreds of gossiping, chattering teenagers, and she tucks a strand of short red hair behind her ear, not because it is loose but because doing so will project a certain appearance; it is something to do, and if Eleanor is in the act of doing something—anything—then she can be forgiven for not hearing Jack and for leaving the cafeteria without acknowledging him.

She will have to apologize, of course. But she will wait until later, when she doesn't feel like such an asshole.

This is not a new problem for her. She shoves him away; he persists, albeit gently. She considers what it might mean, allowing herself to acknowledge and accept his thinly veiled romantic interest; would it transform their friendship into something more? Would it sputter, like her parents' marriage? And if it did, what would she do without Jack, who is always there for her when she falls apart?

Eleanor is fourteen, but she is already a committed spinster in her heart.

So she ignores Jack now and walks through the cafeteria doors, and at the very last moment, she feels something subtle and strange, as if she is made of metal and some magnetic force is tugging her toward it. The tiny hairs on her arms and neck lift up. There is a sharp smell; the air sizzles. Before she has a moment to truly consider any of this, she steps through the doorway—is, frankly, almost yanked through it—and then Eleanor is no longer in the cafeteria, no longer in her high school, no longer even in Oregon at all.

Back in the world, Jack sees her disappear. He drops his carton of milk, bewildered; it pumps like a vein, then dribbles onto the table.

She's just gone.

THE FIRST THING she notices is the change in temperature, then the smell, and then she looks around and realizes that the tiled floor of the high school's entry hall has been replaced with prickly grass. She turns, a little confused, but does not see the cafeteria doors or Mrs. McDearmon or the crowd of talking students or Jack behind her—and then she is very confused.

She does what she learned to do as a little girl. When lost, stay where you are. There is a tree stump nearby, and Eleanor sits down on it, grateful for its existence. She decides, quite calmly, that she will sit here and collect her thoughts and try to understand what has just happened to her.

"Okay," she says aloud, relieved to hear her own voice. "Okay. Okay."

She repeats the word a few times. If she can hear her own voice, then the world cannot be too far off its orbit.

Unfolding in all directions is a warm green meadow. In the distance she can see fences the size of staples, barns the size of Monopoly game pieces, and tiny moving dots that look like insects but are probably horses or cows or sheep. Then one of them seems to grow taller, and she realizes that whatever it is simply has a long neck, and then she says, "Alpacas. Or llamas, maybe."

She looks up and sees a blue sky and fat, happy clouds, and the sun is even higher above, orange and round and warm, and she says, "Okay, so I'm not on Venus or something."

Then she decides to stop talking to herself, because she feels silly doing so. She's clearly not on Venus or in any other strange place. She's on someone's farm, or in between several farms. She can see other distant white houses and red barns and small, moving dots. The air is clear, fresh; a soft breeze rustles through the sheaves of— what is that, corn? wheat?—whatever that is in the distance. The sound reminds her of the ocean. It undulates, just like the sea.

She misses the ocean, not only because it seems to be a million miles from here. Her father sometimes takes her there during visitation weekends, and they sit on the pebbly ground and sweep the rocks away from themselves, exposing the wet and brick-colored sand beneath. He shows her all sorts of interesting ways to build sturdy castles that will stand up to the surf, most of which involve packing small round rocks into the walls and foundation of the castle, and they make bets about whose will last the longest, and then the winner buys ice cream. She's too old for these sorts of excursions with her father—all the other girls her age have their dads drop them off at the mall or the movies, or go to one another's houses and smear blush on their cheeks and glop candy-colored polish onto their nails and speculate about blow jobs and who in their class has given one—but Eleanor doesn't care too much. She knows why she craves these moments. She was robbed of a true childhood, and now, as a teenager, she leaps at every opportunity to regress, even a little.

She is her own psychiatrist.

She told her father this theory once, and his eyes filled up with tears, and so she doesn't tell him things like that anymore. He had wrapped her up in a fierce hug, and she felt guilty, as if the act of acknowledging her fractured childhood was somehow an accusation. But he had to know it was true, didn't he?

Eleanor climbs up onto the stump to see a bit farther, but it doesn't offer much benefit. She can see a tiny bit more of the landscape, of the near-microscopic forests that seem to lie beyond the farms, and now that she squints, she can see an almost invisible mountain towering over the whole scene, snowcapped and dusty against the sky, as if it is a scene that has been painted and then laboriously erased, and all that is left behind is a ghost of its shape.

"Where the hell am I?" she says aloud.

SHE AIMS FOR one of the white houses and starts walking. The grass is long and soft beneath her feet, which she notices now are bare. Where are her *shoes?* She looks back at the tree stump and the grass around it, but her shoes are not there. She looks down and realizes that she isn't wearing her school clothes, either, but a yellow sundress with slim straps.

She doesn't *own* a yellow sundress. With *any* sort of straps.

Eleanor stands still for a moment. The wind ruffles her hair, and she reaches back, without thinking, to knot it behind her head. Her fingers slide into a thick mane of red hair. She is confused, then realizes, with a shock, that this is *her* hair, that her hair is *long*.

This, of all the things she has just experienced, scares her the most, and Eleanor breaks into a run. The white house in the distance rocks on the horizon like a sailboat on a violent sea. Eleanor runs until her lungs burn and she cannot run anymore, and then she stops. The horizon levels out again. She bends over, hands on her knees, heart pounding.

When she looks up again, it is because she hears voices. They are small and very, very distant, but she can hear people all the same.

"Hey!" she shouts.

The voices burble on, seemingly unaware of her presence.

She starts walking again, toward the voices, which seem to be to her right, away from the white house. East? Maybe that's east. Her feet find a mostly overgrown road, one that hasn't been used in years. Two deep furrows in the ground, set apart at a distance not unlike the distance between a truck's tires, have sprouted vivid pink and yellow flowers. She squats and inspects them closely.

They look like flowers from Earth.

"Definitely not Venus," she mutters again.

Despite her interest in the voices, she finds herself slowing to a stroll. The sun warms her skin, and she discovers that she likes the sensation of being nearly naked under a thin dress. The breeze that cools her shoulders also flutters the hem of the dress, tickling her pale thighs. She closes her eyes as she walks, balancing on the ridge of dirt between the flowering ruts. Her breath comes and goes in deep, patient swallows, and her heart rate slows. She enjoys the feeling of the long hair on her neck, a little, but then it reminds her of the accident all over again, of Esmerelda's hair caught in broken glass, and Eleanor pushes the thought away, unwilling to spoil this strange new experience with the worst of her memories.

Her mind drifts to how she arrived here, but the results are inconclusive. She was in the cafeteria . . . and then she wasn't. She had told Mrs. McDearmon that she was going to the principal's office—though that wasn't her intention at all—and then she had walked through the door, and Jack was calling her name, and there had been that strange wash of static—

And then she had found herself here.

In Iowa, or somewhere.

The voices are louder now, and she can tell that they aren't directly ahead, but off to the side of the road. The grass is very tall there, nearly chest-high, and slim white trees form a thatched wall before her. She can see no way around them but straight through, so that's where she goes.

IT CAN HARDLY be called a forest. A wood? A grove? If the trees were fruit-bearing, she might call it an orchard, but they seem like a smaller cousin of the birch tree, their branches deep green with leaves that haven't yet begun to turn with the seasons. Which means that here it's summer, wherever *here* is. The ground here is littered with old, dry branches like bones, the grass replaced by cool, peaty earth. It's soft and refreshing beneath her feet, except for when she steps absently on one of the old branches.

The voices grow louder as she makes her way through the grove. She comes upon a tree, the bark of which has been carved with a knife, its narrow trunk scarred with words that have healed over and are difficult to read. But there are more, she notices; now that she has spied the first carving, they seem to be everywhere. Some are legible: one reads *boogerman getcha,* and she cannot tell if that is a misspelling or a sincere threat made by a man constructed of boogers. There are more—*sleep with your eyes open,* reads another; *dont tell your mom im gonna getcha*—and Eleanor is amused by their childlike naïveté.

Then she comes across one that is very fresh, still damp, with a different tone altogether.

## J LOVES E 4EVER

The tree is too narrow for the words to be wrapped in a heart, so a smaller heart has been carved beneath.

The carving speaks to her, or seems to. She touches it with her fingertip. The wound is damp and smells of green. There are curled strips of bark at the bottom of the tree. She bends over and picks them up, feeling their softness. The carving is fresh, maybe only a few minutes old.

She turns in a circle, studying her surroundings, but no one is around.

Instead, she spies a tree house, quaint and lemon yellow, like her sundress. It rests in the lower branches of a stubby tree. Its blue roof and door and little window look as if they were borrowed from a real house—wood shingles, blue shutters. A short ladder leads up to the door.

She sidesteps more dead branches and climbs two rungs to peek inside. The wooden floor is dusty, and it appears that no one has been inside for a very long time. A bench has been built from two-by-fours and is attached to one of the walls. Stacked on the bench are books—Hardy Boys mysteries, plastic binders open to reveal transparent pages full of baseball cards, Archie comics. There is a dartboard on one wall, but the tree house is far too claustrophobic to permit accurate throws. She can see a cardboard box labeled CLUB SECRETS, and she steps up one more rung on the ladder to peer inside it. There's a plastic spatula, a tin flute, and a baseball.

The voices are louder now and have sharpened: a boy's bold shout, a girl's delicate laughter. Eleanor climbs back down the ladder and looks through the trees. She picks her way through them and comes to the edge of the grove and a scruffy wall of azalea bushes. The bushes are pink and flowering, and bees and humming-birds float dreamily around their blooms.

She spots a gap between the bushes and heads for it, ducking low to avoid a plump hummingbird. She plunges through the foliage and emerges into a beautiful, manicured meadow, surrounded on all sides by the same narrow white trees. It is as private a place as one might hope to find in the middle of farm country, Eleanor thinks, and as perfect a place as one might long to ever find anywhere.

A black pond lies in the middle of the open space, and even from the meadow's edge she can see dragonflies flitting along the water's surface. Someone has built a small footbridge over the pond; a huge yellow parasol stands at its center, casting a wide shadow over the water.

Beyond the pond she can see a makeshift baseball diamond with lovely white chalk lines and a bright, clean home plate. Suddenly two children burst out of a thatch of shrubs along the first base line, and Eleanor retreats into the azaleas. She stands there, oblivious to the bees that hum around her, and watches.

They are young—no more than eight, perhaps even younger. The boy is rambunctious and silly and has a full head of unruly brown hair. He is shirtless and tanned and, while not yet gangly, full of that promise. He will be tall and lanky by thirteen, will grow into his frame by seventeen, and by twenty he will be well-built, and older men will envy his youthful metabolism.

The girl twirls along the line between the pitcher's mound and second base, her red braids spinning like propellers.

*Jesus,* Eleanor thinks. *That's me.*


WHICH MEANS THE boy is Jack.

She hardly recognized him; he is effusive, light, bounding around like a gazelle. The Jack she knows is weighted with things he doesn't often talk about. This little boy hasn't experienced such things yet. For that matter, neither has the younger Eleanor who chases him.

Her legs feel weak, but if she sits down, she won't be able to see the children clearly, and she is captivated and horrified by their very existence. Her stomach turns, and a cool sweat breaks out on her arms and neck.

This might be Venus, after all.

The boy—Jack—explodes into motion, running the bases once, then twice, then a third time around. He takes a spill, sending up a cloud of red-brown dust. He laughs and laughs, and the little red-haired girl runs to him and slides to her knees. Grass stains appear on Eleanor's young doppelgänger's dress.

The children laugh and tussle. Eleanor cannot hear their words, but she recognizes their sounds: the shout of excitement from Jack and the squeal from little Eleanor. The two of them run in crazy loops around the field, Jack trying to tag Eleanor, Eleanor barely escaping. They collapse into the grass and pull up big handfuls of it, and Jack finds a honeysuckle bush, and they pop the blossoms off and suck them.

Eleanor leaves the safety of the bushes and walks out into the field. She cannot help herself. She is entranced—fearful but compelled to see her younger self up close, to peer at her like a captured moth. She remains as quiet as can be, afraid she might startle the children, but they don't seem to notice her at all. She watches them discard the honeysuckle blossoms and practice somersaults and handstands in the grass, their clothes growing progressively dirtier.

"Hello," she says when she reaches the boundary of the infield.

The children do not acknowledge her. Eleanor wonders if they can see her. She walks boldly across the field, inserting herself into the middle of their gymnastics routines, and little Jack tumbles right past Eleanor's feet without spying her. He sprawls on his back, giggling madly.

"Hello," she says, looking down at him.

He looks past her, unseeing. Eleanor decides that this is a dream. Then she laughs at herself softly for not realizing that sooner. One doesn't simply bump into one's younger self without some serious dream action taking place.

What does that mean for her body back at the school? She imagines falling asleep suddenly, narcoleptic, face-planting on the hallway floor.

She certainly hopes not. She doesn't want to wake up in the hospital or in the nurse's office with another broken nose.

Eleanor sinks to the ground, resigned to watching the children play. She remembers days something like this. She and Esmerelda and Agnes would meet Jack and his mother at Franklin Park, and while the children would scamper over playground equipment and dig in the sandboxes, their mothers would chat happily over a thermos of coffee.

She looks around now, but though there are benches, there are no mothers, no coffee, no playground equipment.

No Esmerelda.

Above her, the sun has moved on, and the rich blue sky has turned watery and pink. The children run to a duffel bag on the ground. Little Jack comes out of the bag with a handful of slim gray sticks, and Eleanor wonders what they might be. Jack produces a lighter from nowhere—Eleanor looks around for adult supervision, then remembers that this is a dream—and touches it to one of the sticks. The tiny stem bursts into staticky orange light.

Sparklers! She remembers these.

Jack hands one to little Eleanor. They dance around the meadow, painting elegant loops and spirals in the dusk with their sparklers. Eleanor smiles, recalling a time, in the years before the accident, when her family would recline in the yard as the sun fell into the sea, sometimes plunging behind Huffnagle Island, silhouetting its outcropping of rock as it sank. They would wait for the fireflies to come out, and then the girls would run around the yard with Mason jars, trying to capture the insects before bedtime was declared.

She sighs, calmed by the memory.

In the falling dark, the sparklers finally run out of light. Eleanor's tiny self takes Jack's hand, and the two children vanish through the same bushes from which they had appeared.

Eleanor follows. She cannot see beyond the bushes, but she pushes into them anyway, expecting to find the children hurrying across the meadow toward one of the distant farmhouses, but the bushes are full of night and shadow and strange, decidedly unnatural smells. She pushes through them and stumbles suddenly onto the damp tile floor of her high school's third-floor bathroom.

She trips, falls, and scrambles backward frantically, as if retreating from an attacking animal, until she collides with a stall divider. When she discovers that she is alone and recognizes her surroundings, she wraps her arms around herself, shivering. The bathroom is lit only by the late-evening sun that pierces the square window high above the sink.

She is back.

She is aware that this is all wrong, that everything is wrong, that it is too late in the day, that she was nowhere near this bathroom when she—what? Fainted? Fell asleep?

Her brain seems to short-circuit. She cannot grasp a single clear thought. She just sits on the floor, trembling.

She wishes Jack were here.

## *mea*

It doesn't work, so Mea tries again.

She burrows backward in time, sifting through the moments captured in the diaphanous membrane until she finds the red-haired girl. She's crossing the large room, walking toward a door. Mea waits for the right moment and prepares to throw herself against the membrane with all the force she can summon, but suddenly the membrane clouds over, obscuring her view of the girl.

Mea would cry out if she had a voice. Instead, she thrums, surging with disapproval. But the membrane only flexes as it usually does, ignorant of her frustration.

Outside the fishbowl, Efah watches quietly, furtive in shadow.

Mea is aghast at this unexpected result. She flattens herself against the membrane, stretching herself as wide as the sky, as if she might see the girl from one of a thousand other angles. But the membrane's ghostly veil remains shut.

For a moment Mea wants to shout into the great dark of the rift, but she contains herself. She has not given Efah the satisfaction of hearing her speak, and she will not do so now.

So she waits, holding herself beside the membrane, the gentle, sweeping tide of blackness breaking around her. She is a rock in its stream. In time, ordinary memories drift by again, but she pays them no mind. She has little interest in comets or volcanic eruptions or a bear cub's first salmon catch.

She waits for what feels like an eternity.

Then the fog that blinds Mea to the red-haired girl's history dissipates, and Mea sees the girl curled on a different floor, afraid and shaking. A powerful desire to enfold the girl rushes through Mea— but the membrane, though thin, is a chasm that Mea cannot cross.

## eleanor

Few places are as unnerving as an empty school at night.

After what feels like hours—the orange glare of the sun through the little square window has turned pink, then purple, then has smoked itself out—she finally gets to her feet. The tremble in her hands and knees has faded, but her first steps are uncertain. She is a spindly-legged pony, just born.

The hall outside the bathroom is dark and empty. Eleanor peers up and down its length and tentatively calls, "Hello?" Her voice echoes softly off the lockers and closed classroom doors.

The bathroom door creaks, magnified by the silence around her, and Eleanor cringes. She steps into the hall. The bathroom door hisses shut behind her.

Her feet are bare on the cold floor. The yellow sundress from her dream hangs lifelessly upon her shoulders.

Eleanor turns and pushes the bathroom door open again and feels for the light switch. She finds it and flips it, and the fluorescent bars overhead hum to life. The bathroom looks the same at night as it does during the day, at least when the lights are on, and for a moment Eleanor convinces herself that if she goes back into the hallway, she'll bump into students migrating from class to class, and someone will mutter at her for getting in the way, and all will be right with the world again.

But the square window still displays a darkening sky, and Eleanor feels the emptiness of the school in her bones. She walks across the tile floor, feeling the faint stickiness of floor polish, the gentle *rip-rip* sound as she lifts one foot, then the other. She pushes open the stall doors, hoping that she will find her own clothes there, perhaps, but the stalls are unoccupied.

She pushes her fingers through her hair and massages her scalp the way her father once showed her—the way he would ease his headaches after a long and stressful day of selling houses to ghosts—and she stops suddenly in horror. Her hands still buried in her hair, she dashes to the mirror.

The mirror is smeary—someone has scratched the sentiment WE ALL WHORES into the glass, words that Eleanor has often contemplated, searching feebly for the life truth that might be buried in such an unseemly phrase—but she can still make out her reflection well enough.

Her reflection stares back at her with long, beautiful red hair.

She runs.

THROUGH THE BATHROOM door, down the long and haunted hallway, past the lockers stuffed with homework and forgotten lunches and letter jackets, past the classrooms and their abandoned desks and blackboards with swirls of smudged lessons and assignments, toward the tall staircase that anchors the west wing and leads down to the lower floors. She cannot outrun her sundress or her red hair, and so on the second story she stops to finally catch her breath.

The scene of the crime is on the first floor. When she reaches it, the cafeteria's two pairs of double doors are closed but not locked. Eleanor leans against one, pushing it open. The cafeteria is hollowed out, its long lunch tables folded up and pushed to the perimeter, the accompanying hard plastic chairs stacked like leaning chimneys beside the tables. The buffet serving counter is shut up tightly, a metal shade pulled over its glass front.

Eleanor stands in the doorway and pictures the scene.

She'd been leaving the cafeteria. She'd walked past Mrs. McDearmon's stern face, had heard Jack calling for her. She had gone through the door, intending to—what? She hadn't thought about it then, but she probably would have ended up in one of the bathrooms, maybe the same one upstairs, hiding inside a stall until the lunch hour had passed.

Instead, she had walked through the door and into—someplace else. She thinks of it as Iowa, because it reminds her of her father's favorite movie, the one with the ballplayers who disappear into the tall corn. She remembers one of the players asking if he was in heaven, and the other guy says, no, it's Iowa.

So. Iowa.

How had she gotten there, anyway?

She stares skeptically at the cafeteria doors. She steels herself and pushes the second door open until it locks into place. The doorway is wide open now.

She remembers the static, the *hum* that she felt—like being at the science museum and putting her hands on that clear globe with the forks of electricity arcing inside it. The tiny hairs on her skin had stood on end, and she had felt—something. Something wavery.

She wiggles her hand at the doorway, but that strange field of energy isn't there now. There's no tingle in the air, and her hair—somehow long again—stays where it is.

Should she? What if she found herself somewhere else, someplace not as gentle as Iowa?

She takes a deep breath. Puts one foot through the door.

Then the other.

\* \* \*

NOTHING HAPPENS.

She crosses the threshold of the cafeteria once, twice, again and again, but nothing happens. Each time she finds herself either in the entry hall—surrounded by trophy cases, dangling pennants, vending machines, hand-lettered poster boards advertising the Sadie Hawkins dance or the Anchor Bend–Roseville game—or in the cavernous cafeteria, its empty belly lit by pale windows.

"I'm going crazy," Eleanor mutters.

She closes the cafeteria doors behind her and thinks about going home. She can't explain where the time has gone—it was noon, and now it is night. Did anybody see her when she left? Did they see the grassy farmland through the cafeteria doors, too? Surely Mrs. McDearmon would have noticed if Eleanor had simply winked out like a firefly, wouldn't she? Maybe Eleanor didn't go anyplace at all. Maybe she had simply wandered up to the third floor, in a trance or something, and just fallen asleep in the bathroom. No—wouldn't someone have found her?

She can't explain her missing clothes.

Or her hair, which has grown ten inches in a day.

"They're going to lock me up," she says.

But she is locked up already. She turns her attention to the problem of escaping the school. She has seen the large chains and padlocks that bind the doors shut. Most mornings she arrives early and has to wait outside for a faculty member to unlock those chains.

She wanders the halls, stops at every exterior set of doors, but they are all, indeed, chained shut. She feels a little bit like a ghost, and perhaps she is one. Maybe she died when she passed through the magical cafeteria doors, like a video game character who attempts to pass through a sparking electrical field, and now Eleanor is doomed to wander and haunt the school forever.

She makes her way around the outer hall, pausing to test more doors. What sorts of things might a ghost do to occupy itself in a dark and empty school? She could leave messages on blackboards to frighten students, scratch creepy messages into the mirrors—maybe a retort to the WE ALL WHORES author: NO, JUST YOU—or she could rain basketballs across the gymnasium floor during assembly. Eventually, she worries, she would get bored, and then what? More than that, schools eventually are torn down, and where would she go then? Haunt the empty grounds? The strip mall that would inevitably spring up in place of the high school? Or would she perish with the building, her ectoplasmic self dissolved, evicted?

None of the doors is unlocked.

She finishes her perimeter check at the front of the school. Through the doors she can see the shadowy parking lot, empty of vehicles, and the bus loop, also empty. For the first time it occurs to her that she might be trapped here all night long, and what will she do tomorrow when the students and teachers arrive and she's here with strange long hair, barefoot, like some second-rate Robinson Crusoe, washed up on a tile beach, living ferally in the janitor's closet?

*The janitors.*

As if she has conjured them with her thoughts, a small caravan of vehicles appears outside, headlights blinding her as its drivers turn into the parking lot. Eleanor watches as five people climb out and unload equipment: vacuum cleaners and mops and what looks like a giant sander.

The cleaning crew laughs among themselves. They gather around the front doors and wait, chuckling, while their leader unlocks a faculty access door in the side of the building. He enters and a moment later appears at the front doors, removes the chain, and pushes one of the doors open. The crew starts to filter in, dragging their cleaning supplies behind them on casters and in buckets. Before the door closes, Eleanor darts out from behind the trophy case and runs through the door and into the cold evening.

The very, very cold evening.

She turns around and runs back inside, teeth chattering. The five cleaners stand frozen in the hall, staring at her.

"I, um, got locked in," she says to the startled crew. "Does anyone have a quarter for the pay phone?"

HER FATHER'S BUICK is warm. The stereo is on, and her father's favorite band, Bread, sings her father's favorite song. The singer's voice is warm, too—comforting, Eleanor thinks, almost a bit like warm bread itself. The song triggers an old memory—a fragment of a memory, really—of Eleanor and Esmerelda zipped into the snugglebun: a strange, sleeping-bag-like construct with flaps that folded over the occupant's shoulders and snapped into place like oversize sleeves. The girls are perhaps five years old, small enough to lie together in the contraption. They're stretched out on the floor in front of the crackling fire. Eleanor's father reads *National Geographic* and sips his coffee. Her mother knits in the rocking chair, moving slowly back and forth.

Eleanor can't remember what happened next; the memory is isolated, free of any larger narrative. The moment is as comforting as the warmth of her father's car right now, as perfect a recollection as she could hope to conjure. She has not thought of it in a very long time.

"Want to tell me what happened?"

The streetlights slowly pass over the windshield, their reflections distorted into long, shining bars. There are few cars on the street and fewer shops open. Anchor Bend rolls up the sidewalks early, which means it has to be at least seven o'clock.

"What time is it?" she asks.

Her father pushes a button on the console. On the stereo face, the luminous blue CASSETTE is replaced with a digital readout.

"Seven forty," he says. "So? How does my smart girl manage to get locked up in the school?"

Eleanor looks out the window so she doesn't have to lie to his face. "I went to the nurse's office," she says. "I wasn't feeling well."

"How do you feel now?"

"Okay," she says with a shrug. "I guess I fell asleep there."

"Nobody checked on you?" Paul thumps the steering wheel. "Irresponsible sons of—I'll call the school tomorrow and give them a piece of my mind."

"Dad, it's okay," she says. "It was probably just an accident."

"Okay?" he asks. "You think it's okay for the adults in charge to just forget about a student? To lock her in the school overnight?"

"It wasn't overnight."

"It could have been, though," he says. "That's the point here. It's irresponsible behavior."

Eleanor sighs. "Okay, Dad."

"What?" her father asks, noticing her dissatisfaction. "It's uncool for a father to worry about his daughter?"

"It's fine," she says.

"Maybe it is uncool. But I'm uncool, so it works out."

"You're fishing, Dad," Eleanor says.

"Hey, what's going on with your hair?" he asks, reaching across the seat and taking one long lock in his fingers. "How did I not notice you were growing it out?"

She feels a pang of alarm. She has forgotten to tie her hair back so that he won't notice the difference.

"Um," she says, and then the stoplight ahead of them abruptly flashes red.

"Crap," her father mutters. He holds his arm out in front of her like a turnstile and brakes hard. "Sorry."

"It's fine," she says, grateful for the distraction. "Thanks for coming to get me."

"Yeah, well," he says. "That's what *good* parents do."

Eleanor chooses not to comment on her father's disparagement of her mother, though it will only drive him to continue. He does.

"Did your mother even pick up the phone?" he asks. Then he answers his own question. "I'll bet she didn't."

"I called *you*, Dad."

Paul flips the turn signal and takes a slow right. "Yeah, but you did that for a reason, didn't you?" he says. "You knew I'd answer. You knew that *I* would be—"

"Dad," Eleanor cautions.

"No, Eleanor, come on, now," he says. "What if something had happened and I wasn't around? What would you have done?"

"I don't know, Dad."

"Well," he says, talking almost to himself now, "I know your mother wouldn't have been there for you. Maybe you could have called Jack, if he was old enough to drive, but you know how his father is." He turns to Eleanor sharply. "Don't you ever get in a car with Jack's dad, do you hear me?"

Eleanor looks away. "I know, Dad."

"I know you know. We've talked about it a hundred times. I know. I just worry. I don't like not being there for you every day."

"We've talked about this, too."

"I just don't see why you couldn't have come to live with me," Paul says. Eleanor can hear the unspoken question: *Wasn't I good enough for you?*

"Mom needs me," Eleanor says. "You know it wasn't personal."

"Listen to you," Paul says. "You sound like such an adult. Grown-up women say that a lot, you know. *Nothing personal.* The context is usually very different, but the words sound so mature when you say them. *You* sound mature. You're not growing up too fast, are you?"

"Dad," Eleanor groans.

"Your mother doesn't need you," Paul blurts. Then he pauses, as if he can hear Eleanor's jaw fall open. "Wait, I didn't mean it like that. Came out wrong. What I mean is, your mother needs *some-one*. She needs—I don't know. A caregiver. Actually, no, what your mother needs is a detox."

"Dad, stop it."

"I just don't—"

"Stop it. I'll get out and walk."

Paul falls silent, and Eleanor folds her arms.

"I'm sorry," he says. "It isn't your fault that you love your mother. It isn't your fault that she's—"

"Dad—"

"—the drunk that she is," he finishes.

Eleanor unbuckles her seat belt, and a small red square lights up on the dashboard in front of her father, and a chime sounds.

"Let me out," she says.

"Eleanor, buckle your seat belt."

"Let me out right here or I'll jump out," she says.

"Buckle up and don't be a child," her father says. "We're almost there, anyway. I promise I won't say anything more about your mother."

Eleanor fastens her seat belt. She wraps her arms around her knees and rests her heels on the seat. For the remaining few turns, neither she nor her father says anything at all. There is only the sound of the tires gripping the asphalt, the hum of the heater, the dulcet sounds of another Bread song, and then the car thumps up onto the inclined driveway.

Eleanor unbuckles her belt and grumbles, "Thanks for the ride," and before she closes the door, she can hear her father say, "Bet she won't even answer the door," and Eleanor knows he's right, that Agnes is probably somewhere in the dark womb of the house, passed out as usual, unaware that her daughter has been missing for hours— and the worst part of all is really so much worse: that even if she knew, she probably wouldn't care very much. Not very much at all.

Eleanor scoops the extra key out of the planter beside the door, shakes off dry potting soil and little foam beads, and waves the key at her father. She can see him nod and wave back, and then the car reverses out of the driveway. The Buick's frame sags a bit as it meets the road. Paul waves again as Eleanor unlocks the door and slips into the dark house.

## *mea*

The red-haired girl has changed.

She isn't dressed as she was before, and her hair is longer. It sways against her back as she wanders through the school, poking at locked doors and peering through windows.

She is beautiful—and strangely familiar.

Mea *knows* her.

She does not understand this feeling. Mea is one with the ancient darkness that is her home; she is divorced from the memories that swim by. Beyond the membrane is the great and unfamiliar dark of the rift, which she has never ventured into. She cannot describe this sense of recognition. She aches to communicate with the girl.

In the dark tide, Mea waits for another opportunity.

## *agnes*

Agnes stands in a pale rectangle of light. Around her the house is dark. The refrigerator door is open. Did she open it? There's food inside that she doesn't remember buying. Milk and eggs and a loaf of bread. Some packaged meat. A plastic blue container with a yellow sticky note affixed to it.

She leans over. The note reads: *Mom. Egg salad.*

There's a small heart scrawled beneath the words.

And a letter *E*.

This is how it happens. She forgets, almost every time. She sees a note like this, the letter *E*. She forgets—just for a moment—that

Esmerelda has been gone all these years. She mistakes the note for Esmerelda's, a kind message to her mother.

The note is Eleanor's, of course.

Esmerelda has been gone for nearly eight years, but Agnes sees her every time she opens her eyes. She told Eleanor to put away the family photos years ago, but it is as if they still stand on the mantel, still hang on the walls. The empty spaces they once occupied still appear full to Agnes, with Esme's small round angel face staring back at her.

Agnes takes the blue container out and peels the note off and crumples it on the counter. The refrigerator thumps closed beside her. She pries open the lid and looks inside. Chopped egg whites, yellow paste of yolk and mayonnaise and pickles. She wants to eat it, knows that she should eat it, or anything, but she can't. The smell turns her stomach, and she barely makes it to the sink. What comes up is mostly liquid. She isn't sure when she last ate, but her stomach tells her it definitely hasn't been today. Probably wasn't yesterday, either.

She runs the faucet, then sinks to her knees and rests her forehead against the cool metal of the refrigerator door.

The worst of it is Eleanor.

Agnes sees her living daughter through a haze. Now and then Agnes will wake in the chair and find her child drawing a blanket over her, and she'll say, "Esme, my dear," and then the girl's mouth will open and speak in Eleanor's voice, shattering the illusion. It isn't Eleanor's fault that she has her sister's face. Agnes knows this.

Still, she cannot look at Eleanor.

She stands up shakily, knowing she should eat something, at least drink some water, but, instead, she goes to the china cabinet in the dining room and kneels down and opens the lowest door. She knows the arrangement of the tall serving platters by heart, the wide rectangles of bone china that stand on little pedestals, and she finds the bottle behind one and takes it out. She barely glances at the label. She knows it is whiskey by its shape, knows by its weight that it contains enough to sink her again into the dark long before Eleanor gets up for school.

She carries the bottle through the hall, and her reflection appears in the window, and Agnes stops and looks at herself. In the thin glare of moonlight she can see her face, gaunt beneath unhealthy hair. She barely remembers what her own mother looked like; she cannot find her there, among her own reflected features. But she sees her father there, a little, and that reminds her of her mother, of how much her father cried when she—

Agnes thinks that if she wasn't somewhat sober right now, she might have pitched the bottle at the mirror.

It is as good a reason as any to start drinking today, so she does.

She is young but does not look it. She feels like a woman who has lived through the Depression, a woman who has watched her babies die, who is beaten down by circumstance and who succumbs to it, who doesn't fight back, because why fight back? Why would you ever fight back when it hurts so much less to just lie down?

Agnes settles in the chair with the bottle. The cheap whiskey smell calms her. That hint of ash and charred oak, with a sharp tang not unlike kerosene, eases her nerves just enough that she thinks to herself, *All isn't lost; I still have Eleanor*—but thinking of Eleanor means seeing Eleanor's smiling green eyes, paired so cleanly with her red hair . . . and then she can only see Esmerelda's hair, shreds of it caught in the broken windshield, blood streaked on metal and vinyl, the smell of exhaust and burned rubber, the coppery charge of blood. In these moments, Eleanor becomes a monster.

Agnes tips the bottle back, and her eyes flutter shut, and she swallows, then swallows again, and the burn of it tells her it will be okay, that everything will be just fine, because the burn is always followed by the dark, and the dark is followed by . . .

Peace. Or something very much like it.

She drinks, and eventually her grip loosens on the bottle, and she slips into that place where Esmerelda, where Eleanor, where nobody else is permitted.

# *eleanor*

E leanor's mother is asleep in the blue chair, shivering, dressed only in a thin T-shirt and underwear. An open bottle is slanted against her hip, one hand loosely curled around its neck.

Eleanor studies her mother. The woman before her is delicate, with bones that show through her skin in strange places. Her mother's collarbone is pronounced, her skin wrapped around it like a leather grip on a piece of bone knife. Her chest is hollow, almost concave.

Eleanor thinks back to the memory of the fireplace, the snugglebun, and tries to picture her mother as she was then: her face fuller, cheeks round and bright, eyes that caught the orange light and almost seemed to glow. Her mother was never heavy, but there had been a roundness to her then that Eleanor loved. Her mother's hugs had been soft and encompassing, where her father's were firm.

The woman before her now looks nothing like the woman of the memory.

This woman barely eats or leaves the house, though she must leave sometimes, because mysterious new bottles of liquor appear in places where there were none previously. Eleanor hates to think about these daytime excursions to the liquor store. Her mother is almost never sober, and it seems inevitable that one day she will put her car into the side of a building or sail through a busy intersection without stopping.

Eleanor exhales slowly. "Mom?"

Agnes doesn't stir.

Carefully, Eleanor extricates the bottle from her mother's grip. Agnes's fingers fall limp against her body. Eleanor collects the smaller bottles from the side table, too, the glass clinking loudly, but her mother doesn't notice. Eleanor carries the bottles into the kitchen and considers upending them all into the sink, but then she thinks about her mother getting behind the wheel of the Honda in their garage, intent on restocking the vanished supply. She puts the bottles aside instead and replaces their caps.

The blanket that she usually draws across her mother is on the floor in a heap beside the chair, and for the briefest moment Eleanor almost hates her mother for lying there, paralyzed and freezing cold, with the warm blanket only a foot away from her.

*Your mother doesn't need you, Eleanor.*

"There should be someone in the world who loves you despite you," Eleanor whispers. "I guess that's me."

She unfolds the blanket and spreads it over her mother's sleeping form, tucks it tightly beneath her weight. She adjusts the thermostat upward a few degrees, then stands there until she hears the hammer of the heating system coming to life. The floor vents push warm air out in a rush, and Eleanor sighs, aware in that moment that her entire existence—at least since the accident—is one enormous sigh, made up of a million smaller sighs.

She goes upstairs, and then, too late, she feels the hum of static embrace her as she steps through her bedroom door.

## mea

Mea is unnerved by the woman in the chair. She seems little more than a shell, alive but without purpose. The red-haired girl cares for the woman, and Mea feels another strange feeling: a deep wellspring of coldness.

Mea cannot tolerate the mystery any longer. Soon the girl climbs stairs to a new doorway, and Mea fears she will escape somehow. She throws herself against the membrane, pressing with all the force she can muster.

The membrane sings, quivers, and then, with a soundless *pop*, a new vortex punctures the membrane's surface.

Ambient light floods into the dark fishbowl, and Mea turns her attention from the red-haired girl for just a moment, distracted by the glow. It penetrates the blackness only so deeply, then falls prey to it; it illuminates only a small space around Mea, space that seems utterly solid and utterly empty and utterly obsidian, even in the light.

Sound filters through the vortex, too. Mea can hear the crush of the girl's feet on the carpet, detects every single fiber that is compressed beneath her heels. The girl's breath sounds like a furnace, amplified somehow by the funnel of the impossibly small vortex.

*Come to me*, Mea thinks, and the vortex seems to distort the membrane. Her view of the house and the stairs and the hallway deepens, and for a moment the red-haired girl appears almost close enough for Mea to touch.

Mea reaches for her.

The vortex skitters sideways, to Mea's surprise, its momentum abrupt and vicious, and the red-haired girl's eyes fly open wide, and then she steps through the doorway of her bedroom, and Mea watches the girl blink away, vanished.

*No*, Mea cries silently.

The vortex, like a miniature waterspout, collapses upon itself, and the membrane undulates as before, then falls still.

And this time, as Mea stares into the red-haired girl's world, she sees where the girl goes.

She falls, tumbling into a crevice between her world and Mea's, like falling down an elevator shaft. She slips into this un-space with stunning speed, tumbling away from Mea and from her own world, becoming nearly transparent, growing smaller as she plummets until she is only a tiny red spark, a particle that floats away on some other current like a dandelion seed.

Mea panics, afraid that she has somehow lost the girl forever. She whirls the time stream back, moving in reverse through the membrane's memory of this moment until the red-haired girl is there again, climbing the stairs.

But as Mea watches, the scene clouds over again.

*NO,* Mea thunders soundlessly.

The girl is gone, and Mea impatiently attempts to navigate through the river of time, moving forward now, seeking the girl a little later—a month, a day, a year—but sees no sign of her anywhere. It is as if she has vanished from time entirely.

Mea throws herself into the dark, tearing herself away from the membrane, and throbs with anger and terror at her mistake.

Efah is still and small in the rift beyond the membrane, bewildered by what he has seen, suspicious of the strange goings-on in Mea's cell.

He is curious, so he does nothing.

He waits.

# *eleanor*

It happens again.

The roiling static, the not-so-subtle tug of *something*—as if a black hole has opened up in her bedroom and is trying to suck her right through the doorway. She doesn't have time to say a word, but a terrible thought unfolds in her mind like a vortex of its own—*What if nothing is real; what if everything is just made up, and anything can happen?*—and she feels a powerful urge to resist the thought, because to give in to it, to even consider it, would unhinge her completely.

Because there is no reason that Eleanor should be doing anything other than stepping into her own bedroom right now, to remove the strange yellow sundress, to put on her coziest, safest flannel pajamas, to tuck herself into her bed. Perhaps she would even find the old boxes in her closet, unearth her softest childhood stuffed animals, and bury herself in them until she sleeps.

She would give anything to be five years old again, inside the snugglebun with Esmerelda.

All of this tears through her mind in an instant, and then Eleanor is no longer in her bedroom, or even in her house, anymore.

THE FIRST THING she notices is that this is not Iowa.

She isn't in a lush green meadow. There are no cornfields, no wheat fields, no amber waves and violet skies and footbridges and distant red barns. There is no Jack. No young Eleanor. She is surrounded by gray trees with gray fronds of gray needles. Above her the trees recede to very tall, very narrow points, a bed of nails for the sky to rest on. The gray, gray sky. Around her is a crater of kicked-up mud and rocks, and at its edge, several trees are shattered: bark torn, the hardwood inside bone-white and glistening.

Eleanor does not know this place any more than she knew the picturesque, Venusian Iowa in which she spent her entire afternoon. She is again barefoot, but this time she is entirely naked. Her red hair is still long—she can feel it against her back—and she is dirty, as though she has been running through mud. Her legs are flecked with wet earth, and there are gray pine needles plastered to her damp skin.

A very fine rain mists upon her, beading on her skin and turning her hair into dead weight. It would pull her to the ground if she allowed it to.

Whatever this place is, it's as miserable as Iowa was joyous. The color has been sucked out of it until all that is left behind are the grays: clouds, ash, soot. The clouds lumber by, underbellies black like those of automobiles.

She is cold.

The rain is cold.

There is no wind here, but if there were, she thinks it would probably chill her to death in just a few steps. She searches for shelter. The ground slopes away beneath her feet, and she realizes that she is on the side of a hill. The trees are gnarled, battered; some look as if they have been victimized by fire during their long lives, as if they have burned and yet live on, survivors all. Some leak stone-colored sap that has hardened and turned opaque.

Eleanor wraps her arms around her body and clenches her teeth and wonders if she can possibly wish herself back to her bedroom. It is insufferable that she has to face this again, that she has been abducted from her very home and stranded here. She didn't believe in magic before this afternoon—or aliens, or other worlds—and now she thinks that she has to allow for the possibility that there is *something* present in the world. It seems impossible that she would never have heard of such things—but she probably wouldn't have believed them if she had.

She remembers the static—the strange, almost magnetic field that she encountered before she entered both doorways—and her mind stumbles to a stop on the word: *doorway.*

Each time this has happened, it has involved a door. But ordinary doors, doors she walks through several times every day. There is nothing special about the cafeteria door or her bedroom door.

"Apparently there is," she says aloud.

She coughs. The land here smells strange, and it leaves her with an odd taste in her mouth. The rain deposits little dots of grit on her skin. She touches the grit with one finger, pushes it around. Gray streaks follow her fingertip like tracers.

Beneath a broken old tree Eleanor spots a hollow that looks just large enough for her. Under ordinary circumstances she would never scramble into such a hole—she imagines snakes or badgers or, worse, millions of squirming bugs occupying such a prized space—but she is cold and it is raining and she doesn't know where she is, so she climbs into the hole backward, scooting her bare bottom into the shadows, and tucks herself into a ball against the moist soil. It isn't warm, exactly, but she feels less cold. She discovers that the soil is a form of insulation, so she packs handfuls around her body for warmth. The light is draining from the sky, and she tries not to think about what bugs might be snuggling up to her in the dark.

Rain gathers in small puddles at the mouth of her burrow, then trickles down the slope toward her. It's good that the rain is so faint, but if it begins to rain harder, her hideout will flood.

She feels herself getting sleepy. She sags into the mud, the exhaustion of the past few days catching up to her, and falls into a deep slumber inside a hole in the side of a hill in a wasteland far, far from home.

# *the keeper*

The woman trudges through the bleak meadow. She has wrapped herself in scratchy, hand-knit shawls and scarves to seal herself from the perpetual cold.

This meadow is hers, with its damp earth and tall grasses bent flat by the rain. A creek winds through it like a strand of bulky yarn, twisting past the woman's home, a rough-hewn, single-room cabin that keeps her warm. From out here, the cabin is only a distant speck on the horizon. A thread of smoke curls up from its tiny chimney.

Each morning the keeper walks the meadow. Beyond the hills, mountains rise like broken teeth into the sullen sky. Trees swarm like barnacles over the land, crawling partway up the mountainsides themselves before dispersing, interrupted by wide platters of shale. These mountains flank the meadow for miles, cinching it shut at either end. There is no way into or out of the valley; this land is protected from the world beyond.

Sometimes she walks the perimeter of the entire valley, easily seventy or eighty miles, and is away for days.

This morning she awakened with a sense of unease in her belly. She stoked the fire under her coffee pot, then stood on the wooden porch, smoking a black cigarette and surveying the gray land. She knows that the land is sick, has, in fact, been sick since the day she discovered it. Sometimes she thinks that its sickness has infected her as well.

But this morning, for the first time, she is sure of it.

She walks now toward the mountains to the south, the source of her unease. She can feel a change, a vibration in the air that wasn't there the day before. She's felt such a thing only once before, when her great beasts appeared in the valley. But that was long ago, and the keeper is not keen to share her valley with more interlopers.

She is certain this is what she will find to the south.

An intruder.


THE KEEPER'S SHADOW huddles as if it were a mere patch of shade. Without its owner, the shadow is shapeless, which makes it perfectly suited for reconnaissance. It isn't often that the keeper frees her shadow to swarm through the valley, and before it came to the forest's edge, the shadow skimmed the long grasses along the creek, joyful in its temporary freedom.

But now it must work.

It glides quickly through patches of light, through the dark of the trees. It doesn't know what it's hunting for, only that the keeper believes *something* is here.

Not a welcome thing. An *evil* thing.

Not like the beasts, who are strange but gentle.

The shadow sweeps hundreds of acres, repeating its search again and again. Many hours later it finds what it has been looking for, but only accidentally.

The shadow takes pause beneath a redwood. The woods are quiet except for the *plip* of water falling from the canopy to the forest floor. The rain has stopped, for now.

Then *she* appears.

The girl comes out of a hole in the ground some fifty yards away. The shadow almost doesn't see her, but the girl coughs; the shadow feels the air vibrate and turns to discover her. The girl looks filthy and bruised. She coughs once more, then stretches uncomfortably and begins to scrape the debris from her skin.

THE KEEPER ROCKS in a handmade chair, another black cigarette between her fingers. She is thinking about building a new cabin at the northernmost end of the valley, so that she has a place to rest her feet during her long walks. She often is too worn out to make it back to this home.

A dash of cigarette ash falls onto her burlap pants. She brushes it away.

Her shadow approaches from the south, the low afternoon mist parting around it. It moves stealthily, as if it is playing a game with her, then slips over the porch and reattaches itself to her feet.

"What did you find?" the keeper asks.

Her shadow cannot speak, but she can feel its memories pass into her. She takes them in, eyes closed. She sees the gash in the woods through her shadow's eyes. It is as if a wrecking ball has been hurled into the trees. She sees the lumbering clouds, the rich, wet soil. She waits, and then—

*There.*

A naked, pale-skinned girl with soaking wet hair stands in the clearing, smeared with clay and mud. Her face and arms are scratched.

"You're only a child," the keeper says, eyes still closed. "Where are you from, little girl?"

There is, of course, no answer.

"Be gone, little thing," the keeper says, opening her eyes.

She waves her hand in a slow sideways arc, as if sweeping a table of crumbs. The air crackles, charged with electricity. Far to the south, there is a dark flash in the forest, like the flicker of a mirror briefly aimed at the cabin.

The keeper relaxes, then takes a long drag on the cigarette. The girl is gone now, ushered out of the valley, back to wherever she has come from.

"Well," the keeper says, smoke rising from her lips. "If she comes back, we'll know. Won't we?"

She gets to her feet, pulling her shawl tightly around her, then looks down. Her shadow silently agrees, mute but not deaf.

"Come along, then," she says, and she steps down off the porch and into the tall grass. She picks up her stick, turns eastward, and begins to walk.

## mea

Mea drifts in the tides of her fishbowl, and Efah watches her without speaking. She is forlorn. When the tide pushes her against the membrane, she does not resist; she skids along like a twig upon a stream, scraping the earthen banks.

The membrane illuminates suddenly, and Mea comes to a stop, clutching at the dull, glassy surface. The view is unclouded now, and within its depths she sees the warm orange tones of the red-haired girl's bedroom.

The room is empty, the curtains open. Sunlight spills across the bed and turns the brassy bedside lamp to fire. Tiny dust specks filter by, turned white in the fading light.

Beside the lamp, on the nightstand, Mea sees a framed photograph of the red-haired girl. She is much younger in the photo, posed beside another girl.

An *identical* girl.

Mea tries to inspect the photograph more closely, but a tremor in the membrane distracts her. She looks across the surface, her view of the bedroom distorted, and sees something rocketing along just below the membrane's shell. It grows larger as it approaches, and it takes on substance: it is the tiny red spark from before, the red-haired girl, returning from wherever she has been. Mea is alarmed by the girl's vicious speed; in a panic, Mea propels herself against the membrane, generating a new vortex—but she is too late. The red-haired girl is ejected from that strange in-between realm like a torpedo. She explodes into her bedroom, hurtling past Mea's twisting, tiny vortex, winging herself on the nightstand, and crashes into the wall with crushing force. Mea is terrified the girl will just burst clean through the wall in a haze of dust and debris and blood. But the girl is fragile, not heavy enough, like a sparrow striking a window. She crumples to the bedroom floor, still.

The lamp smashes to the floor; the framed photograph shatters but sails across the room, where it is sucked against Mea's tiny hurricane, and then, with a tearing sound, is drawn through and into Mea's fishbowl, where it floats like an astronaut's lost screwdriver, a curiosity surrounded by bits of debris and broken glass and tiny beads of blood.

Mea stares at these things rotating slowly in the dark, floating away from her. The photograph is nearly torn in two, its twin faces staring happily past Mea. She reaches for it and watches it suddenly flare brightly and burn quickly into nothing. A faint, acrid haze is all that is left behind, and then even that fades, leaving Mea alone and lost again in the dark well she has been thrown into, staring up at a different world and the unconscious girl with the blood-red hair.

# *eleanor*

E verything hurts.
  *Everything.*
      Eleanor opens her eyes reluctantly. The pain lifts her out
of sleep, or from wherever she has been, and for a long moment she
is disoriented. Her vision is weak, her surroundings splintered with
light. Everything is too bright, and she closes her eyes. Her eyelids
are bright red from the inside; her eyes throb painfully.

"Turn off the light," an unfamiliar voice says, and the red is replaced, mercifully, with darkness. Eleanor exhales in relief. There
comes a shuffling sound, and then the bed shifts under some
weight—*bed?*—as someone sits. The mysterious voice says, "Eleanor. Can you hear me?"

Eleanor is shaking, utterly confused. Her ears are full of sound—
a white blur of noise that she doesn't understand—but the sounds
of the forest have ceased. The last thing she remembers is climbing
out of her hole, naked, with mud clinging to her skin and matted in
her hair.

Where is she now?

To her great comfort, her father speaks next. "Ellie, sweetie, can
you hear us?"

Her eyes cloud with tears. If she could just go to him . . . She
opens her mouth to answer him, but her lips are chapped and painfully dry.

"It's okay," says the stranger again. "Don't try to talk just yet. Just
breathe, okay? Listen to me. In . . . out. In . . . out."

Eleanor takes in a deep breath and almost coughs it right back
out. She suppresses the reflex and instead lets the air out slowly.
Something rattles in her throat.

"Good," says the stranger. "Now, when you're ready, try to open your eyes. Slowly, okay? We're not going anywhere. Mr. Witt, turn on that lamp, would you, please?"

Eleanor releases another slow breath. The light behind her eyelids returns, but it's less harsh than before. She opens her eyes, then blinks rapidly in the low light.

"Give them a moment to adjust," says the stranger, and Eleanor can see her, sort of, a brownish blur in an otherwise blurry room. Her vision very slowly fine-tunes itself, and the stranger comes into muddled focus. She is a tall, slender woman in pastel blue scrubs. A paper mask is tied over her mouth, but her eyes are dark and kind.

"Hi there," the nurse says, and holds up a finger. "I want you to follow my finger with your eyes, okay? Nothing hard—just want to make sure you're okay."

Eleanor nods her head, too vigorously, and a spike of pain rips through her skull. She gasps, and little red-and-gold fireworks dance across her vision. Her eyes snap shut.

"Careful," the nurse says. "I want you to stay as still as you can. Try not to move your head just yet. Okay? Now, let's try that again."

Eleanor winces but opens her eyes.

The nurse holds up a finger and slowly moves it across Eleanor's field of vision. Eleanor watches carefully as it moves left, then right, then left again, but then she is distracted by other movement, and she sees her father, wide-eyed and worried, hands clasped to his chest as if in prayer.

"Daddy," she whimpers.

"It's okay, Ellie," he says. "It's okay, it's okay. I'm here."

But his eyes are wet, too, and Eleanor feels herself on the verge of a sob.

"Ellie, my name is Shelley," says the nurse. She pulls her mask down, flashing a white smile. "Hey, that's kind of funny, isn't it? Ellie, Shelley. Ellie, Shelley. Kind of want to say that five times fast, don't you?"

Eleanor stares at her uncomprehendingly.

"Eleanor, you're in a hospital room right now," she says. "Do you know how you got here?"

Eleanor shakes her head, frightened, and her tears spill over onto her cheeks.

"Can you tell me when you were born?"

"D-December," Eleanor says.

"December what? Slow breaths, okay? In . . . out. In . . . out."

Eleanor takes a shaky breath.

"Good. Okay. December what?"

"Eleventh," Eleanor says, trying to steady her voice.

"Good," Shelley says brightly. "Very good. Do you remember what year?"

Eleanor closes her eyes, searching her memory. "Nineteen seventy-eight," she says after a moment.

"Very good," Shelley says. "And who is the man here with me?"

"My d-dad," Eleanor says, fighting back a sob. "He's my dad."

"Good," Shelley says again. "Now, Eleanor, I have to ask you this, and no matter what you're feeling, I want you to tell me the absolute truth, okay?"

Eleanor looks at Shelley strangely. A tear trickles down her jaw her neck.

"I want you to remember that this is a safe place and that nothing bad will happen to you here," Shelley says. "Do you understand?"

Eleanor nods. Her father is crying.

"Do you know why you're here?" Shelley asks. "Can you tell me what happened to you?"

Eleanor's eyes flick in her father's direction, then to the ceiling, then back to Shelley. The room wobbles.

"No," she says, and she begins to shake her head from side to side, but the fresh heat of pain she felt earlier lingers at the corners of her consciousness, threatening to return.

Shelley looks at Paul, then back at Eleanor. "Okay. It's okay. We're going to keep you here for a little while, okay? Just to make sure you're doing okay and to give you a little space to maybe re-member some things. Is that okay?"

"Okay."

Shelley steps back. "Right, okay. Your father's here now. I'm going to be just outside. If there's anything you need, or you're in pain, or you remember something and just need to talk, I want you to press the button on that little remote control next to you. See it?"

Eleanor glances down and sees a beige box with a blue button on it. An attached cable snakes under the blanket and out of sight.

"Okay. You're going to feel pretty tired here in a few minutes," Shelley adds. "Don't fight that. Sleep as much as you can. Your body is still trying to recover from . . . from things."

Shelley leaves the room, and Paul comes to Eleanor's bedside, and Eleanor looks up at her father, keeping her neck as rigid as she can, and she doesn't hold back the sob this time.

PAUL IS GONE when Eleanor wakes. The window opposite her bed is pink with the sunrise, gauzy through thin linen curtains. She flicks her eyes this way and that, remaining as still as possible, taking in the details of her room. There isn't much to observe. It's a hospital room. There's an empty second bed to her left, a yellow hard plastic chair to her right. A framed piece of art, dusky yellow flowers in a white vase, hangs over the chair.

Eleanor hears the muffled sound of a toilet, the static of run-ning water. A door in the corner opens, and her father steps out of a small room.

"Private bathroom," he says when he sees that she is awake. "Nice digs you've got here, Ellie."

But his smile is weak. She sees his worry printed on his face.

"What happened?" she asks.

Paul shakes his head as he sinks into the yellow chair. "I'm really not sure," he says. "Your mother is the one who found you."

"Mom?" Eleanor asks dubiously. She cannot imagine her mother getting out of the blue chair for any reason at all.

"She said she heard a loud noise and went upstairs," Paul says. "She found you on the floor of your bedroom, just lying there. She said the wall was—she said it looked like it had been punched in."

Eleanor can hardly process this detail. "You and Mom . . . talked?"

Paul leans forward. "Ellie, do you know what today is?"

She thinks about this. "Yesterday was Monday," she says. "So today is Tuesday. It's the last week of school."

Paul stares at her through watery eyes.

"What?" she asks slowly.

"Ellie, dear," Paul says hesitantly. "Ellie, it's . . . Saturday."

Eleanor works her jaw, dazed.

"You missed the last week of school," he says, taking her hand in his. "Ellie, we didn't know where you were."

She frowns. "That's not right. That isn't possible. It's Tuesday."

"Jack is the one who noticed," Paul says. "He was worried when you didn't answer the door on Tuesday morning for school. He rode his bicycle over to my apartment, and I called your mother."

"And she *answered*?" Eleanor asks. "She never hears the phone."

"Well, she heard it this time, and I asked her to check on you, and she said that you weren't in your room."

Eleanor can feel her hand shaking, just a little. Her father squeezes it harder. She imagines her mother, clinging to the staircase railing, drunkenly shouting up the stairs, pissed when Eleanor doesn't appear.

"Ellie," he says softly. "She said your clothes were just—they were just in a pile upstairs. I came over, and I looked through the whole house with your mother, and you weren't there. We were so scared that—"

"I don't believe that," Eleanor interrupts. "I don't believe she was scared."

"She was terrified," he says. "Terrified. She kept talking about your grandmother."

Eleanor turns her head at this and grunts at the burst of pain that follows. "Grandma Eleanor? She never talks about her."

"I've told you the story."

"She disappeared—right. I know," Eleanor says. "But why—"

"Your mother was afraid that you had . . . had gone away, too," Paul says. "You know she's always felt like it was her fault. I think—I think, maybe she felt guilty. For . . . well, you know. Maybe she had a moment of clarity." He takes a long breath, then rubs his eyes. "I think she was worried that she had put too much on you, and you'd run away, too."

"But . . . Grandma Eleanor didn't run away," Eleanor says. "She—she committed . . . I would never even think about that."

"I know," Paul says. "And, technically, I don't think anybody knows if she . . . killed herself. Someone saw her swim out to sea, and nobody saw her come back. That's not really the same thing."

Eleanor levels her eyes at her father. "Dad," she says. "That doesn't happen for real. She would have drowned."

"Probably true," he says. "But you never know."

Eleanor doesn't argue with him. She knows the story of her grandmother's disappearance, because her Grandpa Hob often told it during his later years, his voice thick with sadness and regret as he talked about her and the child that would have been named Patrick or Patricia. She knows that Grandma Eleanor had been pregnant and that her own mother had been younger than Eleanor herself was when Esmerelda died, and she knows that Grandpa Hob blamed himself, and that her mother blames herself. Nearly thirty years after her grandmother's suicide, the consequences of her final swim still echo like a dark copper bell.

"Ellie," her father says. "Where were you all week?"

She doesn't know what her father is talking about—there's no way that she's been away for most of a week. But she cannot escape the pain he wears upon his face, the worry that he carries upon his shoulders, and she aches, knowing she is the reason for this. Since Esmerelda's death, Eleanor has been careful to tread lightly through her parents' lives. The last thing she ever wanted was to give them a reason to fear for her. It didn't change things very much, though. Her father left her mother after a few terrible, grief-stricken months. Eleanor remembers the fights, the awful words that her father said to her mother—*It's your fault she's dead*—and she remembers her mother's horrible words to Eleanor herself: *Why were you the one who lived?* Her parents took their grief out on each other and on Eleanor herself, in a way.

Esmerelda's death split their family as finely as an atom, and the resulting detonation blinded them all.


WHEN ELEANOR WAKES again, her father is asleep in the yellow chair. He has scooted it up against the wall. His shoes are beside the chair, his socks stuffed inside. He looks uncomfortable, his neck cranked to the side, his chin resting on his shoulder. It's late afternoon, and the sun is on its way down again, bathing the room in gold, and it occurs to Eleanor that several days of her life have disappeared. Four sunrises and sunsets, at least. This thought tumbles around in her mind, and she feels a sense of regret. Regret . . . and heavy, heavy guilt.

She concentrates, instead, on Monday, remembering the things that she doesn't want to tell her father or Shelley the nurse about. She's afraid that saying the words out loud will somehow make her worst fears real—that she has lost some piece of her mind somehow. She has never heard of children vanishing through doorways that make their hair stand on end and suck at them like an undertow. The very idea reminds her of something from one of Esmerelda's science fiction novels.

But she believes that it was real.

She has set foot on strange earth, has buried her body in mud, has felt cold and heat.

It was real.

When she found herself in the third-story bathroom at school, she was wearing the yellow sundress from Iowa. Her hair was long. She has brought pieces of these—whatever they are: daydreams? nightmares?—back with her.

She longs for Esmerelda, suddenly. She needs someone to talk to who won't think she's insane. She wishes her mother . . . no. Agnes was never that sort of mother. There was only Esmerelda, who would slip out of her own bed and climb into Eleanor's and whisper, "Backs," which was Eleanor's cue to turn over. Esme would turn the opposite way, and the twins would scoot together until their backs touched. Eleanor would say, "What's wrong?" and Esmerelda, facing into the dark but warmed by her sister, would say, "I broke the lamp in the attic," and then Eleanor would confess something.

She cannot remember how old they were, but one night Eleanor climbed into Esme's bed. "Backs," she whispered, and then, when she felt the heat of her sister's body, Eleanor said, "I found a picture of Grandma Eleanor."

"Where?" Esmerelda asked.

"A box in the garage," Eleanor answered. "There were a lot of things in there. Grandpa's stuff."

"What was she like? Was she beautiful?"

"I guess," Eleanor confessed. "She didn't look like Mom. Not much."

"I bet she was beautiful in person."

"Why doesn't Mom ever talk about her?"

The conversation had ended there. Eleanor couldn't remember why. Maybe the bedroom door had opened.

"Backs," she whispers, alone in her hospital bed.

But Esmerelda is dead.

Jack is all she has left, and Jack wouldn't understand.

*Jack.* Eleanor feels a pang in her chest. He must be worried sick about her. She'll ask her father when he wakes if he'll call Jack and tell him that she's okay. But that's not really true. She isn't okay. She hasn't asked her father about the pain in her neck, but she knows that Shelley the nurse will probably tell her about it sooner or later. Eleanor can't see any casts on her arms or legs, but her upper body feels as if it has been squeezed in a vise.

She thinks again about the strange sensation that she felt at the door. What's the most outlandish possibility she can dream up? Maybe she's built up static electricity somehow, and the doors have zapped her. But her bedroom door was made of wood, not metal, so that seems unlikely. Her mind turns over ridiculous scenarios, but it stops on one of them, and Eleanor thinks about it for a long time, for hours while her father sleeps, and she cannot find a reason to discard this hypothesis.

Twice Eleanor has walked through a doorway and found herself in an unfamiliar place. If she grants the premise that something unnatural—that something *supernatural*—is happening to her, then it makes sense: for reasons she cannot understand, doors are turning into portals to other *somewheres*. Not all of them. Only some of them.

*Through the looking glass,* she thinks. *Down the rabbit hole. Into the wardrobe. Somewhere over the rainbow.*

"Nonsense," she mumbles.

Sleep overtakes her soon after. The sun falls out of sight, and the hospital room sinks into shadow, and as Eleanor drifts into the dark, she dreams of fairy tales.

## *the keeper*

The keeper's view of the sky is obscured by ragged clouds. Sometimes the keeper imagines that they are simply the bottom of a great column of thunderheads that stretches high into the atmosphere, impenetrable by the sun. They might well be, for the keeper has never seen the sun or very much of its light.

It rains in her valley for months on end. The water pools in the meadow, turning it to a soggy marsh, and on her walks she rolls her pants to her knees and squishes through the wetlands. The valley is a bowl, and during the worst storms the marsh becomes a lake, the earth swallowed up by dark water. When this happens, the keeper retreats into a shallow cave at the base of one of the mountains, where she lives by the light of a fire and waits out the storm. The floodwaters recede. They always have. She has had to rebuild her cabin several times before. She is certain that she will rebuild it many more.

The most recent incarnation of the cabin is small and tidy, outfitted with only the things she needs. In addition to the fireplace, she owns a table and a bed—hardly a bed, more like a cot—and a few pots and utensils. She makes her own clothes from a stash of fiber and thread and material that never seems to diminish. She makes only what she needs.

Her shadow is her only company, except when the seasons change and the cabin darkens in the shadow of the great passing beasts. The thin glass in the cabin windows trembles with the beasts' heavy steps, and sawdust drifts down from the raw pine ceiling. She often stands on the porch with a cup of hot tea, cradling the mug in her hands as the beasts drift by. They are as tall as the mountains, almost mountains themselves, and they walk on long, spindly legs like the tallest skyscrapers. Their shadows might stretch for miles if there were much sunlight, but, instead, they are murky and shapeless, for their bodies blot out most of the sky itself.

The keeper once thought to name the beasts, but she never did. They arrived in the valley as a pair. The first is almost beautiful in its immensity, with a slender neck that vanishes into the clouds. When its feet thud against the earth, the keeper hears music, a resounding oboe note. She is not certain that the beast is female, but its movements do suggest a certain femininity.

The second beast is heavier, bulkier. It is not as tall, and its steps are far less delicate. During the beasts' last migration it seemed that the second beast might be sick. It stumbled often, a rumbling groan issuing from its throat with each ponderous step. The keeper could see huge divots carved into the earth where the beast had dragged one weak leg. Once she saw it stagger, and in its struggle to right itself, it sheared an entire hillside away, uprooting hundreds of trees, exposing dark soil and buried granite. The shock had rippled across the meadow, buckling one of the struts that held up the keeper's porch and nearly causing the eaves to collapse.

The migration of the beasts echoes the subtle change of the seasons, and the keeper knows that when the beasts vanish into the mountains miles and miles to the north, she can expect snow soon after. It will fall gray and poisonous, carpeting the valley floor like soot. There is nothing elegant about winter in the valley. Winter is the only season during which the keeper forgoes her patrol of the meadow. She hibernates in the cabin until the beasts return.

This year the snow is early. She can see the smudge of it in the distance, already drifting upon the faraway peaks, as if one of the clouds has scraped its belly open on the jagged mountain.

The keeper hasn't seen the beasts for some time, has never found the place where they rest. They are a mystery to her, refugees who have claimed asylum in her valley.

She turns her attention to the south again, to the gaping wound in the woods, and thinks of the girl intruder. The child's arrival has changed the land. The keeper can feel a twinge in the air that was not there before. Something strange and new has affected her home, and for a moment—just a moment—she feels a tiny spark of fear.

And then it is gone.

The keeper sips her tea, then looks down at her shadow huddled beneath her.

"She'll be back, I think," the keeper says. "We'll be ready."

Her shadow flattens, as if preparing itself for battle.

"We'll be ready," the keeper repeats.

# *eleanor*

E leanor will have to make up her missed finals in the summer, the school district tells her mother in a crisp letter, but otherwise her sudden absence from school should not present too great a problem. *We are happy that Miss Witt is home safely*, the letter reads. Eleanor folds it and puts it back into the envelope addressed to Agnes, then drops it into the wastebasket.

Her mother takes only a few days to return to her habits, the fright of Eleanor's disappearance not a powerful enough catalyst to disrupt the routine. She curls up in the blue chair with a scowl that lingers on her face long after she has passed out. Eleanor's father stops by the house every day after work. He parks his Buick in the driveway and sits there, engine idling, until Eleanor comes out.

"Come inside," she tells him each night. "I'll make hot chocolate with marshmallows."

But each night he declines, and after a while, when he is certain that whatever happened to Eleanor will not happen again, and when she no longer has to wear the cumbersome neck brace, and the visible signs of her injuries have faded, her father calls Eleanor before he leaves the office, and if all is well, he simply goes to his own apartment. *All is well* occurs often enough that her father doesn't always call; soon Eleanor sees him only on his regular visitation weekends.

Eventually, all things return to normal. Spring becomes summer, and summer is uncharacteristically hot and bright in Anchor Bend this year. Eleanor and Jack bike around town almost daily, sharing a packed lunch among the tourists on the waterfront, parking their bikes at the Safeway and darting inside to score a jawbreaker from one of the nickel machines. Jack asks a few times what happened to her, but Eleanor never quite puts the right words together to tell him about her theory, about the portal to places like Iowa and the gray forest, and so she doesn't tell him anything except that she's okay.

At night she climbs the attic stairs. She sweeps the hardwood floor and tidies up the clutter from her mother's last visit. She misses the sprawling acreage of the models her father built, the magnifying lamp that revealed their tiny flaws and her father's signature. She stretches out on the floor with a stack of notebook paper and a pencil, and she draws what she remembers of Iowa, of the ash forest. In her drawings Eleanor is always a small and startled figure, overcome by the strangeness of all that surrounds her.

## mea

Mea exiles herself into the center of her fishbowl, where she lingers alone, silent, in the black. New emotions charge through her like electricity, and the sensation of each is uncomfortable. Efah comes around, and he seems aware of her pain, but she does not respond to his questions, and eventually he goes away again. She will not tell him so, but she feels as if she has committed a grievous sin.

She sinks into a well of guilt. She is responsible, of course, for the red-haired girl's accident. She dropped the girl into some other world; it was Mea's fault that the girl had been fired like a cannonball back into her own. Mea does not know pain in the way the red-haired girl knows pain, but she knows she cannot put the girl through such things any longer.

Whatever Mea has hoped to achieve from this—this *experiment*—must be forgotten. Whatever she feels about the red-haired girl must be banished.

So Mea allows the blackness to close over her like water, to swallow her into its dark belly. She lingers there, suspended in a state of shame, and tries not to think of the girl.

Efah indulges Mea's isolation, for a time.

Then, when Mea has punished herself for long enough, he appears at the periphery of her vision, a hazy form outside the filmy walls of her fishbowl.

*Mea,* he says. *I can help.*

## eleanor

August arrives with a storm.

On the pier, Eleanor is perched with Jack on the wide base of a lamppost, looking for whales. Word had spread through town that morning that a pod of grays was resting in the harbor, just beyond the marina. The pier is clogged with tourists and locals alike, men and women in shorts and tank tops and flip-flops. The tourists are pink and rosy, scorched by a sun they hadn't planned to encounter along the Oregon coast. This is a mistake Eleanor and Jack giggle at. You can always spot the tourists, the locals say, by their lobster-like faces.

But today the rain comes from nowhere, and the tourists scatter, leaving mostly locals behind. Eleanor and Jack climb down from the lamppost and fill in the gaps that the tourists have left. They lean on the railing, squinting through the powerful downpour.

"I don't think they're really here," says a woman to Eleanor's left.

"Hush," says the man beside her. "They're waiting for the looky-loos to clear out."

Jack elbows Eleanor, and they both grin behind their hands.

Eleanor hasn't thought about her accident in weeks. Her neck has healed; for a long time it hurt to look in any direction, and then one day the pain was gone, and she just didn't think about it anymore. She finished her makeup exams by the end of July and since then has spent her days on her bicycle, patrolling the town with Jack. Today their plan had been to bike to Rock, a neighboring town just down the coast. There isn't anything to see or do in Rock, but Jack had told her that the journey was adventure enough, and she had agreed. Then they heard about the whales sunning themselves in the harbor, and they left their bicycles chained to a street sign, plans forgotten.

"I don't see them," the woman says again.

"Wait," the man says. "Be quiet."

Jack and Eleanor lean over the rail as far as they can, fifteen or twenty feet above the gray sea, and watch the rain spatter on the surface. Seagulls bob on the slow waves, flapping their wings in place. Now and then one lifts off and noisily relocates itself some distance away from the others; then a few seconds later the others follow, and the cycle begins again.

The whales surprise Eleanor. She has fixed her gaze on the water just short of the horizon, expecting tiny whale bodies to bump to the surface, spout a tiny jet of salt water into the sky, and dive deep again. But they appear no more than twenty yards from the pier, three of them, a clear family unit. One whale is as large as the pier is long, and Eleanor gasps.

"There!" the man cries.

"Where?" the woman asks. "Where are they?"

The man grabs the woman's head in both of his hands and turns her face in the direction of the beasts.

"*Ohhhhh,*" she sighs. "They're so *big.*"

A medium-size whale is a few yards away from the largest one, and between them a small one floats, turning over once, then again.

"It's a *family,*" the woman says. "That's the *baby.*"

Jack shakes his head and whispers in Eleanor's ear. *"Tourists."*

Eleanor watches the whales drift by. They seem to be in no particular hurry. The rain patters on their bodies. Their flukes are the size of automobiles.

"Pretty big," Jack says.

Eleanor doesn't answer.

"Hey," he says. "You okay?"

Eleanor cocks her head without taking her eyes from the whales. "What?"

"You all right?"

A fourth whale surfaces, smaller than even the baby. It swims hard to catch up to the rest of the little pod, though they aren't moving quickly. Eleanor feels a sudden urge to scoop it out of the water in a net—a very large net—and take it home and put it in her bathtub and keep it warm and pat its back and laugh when it spouts water all over the bathroom.

"Eleanor," Jack says. He touches her shoulder, and it breaks the spell, and Eleanor looks at him.

"What?" she says.

"You're spacing out."

"*You're* a spaz," Eleanor retorts.

"No, not *spazzing*," Jack corrects, laughing. "*Spacing*. You're so cute when you're mad."

"Oh, shut up."

She peers down at the whales again. The medium-size one dips below the surface, and then the baby sinks, too. The littlest one isn't far behind.

"Wait, wait," says the woman. "They didn't sneeze yet! They have to sneeze. I have the camera out!"

"It's not called *sneezing*," the man chides.

"Maybe it's called *spazzing*," Jack whispers to Eleanor.

The largest whale slowly turns over, flukes churning the water like the paddle wheel on an old-fashioned riverboat, and then it, too, goes below. Eleanor watches until the whales descend too deep, their shapes fading from view, and all that remains are the slapping waves.

"God*damn*it," the woman says. "I wanted to do the one-hour photo and go show Charles."

"We can wait," the man says. "They'll come back up."

But the skies really open up then, as if the ocean itself is falling from the clouds, and in an instant the people on the pier are drenched. The downpour drowns out the woman's shout. She and the man run for the parking lot.

Eleanor stares at the place where the whales were. The rain churns the sea until it seems to boil; it falls hard enough that it leaves rose-colored welts upon Eleanor's skin.

"Hey!" Jack shouts, putting his hand on her shoulder. "I don't know if you noticed, but it's really raining now!"

Eleanor looks up at him.

"You okay?" he asks loudly.

Her red hair is plastered to her face. It frames her eyes in a way that Jack has obviously noticed. Eleanor has always been aware of the way he looks at her but has dismissed it for years. She understands that she can't do that forever—they're growing up, and he's quietly attracted to her now.

He raises his hand as if he might brush the wet hair from her face, and there's a strange, nervous twinge inside her chest. She feels it take her breath from her, just for a moment, so she quickly tilts her face up to the stinging rain and closes her eyes. The moment is severed as cleanly as a clipped wire.

"We should get inside!" Jack shouts.

If he is aware of the moment that almost was, he doesn't show it, and she is strangely grateful for this discretion, if that's what it is.

"Dad's office!" she yells back.

They abandon their bikes, still chained on the street, and run, their feet smacking against the wet road and splashing in deep puddles that weren't there ten minutes before. The waterfront road is empty, and Eleanor glances to her left and sees that every shop is filled with soggy tourists, pressed to the windows, disappointed by this turn of the weather.

For NINE YEARS, Eleanor has walked into her father's little real estate office and been met by her aunt's buoyant smile. Geraldine Rydell mans the reception desk as if it is a great ship; Eleanor has always thought of her aunt as the steady captain of her father's business, despite her own troubled seas. Gerry had worked for Paul Witt Realty through two marriages—the first of which ended shortly after she joined her brother's firm, when, while on her lunch break, she returned home to discover her husband in bed with not only a woman she did not recognize, but another couple, as well; the second of which fell apart when her replacement husband decided that *he* would like to be a *she*, then cardiac-arrested on a cosmetic surgeon's table—and through the loss of her two boys. The marriages interrupted Gerry's course, but the deaths of her children almost sank her. That desk—along with Paul and Eleanor themselves— kept Gerry afloat. Eleanor recognized this even as a child.

Eleanor remembers the last time she saw her cousins. It had been a few years after Esmerelda died, so Eleanor must have been eight or nine. She was flattened on the green sofa in her father's office, drawing pictures on his stationery while Paul sat idle, hidden behind his desk and its uneven skyline of manila folders and property listings and zoning maps and various books. Had her father worked for anyone but himself at the time, he probably would have lost his job for all the time he spent behind that cluttered desk staring blankly through the blinds at the sea.

It had been raining that day as well, Eleanor thinks, though she cannot be certain. It was the sort of day that a storm might attend to. Those were gray months, a year or two into what Eleanor has always thought of as the dim years.

Geraldine had tapped on Paul's office door, nudging it open

slightly. Eleanor looked up at her aunt, who smiled down at her, then turned to Paul and said, "Paul, honey, the boys are due to be on the bus in a few minutes. They just wanted to say thanks before they leave."

"Yes, all right," Paul said. He got to his feet slowly. His face was pale and grayish. He moved like someone thirty years older. He reached out his hand to Eleanor, who took it and walked beside him into the lobby.

Eleanor's cousins waited there, dressed in freshly laundered khaki uniforms and squashed, short-billed caps. Their last name was stitched onto the breasts of their jackets: RYDELL. Eleanor looked up at her father. Paul smiled, though everyone in the room saw right through the smile, and held his hand out. The boys, Joshua and Charles, the former tanned from too much time in the sharp summer sun, the latter pale and red-haired like Eleanor herself, shook his hand in earnest.

"We just wanted to say how much—"

"It's not much," Paul interrupted. "But you're welcome, boys."

"They'll eat like kings," Gerry said. "Not every boy goes overseas with such nice care packages."

"If Josh doesn't eat it all on the plane," Charles said with a grin.

But Paul had only nodded. His plastic smile weakened. Eleanor and Geraldine both noticed, but the boys seemed oblivious.

"All right, all right," Gerry said, flapping her hands at her sons. "Let's get moving. You don't want to be marked AWOL before you even get to boot camp."

Joshua nodded at Paul and stuck his hand out again. "Thank you very much, Uncle Paul," he said stiffly.

Charles bent down and looked Eleanor in the eye. "Your dad's a pretty good man," he said. "You'll be a good girl, right?"

Eleanor felt her eyes well up. She didn't understand why. She just began crying.

Charles looked at Paul and then his mother. "I didn't say anything," he said.

"Go, go," Gerry said, folding her boys into one big hug. "She'll be all right."

Eleanor pressed her face into her father's stomach. He put his hand on her head, but it didn't comfort her the way she so deeply wanted to be comforted. His hand rested there like a weight, as if she was nothing more than an armrest. She had stopped crying. What was the point if nobody was going to tell her that things would be okay?

"They're so young," he said, watching Gerry usher the boys out onto the sidewalk.

Eleanor didn't know what he meant. She turned her head, listening to the inner workings of her father's belly, feeling the little damp spots on his shirt from her tears.

Geraldine eventually came back inside, her eyes shining and wet. She took up her position behind the desk again and shooed Paul back into his office. Eleanor stood alone in the doorway to her father's office until Gerry noticed her.

"You're crying," Eleanor said, which only made her aunt tear up again.

Gerry held an arm out, and Eleanor went to her. Her aunt was soft and warm and large, with rust-colored hair that tickled Eleanor's cheek.

"At least I've still got my little Ellie," Gerry said.

Things returned, for better or for worse, to something like normal. Eleanor spent her afternoons drawing at Gerry's desk, and Paul stared out his office window, and Gerry captained the office, and her two sons flew first to boot camp and then, weeks later, toward their post in Europe.

They never arrived. They never returned. Geraldine came late to work one afternoon, her eyes glazed and distant. Eleanor was startled to see that her aunt's hair had gone almost white since the day before.

The boys' transport plane had vanished from radar somewhere

over the Atlantic. It couldn't be found. It was as if it had been wiped away like a smudge on a window, disappeared right out of the sky.

Her grief almost shook Paul out of his own. He tried to send his sister home, but Gerry wouldn't go. Eleanor understood. If not for her and for her father, Gerry would be alone, and those alone moments are like a deep, deep well that you can't climb out of. Eleanor was quite familiar with that well.

Despite her loss, Gerry didn't miss a day of work after that. She even continued to bring casseroles and potato salad and pot roasts to work, sending them home with Paul. In those days, Agnes had already learned to drink, and Paul stayed in the attic with his little houses. Eleanor often ate alone at the dusty dining table, subsisting on the Tupperware meals Gerry had filled their refrigerator with.

A good night meant that her father let her go home with Gerry, where she and her aunt would eat together on the porch, watching the sun fall behind the pines. Sometimes they would fall asleep together on the porch swing, listening to the crackle of the neighbor's bug zapper. "Close your eyes," Gerry once told Eleanor. "Sounds almost like a campfire, doesn't it?"

When she was a little older, Eleanor experienced her first period at Gerry's house. Gerry comforted her, assured her that the blood would wash out of the bedsheets. It wasn't a big deal, her aunt explained. It just meant you were becoming a woman, and that wasn't such a bad thing. Eleanor never told her mother, and Agnes didn't seem to notice that she had missed this milestone in Eleanor's life. If she did, she never brought it up. Gerry bought the necessary new products for Eleanor, and life continued on.

After her parents' divorce, Eleanor slept over at Gerry's house less frequently. She feared for her mother's safety. Eleanor slept less and less, often waking in the middle of the night to tiptoe downstairs to check on her mother, to make sure Agnes was still breathing. She knew that Gerry saw the dark circles below her eyes, and now and then Eleanor's aunt would appear at the door with a sack of groceries and prepare a fine supper for the two of them. Agnes never joined them. They saved a plate every time, but it always went bad in the refrigerator. Those nights kept Eleanor sane, and she slept deeply while Gerry sat downstairs, reading a book by lamplight.

Some nights Eleanor could hear Gerry talking to her mother. Agnes didn't take kindly to lectures—when Paul delivered them now and then, Agnes responded by throwing things at him—but Eleanor never heard her mother raise her voice to Gerry.

Without Gerry, Eleanor sometimes thought both she and her mother might have been lost. It only occurred to her years later that she might have been Gerry's anchor, as well.

ELEANOR AND JACK can see Gerry now inside the office. The rain hammers the road around them, and Jack dashes for the door.

"Wait," Eleanor says, but Jack zips inside without her.

She can see Gerry leap up. She exclaims over Jack's condition, like a very animated mime, and Jack turns and points outside. Gerry looks past Jack and sees Eleanor standing on the opposite sidewalk. She goes to the door and yells across the street.

"Ellie, dear, for Pete's sake, come inside! You'll catch cold!"

The office is lit up, gold against the darkening gray sky. Gerry is a vision in the doorway, plump and pink-cheeked. The blinds over her father's window are pulled, but she knows he is in there, too. His Buick is parked at the curb. She can go inside and stand on a mat and maybe drip-dry. At least inside it's sure to be warm. The temperature outside has plummeted, and Eleanor feels a shiver course through her body.

But she hesitates.

The sudden summer storm. The whales.

It has been an unusual day. A not-quite-right day.

"Ellie," Gerry calls again. "Dear, sweet Lord, come in! What's wrong?"

Eleanor pushes the worry away. She can practically smell Geraldine's perfume, and suddenly the only thing in the world she wants is to sink into her aunt's arms. She feels as if she has been away for years.

Eleanor forgets to look both ways as she steps into the street, but it doesn't matter. There's no traffic. The sound of the rain on the asphalt becomes a sort of chant. Eleanor crosses the street and stops just outside the door.

"You're drenched!" Gerry exclaims. She steps back, holding the glass door wide for Eleanor. Jack stands dripping in the lobby, looking helplessly at the puddle forming at his feet.

Eleanor takes a deep breath and holds it. She fixes her eyes on Geraldine. Maybe if she doesn't look away, everything will be okay. Maybe she won't lose her way again.

She steps through the doorway.

## mea

Efah assures her that it will work this time.

The red-haired girl's world is dark now. Colossal clouds swell over the little town, emptying themselves of rain. The storm casts a long shadow over the buildings and shops that dot the waterfront. The sea is almost black. Mea sees other humans struggle to moor their boats. The rain thunders down so hard, she can almost hear it.

But in her own void there is only silence.

It is supposed to work like this: Mea will create a vortex that will, for a moment, join the rift and the red-haired girl's world. That's what Efah says, but Mea knows that already. She's done it before. What she doesn't know is how to bring the girl through.

What she doesn't know is if the girl will survive the journey.

She tells Efah about the photograph, the other debris that came through the last time. Efah doesn't immediately respond; he is too pleased that she has spoken to him at all.

*She will live,* Efah tells her, with a confidence that Mea herself does not feel. *She is unique.*

Mea imagines what will happen if she is successful. What will she say to the girl? Will the girl even see Mea? Their shapes are so different. Mea is almost indistinguishable from the darkness of her fishbowl.

*You have excelled at creating the tunnel,* Efah says. *What you haven't learned is how to* place *the tunnel.*

*Place it?* Mea asks. *What do you mean?*

But then she remembers: When the girl was climbing the stairs, Mea jostled the little vortex, and it went skating away from her like a hockey puck.

Efah tells her that she must *pin* the vortex to the red-haired girl's world. Without an anchor, the vortex is dangerous and unpredictable. He tells her that she should learn to fasten the vortex to physical doorways.

*Doorways are intended for passage,* Efah says. *It is a natural conclusion.*

*That's why she keeps falling away from me.*

Efah agrees. *It is so.*

*But why? Where does she go?*

Without explaining further, Efah says, *The dream realm.*

*Dream?* Mea asks, but Efah drones on without answering, describing a successful experiment as the inverse of birth: the red-haired girl will forsake the sun and moon and stars of her own world, trading them for the dark womb of the rift.

*What if she doesn't want to—* Mea begins.

Efah interrupts. *What is the child's name?*

Mea pauses to reflect. She has observed the girl's world for long enough now that the answer should be . . . *There.* She says the name as if it is something foreign, a word she has never spoken. But her heart, such as it is, knows this name.

*Eleanor. Her name is Eleanor.*

Beyond the membrane, Efah's indistinct shape seems to flinch in response to the name. For a long time, he is silent. At last, he says, *Retrieve the child.*

Mea can see Eleanor now. The girl is soaking wet. She steps off the sidewalk and into the street, water squishing in her white shoes. She approaches a building. An older woman, much older than Eleanor—and vaguely familiar to Mea—stands in the building's doorway.

*Only one person may pass through the tunnel,* Efah explains. *Only El—only the child is chosen. It is time.*

Mea presses against the membrane with all her might. It flexes away from her, and for a moment she can see Efah, not so far from her now, on the opposite side, in the shape of a cloud, his edges almost invisible against the darkness of the rift. He seems to be staring right at her, and she just has time to feel vaguely unsettled at being so near him when the vortex appears with a thump.

*The doorway ahead,* Efah says.

Mea brushes the tiny, whirling vortex, and it takes flight, zipping over the surface of the membrane like a firework.

Efah cautions her: *Careful, Mea! Be gentle.*

Eleanor approaches the building at a rapid walk, and Mea tries to ignore her, focusing instead on corralling the little portal. She moves this way and that, herding it toward the glass door of the office building; then, suddenly, she feels it suction into place, and it adheres to Eleanor's world with a powerful tension that even Mea cannot dislodge.

She's done it. The two worlds are firmly joined by the twisting vortex—the tunnel, as Efah calls it. All that remains is for Eleanor to pass through.

*You have done well,* Efah says.

Mea watches as Eleanor steps up onto the sidewalk and climbs the few stairs to the open door.

*She is coming,* Mea says. She trembles with anticipation.

The older woman welcomes Eleanor inside. For the briefest moment, Eleanor and the woman occupy the doorway simultaneously.

*Yes,* Mea urges.

But Efah cries out, confusing her. *Only the girl,* Efah cautions. *Not the woman!*

But the worst happens: The vortex detaches from the doorway and spins away. It passes over the building's brick façade, and bits of chewed-up brick sputter into the rift, then burn away like water on a hot skillet.

Eleanor vanishes from sight.

The older woman shouts in fear and staggers backward. She falls from the doorway onto the floor, the color sucked from her face, her eyes unfocused and full of fright.

Mea is horrified. She throws herself against the membrane, but the vortex has collapsed, and Eleanor is already a tiny flickering pinprick of light herself, far below the fabric of her own world, plummeting into the realm of dreams once more.

*Stop!* Mea cries. She pushes against the membrane, stretching it until she is even closer to Efah's shape on the other side. *Stop her!*

But Efah is still.

*She is beyond my reach.*

*Send me after her,* Mea pleads. *Please, you must!*

*No. You can only wait.*

*How long?* Mea begs.

*As long as it takes.*

In Eleanor's world, a boy bends over the woman, who has fainted. He is shouting, looking over his shoulder, and then a man bolts into view.

Eleanor's father.

He attends to the unconscious woman.

*You,* Mea says, staring at the man. *I know you.*

On the other side of the fishbowl, Efah says words that Mea does not understand, and the membrane clouds as before, obscuring her view of the Eleanor-less world.

*This is not yours to see.*

*I know that man,* Mea says. She lingers upon the fogged-over membrane, the image of Eleanor's father imprinted upon her.

Efah doesn't answer her, but she barely notices.

*I know that man.*

# *eleanor*

The doorway *quivers*.

Eleanor notices it at the last possible moment, but inertia carries her across the threshold. The trembling air, that strange crackling sensation. Eleanor's skin prickles all over. Then her foot touches the floor, and her father's office is gone.

Aunt Gerry stands before her still, but Jack isn't there. Neither is Gerry's barge of a desk or the cool, fluorescent lights overhead. Eleanor cannot hear the rain any longer—cannot hear much of anything at all, which makes her surroundings feel even more alien and unfamiliar.

"Aunt Gerry," Eleanor says. Her voice is honey-thick.

Gerry doesn't answer. She hasn't moved much in the last few seconds. When she finally turns, Eleanor is startled to see that her aunt is younger. Eleanor's mind chokes on this, and she stares, perplexed. Gerry's hair, almost white since the death of her boys, is a warm, woody red. The fold of her brow over her blue eyes has receded, and the crinkled skin above her lip has gone almost smooth.

Eleanor steps closer and opens her arms and says, "Aunt Gerry, what's going on? I'm—"

She passes right through Gerry.

She has never felt anything so unpleasant in her life. Not the car accident, not the strained neck and broken collarbone she suffered in the spring. A sizzling sensation envelops her, as if the outer layer of her skin has burst into flame, as if she is being devoured by a swarm of tiny chewing insects. It is, for an almost intolerable moment, as if she has been swallowed by lightning. Then she emerges on the other side of Gerry, and the feeling passes instantly.

Eleanor gasps loudly and falls hard to her knees. It takes a moment for the shock of it to fade, for her muscles to relax; they have drawn themselves so tight that her entire body trembles.

"Fuck," she groans. A long thread of spittle swings from her lips. Her breath comes in a staccato beat. She can't catch it and tries to swallow huge lungfuls of air as quickly as she can.

She stays on her knees for a long time, then plants one palm on the floor and pushes herself onto one foot and then the other.

Gerry is still standing behind her. If she has moved, Eleanor cannot tell. She steps wide around the woman—if this really is Gerry, really is a woman—and peers suspiciously at her.

"Aunt Gerry," Eleanor says.

Geraldine doesn't answer.

"*Aunt Gerry!*" Eleanor shouts.

Nothing.

But Gerry moves a little, shifting her weight onto one foot, and beneath her the floorboards creak. Eleanor sees that the office floor is gone, replaced with old wood planks. Gerry is standing on a threadbare rug. There are walls to either side of her and a door in front of her, and Eleanor realizes that this is a hallway. It isn't her father's office at all. It's a house.

Gerry's house.

Gerry is tilted forward, hands pressed to the doorjamb. She's risen up on tiptoe and is trying to peer through the fanlight. Whatever she sees has her worried, because she speaks suddenly, startling Eleanor.

"Go away," Gerry croaks. "Go—go away."

Eleanor has never seen her aunt look so afraid. Gerry's eyes are wide and glazed over, and a tear slips down her cheek. Her mouth is drawn narrow and thin, and her skin seems to drain of color before Eleanor's eyes.

"Aunt Gerry," Eleanor says, waving one hand at the woman.

But Gerry doesn't see Eleanor or hear her. She backs away from the door slowly, retreating into a corner of the small foyer. An umbrella stand tips over, spilling its single buttoned-up umbrella onto the wood floor.

Eleanor steps back and looks around. To the right of the front door is a living area. There's a love seat, a recliner, a coffee table, all tidily arranged. A basket of magazines sits beside the recliner, and a television remote is the only object on the coffee table. The television itself is perched on a dark cabinet beside a fireplace. The room smells of potpourri.

On the mantel of the fireplace are framed photographs of her cousins. Joshua. Charles. A couple of photos of the boys with their mother. One of the boys standing below a brown sign with white print that reads FORT SMITH, ARKANSAS. They're wearing fatigues in that one, and their hair glows in the sun.

Behind the love seat is a window with the curtains drawn. Eleanor goes to it and tentatively touches the curtains, afraid of that awful burning sensation. But all she feels is light fabric on her fingertips, and she draws the curtain back. Through the window a small green lawn unfolds. A tall oak looms over the yard, and it must be fall, because the ground is blanketed in brown and orange leaves.

Beyond the lawn, parked at the curb, is a beige sedan. A man steps out of the car. He wears an olive green dress uniform with a field of pins and medals on the breast; he carries a dark hat beneath one arm. The passenger door opens, and a second man, dressed the same way but with fewer medals, exits.

"Go away," Gerry rasps again, softly, and Eleanor realizes what is happening.

\*　\*　\*

ELEANOR HAD CONVINCED herself that it would not happen again. That it, whatever it was, was some sort of delusion. Maybe she'd eaten something bad and gotten sick, and her brain had turned feverish. Maybe she had wandered off.

*All the way to a farm? Into the mountains?*

But here it was, happening again. And this time she wasn't lost in a cornfield in Iowa someplace, watching herself as a child. She wasn't burying herself in mud in some faraway mountain range. This time she was in her aunt's house, years in the *past*, watching the worst moment of Gerry's life repeat itself.

A wave of nausea overwhelms Eleanor, and she wants to vomit, but nothing comes out. Her belly and her throat burn as if acid has worked its way up from her stomach, but there is nothing there.

Outside, the two men have made their way to the front door.

"Go away!" Gerry cries weakly.

One of the men knocks firmly.

Eleanor hears the front door open and quickly goes into the hallway. Her aunt covers her eyes with her palms and shakes her head vigorously.

"No," Gerry moans. "No, I didn't answer the door. You can't come inside. You can't—"

The two Army men stand on Gerry's doorstep, hats beneath their arms, resigned expressions on their faces. The younger man says, "Ma'am, are you Mrs.—"

"Don't you tell me *that*!" Gerry cries. She tries to kick the front door closed but misses and almost falls over. Eleanor claps a hand to her mouth. Her poor aunt doubles over onto her knees, and Eleanor can hear Gerry gasping for air like a fish, sucking it in but not exhaling any of it. Eleanor reaches for her, then remembers how it had burned when she tried to touch her aunt before, and she snatches her hand back, ashamed. Gerry bellows a teeth-rattling wail that sounds as if it comes from the soles of her feet. She lurches forward, her knees gone from beneath her. Both of the soldiers immediately drop their hats and go for Gerry's arms and scoop her up between them.

Eleanor feels hot tears trace down her cheeks. She wipes them away with the heels of her palms.

The Army men help Gerry past Eleanor—Eleanor steps back quickly to avoid colliding with them—and take her to the love seat in the living room.

"Mrs. Rydell," the young man says. "Mrs. Rydell, can you hear me?"

Eleanor doesn't want to watch this. Gerry is slack in their arms, and they place her on the love seat as if positioning a cloth doll. The older man reaches into his pocket, comes out with a small white packet, and deftly cracks it open beneath Gerry's nose. He waves it about, and Gerry's eyes begin to flutter, and Eleanor turns away. She feels like Ebenezer Scrooge, visited by the terrible ghosts of time itself.

*"I want to go home now!"* Eleanor shouts, stomping her feet on the hallway floor. *"Please, please, send me home!"*

Nothing—no *one*—answers her.

But something does catch her ear: voices, distant and small. She whirls around, but nobody is there. The front door stands open, pale daylight spilling across the floor. A few leaves have blown in and snagged on the rug. Opposite the living room is a dining nook, with a circular table in the center. It is draped with rose-colored lace, decorated with a vase of clean, bright lilies.

Eleanor passes the dining room by, listening for the voices. She follows them down the hallway, passing closed doors along the way, and she opens each one to peek inside. She finds closets and bedrooms and the kitchen and a bathroom, and then she comes to the last door. It is at the end of the hallway, down three steps.

The voices are louder now, but they're muffled by something. White noise. A rushing sound. She presses her ear to the door but can't make out the voices clearly. The rushing noise is very loud and unnatural.

Behind her she can hear the faint sounds of her aunt stirring, and she does not want to hear the words that Gerry will say when she realizes where she is and what has happened. So she opens the door at the bottom of the stairs, and a hurricane explodes through the doorway like a wall of seawater.

THE WIND IS fierce and angry, and it tears the hallway to pieces behind her. Eleanor claps her hands over her ears, but it doesn't diminish the howling current. She turns away from it, and she sees the house coming apart. The walls flex and bend and then fold and crumple and collapse as if the entire house were made from balsa wood and papier-mâché. Framed pictures fly off the wall and collide in the air. Glass flies everywhere, embedding itself in the tumbling walls. The wood planks in the floor separate from one another and become weightless.

Eleanor's hair rests straight and smooth on her shoulders, but she scarcely notices.

She is afraid the house will fall down upon Gerry and the two Army men, so she turns and steps quickly through the door. It slams behind her.

Her first thought is that she is in her aunt's garage, and the big door is open, because the room is flooded with pale light. It's so bright that it makes her eyes hurt.

The wind swirls around her, loud as a banshee.

Her eyes adjust, and she is dumbstruck.

The room is not a garage at all, but the cargo hold of an aircraft, and the scene is chaotic. There are large green crates strapped down, and, beyond them, the floor is covered with hundreds of little rollers. The crates are all marked U.S. ARMY. As she looks, one of the crates breaks free of its straps and skids down the carpet of rollers, sliding into a row of wall-mounted jump seats. This has apparently happened before; she can see that many other jump seats have already snapped free. Others are mangled and twisting in the gale. In the few seats that remain, Eleanor sees terrified soldiers, plastic masks over their faces.

At the far end of the cargo hold is nothing but blue sky and white clouds. The door is open, and the stiff, cold winds at thirty thousand feet chew at the inside of the plane. The door looks broken— one end lists to the side, and she sees that the giant hydraulic strut that controls the door is twisted. The other strut still holds, but she can hear it whining in the wind, a terrible, shrill, mechanical cry that can only mean something very bad is about to happen.

Then it does. The strut gives a terrible groan and breaks into several pieces. The cargo door falls open farther, swinging low. Eleanor can feel the entire plane shudder.

It begins to spin.

Another crate pulls free and banks off yet another, and suddenly the three loose crates are not just sliding but are flung about like toys. One of them splinters open, and Eleanor watches in horror as huge burlap sacks full of—what?—are flung around the cargo hold. The other two crates collide with more jump seats, and Eleanor screams. The soldiers in those seats sag limply, and the plane's strange new gravity yanks at their slack bodies so that it appears they are standing straight up with their arms outstretched.

Their broken, misshapen arms.

For the first time then it occurs to her that she has not grabbed on to anything, and yet the wind has not touched her. Her T-shirt and shorts are unruffled by the steep draft. She grabs her hair, holds it away from her face, and lets go, and it falls gently back into place.

There are five soldiers left in the jump seats. Two are unconscious and battered by the stiff winds. The other three look absolutely terrified behind their masks. Eleanor takes a careful step forward. Her footing is sure, so she takes another, and another, until she is next to the first jump seat. The boy sitting there—for that is all he is, just a boy a few years older than Eleanor—is crossing himself and crying, because that's what a boy does when he is faced with death.

And that is surely what is happening here, she realizes.

The plane is all wrong. The angles inside the cargo space are not straight. They are curved, as if the plane has been snatched out of the sky and twisted. The clouds outside the open door are turned the wrong way, and then the right way, and then the wrong way again. She can see a pale blue Earth sprawled high above them—instead of where it should be, far below the clouds.

Abruptly, the two unconscious soldiers are yanked from the plane, a swatch of steel peeled from the wall with them.

The boy in front of Eleanor screams and begins to jabber unintelligibly. Beside him, another boy says something about Jesus, and Eleanor looks at him and freezes.

The second boy is her cousin Joshua.

He and the stranger are strapped into the same rack of seats. Eleanor inspects the eyes of the third soldier, strapped alone into an empty row of vibrating jump seats.

The third boy is Charles.

A loud crack sounds behind her, and Eleanor looks back to see the entire wall of crates shift and tear free of their straps. She instinctively flinches, but the crates pass directly through her. They collide with every square inch of the cargo hold, hurled to the ceiling and the walls and the floors as the plane spirals out of control. Eleanor watches helplessly as a crate smashes directly into the first crop of jump seats, tearing them free of the wall.

The first boy and Joshua are wrenched from the plane, still buckled into their bent seats, limp and bloody, silently sucked into the bright void.

Then there is only Charles.

He has somehow found a strap to clutch, and he hangs on, desperately trying to wind it around his hand. His bladder has released, staining his uniform, and he is too frightened to cry any longer. The jump seats quake and creak as they are pulled free from the wall. Charles clings to the strap with both hands, his wide eyes full of panic.

*He sees her.*

He opens his mouth to speak, to beg for help from this red-haired girl who stands completely untouched by the destruction around her, but then, in the flicker of an instant, he is gone. He collides sharply with the flapping cargo door and sails out into the sky, rag-doll limp, and begins his long fall to—to the sea below, Eleanor realizes, seeing the vast blue ocean rising up so far beneath the plane.

She stands there, rooted in place.

*He saw her.*

Had he recognized her? She didn't think that he had, or if he had, that recognition hadn't penetrated the shrill alarm ring of fear that must have been sounding in his skull.

She hears her cousin's voice in her head as clearly as she heard it all those years ago.

*You'll be a good girl, right?*

Then the plane begins to break apart.


# *the keeper*

The keeper rocks slowly in her chair and listens to the rain. The water has been rising again, four or five inches now. Bits of grass and leaves float on its surface.

There are several leaks in the cabin's roof. She has scattered iron pots around. Water taps rhythmically into them. The keeper hums a low song to the metronome of the drips. Her humming almost obscures a sudden rumble, but her shadow hears it and peels itself free.

The keeper stops humming. "Where are you going?"

The shadow pauses at the stairs, tightening into a dark, flat circle. Then the keeper hears it, as well.

It isn't thunder. Whatever it is, her shadow is unnerved by it. And that bothers her, because in her valley, she is the keeper of the rain, the trees. Nothing happens here without her knowing.

And yet.

She gets up and stomps on her shadow, binding it to her feet again. It cowers beneath her, and she leans on the porch rail and stares out at the rising mist. The rumble comes again, and she follows the sound of it skyward, studying the slow black billow of the clouds. She can see nothing unusual, but the rumbling sound persists, growing louder—

An airplane rips a hole in the sky.

The keeper cries out in shock, so foreign are such things in her valley.

The plane is very far away, an immense hunk of shrapnel; it shrieks through the air like a banshee. She can make out ragged holes in the fuselage, a giant sheet of steel flapping open like the thorny jaw of an angler fish. A funnel of tar-colored smoke corkscrews behind it.

"It will crash," she says to her shadow. The plane spins like the blades of a windmill, its wings boring into the low clouds like an auger. "This is *her* doing. Our unwanted guest."

In the distance, the mountains and the pines climb up, obscuring the falling aircraft's final moments of flight. Then a spray of dirt and stone fans high into the sky. A moment later an orange fist punches skyward, then folds over upon itself, darkening into a charcoal cloud that looms large over the horizon.

The rain will put out the fire; that is the least of her worries. She quickly gathers her things, preparing for a long hike to the crash site. In this weather, across her swollen meadow, the journey will take two days at least. Longer, if the storm worsens. And she knows what she will find: a terrible gash in the side of her mountain, wreckage strewn over hundreds of yards, trees shattered into splinters.

"This must end," the keeper hisses. She glares down at her shadow. "Do you understand? I have had enough!"

The keeper looks again at the distant smoke. The mushroom

plume has widened, settling over the forest, shrouding the mountain in black ash.

"It is settled, then," the keeper says. "We must stop her."

## *eleanor*

A t the head of Pier C in Anchor Bend stands a great white shark. The statue is a curiosity, but it is an impressive one. The body is hammered bronze, and the shark is threatening, the way a great white should appear: body arched dramatically, jaws wide and layered with rows of menacing teeth, eyes beady and absent personality. It is a near-perfect representation of the feared killing machine, but the story of how the statue came to be is much less fantastic. It was inspired by the only such beast ever spotted in Anchor Bend's waters, a shark that was, truth be told, only half spotted, at that.

A fishing trawler had reported the shark's appearance in the early 1960s. None of the ship's crew had seen the actual shark, only its ominous fin. And most of them dismissed the sighting. But one fisherman had come home quite excited by the event, and at Wharfman's Pub had spun the tale into a full-fledged shark attack. A local artist, himself a fisherman, had commemorated the story with the great-white sculpture, and his brother-in-law, a city councilman, had persuaded the city to mount the sculpture near the water. The statue raised Anchor Bend's air of mystique and lured tourists, most of whom had no idea that the story was a fabrication. It was widely believed, in fact, that the artist—who had long since fled Anchor Bend amid scandalous rumors about his interest in another city official's wife—had never sobered up enough to verify the fisherman's tale.

But tourists love to pose with the statue and take turns sticking their head into the bronze mouth, posing for Polaroids.

Which is how so many people came to witness Eleanor's reappearance.

Not one of them could explain where the red-haired girl came from, just that she was suddenly *there*, in the shadow of the great white, splayed out on the wet sidewalk. Someone says, "Oh, my god," and another person says, "Is she okay? Did she fall?" The crowd of tourists tangles tightly around the unconscious girl. A third person says, "Did anybody call an ambulance?" A fourth: "What happened?"

An anesthesiologist from Denmark—who had little interest in the shark statue anyway—takes charge of the scene and kneels over Eleanor, quickly taking the girl's pulse and turning her onto her side. The onlookers crowd in; someone's knee bumps the woman's shoulder painfully.

"Back!" the Danish woman barks.

She turns back to Eleanor, snaps her fingers a couple of times, then lightly pats Eleanor's damp cheek. She is startled to feel how cold the girl's skin is.

"Come on, come on," the woman says. "Let's open your eyes now, dear. Let's go." She claps her hands, loudly, and that seems to do the trick. Eleanor flinches, then squints up at the people hovering above her, the blonde stranger peering down at her.

"Hello," Eleanor says, her voice sleepy. "Who are you?"

The anesthesiologist says, "I'm Cecilie. What's your name?"

"Eleanor," says Eleanor. "Where am I?"

"You are at the piers," says Cecilie. "Are you from here? Do you know where you are?"

Eleanor sees the shark overhead. "Hello, shark," she says.

"Tell me how you feel," Cecilie says.

A darkness passes across Eleanor's face. "I had a dream," she says. "It was—it was very sad."

"Do you live here?" Cecilie asks. "Are you visiting?"

Eleanor sits up and bumps her head on the shark's tail fin. "Ouch," she says, rubbing her head. "I—uh—my father. He works just over there."

She points up the road at her father's office, and the crowd of tourists disintegrates as it becomes clear that Eleanor, while disoriented, is generally okay. Cecilie helps Eleanor to her feet, drawing her away from the statue, and says, "You are okay?"

"I'm okay," Eleanor says. "Just . . . tired."

"Can you walk?"

"I think so," Eleanor says.

She allows Cecilie to guide her, and together they cross the waterfront lawn to the sidewalk and turn in the direction of Paul Witt Realty. They walk slowly, and Eleanor tries to shuffle her thoughts into order.

"What is today?" she asks Cecilie.

"Saturday."

"Saturday," Eleanor says. "The same Saturday?"

Cecilie looks confused. "I don't know what you mean."

"The—the whales! Were there whales in the harbor?" Eleanor asks. "Today. Were there whales today?"

Cecilie says, "I did not see them, but I heard their spouts."

Eleanor frowns. "So it's the same Saturday? It's not the next one?"

"You sound as if you might need to see a doctor," Cecilie says. "You sound . . . hmm. Addled. Are you sure you're okay?"

Eleanor looks around at the damp streets, then at Cecilie. "I'm not addled."

"Do you know what happened? Did you faint? I did not even see you—"

Eleanor puts one hand up, and Cecilie almost walks into it.

"What—," Cecilie starts, and then she stops, following Eleanor's gaze.

A few blocks ahead, a police car and an ambulance are stopped on the opposite side of the road. Their lights wink and swirl, and a few people have gathered around to eyeball the disturbance.

"Dad," Eleanor says. "That's my father's office."

"Here," Cecilie says. "Hold my hand. We will try to go faster."

"I'm fine," Eleanor says, breaking into an unsteady run. She darts across the glistening street.

"Are you sure?" Cecilie calls after her.

Eleanor doesn't answer.

PAUL WITT REALTY is in chaos, as much as three worried people can generate. Eleanor stops on the sidewalk, just short of the police car. A tanned officer in short black sleeves sees her and says, "Wait—you. Come with me."

Eleanor steps back, wary, but the officer takes her by the elbow and leads her past the car and the flashing lights.

"Hey," she says. "Let go of me, please!"

The officer waves another officer over, a woman with a tight, dark ponytail. "Sheila," he says. "This the girl?"

The woman takes two steps in Eleanor's direction, then stops. "Hey," she says.

"Let go of me," Eleanor says again.

The officer named Sheila steps through the office door and a moment later comes outside with Paul Witt, who says, "I don't under—" Then he sees Eleanor, and he runs to her—runs, as she has almost never seen her father do before—and then the first officer is letting her go, and her father's arms wrap around her, tightly, as if he is cinching her in half. Words come out of him in a rush: "Ellie, my god, where—how did you—I was so—are you okay? Goddamnit, where—Ellie, you're safe, you're okay, you're—"

"This your daughter?" the first officer asks.

Paul just squeezes Eleanor more tightly.

"Dad," Eleanor says, confused. "What's going on?"

\* \* \*

SHEILA TELLS ELEANOR's father that she's going to stick around to take down some information for her report, but the tanned officer leaves in the squad car. Eleanor asks about the ambulance.

"Come inside," her father says. He starts walking toward the door, but Eleanor stops short.

Paul turns back. "Ellie," he says. "Come inside."

She shakes her head, staring past him at the glass doors.

"What's wrong?"

"I—I want to stay out here," Eleanor says. She feels a tremor in her throat but can't tell if it's fear or if she's about to burst into tears. "Can I stay out here?"

Paul looks at Officer Sheila, who shrugs. "I guess so. Everyone's inside, though. Ellie, what's going on?"

Through the doors, Eleanor sees Jack inside at the same time he sees her. He claps his hands to his head, then runs outside. "Ellie," he says, and she is surprised to see that he is distraught. "Ellie, Ellie."

He just says her name again and again, and Eleanor looks at her father and then at Jack, and she says, "What's going on?"

Officer Sheila says, "We were told you were missing. Do you want to tell me where you've been this morning?"

"This morning?" Eleanor asks cautiously. "Only this morning?"

Jack's eyes fill up with tears. "You. Just. *Disappeared*," he whispers.

"Aunt Gerry," Eleanor says suddenly. "Where's Aunt Gerry?"

ELEANOR GOES INSIDE. Walking through the door is terrifying, and at first she cannot do it. She puts her hands on either side of the open doorway and pushes herself away from it. Her father says, "Ellie," and the note of tension in his voice upsets her, because that means everything is back to the way it was, because she was gone and now she's home and he is already parenting her, but then Jack is next to her, and he says, gently, "It's okay. Everything is going to be okay."

Eleanor inhales sharply, and that's when she realizes that she doesn't feel any of it—doesn't feel a charge in the air, doesn't feel anything pulling at her.

She goes through the doorway with her eyes closed, and when she opens them again, she's in the lobby of her father's real estate office, and everything is quite normal—except for Aunt Gerry lying on the couch with an oxygen mask over her nose and mouth, except for the paramedic kneeling beside her, capping a syringe and depositing it into a biohazard bucket.

Eleanor turns to her father and says, "What happened?"

But Jack says, "He didn't see. I did, though."

"What happened?" she says again.

Eleanor's father and Officer Sheila tower over her as she stares at her aunt. Gerry's breath is labored.

"She fainted," Officer Sheila says. "Or something."

"She's getting older," Paul says. "She's got high blood pressure. And diabetes."

Eleanor begins to cry. Her father pats her shoulder, but then he and Officer Sheila turn away and continue talking. Jack opens his skinny arms, and Eleanor covers her face and steps forward into them. His embrace is warm and strong. She allows herself to sink into this feeling, this feeling of being held, of being essential. With everything that has gone wrong, she realizes how long it has been since she felt anything like that at all.

"Ellie," Jack whispers. "You—it sounds crazy, but you—you *disappeared*. Just—*poof*. And it scared her. And me," he adds.

In the quiet she hears the hiss of the oxygen mask upon her aunt's face, and the sensation goes away. Things aren't okay.

Things aren't even a little okay.


ELEANOR SITS ON the couch in her father's office. The paramedic has given her a blanket. It's rough and folds around her like—*like burlap,* she thinks regretfully. But it warms her. She didn't know that she was cold until now.

The sounds of the office are unnatural: Gerry's rattling breath, the paramedic's equipment scraping and knocking around, Jack pacing restlessly. Eleanor feels responsible, somehow, for the wrongness of the world. That's what it is: *wrong.* She struggles with her thoughts, but they don't make any sense. She feels displaced, as if the world she inhabits has shifted, has become foreign.

A blur in her vision distracts her. She looks up to see her father standing at his office window, hands locked behind his back. He stares through the window at the sea wall. The shark statue is visible in the distance, and she wonders if he saw her there before. The sun is going down, and the statue flares gold as the light seeps away. Her father is a dark silhouette, pink around the edges.

He sighs heavily, and Eleanor can almost feel it in her bones. Her father doesn't look well, and that is surprising to her, because just yesterday—was it yesterday?—he was fine. Just yesterday the world rested firmly on its axis, and all was well. The summer had been pleasant, even easy. But now her father looks as if he has endured a battle. He is tired—she can see it in the slump of his shoulders, the curve of his spine. He hasn't shaved. His face is prickly under a few days of stubble. His clothes are wrinkled.

Were his clothes wrinkled like that earlier in the day, when she and Jack stopped by to steal bottles of orange juice? Eleanor can't remember.

She thinks of her mother, then, because her father's condition is not altogether unlike Agnes's. Agnes, who isn't here, who is probably at home, as usual, tucked into her chair with a bottle of . . . something. For a moment, Eleanor resents her mother, but this is nothing new. There have been many such moments during the past seven years. There will be many more. This is what it is like when a child must raise herself *and* her parent.

Eleanor stopped fooling herself long ago. She knows that her mother doesn't care about her; she suspects, sometimes, that her mother might even *hate* her. When Agnes is lucid, Eleanor can see the pain that inhabits her eyes.

Did Agnes even love them when they were both alive? Eleanor cannot remember. Her sister seems to have taken on a new shape in death, a regal one, as Agnes has built up Esmerelda's memory into a towering memorial in their dark home.

What would Eleanor ever have done without Gerry?

In the lobby, Jack sits behind Gerry's desk, turning idly this way and that in the chair. He looks helpless, forlorn, as he stares down at his hands. He notices Eleanor watching him, and he glances up, then away, then back. He mouths something—*Come here,* perhaps?—and jerks his head to indicate the office kitchen.

The couch springs creak when Eleanor rises, but her father doesn't notice, and again she feels as if something critical has changed. When she was small and tripped and bumped her head and cried, he would scoop her up and lock her in his arms and press his cheek to hers and whisper into her ear: *You're okay. I'm right here. I love you.*

And that would make everything better.

Her father sighs again.

Eleanor follows Jack into the kitchen. She doesn't look at her aunt, still laid out on the sofa, still rattling like a loose gutter.

Jack pulls open the refrigerator and takes out a box of cranberry juice. He holds it up for her. Eleanor shakes her head, and he takes it for himself, puncturing the foil cover with the straw and bumping the refrigerator door closed with his hip.

"Is your dad okay?" Jack asks.

"I don't know. He will be."

"He was really upset," Jack says.

"Aunt Gerry—"

"She just—she just went empty," he says. He wrinkles his nose. "Not empty. But—you know? She just fell down."

Eleanor looks at her feet. "Did you—? Never mind."

Jack says, "You're going to tell me what happened now, right?"

"Jack," she says, "I don't know what happened."

"No," he says. "I think you do. I think you have an idea, even if you don't really know."

She's quiet. "I really don't know."

"But *something* happened," he says. "Don't lie to me. And it happened before. Didn't it."

Eleanor takes a slow breath, then looks at Jack solemnly. "Yes."

"What did it feel like?" he asks.

He pulls out a chair for her, and she sinks into it, bundled in her scratchy blanket. He pulls out another chair for himself and sits next to her, facing her, the juice box cupped in his hands.

"I don't think I can explain it," she says.

Jack doesn't look away.

"Try," he says.

So she does.

In the little kitchen in her father's office, while her father stands like a frozen statue at the window in the next room, while his sister lies damaged on the sofa nearby, Eleanor tries to put into words what is happening to her, and she discovers that she has plenty of words for it, indeed.

## *the keeper*

I t takes three days to reach the foothills below the crash site. Three days of slogging through muck and rising water. The keeper grips her walking stick, and her shadow flits upon the surface of the deepening lake. The water is bitterly cold, but she barely feels it. If she wanted to, she could warm the water to a boil with a thought.

But she is weary.

Beyond the crowns of her great pine forest she can see the crash smoke. It has thinned to small, curling threads.

"A few more hours," she says to her shadow.

As SHE CLIMBS, the ground warms. She can already smell the acrid tang of burned fuel. A mist swims up, obscuring the earth.

This forest has burned and regrown twice since the keeper has lived in the valley. The earth here has never forgotten its pain. It cradles the heat of its own death, always just beneath the surface, as though releasing the memory would be to forget it forever, to risk succumbing again. But forests burn. They always return. The keeper's valley is an open wound, doomed to scratch itself until it bleeds and bleeds.

She prefers it this way.

She crests a small rise, where the trees thin, and surveys the land far below. Her cabin is a distant speck. The chimney smokes, and she wonders if the place will burn down while she is gone.

But what interests her most is not the cabin.

The beasts are lumbering down from the distant mountains. The largest comes down first, her head and neck lost in the low clouds, stepping almost gracefully down the mountain slopes. The smaller beast follows, its limp more pronounced, stumbling down the incline.

"What happened to you?" the keeper asks from afar.

The beasts will bed down somewhere in the valley. They don't seem to mind sleeping in the water. That the beasts are visible to the keeper even here, all these miles north, is a testament to their stunning size. But she is perplexed by their migration. The beasts should be moving southward, but they are there already. That they appear to be marching north is irregular, worrisome.

The keeper senses that the world around her has fallen out of time with itself.

\* \* \*

THE PLANE'S WRECKAGE is a marbled glow beyond the trees. It turns their branches and needles blood red in the dark.

"That damned child," the keeper grumbles.

Damned child, indeed, leaping from one world to the next as if she were some sort of damp, fresh god, toddling about in the dark, wrecking everything.

The keeper has never encountered anything like her before.

"Have you?" she asks her shadow, almost invisible in the dark. "Have you seen *anything* like her before?"

Her shadow does not answer.

"No," the keeper mutters. "No, she is something new."

She begins to climb again.

## *eleanor*

Eleanor is quiet during the car ride to her father's apartment. The car sways over the wet asphalt, triggering a strange new sensation, one of being unhitched from the world that passes by, as if Eleanor rides on some current that moves at a different pace. She rests her head against the passenger window. The glass is cool and pleasant on her skin. It grounds her, a little.

Paul drives carefully, more slowly than usual. He is still quiet himself but casts sideways glances at Eleanor as he drives.

Finally he says, "Penny for your thoughts?"

Eleanor gives him a half smile but nothing more.

Paul coasts to a stop at a red light, and it changes almost immediately, casting a sickly green glow on his face.

"Are you worried about your mom?" he asks. "I left her a message."

Eleanor doesn't look at him. "I'm always worried about her."

"She's drinking again, isn't she?" he says. He exhales worriedly. "Gerry—she said she talked to Agnes. Your mother told her she was going to quit."

Eleanor doesn't answer. She doesn't need to. Agnes tells the familiar lie now and then, has for years.

"I'm sure she knows you're safe," Paul says.

"Not likely," Eleanor says in a voice so quiet, she can barely hear it herself.

"What?"

"I said, I'm sure she does."

Paul nods, then says, "You know it's killing me, right?"

Eleanor lifts her head off the glass. "What's killing you?"

"Not knowing what happened," he says. "I don't know what's happening with you, and it scares me."

"I don't want to talk about it right now," Eleanor says.

"I know," Paul says. He shifts in his seat so that he's facing her, just a little. "I know you don't want to, but—Ellie, I can't *not* know. You're my little girl."

Eleanor doesn't say anything.

"This is serious," he says. "Don't you realize—"

"Of course I realize," Eleanor snaps. "It happened to *me*."

Paul falls silent, and Eleanor immediately feels guilty.

"I mean—it must have been the most awful thing for you to—"

"It was," Paul interrupts. "It was exactly the most awful thing ever, Ellie. If I prayed, then I would pray every day and every night that you never have to go through anything like it. This has been the worst year ever."

Eleanor feels his words like a fist. "The worst," she says, aware of a hollow inside her chest. "No. It isn't the worst."

Paul opens his mouth, closes it. "I—I didn't mean—"

"And I *did* go through it, Dad," Eleanor says. "Do you think I *wanted* to? Do you think I have any idea why—"

She falls quiet and sulks in the passenger seat, suddenly angry with her father. How could he make this about *him*?

"Goddamnit," Paul says. He thumps his palms on the steering wheel in frustration. "Goddamnit, Eleanor. I wiped your bottom. I gave you baths. You used to run around in circles and then fall down, dizzy, and say, 'Dada, up.' If you ever got hurt, it *killed* me—so do you know what it felt like to find out that you were just—just *gone*?"

Eleanor crosses her arms and slides down in her seat.

"It felt like someone ripped my bones out," Paul says. "Like I couldn't stand up. I was imagining my little girl—my baby girl, just knee-high—out there *all alone*."

"I'm not your baby girl anymore," she says. "I'm not knee-high. I'm taller than Mom."

"You know what I mean, El—"

"Stop making this about you!" she says. "Who *are* you?"

Paul flinches at this.

"Take me home," she says.

"We're going home," Paul answers, reeling.

"Not *your* home," Eleanor says, teeth flashing. "*My* home. The one that *I* didn't *leave*."

Eleanor feels an immediate and cold crush of regret, but Paul smacks his hand on the dashboard, hard, and says, "Does your mother even ask you about your day when you come home from school? Is she ever even coherent? Do you have to feed her like a fu— like a baby? Is she even really your mother anymore?"

"I want to go home," Eleanor says quietly.

"*My* home," Paul barks, and then his voice drops to a sulking growl. "You'll stay in *my* home on *my* weekends, and this is *my* weekend."

Eleanor doesn't answer him. She sits in the pale dashboard light, staring straight ahead into the dark, and Paul seethes behind the wheel.

"Your mother can take care of herself," he adds. His nostrils flare when he says it.

Eleanor says softly, "No, she can't."

Paul swings the wheel, and the car thumps up the ramp into the apartment parking lot. He pulls into his assigned space and turns the key, and the engine cuts out, and the car falls into a tense hush. He sits still for a moment, his hand frozen on the key, and then he exhales in a rush and turns to Eleanor. His eyes soften, and he starts to say something, but Eleanor just pushes the door open, climbs out, and closes it behind her.

She's halfway up the exterior staircase before he opens his door to follow. She can hear him trudge up the stairs behind her. She knows what he had hoped for tonight: a comfortable evening, one that would restore the balance of things. A bowl of soup, a Saturday-night movie. She would fall asleep on the couch, and he would put a blanket over her. He would feel like a good parent, and Eleanor would be safe.

Not tonight.


SHE TURNS OUT the light in the bedroom that will never feel like hers, climbs into the bed that still doesn't feel broken in, and pulls the blankets up to her chin. She sees her father's shadow interrupt the sliver of light beneath the bedroom door. He lingers there for a minute, then two, and she hears him mumble something, then shuffle away.

She remembers a brighter time. When her mother was young and stern but not so poisonous. Her father would come home from work and shrug off the weight of his day, and Eleanor would wait for the sound of the attic door opening and follow him upstairs to watch him build entire worlds out of sticks and paper.

Now it seems as if all anybody ever does is tear the world apart.

\*    \*    \*

A BOWL OF chocolate ice cream. Coca-Cola poured over the top, the cold scoops crusted over, caramel brown. Eleanor taps at the brittle layer with her spoon, satisfied by the tiny cracking sound it makes.

"That's no kind of breakfast," her father says, yawning.

"It's all you have," she says without looking up.

"That's not—," he says, but then he opens the refrigerator and stops. "Yeah. It's all I have."

He takes containers out of the refrigerator. They were transparent, once, but the plastic is clouded, and the contents are indecipherable and mushy with mold. He drops them unceremoniously into the garbage can, one by one.

"They'll smell by afternoon," Eleanor chides.

"I'll take the trash out," he says.

"No trash collection on Sundays."

"Yeah," he says, "but there's a dumpster, and—"

"Dumpster's full," Eleanor says. "Might as well leave them in the fridge until Monday."

Paul closes the refrigerator door, then tousles Eleanor's hair. She cringes away from him.

"Wash your hands," she says.

He lathers up in the sink. "We should go to Dot's."

"I'm already eating."

"Come on," Paul says. "Breakfast. It'll be good."

"It's already almost nine," she says. "It'll be packed. We'll have to stand in line."

"When's the last time you saw a line anywhere in this town?" Paul dries his hands on a towel, then leans against the counter. "What's going on?"

"Nothing."

"I'm sorry about last night," he says.

"I don't care," Eleanor says. She drops her spoon into the bowl, then pushes away from the table and dumps the dish into the sink.

"Hey," he says, putting his arms out.

She sidesteps them, maneuvering around the small folding table that serves as his dining table.

"Ellie," he says. "You're having a rough week."

"Understatement," she scoffs.

"I'm worried about you."

"Good for you. Mom probably isn't. You're father of the goddamn year."

"Hey, now, Eleanor—"

"I bet she's in the same spot where I left her two nights ago," Eleanor says. "Or maybe not. Maybe she realized I threw away her bottle."

"Ellie—"

"I always regret that. Throwing the bottles away," Eleanor continues. "Because when she finds out they're gone, she just finds some way to get out of the house for another one. And Mom drunk in her chair is much better than Mom drunk anyplace else, right? But sometimes I do it, anyway. Do you know why? Because I hope she'll stop. But she can't. And you know what? If she wrecks the car on the way to the store and dies, then I'll be the girl who killed her own mother because I tried to save her."

"Eleanor—"

"But it's refreshing, you know? At least she's honest about who she is. She might hate me, but she doesn't ever pretend she doesn't. What do you do? Besides yell at me all the time now."

"You have to come live with me," Paul says. "You can't live with her anymore. She's killing herself! She's killing *you*. I won't let you—"

"Won't let me *what*?" Eleanor demands. "Make my own choices? Right, because you're so good at making them for all of us, aren't you? You send a check every month, but that doesn't mean you own me!"

Paul recoils, stunned. "Ellie, I—"

"I live with her," Eleanor says firmly, "because without me, she will die. She'll give up. And *you* made this choice for me when you fucking *left*."

Paul opens his mouth, but Eleanor steps forward and pushes him.

"I'm the only thing keeping her from drinking until she's dead," Eleanor says loudly, pushing her father again. "Me! And do you know what I get for that? She looks at me, and she sees Esmerelda, and she *hates* me. And do you know what? *I don't blame her.* I feel the same way. I have to wear this face forever. So don't talk to me about choices, *Dad*. Because the rest of us don't have *any*."

Her father's eyes swim with tears. He's speechless.

She stops pushing and takes a few steps back, breathing hard. "Do you know what happens if I come to live with you?"

"Ellie—"

"I'll get up in the morning, and I'll walk through the apartment, and you'll catch a glimpse of me, and you'll mistake me for her," Eleanor says. "That's how it starts. Then *you* start to fall apart. And the only thing that keeps that from happening is me *not* living here."

Eleanor chokes back a heavy sob, and Paul says, "Ellie, sweetheart—" and he steps forward.

"Leave me alone!" she shouts.

She storms out of the kitchen.

But a moment later she returns.

"Look," she says, staring at the floor. Her voice is brittle. "I don't know what's going on. Things are—I can't explain it. I just want to be left alone. Just for one stupid minute. Okay?"

There is only heartbreak in his eyes. "Okay," he whispers.

Without a word, she goes to her bedroom, gathers some clothes, and stomps down the hall to the bathroom. She can hear Paul on the phone, leaving another message for her mother—"She's safe and she's with me; call if you get this"—and she wishes she could just disappear for real.

Who would choose this life?

She stacks her clothes on the bathroom counter, then stands there staring at herself in the mirror. She looks angry. It *hurts* to look so angry all the time. Her jaw is tight, her brow furrowed severely. She exhales and tries to soften her face, to let go of her quivering anger.

But she just looks tired, though she somehow slept all night. Her hair is tangled and dirty, stiff from the salty sea air. Dark hollows nestle beneath her green eyes, ominous against her pale skin. She has a sour taste in her mouth from the Coke and chocolate ice cream. She brushes her teeth, staring herself down.

She wishes she could rewind the past day and start again. She would bike to Rock with Jack. They'd eat sandwiches in the park and walk around the small main street, looking through shop windows at the businesses on life support. She always wondered how little niche shops like those survived in a town with only a couple of hundred residents. Are there that many people in small towns who need hand-painted novelty cows to hang in their kitchens?

If she could begin again, then this morning she and her father would have gone to the store for groceries, and they'd have made French toast and scrambled eggs, and they'd have laughed over breakfast. And maybe she would have confided in him and told him what frightens her. Because if there is only one thing in the world that she can trust, it is that she is afraid. And alone.

She misses her family.

The telephone rings in the kitchen, and she can hear her father answer it. She ignores it, but then he says, "—you're okay?" and she listens.

"—so glad you're all right," her father says. "Did the doctor say what—wait, a minor *stroke*? Gerry, that's—"

Aunt Gerry.

Her father is quiet for a moment, listening. Then he says, "Should you even be on the phone? You sound upset. Is your doctor there? Can I—"

More silence, then: "What do you mean, she saw something? Saw what?"

A chill passes over Eleanor.

*Aunt Gerry knows.*

"—under a lot of strain," Paul says. "You need to rest—"

Now Eleanor can hear her aunt's voice, a faint but insistent buzz. She sounds scared.

"Gerry," Paul says. "Gerry. Gerry. Listen—if—listen to me. *Gerry*!"

*Buzz, buzz.*

"A stroke is serious business," Paul says. "Do they know you're on the phone?"

Eleanor has gone pale. She steps into the hall. Her father is framed in the kitchen doorway, telephone cord dangling around his knees.

"We're on our way," he says. "We'll be right there. Okay? Please. Rest. I'll come see you today. Okay? You need to rest."

*Buzz, buzz.*

"Okay. Okay, I promise. Okay, Gerry."

He hangs up the phone, then turns to see Eleanor standing there.

"Ellie," he says. "Your aunt—she—"

Eleanor just stares at him.

"She said you—she said you—no, it's crazy." He trails off, bewildered.

"She says I saw Charles and Joshua," Eleanor says.

Paul's mouth falls open. "That's what she said. How did you—"

"I *did* see Charles and Joshua."

"Ellie, what—how did you . . ." Her father looks frightened. "What in the world is going on here?"

*Poor Aunt Gerry.*

"No," Eleanor says, and she feels a rush of nausea, and she turns to the bathroom door, and once again, too late, she feels that unwelcome tingle of electricity, and she protests: "*No*—"

The apartment explodes around her.

# *the keeper*

S he arrives at the site before morning.

She pauses at the edge of the pine grove, which only a few days before was the heart of these mountain woods. She thinks back to the plane's sudden appearance and ferocious descent, and she stares now at the crime scene before her. She had hoped—in some childlike corner of her cold heart—that the plane was a hallucination.

It is real.

The trees are scattered like toothpicks. A great swath of forest has been torn open. Many of the trees have become spears, tangled high in the branches of others. The plane has dived into the ground like a spade, carving its own long grave. It does not much resemble a plane now. Hollow sections are crumpled and shredded. The keeper sees a few broken seats, the crushed tail. A wing stands almost upright in the dirt.

Pine needles and ash float lazily down from above. The rain has slowed.

She is relieved to see that most of the burning wreckage has been extinguished. Damp or not, if the forest had caught fire, thousands of acres would've gone up in a few days' time. The keeper would have survived, perched atop her cabin—almost a boat now—in the middle of her watery meadow. She would have rested there for decades, patiently watching as the forest slumbered, black and smoldering, until its slow rebirth began. She would have waited a century for it to creep across the foothills and into the mountains again.

She sees no survivors, no bodies, whole or in pieces, and she is relieved by this. She remains the only human to have walked this valley.

Except for the stranger, she remembers.

The rain falls harder.

The keeper turns her face up into the downpour. The rain blends with the ash on her skin, tracing fine black lines down her face. The falling ash has soured the rain. She can smell the bitter tang of airplane fuel and scorched metal.

She feels her shadow leap at her feet.

"What is it?" she asks, glancing around, then up.

A pulse of light echoes in the heavy clouds high above the mountain. It is not much, can hardly be called lightning. It is simply a heartbeat, a single, muted note. It blooms deep within the clouds, then contracts, flickers, and is gone. The keeper stares, but it does not return.

"I saw you," she whispers.

She looks down at her shadow.

"We're losing our grip, I think," she says quietly. "Strangers in our home."

She turns back to the clouds, but the flare of light has gone.

She knows what it was.

*Who* it was.

"This is my home," she whispers. "You cannot have it."

The sky thunders in response, and the rain becomes a torrent.

## mea

What am I doing wrong?

Mea rides the tides around her fishbowl, skimming past the membrane and its eons of memories. She passes the view of Eleanor's body again and again and is unable to look away from the damage she has wrought. The black ocean swells around Mea like a storm, coursing over every ebb and flow of her shape. Outside her prison, Efah keeps pace alongside her, his shadow coursing over the outer wall of her enclosure.

*You have been impatient,* Efah says. *You should know better.*

*How?* Mea exclaims. *This is not my home! This isn't a home at all. You've trapped me here! Just how should I know better?*

Efah is not stirred by her anger. *You might well have taken her life,* he says.

Mea had leaped at the opportunity to take Eleanor out of her father's apartment, had quickly created a new vortex—but Eleanor didn't plunge into the dream realm, as before. This time the vortex seemed to act as a cannon, firing Eleanor like a lead ball into the bathroom wall.

This time was much worse than the last.

Eleanor lies in a heap on the floor. The tiles on the bathroom wall have shattered and fallen down upon her. The wall is crushed inward—there is a huge hole in the drywall, and Mea can see exposed studs and wires beyond it. The overhead light flickers. A single violent crack splits the mirror.

Eleanor's father stands paralyzed in the doorway, aghast at the sight of his daughter crumpled amid plaster dust and broken tile. The toilet tank is fractured, and water gushes onto the floor.

Eleanor groans and stirs, and both Paul and Mea are horrified to see that one of Eleanor's eyes is filled with blood. Then both of her eyes roll back, and her head clunks onto the floor. Paul snaps out of his paralysis and runs to her, sliding to his knees in an inch of water and debris.

*Why is this so hard?* Mea demands. *I'm killing her!*

*You wish to bring a human into the rift,* Efah says. *It has never been done.*

*You told me that it* can *be done!*

*I told you that I* think *it can be done. She is special.*

Mea whirls angrily away. She watches as an ambulance arrives, and Eleanor is loaded into the back, and the paramedics prevent Paul from climbing in with her. Paul yells and yells, but a police officer arrives and steps between him and the ambulance, and the vehicle rushes into the night.

*She needs me,* Mea says.

*You must take care,* Efah says. *You must not fail again.*

Mea does not reply.

MEA SETTLES DOWN against the membrane like a child pressed against a window to watch the snow fall. Eleanor's next days unfold painfully slowly.

One more chance may be all Mea can afford. Eleanor might not live through another of Mea's mistakes. Should she try again? If she fails, it will be the people in Eleanor's world who suffer the most. And for what? For Mea's strange and trivial desire to meet this particular human?

But she knows she will try again.

Efah will help her.

First, though, Eleanor must heal, and that road is long, long.

## *eleanor*

She blinks up at a grid of fluorescent lights and acoustic tiles. There is something off about her vision. She closes her left eye. The ceiling is clear. She closes her right, and the world is underwater, murky.

She tries to lean forward, but something holds her back; she tries to look at her feet but can't see much beyond her chin from this angle. Her hands are free, however, and she lifts first one, then the other. There is a bandage around each of her arms. A slim IV tube is lodged in the pit of her right elbow.

*Oh, no,* she thinks.

She sags against her pillow and turns her head. There is a window covered with a dull gray curtain. There is a lamp. There's a reproduction of a Monet on the wall, behind smudged glass. To her left—it is hard to crane her neck—there is more glass, a window that looks into the building instead of outside, and through it she can see a nurses' station, and just to the right of it is her father, in conversation with a doctor in a white jacket and a police officer in uniform. She can hear their muted voices, the muffled crackle of chatter from the radio on the cop's shoulder. A pair of shiny hand-cuffs hang on his belt.

Her father glances toward her then, and his face changes when he sees that she is awake. He starts in her direction, and Eleanor smiles at him. Then the doctor and the police officer take her father by the wrists and arms, and Eleanor's smile fades. Something isn't right. Her father looks surprised, and she can hear his voice grow loud, and then there is a tiny beep from a machine beside her bed, and Eleanor feels the world fog over.


THE NEXT FEW hours are a blur of paperwork and instruction. A doctor comes in, leaves, and does not return. Shelley, the nurse from Eleanor's last hospital visit, sits beside Eleanor's bed, explaining what the back brace is for and how to change the bandages on her arms. She helps Eleanor sit up and removes the IV needle; Eleanor gasps a little when it comes out.

The nurse draws the curtain over the hallway window. She holds Eleanor by the elbow and guides her out of bed. Eleanor hobbles, then smiles ruefully.

"I'm a hundred years old," she says.

Shelley chuckles. She unsnaps the hospital gown and helps Elea-nor step into her pajama pants—the ones she came into the hospital wearing, still white with drywall dust—and hospital slippers.

"Now, when you're in street clothes, the brace will go over your bra," Shelley says. "Just a little."

"How bad is it?" Eleanor asks.

Shelley cocks her head. "You haven't seen, have you?" she asks. "Well, you're a strong girl. Do you want to see?"

Nervously, Eleanor asks, "*Do* I?"

"You'll see it at home, first time you look in the mirror," Shelley says. "Might as well see it here with me, now."

She leads Eleanor into the private bathroom.

"Raise your arms," Shelley says.

She puts her hands on Eleanor's waist, and they face the mirror together.

"Here." Shelley points at Eleanor's right side, below her armpit. "You can see a little of the bruising here. Do you see?"

The skin Shelley points at isn't dark like a bruise. It's just pink, like a fierce sunburn.

"That's not so bad," she says.

"Let's turn," Shelley says. She gently pushes on Eleanor's hips and helps her turn sideways.

Eleanor's back comes into view in the mirror, and she cannot stifle a gasp or the tears that spring to her eyes.

"There," Shelley says. "Now you can see it."

The pink deepens into a severe, continent-shaped blotch of purples and blues. The discoloration spreads over most of her back. Only the edge of her left side is unmarked. At the low center of her back, the blotch is almost black. To Eleanor it looks as if some poisonous tar has been injected just beneath her skin.

"That's why putting your bra on later might hurt just a bit, you see?" Shelley says. "And it's also why you have to wear the brace for a few weeks, okay? You can't take it off. It's there to make sure you're staying straight and strong while you're healing up, so you don't do any lasting damage to yourself."

Eleanor cries as she watches the nurse fit the brace. Three straps circle her torso, attaching around her belly, her hips, and below her small breasts. Shelley cinches the brace tightly, and Eleanor gasps again.

"Tighter is better," Shelley apologizes. "Kind of like wearing a corset in the old days, isn't it?"

"Thank you," Eleanor says. "For helping me."

"You don't have to thank me, honey," Shelley says.

Eleanor turns away from the mirror, slowly. "They think my dad did this."

Shelley looks forlorn. "I don't want to ask, but, honey . . . are you sure he didn't?"

Eleanor shakes her head.

"No," she says. "I think *I* did."


PAUL DRIVES EXCRUCIATINGLY slowly through town, and other vehicles stack up behind him. None of the drivers honks at Paul, but he pulls over now and again to let them pass.

From the vantage point of the reclined passenger seat, Eleanor watches the tops of buildings and trees and power lines glide by. Each time the car thuds into a rut, she winces, and her father apologizes.

"How do you feel?" he asks her, and she says, "Okay," and a few minutes later he asks again.

Finally she says, "Are *you* okay?"

Her father glances her way. "How much of that did you have to hear?"

"It isn't fair," she says. "That they did that to you. That they *thought* it."

"It's not always a nice world," he says. He's quiet for a minute. "I understand their reasons."

"It's not fair," she says again.

They ride in silence a while longer, and then Eleanor says, "I'm sorry, Dad."

He nods. "Me, too, Els."

The car comes to a stop, and through the window Eleanor can see her father's apartment building looming. Her father doesn't turn the engine off, and she looks over to see him gazing at her. His eyes are damp.

"I don't know what happened up there," he says. "But whatever it was, I— It *can't* happen again."

She doesn't say anything.

"I'm going to go upstairs, and I'm going to get your things," he says. "Then I'm going to drive you to your mother's house. I think it's probably safer for you there until I figure out what happened upstairs here. I want you to be safe."

He opens the car door and starts to climb out, leaving the heater on.

"Dad," she says.

Paul stops.

"It wasn't your fault," she says. "It—it's the same thing as before. It doesn't matter if I'm at your place or Mom's. This wasn't the first time."

"Like when your mother found you," he says. "Ellie, *what*—"

"I don't know," she says. "I really don't."

"It's scaring me," he admits. "Gerry—"

"Aunt Gerry isn't crazy," Eleanor says. "I saw her boys."

"I don't understand."

"Neither do I."

Paul slumps back down into the seat and stares through the windshield at nothing. "The world isn't supposed to be like this," he says. His voice is flat. "It's not supposed to be like this for a kid."

Something occurs to Eleanor then.

"Dad," she says. "What time did you get up this morning?"

He regards her strangely. "I don't know," he says. "A little after eight?"

"Did you come right down to the kitchen?" she asks.

He thinks. "I checked your room. To see if you were sleeping."

"Then you came to the kitchen," she says. "And you said we should get breakfast."

"That's right."

"I said it was almost nine, and Dot's would be packed," Eleanor finishes. "What time did they check me in at the hospital?"

"What does—"

"Just think," Eleanor says.

"I don't remember. Maybe a few minutes later? Gerry called, and then—and then—"

"Think," Eleanor says again. "Are you sure you don't remember?"

He closes his eyes. "There was the ambulance, and the cop," he says. "And I had to follow in my car. And the cop followed me."

His voice is bitter.

"They unloaded you straight into the emergency room," he goes on. "They—they stopped me. They made me do *paperwork*."

"Insurance stuff," she says.

"Right, insurance stuff," he says. "And then I had to sign in."

"At the desk?"

"Yes," her father says. "I had to sign in, and I didn't know—I had to ask—"

"—what time it was," Eleanor finishes. "And?"

Her father goes pale.

"Dad," she says.

"Eleven twelve," he says, clearly remembering the nurse's answer to his question. "Ellie—"

Eleanor lets out a long breath. "Two hours later," she says.

"I remember because the numbers were consecutive," he says. "Like when you look at a digital clock right at twelve thirty-four."

"One, two, three, four."

"It was eleven twelve," he repeats. He looks as if he can see a ghost standing right outside the car. "Ellie—what does it mean?"

"I don't know," she says. "But it keeps happening. Every time I—whatever it is. I lose hours. Sometimes more."

"I think this is a dream, and we should wake up," her father says slowly.

"It's not," Eleanor says. "I already tried."

They sit in the car without moving.

"Dad," Eleanor says after a few minutes. "Let's go."

Her father looks over at her, still pale. "Your things," he says.

"There's nothing up there I need," Eleanor answers. "Come with me to Mom's."

On the way home, her father begins poking holes in the lost-time problem. Eleanor doesn't listen. She knows that he's just feeling the real world rush back in. He's driving through neighborhoods and along the main road and seeing people walking around with children and dogs and ice cream cones.

Reality is a terrific drug.

When he finally pulls into the driveway at Agnes's house, Paul kills the engine, then turns to Eleanor and says, "How would you feel if I said I thought maybe it would be a good idea to talk to someone?"

Eleanor says, "Like a shrink?"

"Like a therapist," Paul says. "Your aunt talked to one after . . . after the boys went missing. She said it really helped her make sense of what happened to her. To them."

Eleanor considers it. "Sure."

Paul is surprised. "Really?"

"It couldn't be any weirder than what's already happening," she says.

"Well, okay, then."

Eleanor unbuckles the lap belt, and it retracts noisily. "Help me up," she says.

Her father is elsewhere now, lost in thought.

He says, "Your mother hates seeing me. She was so angry the last time I was here."

"Dad," Eleanor says. "I need your help. You have to come in."

He looks at her and seems to snap out of it.

"Right," he says. "Right. Okay."

## *mea*

*S*he is weak. I know you are eager, but you must take care.

Efah is wise—and correct. Mea watches Eleanor shuffle across the driveway, leaning on her father for support. And Efah observes Mea through the membrane.

*You watch her too much,* he suggests. *The child's present is painful. Give her time.*

Mea doesn't reply. She waits.

The days, the weeks, must pass.

Eleanor must heal.

Again.

## *eleanor*

*E*leanor and her father creep up the walk like two invalids.

To her surprise, Jack waits on the porch, standing in the shadows cast by the late-afternoon sun. "I didn't mean to scare you," he says.

Eleanor looks up, and she can tell by Jack's reaction that she has scared *him*. She knows what she looks like, with her bandages and her blood-filled eye and her bruises and scrapes and stitches. She knows that the brace is visible beneath her T-shirt, a knobby shelf below her breasts. Her shoulders are stooped, her knees weak. Her father's hands are below her elbows, guiding and supporting her.

"What happened?" Jack asks, his expression pained. "Are you okay?"

Eleanor smiles weakly at him. "Hi, Jack."

"Hi, hi, yes," he blurts. "*What happened?*"

Paul gives Jack the door key, and the boy stares dumbly at it.

"I don't want to let go of her," Paul explains.

Jack seems to notice Paul's hands on Eleanor's arms for the first time. He nods, understanding, and unlocks the door.

"Don't tell your mother I kept a key," Paul says to Eleanor.

Jack holds the door open. Paul and Eleanor walk awkwardly through—no static charge here, Eleanor notices with relief.

"It happened again," Jack says. "Didn't it."

Eleanor shoots him a stern look.

Paul stops. "Jack knows?"

Eleanor looks sheepishly at her father. "Yes," she admits.

Paul sets his jaw. "Jack, don't you tell a soul until we know what it is," he says. "Do you understand?"

Jack nods emphatically, then says, "I think I should sleep over."

Eleanor can't help but smile. "It's fine," she says. "Dad's here."

Paul flips the hallway switch. "Hello?" he calls. "Aggie?"

Jack says, "I should still stay over and help."

"That's sweet," Eleanor says. "But it's fine."

"TV's on," her father says.

He's right. Eleanor can hear thin strains of laughter from another room.

"Mom doesn't really watch TV anymore," she says.

Paul helps Eleanor take the step up into the foyer. Jack closes the door behind them. Deep in the house, the television's laughter grows louder, and then there's singing, and Eleanor feels her father go very still.

"Dad?" she asks.

He shakes his head as if trying to clear it. "I—uh—"

"What's wrong?" she says.

"I know those sounds," he says. His voice is raw. "Don't you?"

Eleanor listens, then shakes her head. It just sounds like television noise to her.

Paul tilts his head, listening to the singsong voices, then joins in, lightly, anticipating the next lyrics. His head bobs. "You girls always loved 'Billie Jean.'"

And that's exactly what it is. With that frame of reference, Eleanor knows exactly what her mother must be watching. It isn't television at all. It's old home movies. It is, quite specifically, the last Fourth of July they celebrated together. There was a backyard barbecue, a picnic table, a dozen people, streamers.

"We were six," Eleanor says.

"Your mom invited her gardening friends," Paul says. His eyes are closed, and he sways a little. "I overcooked the burgers, and Jim took over."

Jack stands back and just watches the two of them.

"You made us perform for everyone," Eleanor remembers. "Like little dancing bears."

"No," Paul says. "It was your mother. She loved it when you both sang."

"She loved it when Esme sang," Eleanor corrects. "I wasn't good at all."

"You were both lovely."

The sounds are tired and old, the quality of the tape degraded after years of lying in a box somewhere. There are gaps in the video, garbled bursts of noise between segments. "Billie Jean" abruptly ends in a fit of laughter, and then there's a noisy, staticky break, and then a soft voice, speaking all alone from the past.

Esmerelda.

Paul makes a choking sound and says, "Esme," and then he plunges headlong into the house, looking for the source of the sounds. Eleanor starts to follow and almost falls over. Jack is there, though, and puts his hands beneath her elbows just the way her father had done. She smiles gratefully.

"It's nice having him home," Eleanor says. "Even like this."

They walk into the living room together. The blue corduroy chair is empty, but the side table isn't. A single bottle of Jameson. Empty. If Jack notices it, he doesn't say so, and Eleanor is grateful.

She and Jack follow Paul through the living room to the stairs. Her father takes the steps slowly, almost dazed. She worries for him. She knows what's on this part of the tape, even if he can't exactly remember. They were little thieves, she and Esmerelda. They found her father's old video camera in the closet one afternoon and spent hours running around the house together, filming fake news reports and music videos, then pretending to be burglars, creeping through the house, shooting every object and musing aloud about its value.

When they got tired of the game, Eleanor went to her bedroom to read but was distracted by Esme's voice coming through the wall. Eleanor walked lightly to her bedroom door and peeked out. Esme was at the opposite end of the hallway, facing the antique table next to their parents' room. The video camera was resting on the table, and Esme had been performing for it, only a little bit self-conscious.

Jack helps her climb the staircase now. Paul stands at the top, listening.

"Mom?" Eleanor calls, at the same time that he says, "Aggie?"

There's no answer. They follow the sounds into the bedroom that Eleanor's parents once shared but that now belongs only to Agnes. The bed inside is carefully made but empty. Agnes simply falls asleep wherever she happens to pass out these days, and only rarely is that on her own bed. Eleanor doesn't mind; she worries about her mother climbing the stairs. She has nightmares, now and then, about Agnes stumbling drunkenly up an endless staircase. The dreams always end with her mother tumbling, head over heels, down a thousand steps.

The old tube television that used to be in the living room is now on the dresser. It faces the bed, spilling light into the dark room. The VCR beside it flashes *12:00*. Paul covers his mouth when he sees what's on the television's milky screen. He sinks onto the bed and stares, and Jack helps Eleanor sit beside him. Then Jack stands there, uncertain of his proper place.

Eleanor is transfixed by her sister, who is framed in the center of the screen. She recognizes the Disney T-shirt that Esmerelda wears. Printed on the front are Mickey and Donald and Goofy, following a

silly mule down a steep path. A beautiful pink vista spreads out behind them, and printed in wooden letters are the words THE GRAND
CANYON. Esmerelda loved it dearly.

Eleanor still has the shirt, folded carefully in her dresser drawer.

"What do you mean, she *broke* it?" Esmerelda protests on screen.

Eleanor laughs, startling Jack and her father. She had forgotten
about this, about Esmerelda's habit of affecting an awful, stodgy
British accent. If ever a person's voice could sound *fat,* this accent
certainly did. Esme seems to transform before their eyes into a
stooped, overweight, elderly British socialite.

"Well, that's *un*acceptable," Esme continues, a hand to her throat
in shock. "Do you hear me, Jarshmerschar? She must pay for it. You
will not allow her to leave until she does. That lamp cost six dollars!"

"*Jarshmerschar?*" Paul blurts. He bursts into laughter and tears at
the same time.

Eleanor laughs until she, too, is crying. On the screen, Esme
stages an entire soap opera as a one-girl show, playing the parts of
the socialite and her butler—Jarshmerschar—and the offending
guest, a bratty child with an overemphasized Southern twang. It's
entertaining on its own, simply for what it is, but it's more than that.

It's a hot shower after seven years lost in the woods. It's the first
glimmer of sunlight after the rainy season. It's a fresh breath of air
after a decade underground.

Eleanor looks up at her father. He looks down at her.

"I miss her," Paul confesses, and he weeps.

Eleanor cries, too, and Jack starts to ease slowly out of the room.
Until he spots Agnes.


SHE IS ON the floor, almost hidden behind the bed. She's clearly
been there for a while, and she isn't a pretty sight. Her bare feet are
the only part of her visible from the doorway, and that's the reason
Jack noticed her.

Jack shouts, and Eleanor jumps. Her ribs rattle in pain. Paul almost falls off the bed, so rudely is the moment interrupted.

"Jack, Jesus," Paul starts to say, and then Jack says, "Mrs. Witt!" He goes to his knees on the floor and repeats himself: "Mrs. Witt, Mrs. Witt! Wake up!"

Paul leans over and sees Agnes on the floor, and he says, "Oh, fuck, Aggie," and he vaults over Jack and into the space between the bed and wall. Eleanor struggles to follow but can only lie down on the bed and crawl to its edge like an earthworm. She instantly wishes that she hadn't. The pain is searing, awful.

Her mother is on the floor in her nightgown. She's on her back, hair tangled, skin pale—almost blue, Eleanor thinks. Her chest moves, barely.

*Jarshmerschar.*

They hadn't even been thinking about her mother.

"She tried to kill herself," Eleanor whispers, her voice husky.

Neither her father nor Jack seems to hear her.

"On her side!" Paul says, and Jack takes Agnes's feet and Paul grabs her shoulders, and they turn her over. She weighs almost nothing, and they almost flip her onto her belly by mistake.

The rattle of her breath is replaced by a delicate wheeze. Almost immediately color begins to return to Agnes's face, but her eyes remain shut.

"It was her tongue," Paul says. "Caught in her throat. Aggie?"

"She was choking," Jack says.

Eleanor feels as if someone has yanked her batteries out. She stares at her poor mother, and a hideous wave of guilt submerges her.

"I should have been here," she says. "The things I've said to her—this is my fault, my fault—"

She begins to cry.

"Jack, nine-one-one," Paul says, ignoring Eleanor. "Now."

Jack runs out of the room, and Eleanor looks tearfully at her father.

"Dad," she says.

He puts his hand on Eleanor's cheek. "It isn't your fault," he says. Then he crouches down beside Agnes and takes her hand and says, "They're coming, Ags. They're coming now."

*Ags.* He hasn't called her that in years.

Jack comes back. "They said three minutes," he says.

"Three minutes," Paul repeats. He says the words into Agnes's ear. "Just three minutes, Aggie."

"Should I get rid of this?" Jack holds something up. "It was under the bed."

Eleanor's eyes are blurry, but she recognizes the shape of the whiskey bottle. She can't form words. Jack leaves the room, and when he returns a moment later, his hands are empty.

Eleanor watches her father squeeze her mother's hand, and the four of them wait silently for the second ambulance of the day to arrive and make everything okay. On the television, the ghost of Esmerelda turns in slow, balletic circles, then collapses to the floor in a fit of giggles.

part two

1994

# eleanor

S plinter Beach," the bus driver calls.

Eleanor stares through the window. It's raining. Big surprise. The clouds blot out the sky, and a soft, late-morning mist blankets the shore.

"Maybe this isn't a good idea," she says.

"It's a good idea," Jack answers.

He's carrying a duffel bag and wearing a backpack over his windbreaker. The hood is cinched tightly around his face. Water beads on his jacket. She is grateful for her own raincoat, but she still wishes she was in her mother's hospital room.

Although, she must admit, it is nice to breathe some fresh air.

"Come on," Jack says. "Field trip."

He steps off the sidewalk and down into the beach grass. Eleanor stays on the sidewalk and watches the bus trundle away, belching black smoke. She takes a deep breath, filled with carbon monoxide, and lets it out.

"Ellie," Jack says, out in the hip-high grass. "Come on."

"I'm not sure," she says again.

Jack trudges back to her. She's tall, but he's taller. He kisses her forehead and says, "Ellie, your mom is going to be just fine."

"I shouldn't have left. She could wake up."

"Look," Jack says. "Things are bad. I know they're bad, but you have to take care of yourself first."

"Or what?" Eleanor asks. "Or I won't be any good for her?"

"Right," Jack says.

"She's pretty messed up," Eleanor says. "I could be a thousand times more tired, and I'd still be better company than an empty hospital room."

Jack points to the sea and the distant island. "Look out there."

"It's foggy," she complains.

"It'll burn off before we get there," Jack says.

"There's no sun to burn it off."

"There will be," he says.

"We'll get lost."

"We won't," he says. "It's a straight shot from here to there." He draws an imaginary line between his chest and Huffnagle.

"The boat'll turn over."

"I'll flip it right-side up," Jack says.

"We'll freeze and drown."

"It's pretty cold," he agrees. "So let's agree not to turn the boat over."

Eleanor wraps her arms around herself. "It doesn't seem safe."

"I bet it's safer than that bus ride," Jack says. "I thought he was going to run all three red lights."

"Sharks."

"Too cold."

"Undertow."

"That's why we stay in the boat," Jack says, laughing.

"There's nothing to do out there," Eleanor says.

"That's the point."

She watches her breath turn to steam. "I'm too cold already."

Jack holds up the duffel. "I brought all kinds of things that my mom used to knit," he says.

His cheeks are flushed with color, and his eyes are bright and nervous, and it hits her then: Jack is trying to take care of her. She didn't recognize it at first, because nobody has tried to take care of her in years.

"May I see?" she asks.

He unzips the duffel and pulls out a wool scarf and a cowl and a pair of bulky mittens. Eleanor takes the mittens and pulls them onto her hands.

"Mm," she says. "Oh, that's nice. Scarf."

He loops the scarf around her neck once, then twice.

Eleanor peers into the bag. "How about a hat?"

"Take your pick," Jack says. He produces a goldenrod beanie and a burgundy cap with a pom-pom.

Eleanor takes the beanie and pulls it on. Her red hair curls from beneath the hat. She immediately feels cozy and warm.

"I wish I'd met your mom," she says.

"Me, too," Jack says.

Eleanor kisses his cheek. His skin is cold and pink. He flushes and looks away, his face suddenly a red balloon.

She says, "What's in the backpack?"

He shrugs out of the straps and opens one of the flaps to show her plastic baggies stuffed with sandwiches, a red cotton blanket, and a green-plaid-printed thermos. Eleanor eyes the blanket suspiciously.

"I thought it would be nice to just go somewhere quiet and just—I don't know. Breathe, I guess," Jack says, embarrassed. "For a second."

Eleanor looks closely at his brown eyes, then looks at the fogged-over ocean and the distant, pale island.

"Where's the boat?" she asks finally.

"I DON'T THINK it belongs to anybody," Jack says.

They trudge across the beach, and the mist kicks up around their feet, exposing the gravel below. There isn't any sand, not really, just a trillion million pebbles, damp and smooth and gray. Jack leads her to the stubby pier. It's wet and dark, its planks slick and worn glossy by the sea and the rain.

"My dad told me once that he can't remember ever *not* seeing the boat here," Jack says, and as he says it, the gloom over the water thins, and the boat appears, a small thing that looks a hundred years old, maybe more. "It was yellow once," he adds, but the paint has flaked and bleached, and it is now bone-colored and pale. It bobs gently on the calm water.

The dock creaks beneath their feet.

"It's going to sink," she says.

Jack only smiles and takes her hand.

ELEANOR SHIVERS DESPITE her scarf and hat and mittens and rain-coat. She thinks of the blanket in Jack's backpack, but she worries that she'll seem greedy.

Aside from Jack's voice, the only sounds out here are the churn of the oars in the water, the worrisome groan of the boat itself, the quiet lapping of the sea.

"I've been out here before," Jack says.

"You never told me that," she says, her teeth chattering audibly.

"Cold?" he asks.

She tries not to nod, but she can't help herself.

"Here," he says, taking off his windbreaker. Underneath he is wearing his hooded sweatshirt, and he lifts it over his head. There is only a T-shirt beneath it. He stops rowing for a moment and tosses the sweatshirt to Eleanor.

"You're going to freeze," she says.

"I'm built for the cold," he says. "I'll be fine."

"No," Eleanor says. "You'll freeze, and then I'll be out here alone, and that will make me very sad. And then I'll be very angry with you for being so stupid."

She throws the sweatshirt back.

"Come on," he says. "Are you sure?"

She nods. "But give me the stupid blanket."

He grins at her, and it makes her smile, too.

\* \* \*

HUFFNAGLE ISLAND HAS never been a tourist attraction. It has no shops. No roads. Nobody lives there. It juts up from the sea like a hunk of shrapnel, twisted and dark. The view from its summit is lovely, but to witness it, a visitor must scale a jagged, steep path to the island's flat peak. There are no handrails. There's no proper dock for a boat. The island's condition serves as its own NO TRES-PASSING sign.

The shops along the mainland's waterfront sell T-shirts with Huffnagle's silhouette printed in the center, above a legend that reads THE ISLAND OF LOST BOYS. Eleanor has never been fond of the shirts. No boys were ever lost to the island.

"Dad told me that nobody goes to the island anymore because it's too much work," Jack says, pulling the oars, lifting them, pulling them again. "He said that now and then someone wrecks a boat on the rocks and gets stranded or gets hurt, and the Coast Guard has to send out a special rescue boat, and it's embarrassing and expensive."

"No," Eleanor says. "People go to the island. They just don't talk about it."

Jack grins.

"What?" she says. "I'm not lying. Kids go out there to have sex. It's, like, the worst make-out point in the whole state."

Jack laughs. "I don't think you're lying," he says.

"Good."

"I know you aren't lying."

She doesn't take his meaning and stares at the faint shape of the island, growing slowly darker as they draw nearer.

"I told you: I've been there," Jack says. "I told my dad I wanted to. You know what he said to me?"

Eleanor shakes her head.

"He said, 'I've been there,'" Jack says.

\*   \*   \*

JACK WAS ALWAYS a climber. He scaled the water tower behind the school. He skipped class and climbed onto the roof of the school itself. During a basketball game—the last game before they threw him off the team—he ignored a pass and shimmied up the goalpost instead, then just sat there, behind the backboard, kicking his feet and dodging projectiles chucked at him by the crowd.

"I thought about swimming out there," Jack says. "But it's a really long way. And Dad said he heard a rumor that someone drowned swimming out there, a long time before we even moved here. He was the one who told me about the boat, and how he went out there once when my uncle was in town. They didn't do much, just got drunk and then rowed back, but he did it, so I figured I could, too."

"My grandmother," Eleanor says. "Who drowned. It was my grandmother."

Jack's jaw slides open. "I— Are you serious?"

"My mom's mom," Eleanor says. "I was named after her. She was a competitive swimmer or something. This was where she used to train."

"Oh, my god," Jack says. "You never told me."

"It's okay. I never met her. Mom was only . . . five, I think."

"Jesus," Jack says. "I'm sorry. I didn't know."

The blanket keeps her warm, though the ocean spray nips at her exposed face.

"What did you do?" she asks. "On the island. Did you take some girl out there? Was it Stacy?"

"Stace?" Jack wrinkles his nose. "Ha! I went by myself."

"I bet it was boring," she says, smiling behind the scarf.

"Did you know they call the water around the island 'the boneyard'? Did you know that?"

She shakes her head.

"Because of all the rocks," he explains. "I guess way back in the old days, pirate ships used to run aground on them. Before the light-house."

"There weren't pirates out here," Eleanor says.

"Well, old ships. Whatever."

"This boat is going to crash on those rocks, isn't it," she says. "We're going to die. Aren't we."

"We're going to be fine," Jack says. "I know where to land. Try to relax."

She does. She tries very hard to relax, but *trying* seems counter-productive. Jack falls silent and works harder at the oars, and Eleanor closes her eyes. She thinks about her mother, alone in the hospital room. Being diagnosed with liver cancer has not improved her disposition—or made her any less inclined to drink. Eleanor has taken to staging daily interventions, and Agnes, her eyes fiery and her breath toxic, has slapped her a few times and pushed her to the floor once. There have been no apologies, and Eleanor expects none to come.

She cannot relax. The world around her is a living, breathing metaphor. The boat is her mother's frail body, groaning under Eleanor's weight. The sea is the poison that waits below, ready to consume her when she stumbles. The island is death, and she carves a resolute path—"a straight shot," as Jack said—to death's very door.

Eleanor's hips throb. Her body aches from the cold.

"Is she doing okay?" Jack asks. "Your mom?"

Eleanor looks up at his face, registering his concern. She sighs.

"They're doing more donor tests. Apparently my mother's body won't accept just any new liver."

"I wanted to see you sooner," Jack says. "Your dad wouldn't let me. He said you weren't taking it well and that you needed some time. But he didn't look so good, either."

"He's . . ." She trails off, not knowing exactly what to say.

That day, when Jack had discovered her mother on the bedroom floor, Eleanor had watched her father take her mother's hand. She'd rather stupidly pinned a hope on that moment, a hope that one day her family might reunite, that she might be her father's daughter, her mother's daughter, again. Her father has hated her mother for years. Hated her for the accident, blamed her for Esmerelda's death. Despised her for failing Eleanor. But at that moment in the bedroom—*"Ags,"* her father had whispered—Eleanor had thought that maybe her father would discover how to forgive her mother.

She thinks now that his anger has only retreated temporarily. She can see the signs. It will come back. And it is miserable to think that this is what adulthood is like: two people, cowering behind their grief, lashing out at each other like injured animals.

"You aren't the only ones who miss her," Eleanor mumbles behind her scarf.

Jack doesn't hear her. He rows and rows.

And Huffnagle looms, ominous and large, with every fresh pull of the oars.

## *mea*

Time is a river, and it flows in a circle.

While months pass in Eleanor's cold, gray world, Mea watches in silence. Eleanor sleeps and wakes and eats and quietly attends to her sick mother. Mea observes Eleanor's galaxy of bruises fade, sees the girl slowly grow stronger.

And eventually Mea begins to think of trying again.

She worries often that Eleanor will never cross the boundary of her own world, that Mea is not a competent guide through these strange hinterlands. She is a failed shepherd, one who has grievously injured and sometimes lost her flock of one.

Eleanor's mother is pale and damp and unwell. Her bathrobe seems to swallow her whole. Even as Eleanor cares for her mother,

Agnes withdraws. She complains when Eleanor brushes her stringy hair. She shouts at the girl, unprovoked.

In the past year of Eleanor's life, Mea has become an expert on the girl. In Eleanor's world, Mea would be the neighbor who peeks through the blinds with binoculars, a suburban version of the researcher who hides in the jungle, watching indigenous tribes from afar, journaling their behaviors. But Mea has become a part of Eleanor's story. She has interfered, with consequences that cannot be retracted.

If she can guide Eleanor into the rift, the girl's life will be forever changed.

If she fails, she may very well doom them both.

THE ROWBOAT TRACES a watery path across the bay, lazy loops of froth spilling out behind it. Mea thinks Eleanor's world is beautiful: this strange disturbance of the sea, the stodgy gray clouds, the rain that stabs through the mists like falling needles.

*She is special,* Efah explained before. *But only to you.*

This is not entirely true. With Eleanor is a boy, one who sees what Mea sees: a well of beauty tucked away inside the girl, masked by drawn expressions and tired shoulders. She carries unseen weights. Were they removed, Eleanor would almost glow.

The boy leans into the oars, pulling with all his might. He doesn't speak now, though he was laughing a few minutes before. He is determined, his lips tucked between his teeth. Mea wonders what he is thinking. She is learning to read Eleanor, but the boy and the other people in Eleanor's world are a puzzlement to her.

He navigates between baleful rocks, and the sea coughs the vessel onto the island shore. The boy clambers out of the rickety little boat and tugs it onto a gravelly beach.

Mea follows Eleanor's worried gaze to the towering cliff above, framed against scratchy wool clouds. Something occurs to Mea— the beginning of an idea.

She turns to Efah, who has lingered, watching her. He knows her question before she asks it.

*Yes*, he answers. *I think it might.*

## eleanor

The island rises up from the sea like a broken old fortress, like a villain's lair in a movie. The rocks surrounding it are sharpened by storms and the bones of dead sailors—dead *pirates*, she thinks with a smile. What little grows on the island is hardy and tough, weeds and vines and scrubby, twisted trees. She can see the beginning of the cliff path from here, cluttered with boulders and overgrown with reedy brambles. The side of the sheer cliff is streaked with white.

"Bird shit," Jack says, and he splashes out of the boat.

Eleanor gasps involuntarily.

"Oh, hush," Jack chides. "I have waders on."

She wonders how she failed to notice that before, but he does. He's wearing rubber fishing waders that reach to his waist. She watches as Jack grips the bow of the boat and pulls, leaning almost parallel with the water. She worries that he'll fall in, anyway, and soak himself, then freeze while she ineffectively tries to row the stupid boat back to shore. She also thinks that he's lying about not being cold. His face is pink and pale, and he's shivering.

"This was a stupid idea," she says.

He just grunts and drags the boat, and then Eleanor can feel a tiny tremor in the hull as it strikes gravel. It grinds over the rocks, and then it stops, firmly embedded in the little stones, and Jack lets go and falls on his butt on the beach, breathing hard.

"Is this the spot?" she asks. "Where your dad and uncle landed?"

"Yeah." He sticks out his hand. "Hop out. Careful."

She takes his cold hand and steps delicately across the boat's bottom, then over the side. Jack urges her away from the boat, then turns back and tries to pull it farther onto the beach. It budges only an inch or two and seems to freeze in place. Water laps at the boat, and Eleanor says, "It's going to float away."

Jack kicks the boat. It doesn't move. "It's not going anywhere," he says.

"I think the ocean is a little stronger than you," Eleanor says. "What about the tide?"

"Islands don't have tides," Jack says.

"Don't be stupid," Eleanor says. "Every piece of coastland has tides."

"I didn't even pull the boat up this far the last time I came out here," he says. "It was fine."

She stares at him. "It's going to get sucked out to sea, and we're going to be alone on the island, and nobody will know where we are, and we'll die," she says. "Slowly."

"What happened to your grandmother?" Jack asks. "Did she really drown?"

Eleanor looks up at the cliff wall. "I don't think 'bird shit' is the technical term," she says.

Jack is still breathing hard. He stares up at the white streaks on the rocks. "Guano?"

"Guano is bat shit," Eleanor says.

"You're bat-shit," Jack says.

Eleanor gapes at him; then they both dissolve into laughter.

"Let's climb up," he says.

"I don't know."

She cranes her neck and sees the quilt of clouds beginning to pull apart, separating like cotton. On the other side, the sun is a pale white ball. She stares at it for a second, then squeezes her eyes shut, trying to clear the purple afterimage.

"Hey," Jack says. "We're here, right? We might as well get our money's worth."

Eleanor looks skeptically at the path. "Okay," she says. "But if I die out here, I'm blaming you."

The path is not altogether untamed, she discovers. Enough people have climbed it that there is some hardpack, but the brambles she saw from below choke the path completely in some places. Now and again Jack has to help her across, and the scraggly branches and roots snag her jeans. They climb in silence, their feet crunching on the rocks and skittering pebbles. She can hear the distant call of seagulls, the slow crush of waves on the shore as it falls farther and farther below her. The faraway bellow of a foghorn. Jack's labored breath. Her own.

And nothing else.

Not the hum of traffic, the buzz of streetlights, the bustle of tourists. Not the rumble of garbage trucks in the neighborhood. Not the clink of her mother's bottles, keeping her awake in the small hours of the morning. Not her father's disappointment, palpable in every quiet breath.

She concentrates on every step, focusing all her energy on a single task: *Don't fall down.*

The entire world seems to have been scraped away, and she realizes that she is grateful to Jack for bringing her here. It feels, a little bit, as if she has left reality behind her and has entered a place where there is only the island, this place of death and strangeness, this secret world so close to her home and yet so very far from anything she knows. There is only the island and Jack and Eleanor, and she is—for this moment—happy.

She blinks away tears before Jack sees them.

# *the keeper*

Her breath comes heavily. The cords of her neck tighten. Strings of her hair, damp with sweat and rain, cling to her skin. The keeper clenches her teeth, feeling her strength dwindle. She rises up on tiptoe and *vibrates*, as if she is trying to rocket into the sky.

Her shadow watches from a distance. She points at the airplane wreckage, raises her hands theatrically, straining; the metal screeches, rattles, tilting into the sky, shaking gravity off like a frayed rope. The keeper almost collapses with the effort of lifting the wreckage. The last section of the tail levitates, groaning in midair. With a shout of pain, the keeper flings her hands toward the sky.

The twisted shrapnel launches into the sky, punching a hole in the clouds. For a moment the keeper can see through to the darkness beyond—no stars, no moon, just pure, obsidian black—and then the clouds pinch the void shut again.

She sags to her knees in the clearing.

The crash site is, at last, bare. The grass is still charred and black, and there is still an immense scoop of earth missing, but the plane itself—all its shattered bits of glass and metal—is gone.

Her shadow returns to her. She exhales, feeling tired but whole again.

"My valley," she breathes.

She has worked for months on the wreckage, moving only a few pieces per day. There is still so much to do, she knows. The holes must be filled; the forest must grow again. She could have done it all in a day, she thinks, when she was younger.

"Now we rest," she says to her shadow. She reclines against a tree, and her shadow curls around her like a puppy.

Rain falls through the branches above her. It might heal the valley on its own, she thinks. She would not have to trouble herself with the repairs. Grass would grow again without her direction. She could rest for a few years, allow her valley to take care of itself for a time.

Spent, the keeper lets her eyes close, and she falls asleep.

# *eleanor*

The top of Huffnagle Island is almost perfectly flat. The rocks are beaten smooth, the dirt planed away, as if some god or another had taken a wide saw to the cap of a mountain.

The sun peeks out, warming the rocks and Eleanor's skin. The rain stops. The mist far below boils away, just as Jack had said it would, and color seems to rush back into the world. The island is no longer gray and threatening but a warm, chocolaty color. The sea is crushed pigment, peacock blue. The sun is golden, the clouds tinged with pink.

Jack takes off his waders and jeans and stretches out on the ground, his legs dangling over the edge of the cliff. Eleanor sits down beside him on crossed ankles.

"You took your pants off," she says.

"It's warm," Jack says. "Too warm for jeans and waders now."

"It's weird."

"It's not weird. It's like shorts."

"No, it's weird."

"You can hang your feet over," he says. "It's nice."

"No, thank you," Eleanor says.

Jack closes his eyes and is still.

"You look like a turtle," she says.

He opens one eye. "A turtle?"

"Sunning itself," she says.

"Ah. What sound does a turtle make?"

"No sound, I think," Eleanor answers.

Jack opens his mouth and closes it again, and nothing comes out.

"It would have been funnier if turtles made sounds," he says.

"It wouldn't have been funny either way."

She tugs her feet closer, rocking back and forth on her butt until they are wedged tightly beneath her.

"It's nice," she says.

"I knew you'd like it. Aren't you glad you came?"

"I am," she says. "I still feel guilty, though."

"She's going to be okay," Jack says. "My grandpa was in the hospital once. For, like, three weeks. We were there all the time, and then he told us to go home. Dad didn't want to, but Grandpa made us. We went home to eat and sleep and came back to see him every night. It was very—I don't know. Balanced."

"Was he okay?"

"My grandpa?" Jack asks. "He died."

"Were you there?"

"My dad was," Jack says. "I was at school."

"Don't you wish you were there?" Eleanor asks.

Jack is quiet for a moment. Then he says, "No. I wouldn't want to remember that."

"But what if he had things to tell you? What if he wanted to say good-bye?"

"Grandpa had told me everything already," Jack says. "We said good-bye every night, just in case."

Eleanor regards the sea worriedly. "My mom hasn't told me anything. I haven't said good-bye."

Jack leans up on his elbows. "Yeah," he says. "But your mom isn't dying. It's different."

"She almost did," Eleanor says. "She still could. It's really serious."

"But she didn't. And she isn't going to. At least not today, and probably not for a long time."

"She's still in the woods," Eleanor says. "That's what the special-ist told Dad. 'She might come out of the woods if we find the right donor. Or she might go deeper into them if we don't.' That's what she said."

"Doctors have to say those things to cover their asses," Jack says. "Just in case."

"I don't know. It sounded . . . true."

They're both quiet for a few minutes. Jack scoots closer to her, shaking little bits of gravel from the edge of the cliff. Eleanor watches seagulls, specks against the peach-colored sky, and thinks that sometimes, when Jack's this near, he's planning to kiss her. It isn't as if he hasn't tried before, and it isn't as if she hasn't kissed him back, at least once. He is, now and then, charming entirely by mistake. It's when he means to be that Eleanor sees right through him. His shoulder brushes hers as he slings a rock out over the ocean.

If he tried to now, would she let him?

She doesn't like thinking about it. If it's going to happen, she would rather it just happen, and she'll decide how to feel about it later.

But he doesn't try. He stands up suddenly, startling her.

"Want to see something cool?" he asks.

She looks up at him, shielding her eyes from the sun. "What?"

"Keep looking out there," he says, pointing at the horizon. "See those boats?"

"What boats?" She squints into the distance, scanning the water, but sees nothing. "Jack, I don't see—"

She hears the slap of his feet and turns, and Jack is running to-ward her from behind, a blur of legs and elbows. Then he flies past her, and Eleanor whips her head around to watch him sail over the edge. He falls away from her horrifyingly fast, shouting something, and Eleanor screams and jumps to her feet. His laughter rings out as he tucks his knees to his chest.

He hits the water like a stone, with a wide and mighty splash.

"Jack!" she shouts.

He surfaces a pregnant moment later, slicking his hair back with one hand.

"You are an *asshole*!" she yells.

"That was *awesome*!" he shouts back.

"You could have killed yourself!"

"What?"

"You could have killed yourself!"

"What?"

"*You are an asshole!*"

He laughs. "Come on down!"

Eleanor turns away from the edge and folds her arms.

"It's only a little cold!" he yells. "And, look, no dangerous rocks back here!"

She looks back down at him, watching as he treads water. "I am not jumping off a cliff!"

"Ellie, you'll love it! It is *awesome*!"

She should be with her mother. Her mother, tiny under the beige hospital blanket. Eleanor should be in the hard plastic chair beside the bed, listening to carts wheeling by in the hallway, listening to the faint beeps from other rooms. She should be under fluorescent lights instead of the sun, reading hospital pamphlets for the hundredth time, waiting for her mother to wake up and ignore her, waiting for the nurse to shoo Eleanor from the room for her mother's daily checks and tests and sponge bath. She should be there, amid the smell of Lysol and sweat; there, where it is hard to breathe, where there are no real windows, where strangers sometimes pop into the room and say, "Oops, wrong room," and then get to walk away, leaving Eleanor's reality behind in favor of their own, which she always imagines is far, far better.

She should be there when her mother needs someone to blame, to accuse. She should be an ear for her father to bend about the medical bills, about the divorce, about hospital red tape and medical insurance and legal obligations. Lately, about his threat of litigation.

*We aren't even married,* he would insist, the words falling on his daughter's ears like broken glass. *She isn't my responsibility.*

Eleanor squints down at Jack, bobbing in the sea. His wide smile and wet hair and shining eyes. So small, so far below.

"Does it hurt?" she yells.

He shakes his head.

Eleanor takes a deep breath.


# *the keeper*

Night has fallen.

The keeper wakes, facedown in damp earth. Her tongue is coated with grit. She coughs, then clears her throat.

"Was I asleep long?" she rasps.

Her voice is grainy, as if she has screamed herself hoarse. She coughs again, and a fine mist of black dust appears, glittering subtly in the faint light. Puzzled, she touches her tongue, then holds the finger up to inspect it.

It is stained with damp black ash. She rubs her fingertip and thumb together. The stuff is dark and sludgy and fine.

"What is this?" she croaks.

Her shadow has no answer. It stares blindly at her.

She cups her palm and spits into her hand. Her saliva is murky, viscous.

"No, no," she moans. "What is this? What is this?"

She wipes her palm on her wet clothes.

"We must go home," she says. "Back to the cabin."

But as she stands, a horrible fire erupts in her gut, and she falls to her knees.

# *mea*

Y ou're certain it will work?
  *I think it will.*
        Mea remembers how she lost Eleanor before, watched her tumble into the other realm, the one into which Mea cannot see nor follow. She dwells on Eleanor's injuries, her lost hours and days. She is unsure.

*Do you promise?* she asks Efah.

*I hope you have prepared for her arrival. She will be frightened.*

Mea turns her attention back to Eleanor's world.

The boy is in the ocean, shouting at Eleanor, who stands above, on the cliff. The girl is fearful but lit with determination. Eleanor pulls off her raincoat, her scarf, her hat and mittens. She places her shoes carefully beside each other but leaves her socks on.

Here on the cliff there are no doorways to which the portal can be fastened, only sky. But a doorway isn't strictly necessary, and Mea has a hypothesis. Something was missing from her past attempts to steal Eleanor from her world.

Momentum. Like Mea's own when she entered the rift, ages ago.

*If you fail now,* Efah says unnecessarily, *the girl will die.*

Eleanor backs up for a long time, then begins to run.

*I know,* Mea says.

There are no rocks in the water on the back side of the island, and the sea is not as gray. Treading water, the boy waits, a little nervous. Eleanor's red hair is a vibrant cape whipped by the wind. She runs to the cliff's edge and, with a frightened shout, launches herself into the void.

Jack's expression changes—there is something not quite right about the way Eleanor falls. For a moment she is graceful—the arch of her body, the ribbon of her hair—a swan framed by the pale sun.

But the moment passes quickly. Her body remembers that she is a fifteen-year-old girl, fresh and new and graceless.

She tumbles, arms flailing, her head aimed toward the ocean, then her back. Jack shouts, his voice cracking in fear, and he begins swimming hard to where Eleanor will strike the sea. If she lands flat, the churning water will be as hard as a slab of concrete; she will not pierce it cleanly. Eleanor will collide with it, and her bones will shatter; Jack will have to dive deeply to find her unconscious body before the deep-water currents collect her.

*Now?* Mea asks, her fear gone. If she doesn't intervene, Eleanor might not survive the fall.

*Now*, Efah commands.

Mea takes her, and Eleanor vanishes from the sky.

*the rift*

# eleanor

The sun goes out.

Jack disappears, along with the sea. His terrified cry is interrupted, silenced. The clouds are swallowed by sudden darkness. The frightening sound of the wind ripping at her clothing ceases. Eleanor has fallen into a well, and the lid has been drawn over the top. Everything is black, and she wants to scream—but she was already screaming, and she can't hear anything. Did she stop screaming?

She feels ... different. The space *around* her is different, neither warm nor cool. She can see no variations in the darkness; it is complete, and it wraps around her as water would, sliding into the crevices of her elbows, into the small pockets behind her ears. She gasps—and makes no sound. The darkness, like the sea, enters her nose and her mouth, swelling inside her lungs.

What is she supposed to do?

She tries to think, but thinking is hard. Where is she? What happened to her? Is she still falling? Has she plunged deep into the sea? Where is Jack?

Her mind races back over the past year. Is this a new place, like the cornfield, like the woods? Like the airplane? She has pushed those memories away for months now, and each time she walks through a doorway and doesn't find herself in Siberia or New York or a swamp or an icy lake, she challenges those memories just a little

more, until they are like remembered stories instead of memories—
fairy tales to pass on, not experiences that she lived.

Something is happening. The darkness has a softness to it. The
definition of Eleanor's own body has begun to blur; she cannot tell
where her skin ends and the dark begins.

The darkness cups her gently, cradles her, *becomes* her, and she
becomes *it*.

If she moves, the darkness moves with her.

She has become enormous. She is a galaxy, a thousand galaxies.

Calmness descends upon her. This—whatever is happening—is
okay. It is *good*.

She can no longer tell which way is up, if "up" even exists. The
sky that she leapt into is gone. Was it behind her? Above? It doesn't
seem to matter. In the dark, she is all things and nothing. She is the
before, and she is the after.

Eleanor feels pleasantly intoxicated.

*Floating,* she thinks. *I'm floating.*

She is, or may as well be, for in the darkness she has no sense of
weight, of substance. Gravity itself has been dispensed with.

She wonders if she is still capable of moving. She cannot feel her
legs, her hands. Are they even there? Does she still have a body? If
she cannot feel it, does it exist? If she cannot see herself, what is she?

She tries to lift one hand so that she can see it.

The dark bursts into color around her.


THE COLORS ARE hypnotic. They dance, and their warmth surges
through her. The colors are not separate from the darkness—they
are a part of the darkness, which means that they are a part of *her*,
and she has power over them. She feels joy like a sunrise, and the
darkness flares in a great wash of pink and orange and yellow, the
colors so vibrant that they suffuse her with happiness.

Then she remembers Jack—and the colors shrivel into ash and
dissipate into the dark.

*No!* she thinks. *Come back.*

And the colors do, playfully returning, arcing through her like comets trailing vapor. She feels oddly powerful. Is this a dream? If it isn't a dream—if it is not a dream, then is she . . . has she died? She feels . . . She hesitates to put her feeling into words, but she thinks it, and the darkness surges with colors that overlap and collide and create entire new palettes she has never seen.

She thinks, *I feel like a god.*

But the image of Jack, helpless in the ocean, rushes back. She thinks of him there, alone, terrified, unable to find her. She knows Jack well, knows that he will not leave the island without her—but she is no longer there. She wishes she could tell him, somehow, that she is okay. She knows that she is, even if she doesn't know *where* she is. If he knew that she was okay, he could row home without her and not feel the way she knows that he will: heavy with guilt, frantic, frightened.

The colors wither around her.

SHE DOES NOT know how long she has been in this place. Time seems elastic, or perhaps absent. In the void, she worries for Jack, worries about her mother, her father. She worries about her own body—is it still behind her, suspended in the air between the cliff and the sea? Has she plunged into the water already, an empty shell that sinks under its own weight?

Maybe she really is dead.

The darkness around her is silent, vast, and Eleanor feels achingly small.

## the keeper

She feels as if death itself has taken up residence inside her but will not permit her to die. She scoops handfuls of the black sludge from her mouth, but it never goes away. Every time she swallows, more rises from her throat.

She spits a mouthful of grit onto the earth, and something pale winks up at her. The keeper bends over and sifts through the wet mass until she unearths it: a molar, brittle but intact. She pushes her tongue frantically around her mouth, counting her teeth, until she finds a grimy, soot-packed socket.

Wildly, she turns to her shadow. She looks like a madwoman: her gums are black, her lips and chin streaked with the poisonous, awful stuff.

"What is happening to me?" she asks.

Her shadow, though, isn't paying attention. It sways like a cobra, pointing at the oily sky.

The keeper turns her face upward in time to see the first meteor pierce the clouds.

## mea

*You did not fail.*

*She is here?* Mea asks, stunned.

*She does not know what has happened,* Efah says. *Where she is. She is like you, when you first arrived.*

Together, they observe Eleanor, transformed. The black tide within the fishbowl moves slowly, carrying Eleanor with it.

*She is becoming,* Efah says. *She learns. Watch.*

Far away in the dark, an explosion of color flares brightly, then dies away. It reappears, dancing like a nova.

*She deserves an explanation,* Efah says. *Go to her.*

# *eleanor*

E leanor feels a change in the darkness, as if something has brushed her leg beneath the surface of a murky sea. Her colors fall into shadow again, and she expands herself so that nothing else can frighten her. She tests the farthest reaches of this black country, searching for anything unusual, but she encounters nothing, no one.

And yet she senses that she is no longer alone.

A tiny tremor ripples across her form, as if she is the sea and a ship's wake has sent a long wave rolling across her surface.

Eleanor has not moved; the wave does not belong to her.

She waits, hyperaware, and is rewarded when another wave, slow and languid, passes over her. She imagines two rivers merging into one, their waters mingling, their currents colliding, wrestling for dominance.

Another wave breaks, and with it, this time, comes something else.

*Music.*

IT SOUNDS LIKE no music she has ever heard. There are no progressions, no chords, no lyrics or discernible tempo. She does not hear it as she would have back in the world—which is how she thinks of her past now, as her time *back in the world,* as if Earth was a place where she once summered.

The music hums through her, chasing the slow wave that brought it. It expands within her, thrumming delicately, like a tiny drumbeat.

She thinks that this is what it is like for a person to feel music instead of to simply hear it. Her suspicion fades away; she is overcome by its beauty.

It occurs to Eleanor that she could remain here, in the dark—*as* the dark—for a million years and never learn everything that it has to teach her. She absorbs the dancing music, each tremble and ripple and rise and fall. Music that belongs to someone else, some*thing* else.

But there is more than music. Rather, it is not music; as she takes the vibrations deeply into herself, she discovers that she can parse them, that they have meaning and substance. The music is not music at all.

The music is language. It is words of a sort.

Some other being is communicating with her.

Eleanor billows in the dark, fluttering, listening.

Feeling.

*You have come,* the Other says.

SHE ENTERTAINS THOSE words for a long, long time, until they dissolve into tiny embers, each letter a flash of warmth inside her.

*You.*

*Have.*

*Come.*

Three words, and yet if Eleanor had any sense of time left, she might have thought that in the time it took for her to feel them, to understand them, that one million human lifetimes could have sparked and sputtered.

Eleanor considers her reply for eons, plenty of time for millions more lifetimes to come and go, but before she can speak, the other entity speaks again. Its words wash over her.

*You must have questions,* the Other says.

Eleanor does, and she speaks them, and a thunderous, beautiful melody escapes her, forming a ribbon that unfurls and recedes into the darkness, like a rainbow taking flight, lifting from the earth.

She watches her reply grow thin and small, traversing an enormous gulf of black space.

And then, so far away in the dark, the light of her words shatters into thousands of glittering shards that twinkle, then fade to night, briefly revealing the dark outline of some mysterious, feathery form.

The Other.

## *mea*

Mea vibrates happily to hear the girl's voice for the first time. She is aware, but only dimly, that Efah lingers beyond the membrane, watching silently. It doesn't matter; Mea's elation is almost overwhelming.

"Yes," Eleanor says.

Mea says, *Ask. I will answer.*

Before Eleanor can reply, Mea adds, *I do not know all things.*

"That was my first question," Eleanor says.

*What was your first question?* Mea asks.

The girl hesitates and then says, "I was going to ask if you are . . . are you a god?"

Mea says, *You may still ask.*

"I don't need to," Eleanor says.

*Why not?* Mea asks.

"If you were a god, you *would* know all things."

*Do you believe in gods?* Mea returns.

"That's a very human question."

*You are a very human girl.*

"I don't seem to be. Not anymore."

*This is temporary,* Mea says.

"Oh. But if I'm human, what are you?"

*I am . . .* Mea hesitates. *I . . . I watch.*

Eleanor is silent for a long time, as if considering the gaps in Mea's reply. When she speaks again, she asks, "Where are we? Is it a place?"

*It is called the rift.*

"Am I dead?"

*You are very much alive,* Mea says.

"Then how did I get here?"

*I brought you here.*

"But why? Who are you?"

*Because I have questions for you, as well, Eleanor.*

"You know my name."

*I have watched you,* Mea says. *I have always admired your curiosity.*

Across the void, Eleanor flares purple, confused.

Efah whispers, *You have frightened her.*

*I didn't do anything.*

*You are too familiar,* Efah says. *Calm her, or she will flee.*

Mea says to Eleanor, *Don't be afraid.*

But Eleanor's voice is angry, fearful. "Where am I? How did I get here?"

*Don't be afraid,* Mea repeats. *You're safe here.*

*"Answer my questions!"* Eleanor thunders, her voice urgent. "Why won't you answer my questions?"

*You are losing her,* Efah says.

Eleanor contracts into a hard red ball of light.

*Wait,* Mea says. *Don't—*

*She is lost,* says Efah.

The membrane seems to unravel, and the vortex appears, un-bidden, a whirling cone that stabs into the dark of Mea's fishbowl, violently enfolds Eleanor—whose scream explodes like fireworks in the black—and retracts as quickly as it appears.

Eleanor's wild cry lingers in the dark, a brilliant wisp of fiery purple that dissipates slowly, like smoke.

Mea cries out in anguish.

# *eleanor*

E leanor wants to scream at the Other—"Why bring me into this place *if you don't know what you're doing?*"—but the darkness around her begins to separate. She can feel it withdrawing from her, tearing from her lungs and escaping her mouth like a long, smoking worm. She would vomit if she could.

The darkness becomes wispy, and through it Eleanor sees water, dark and glinting with pale light.

The blackness expels her from the rift, and Eleanor plummets to the sea far below.

1996

# eleanor

She crashes into water. It folds over her, utterly unlike the gentle, warm ocean of the rift. This water is black and icy. It invades her open mouth. She screams to keep her lungs clear. Her eyes are open, but the water is opaque, black and blue and freezing and—

—then she hits bottom.

She plants her feet and pushes off with all her might.

She surges upward through the blackness and breaches the surface, which is wrong: the surface should be farther away than this; the bottom of the sea cannot be so close to the top—

Eleanor sputters in the cold air. Her feet again find the bottom; she does not have to tread water. This frightens her, dislocates her. The ocean isn't this shallow.

Something falls over her face, and she shrieks and bats at it, but it sags over her like a sheet. She panics and flails about, but it only seems to cling to her more closely.

In the barest hint of light she catches a glimpse of the thing, a glistening dark shadow swallowing her up, and she recognizes it, dimly: a tarpaulin.

A swimming pool cover.

Struggling only seems to wrap it more tightly around her.

*I'm on top of it. I fell into it . . .*

It blots out the sky, and she cannot find its edges. She tangles in it, loses her footing, and sinks, thrashing, into the water. The bottom isn't there—she has no sense of direction anymore; down has become up. As she wrestles with the plastic sheet, the air in her lungs burns away, and she thinks to herself that she is fourteen years old and she is going to die because of a piece of plastic, and then that's all the thought she has time for—she has to breathe, she *has* to, she has to open her mouth, she can't breathe, *she has to breathe, she can't breathe, she has to breathe, she has to breathe, has to—*

SHE IS FACEDOWN, her cheek squelching against mud. It gets into her eyes, her mouth; it clogs her nostrils.

Someone roughly flips her over. She tries to blink, but water courses over her eyelids. Raindrops spike down at her.

Something immensely heavy falls on her chest, and she thinks vaguely, *I should push that off me.* The pressure on her chest recedes but comes back immediately, harder, and she feels as if her sternum is going to splinter, that her lungs will be pulped, her heart crushed into mulch, and—her eyes fly open wide, and she feels the sea rising within her, angry, violent, and she snaps forward at the waist, and water explodes from her mouth, and then she can take a breath, so she does, but the breath only stirs more of the ocean inside her lungs, and she vomits, twice, three times, then sags forward, coughing. A strong hand pounds on her back, right between her shoulder blades.

A voice says, "Oh, thank god, thank god."

A different voice—a man, his mouth right beside her ear—says, "You're all right, you're okay. Take it easy. Just breathe."

His cheek is scratchy, his voice throaty and old. She leans against him, depleted.

"You called nine-one-one?" the man calls out.

A woman's voice, behind him: "Edna did."

Farther away, a second woman: "I did. They're coming."

Eleanor can hear the two women talking quietly.

"How on earth did she wind up in your pool?"

"Beats me. Maybe drugs."

Eleanor coughs again. She is naked, trembling in the bitterly cold rain.

"Get her a towel or something, will you?" the old man chides. "Thing's shivering like a banshee."

She rests her cheek on his shoulder and closes her eyes. The calm wash of the rift feels unreal now, a dream that happened a billion years ago. She feels a little like something that it coughed up, a fish it has thrown back. Her body aches; her mind whirls, disoriented.

She feels as if she has just been born.

ELEANOR COMES ALIVE in the shower, steam rising around her as her skin's color returns. The bar of green soap smells like fertilizer. One of the old women sits on the toilet lid on the other side of the shower curtain.

Eleanor's body feels strange and different. She could swear that she is taller—not just a little taller but two inches, maybe more. Her hair rattles her—it is longer than she has ever worn it, hanging almost to her bottom. Her hips are different—flared, somehow—and her breasts are larger, and . . . and there's an awful lot of unexpected hair beneath her arms and down *there*. Her legs are fuzzy.

She thinks about the rift and wonders if it has done something to her. What if it was radioactive? What if it mutated her, like the dogs near Chernobyl?

The bathroom door opens, and Eleanor hears the old man's voice, low. The toilet lid clanks a bit as the woman gets up and goes to the doorway, and Eleanor listens to them whisper loudly.

"Three in the godforsaken morning," the woman says. "What was she doing running around naked in the middle of December? She's apt to have killed herself."

*December?*

"Paramedics are here," says the old man. "I told them to wait, let her make herself decent."

Behind him, a male voice—a paramedic?—protests. "Sir, we really have to—"

The woman named Edna interrupts. "She'll be out when she's out. Now sit. I'll make some tea."

"She okay?" the old man asks.

"Didn't want me to help her shower," the woman says, as if Eleanor can't hear her. "I think so."

The old man is quiet for a moment. "Well, send her out when she's warmed up. They want to at least look her over, just to be safe. Did you get her name?"

The woman shuffles over to the shower curtain. "What's your name, dear?"

"Uh—Jennifer," Eleanor says.

"Jennifer," the woman repeats to the man, who grunts, then closes the bathroom door.

Eleanor looks down at her prickly legs and scruffy armpits and eyes a pink razor hanging from the shower caddy.

"I've got some of our granddaughter's clothes in the spare room," the woman says. "I'll go get you something."

When Eleanor finishes shaving—not without some angry red nicks; after all, she has never used a razor—she steps out of the shower and onto a gray shag rug. She deliberately leaves the water running and quickly dries herself with a rough towel. There are fresh clothes stacked beside the sink. The old couple's granddaughter is a little smaller than Eleanor. The jeans are snug and too short, and the T-shirt has a printed image of a unicorn on it.

Then she opens the bathroom window and steps onto the toilet lid and hoists herself up onto the sill.

She drops down, too-small shoes squishing in the cold mud, then sneaks past the waiting ambulance, across the black lawn, and into the night.

\* \* \*

SHE RAPS LIGHTLY on the window.

*Please, Jack,* she thinks, and she knocks again, louder.

A light goes on inside, and then the curtain is yanked back, and Jack peers sleepily into the dark. He cups his hand against the glass, squinting past his lamp's reflection. She waves, and Jack's face turns white, as if he's seen a ghost. He staggers backward and out of sight; the curtain drops impolitely back into place.

Eleanor stands in the rain, shivering, and then Jack appears beside her, scaring her half to death. He throws his arms around her, grips her tightly. Her ribs flare in pain, but she only grunts. He releases her and clutches her face as if she might vanish, and before she can say a word, before she can prepare herself, he kisses her, hard, as though he is drowning and her lips hold the air he needs. He kisses her cheeks, her nose, her eyes; he seems almost desperate to prove that she is real. When he stops, she doesn't have time to breathe before he draws her in fiercely again. His lips move against her ear, and Eleanor feels her body turn to ice at his words.

"Oh, Ellie, I thought you were dead," he says. "We all thought you were dead."

He's sobbing.

# *the keeper*

The end of the world has come.

She wanders, stunned, through what is left of her valley, shocked by the cataclysm that has befallen it. It feels like a simultaneous declaration of war and victory, an attack that the keeper could not possibly have anticipated or prepared for. The

red-haired girl had been only a scout, she now believes. Whoever—
*whatever*—followed the girl had exterminated the keeper's hope.
Her cabin is gone, obliterated by fireballs. Her forests are charred
and smoking. The earth itself crackles like glass underfoot, steaming, still painfully hot.

She picks her way through splintered trees. All around her the
earth is sooty and black, like the dark muck that clogs her mouth.
She wonders if the fire in her belly is anything like the fire that
came from the sky. Her pain is blinding now.

She feels like a star at its end, collapsing slowly.

"When stars die, they explode," she says.

The shadow hears but does not answer. It follows at a distance,
skirting charred stumps.

*Dead stars explode.*

What will become of her valley if something happens to her?
Will it cease to exist?

Her thoughts are black. Such a day does not feel so distant now.

The keeper is dying.


SHE RESTS BENEATH a fractured boulder, where the ground is not
so hot. Her shadow watches as she coughs, hacking up another wet
mass of the black dust. When she tries to wipe it away, it smears
across her skin, turning everything black.

Then she sees it: a dark stain, spreading across her belly.

Her shadow has seen enough. It flees from her, but she is preoc-
cupied.

She panics at the sight of the black stain. She cups water from a
hissing puddle and pours it onto her abdomen. She closes her eyes,
willing the stain to wash away.

But it is still there when she opens them again.

It is *beneath* her skin, its center black and oily. It has already
spread across her stomach, turning bluish at the tips. The keeper

presses her hand against her belly; something hard and fiery sizzles inside her, and she sobs in pain.

The meteors had presaged something far worse. As the keeper had watched, the clouds had bulged, and a funnel surged down, enormous and horrible. Had she seen beyond her valley at that moment, she might have seen Mea drawing Eleanor into the rift for the first time. In the sky above the keeper's valley, a burning red orb appeared and plunged through the funnel like a falling sun. The air had rippled with heat, evaporating the rain and clouds; the sky had turned blood red.

She weeps over her ruined body now, weeps for her valley. The orb, now long gone, has taken everything from her. Her hair was burned away, her skin fiercely scorched. Most of it has sloughed away now, leaving her pink and raw beneath the apocalyptic, sunless sky.

# *eleanor*

I don't have any marshmallows," Jack apologizes.

"It's okay," Eleanor says.

She takes the mug of hot cocoa and sighs at its warmth. Jack's T-shirt is much too large for her. On the front is a Minnesota Twins logo. A pair of his sweatpants is cinched tightly around her waist, and still she had to hitch them up before she sat down. Her hair is tied up in a damp towel. She can feel the life slowly returning to her cold skin, a faint murmur of warmth rising in her cheeks.

*Two showers in the middle of the night,* she thinks.

"You're sure I didn't wake your dad?" she asks Jack as he sits. He's carrying a blue plastic storage container.

"He just got back from a race weekend," Jack says. "He's probably still hungover."

She sips her hot chocolate. It has almost no taste—it's not much more than hot water with an ineffective sprinkle of cocoa powder for color—but it makes her tongue tingle and reminds her that she's alive.

Which seems improbable; after all, she just fell out of the sky and into someone's swimming pool.

"You look different," she says.

Without saying a word, Jack opens the container and takes out a pile of newspapers. Eleanor watches him place them on the table, then looks at him quizzically.

"What are these?" she asks.

He turns the stack over, takes a folded City section from the bottom, and spreads it on the table in front of her.

The story is about the annual festival of boats. An accompanying photo shows sailboats and fishing trawlers parading through the harbor, lit up with strings of golden bulbs.

"What am I looking at?" she asks, finally.

Jack taps a smaller headline:

## LOCAL GIRL DISAPPEARS
## FROM HUFFNAGLE

"This, Eleanor," he says.

# *the keeper*

She wakes to poisoned rain, hot needles upon her raw skin. At the periphery of her vision, her shadow hovers, watching.

"Good morning to you," she says coldly.

She rises, bones cracking like bullets, mouth thick with ash. Abruptly she vomits; what comes out of her is as black as the land.

Her belly is now consumed by the toxic stain, and its bluish tendrils creep upward toward her breasts.

She climbs up on the boulder that has shaded her. Shakily she stands and surveys the wreckage of her valley.

For the first time she can see the red orb's impact point. She had expected a crater, perhaps, but it is far worse. A gaping chasm, miles across, exposes glowing bedrock. Smoke rises in a wide column from the fissure.

The stain has weakened her mind. She doesn't know how much time has passed. More than days, than months? Years? But the hole still glows hot. The basin around the impact point is barren. The river is a blackened furrow. The mountains have crumbled into heaps.

For two days she journeys to the chasm's edge. Wide crevasses have opened around it, rendering the earth unstable. More than once she steps on rock that crumbles into yawning darkness beneath her. The enormity of the pit takes her breath away; its farthest bank is hazy in the distance.

The keeper has patched up the valley before, but this is beyond her ability to heal. Magma leaks like glowing taffy below her. A pungent, blistering wind rises up from the hole. She cannot see the bottom.

There is no sign of the orb itself.

She remains on the edge of the pit for days, watching as the steaming rain cools lingering fires. In time, perhaps, the rocks will cool; in a year or two the hole might be a cold black tomb.

But her valley will never heal. It can never recover from this.

When she has enough strength, the keeper begins searching for life—a standing tree, some grass—but there is nothing left. She looks for the beasts, hoping that they found their way out of the valley before the end came.

She looks for bones.

One dark morning she skids down another ash-crusted hill. The stain has spread fervently; it has moved up her chest, over her heart, and now scales her neck. Her skin has scabbed over in places, but it cracks and bleeds as she walks. She falls often, each time wondering if she will have the strength to stand again.

But she forgets herself at the bottom of the hill.

There she finds the beasts bedded down among the rocks, their bodies as black as the earth, perfectly camouflaged among all this death. The large beast sleeps, its sooty body rising and falling.

Beside it, the smaller beast sleeps, too.

Breathing.

But barely.

## eleanor

Eleanor puts her mug down and stares at the words.

*Disappears.*

"What is this?" she asks, bewildered.

"Look at the date," Jack says.

*August 24.*

Eleanor's mouth dries up. "That's—that's—"

"Two days after I took you to the island," Jack says. "More than a month after you disappeared the first time."

"The first time," Eleanor repeats.

"Yes," Jack says. "Now look at the year."

"Nineteen ninety-four," she reads slowly. She looks up at Jack. "I don't understand."

Jack turns over the next clipping.

### COAST GUARD CONTINUES SEARCH FOR MISSING GIRL; BOY CLEARED AS SUSPECT

"Four days later," he says. "Nineteen ninety-four. They sent divers down, Ellie. They didn't find anything."

He flips through several more folded newspapers, then pauses. He taps another date. "See?"

She leans forward, almost knocking her cup over. A chill grips her.

"February," she says hoarsely. "Nineteen—"

"Ninety-five," Jack finishes.

Eleanor taps the headline. "What does this mean, 'cleared as suspect'? They didn't—they thought *you*—"

Jack shrugs. "I was the last person to see you. Why wouldn't they?"

## FAMILY STILL HOLDS OUT HOPE
## FOR VANISHED DAUGHTER

Jack spreads the clippings out on the table as Eleanor looks on, speechless.

## MISSING GIRL STILL UNACCOUNTED FOR

## NO NEW DEVELOPMENTS IN WITT CASE

The stories have gotten shorter, smaller.

"August," she whispers.

Jack turns over the last of the clippings.

## MISSING STUDENT PRESUMED DEAD

She covers her mouth in horror.

Jack taps the date.

*March 3, 1996.*

Her chest tightens, and her eyes fill up with tears. "Nineteen ninety-*six*?" she rasps. "Jack—it's—it's—"

"It's not a joke," he says. "I'm not messing with you. There was a service at the high school. The whole town came, practically. Stacy's father gave the eulogy."

She grips Jack's hand and squeezes it hard. "My parents," she says urgently.

Jack takes a sheet of pink copy paper out of the storage container. Printed in black ink is Eleanor's eighth-grade yearbook photo. Beneath it, a bold headline reads:

## REWARD FOR INFORMATION

"Your dad put them up all over town," Jack says. "They were everywhere. You couldn't turn a corner without seeing twenty more."

"Oh, god, my mother," Eleanor whispers, a hand over her heart. "She—Jack, two years? Is she—is she—"

"Shh," Jack says. "No liver came. Your mother was sent home. The doctors wanted to send a nurse home with her. A home health care worker? But I think your dad decided to do it. I haven't seen his office lights on in at least a year. I think he just . . . quit his job. I don't think he could handle it, going to work, selling houses every day with you d— while you were wherever you were."

"I can't breathe," she says. "I can't—two years?"

"You're almost eighteen now," Jack says. "I—your birthdays were . . . hard."

She stares, her eyes clouded by tears.

"You scared the shit out of me," he says. Then, suddenly, he's angry, almost shouting. "Two whole years, Ellie! No more bullshit. Okay? What the hell is happening? Where did you go? I thought I'd gone crazy. I thought I'd blacked out or something, because you—I couldn't find you anywhere. Do you know how that felt? What that was like? I dived under, over and over again, looking for you. I couldn't find you. And eventually it got too dark to see, and I had to row the boat back to shore alone. The whole way was torture. I kept thinking, what if she's still back there, and she can't find me? What if I'm abandoning her?"

She grasps his arm. "Jack—"

But he shakes her off. "No. I kept thinking: I did this. It's my fault for taking her to that fucking—I had to tell the police that you—that you just fucking disappeared in midair!" he cries. "They thought I was high!"

Eleanor swallows the hard knot in her throat. "I'm sorry! I didn't—I—"

Jack angrily swipes tears from his cheeks, but more just spill over. He's embarrassed, but he doesn't turn away, and Eleanor wishes—as powerfully as she has ever wished anything—that this wasn't her life, that her sister had never died, that her parents were happy and well-adjusted, that she was boy-crazy and begging her dad for a car, sneaking out at night, all the things that a teenage girl ought to be doing.

If only she were *normal*.

She sees it in Jack. Every time he looks at her. Every time he swallows down the things he wants to say and makes a joke instead. Every time he mock-punches her arm when what he really wants—what she knows he really wants—is to dart in and kiss her. He deserves normal, too.

But the rest of the world is too big. The rest of *her* world is too much. Too dire.

She puts her hand on the back of his head and leans in close.

"Jack," she says, brushing away his tears. "Jack, I need to see my parents."

He looks at her calmly, exhales slowly. His emotions seem to vanish, as if he has flipped a switch.

"Okay," he says. "I'll call your dad."

Jack goes to the telephone. He looks older—not just two years older but ten, maybe more.

"Wait," she says.

Jack stops, holding the handset.

"Hang up," she says. "There's something I have to tell you first."

\* \* \*

SHE'D TOLD HIM everything that day in her father's office. About the alien Iowa cornfield, about the mysterious ash forest, about the lost minutes and hours. But she hadn't known about the rift then. He listens intently, barely blinking, not saying a word.

"It's crazy," she says finally. "I know it sounds crazy."

"It's a lot more than crazy," he says.

She tells him about the last part. About the Other, deep in the rift. When she finishes, Jack doesn't say anything.

"Something is happening to me," she says. "I don't have any control over it."

"What happens if you—if it happens again? What if you never come back?" He is pale. "Two *years*, Ellie. That's a lot longer than before."

Eleanor closes her eyes. Jack's question triggers something within her.

"I have to say something terrible," she says softly. "It's okay if you think I'm horrible."

"I won't," Jack says.

"My father thinks I'm dead, right?" Eleanor says. "My mom, too?"

"Everybody thinks you're dead," Jack says.

Eleanor rubs her eyes, then massages her temples. "I think that there's something I have to do now," she says. "And I think that if I go home first—"

"And your parents see that you're alive—"

"—then they'll be devastated all over again when I leave," she says. "They've been through too much already."

"Wait," Jack says. "What do you mean, when you leave again?"

Her meaning dawns on Jack slowly, and he pushes back from the table sharply. "You can't," he says, his voice escalating. "*Jesus*, Ellie."

"Something strange is happening," she says again. "Don't you think it means something? Don't you think there's a reason for it?"

"This isn't a movie," Jack says. "You aren't the fucking *chosen* one.

You can't mess around with life and death just because you experienced something you can't explain."

"I think I was supposed to learn something," she says, ignoring him. "In the rift. From the . . . Other. And I didn't. I got scared."

"Ellie," Jack says. He paces wildly about.

"I don't expect you to believe any of this, you know," Eleanor says. "I know it sounds crazy."

Jack stops, slides back into the chair, and leans close to her. "But I *do* believe you," he says. "I *saw* you. I watched it happen."

"Then you know—"

"But you can't do it again," he says. "You just can't. It's too much. It's too dangerous. *This isn't natural.*"

"Jack." She puts her hands on his. "You have to take me back to the island."

"I won't," he says, snatching his hands away. He presses his palms against his eyes. "I won't do it."

"I'll go by myself, then," Eleanor says.

"Ellie, please," Jack begs. "Please don't do this."

"Then take me," she says. "I want you there. I need you to be there."

He shakes his head. "I can't. It's not right, Ellie. You don't know what it was like, watching you . . . and then losing you. I've been fucking lost myself for two whole years."

"Then don't watch," she says. Gently she places a small, soft kiss on his cheek. "Just be my ride. Okay?"

THE SKY IS a frayed gray blanket. There's no moon.

Jack rows in silence. Rain patters upon the sea around them. Eleanor reads his fear in every pull of the oars, finds his worry in the hard slope of his tucked shoulders. She cannot see the furrow in his brow, but she knows that it is there, so deep it must be almost painful.

"There's water in the boat," Eleanor says.

Jack doesn't answer. For the duration of the bicycle ride that brought them back to the beach and the moored rowboat, he has been quiet.

"Only a little," she adds.

She would be lying if she said that she didn't share Jack's fears. The memory of the rift has begun to slip away from her already, and more of it fades by the minute. If she waits much longer, she might forget her journey there entirely. It is too strange and fearsome and wonderful a memory for her to permit such a thing.

The sky rumbles. Little sparks of lightning rattle about on the horizon, illuminating other boats bobbing on the rolling waves, and once she spies their distant silhouettes, she can also make out their tiny stuttering lanterns, like little campfires at sea. The sun hasn't yet begun to rise; maybe it won't rise today at all.

It feels like the end of the world, a little.

It feels as if anything could happen.


NOT CONTENT TO just be "her ride," Jack walks behind Eleanor. She can feel him watch her as she climbs, ready to catch her if she stumbles. And she does, a little, sliding backward in the gritty mud with every short step. The brambles that hang over the dark path are sharp and invisible until she's right upon them, and more than once she staggers through the branches and hears Jack's grunt as their bristly limbs smack him.

But they reach the pinnacle of Huffnagle without much more trouble. For a time Eleanor stands there, Jack at her side, staring at the edge of the cliff. The sparse grasses on the rocky summit are matted down with mud. The crown of the island shimmers in the damp dark.

She imagines what Jack is thinking as he stands beside her, sharing the view. He will worry about the leap, yes, but also about her approach to it. About the few running steps she must take, barefoot on the slick rock. One bad step and she might fall too close to the cliff wall, maybe even dash herself against some jagged outcropping.

He finally speaks. "I'm actually terrified."

"Me, too."

"This doesn't feel real," he says. "It feels like I'm dreaming. There just aren't places like that. Like your . . . your rift."

"I've thought of a thousand possibilities," she says. "But it's real."

"Were you really there for two years?" he asks.

"It felt like a few minutes."

He shivers. "I don't know if I can watch again."

Eleanor feels for his hand.

"Just hold my hand for now," she says. "This will be okay."

The rain picks up, lashing their faces.

"Promise?" he whispers.

She kisses him tenderly, startling them both. "I can't."

Their clothes are soaked through, so they strip down to their underwear on the cliff's edge. Eleanor steps right up to it, her toes curling over the rocks. Jack takes her hand and suddenly pulls her back. She is unselfconscious in her state of undress. He doesn't even seem to notice her exposed skin; there are much more pressing things on his mind.

"I have to say this now," Jack says. Rain sluices down his face and drips from his nose. "I have to say it now, because I'm afraid you won't come back. I'm afraid I'll never have the chance."

Eleanor pushes her wet hair back. "No," she says. "You will."

He opens his mouth, shaking his head, but she is firm.

"You will," she repeats. "But if you tell me now, I might stay. And I have to do this."

She kisses him once more, slowly; everything that makes her who she is goes into that moment. Despite the rain, their bodies are warm as they touch.

Jack's chest is heaving when they part.

"I have to go now," she whispers.

His mouth opens and closes; then he nods his agreement. "Okay, Ellie."

He takes her hand, and they jump from Huffnagle together, their skin blue, their bodies pale like ghosts. Eleanor thinks of her grandmother, slicing through waves, sinking to her death. She thinks of her father, of the terrible grief that he must carry like an iron ball hanging from his neck. Of her mother, self-medicated nearly to death's door.

She hears Jack shout something she can't understand; the wind rips his words and his hand away from her. The senseless sound of his voice is the last thing she hears.

Only one of them crashes into the sea.

## mea

Eleanor tumbles into the rift.

*I am pleased,* Efah says to Mea. *She is here. You have done well.*

Eleanor is a distant glob of shadow. She sends out an immediate warning, defiant, aggressive. It sizzles outward, a burning red wave. A challenge. *I'm not afraid of you,* it says.

*Give her time,* Efah warns. *Be patient. Do not lose her again.*

*I won't,* Mea says.

Efah's words strike hard within her. *If you lose her again, I will be displeased.*

Mea says nothing. But she understands.

# the keeper

She wakes, her singed lashes crusted with ash. Silt collects in her nostrils, in the corners of her eyes, in the creases around her fingernails. She feels as if a shell of grime is slowly hardening over her. Her bones ache. She wishes she could simply lie here and fossilize.

But something had woken her.

The largest beast rests on its haunches, its great forelegs posed mantis-like before it. Its long, pebbled neck curves down to the earth in supplication. It lows, rumbling like a foghorn, and the keeper can feel her own lungs vibrate in response. She has slept in the beast's shadow for—weeks?—and yet she has never touched it. But now she stands up and places her hand against its belly. Despite the reptilian look of its hide, the animal burns like a furnace.

The beast grunts and raises its head sharply into the sky. The keeper cranes her neck to follow its movement and is startled by what she sees above.

The clouds are fiercely red, the color of blood again.

The beast sings a long, worried note, and the keeper sees the clouds rupture as a fresh assault begins, and not so far away this time. The clouds twist and tear, and a fork of steam rushes to the earth like a striking snake.

Deep inside that fuming artery, the keeper sees the orb again. As before, it hurtles toward the earth—*her* earth—as if it intends to repeat its earlier, terrible performance. As the keeper sucks in her breath, the thing spears into the remains of a mountain.

The peak shatters like a sculpture carved from ice, sending glowing shrapnel into the sky. The detonation echoes through the valley like a thousand bomb blasts. Veins of steaming magma spill from the wound.

The keeper huddles beneath the beast as missiles sizzle down from above.

The red orb—*that hateful bitch!*—is already gone, shot through the earth as before.

The beast above her continues to sing, but the smaller one begins to kick and spasm on the ground, its legs shoveling up geysers of dirt and rock that almost bury the keeper where she stands. The keeper darts into the open, away from the beasts, dodging falling debris. This time her shadow follows, alarmed.

The small beast lifts its tail into the red sky, and it hangs there, framed against the bleeding clouds; then it falls limp, smashing a ravine into the ground. The beast thrashes about, wrecking what remains of the land.

The keeper covers her head, stinging rocks whistling around her. The valley flushes with fresh heat, twitching in great seismic up-heavals.

"Please," she moans. "Please, enough. You'll leave me with noth-ing."

Her shadow draws near for the first time in months.

Rain falls like a bitter plague upon the valley.

## *eleanor*

The Other's first words come in time, after Eleanor has grown accustomed to the darkness again. She feels strangely enlarged, separated from the fibers of her nerves and the pores of her skin and the damp weight of her hair.

Long before the Other speaks, she discovers that her thoughts are like commands.

She thinks of Jack as she hangs in the darkness and wonders

what it must have felt like when she disappeared from his grasp, when he struck the water alone. She wishes she could see him now.

In the darkness, Eleanor collides with a viscous membrane that, until now, she had not even noticed. Her wish is granted: just like that, the milky surface of the membrane thins, and she *can* see Jack. She gazes down upon him from a great height, as though she were a bird drifting upon a current of salty air. He is a bead of white against the dark slate of the sea. It takes time for her to realize that Jack isn't moving. He hangs, suspended like her, partly in the sea, partly in the sky. The waves are frozen against the base of Huffnagle's cliff like gelatin.

She is staring at a painting of the world that she has left behind, a photograph of it.

*I have been waiting for you,* the Other says.

The words splash upon Eleanor like a waterfall. The sensation is calming, comforting, much like her grandmother's old blanket, like the smell of her mother's coffee when Eleanor was only a girl. The words are heavy with memory.

"Is he okay?" she asks, still looking down at Jack, frozen in the northwestern sea, while at the same moment the Other says, *How do you feel?*

Eleanor turns from the membrane, searching the darkness for the invisible shape of her strange new companion.

"You frightened me," she confesses.

*It was not my intention.*

"What happened to my friend?"

*He is safe. Don't fear for him.*

"He's not moving," Eleanor says.

*Do you remember your last visit to this place?* the Other asks.

"You called it the rift," Eleanor answers. "I remember now. I was starting to forget."

*Good,* the Other says. *That you remember.*

"You have to tell me why I'm here," Eleanor says.

*When you were a little girl, you were not good at many things,* the Other says. *But with time, as you grew, you became good at those things. Is that true?*

"Yes."

*For a very long time—time is relative, but especially here—I have struggled to bring you to this place,* the Other says. *Do you remember?*

"No, I—," Eleanor begins, but an image of red barns and yellow corn surfaces in her mind. "Wait. Iowa?"

The cornfield, the scorched mountain, the plummeting airplane.

"That was you," she says.

*I, too, grow better at things with time,* the Other says. *I have been here for what you might consider a very long time, Eleanor, but for me—as I said, time has little meaning here. I have had much time to learn, to grow.*

"What are you trying to say?" Eleanor asks.

*I have learned how to . . . preserve your timeline when you enter the rift,* the Other says. *That is why your friend is not moving.*

"I still don't understand," Eleanor says.

*You would call it stopping time.*

"That's absurd—you can't stop—"

But she feels the truth of it even as she denies it.

*You know that it is,* the Other observes. *I feel it.*

"So he's okay, then," Eleanor says. "He's really okay."

*Yes.*

"Why am I here?"

*I will tell you what I can. The rift, as it is called, is a . . .*

The Other thinks for a long time. Eleanor has the sense that the Other has gone away altogether, when, finally, an answer comes.

*You might call it a waiting room.*

"A waiting room," Eleanor repeats, as if such a thing makes sense. "But for what? What are you waiting for?"

Another interminably long pause.

*I wait for passage,* the Other says at last, *into the light of the after. I do not know what waits for me there.*

"Purgatory," Eleanor says. "The rift—it's purgatory."

*Purgatory,* the Other muses. *Yes, it's like that.*

"So there's really an afterlife," Eleanor says. "You're dead. You're waiting for it."

*Perhaps,* the Other says.

Eleanor considers this. "Does that mean that I'm dead, too?"

*The rift does belong to those who have passed from life,* the Other says. *All sorts of lives, in all sorts of places.*

"So I'm dead."

*No,* the Other replies. *You are . . . unique. Few can enter the rift from life without passing first into death.*

"But I'm not dead?"

*No.*

"Then I don't understand," Eleanor says. "Why am I here?"

## mea

*I* *cannot answer her questions.*

Efah waits beyond the membrane, pensive.

Mea is impatient. *Everything she asks me—what do I say to her?*

Efah says, *Whatever you want to say to her. Why* did *you bring her into the rift, Mea? Do you even know?*

Across the wide gulf of Mea's fishbowl, Eleanor is alone in the dark. Mea can hear the girl asking after her: "Hello? Where did you go? Are you there?"

Why, indeed?

Efah is no help to her. He has supplied her with a few answers to the girl's questions, feeding them to her silently. But the girl's questions are stirring, and they come more quickly now, and Mea reels from them. They are questions that Mea herself has asked of Efah, which Efah has not answered for her.

*That's it*, she thinks. *Efah is not so wise after all.* Caught up in the game that Mea plays with Eleanor, Efah has, in fact, been answering Mea's own questions, the same ones he refused to answer during her first days in the rift.

*The rift belongs to those who have passed from life*, he had said, supplying Mea with an answer to Eleanor's question.

*I'm dead*, Mea says. She leans against the membrane, and Efah's cloudy shape retreats from her. *I'm dead. You just said so.*

He doesn't answer, but it doesn't matter. Mea whirls and forces her way through the membrane's vast river of memories. She rushes through them adeptly, focusing her attention only on Eleanor's particular current. She watches Jack and Eleanor in the boat, moving in reverse over the sea; skims over the period of Eleanor's recovery, watching the bruises and cuts rewind, growing fiercer and brighter until Eleanor flies away from the bathroom wall, into the kitchen, arguing with her father.

Mea stops when she arrives at Eleanor's bedroom, before she took the girl and failed. The room is familiar to her, as it was before, but she does not know why. The two faces in the framed photograph beside Eleanor's bed seem to stare right through Mea, across the years of memory.

She looks up. Efah is gone.

Mea burrows through Eleanor's past, furiously flitting over Eleanor's high school years, her middle school years, until, suddenly, there's Eleanor, hospitalized, bandaged, small in the children's ward.

*She's so little*, Mea thinks.

"Hello? Where did you go?" Eleanor calls out from the depths of Mea's fishbowl, but Mea barely notices her.

She pushes backward in time once more, and then she stops, stunned by what she sees, by the bright, searing pain of real memory.

"I'm scared," comes Eleanor's voice, a faint swell of panic evident in the colors that issue from her, carrying her words to Mea.

Mea stares at the memory she has found.

*Me, too.*

# *eleanor*

E leanor panics, abandoned to the darkness.

"Hello? Where—"

*I brought you here,* the Other says, returning suddenly. *For you, the rift is . . . different.*

Eleanor is relieved to hear the Other's words booming into the darkness.

*For me, the rift is as you said: purgatory, sort of. For you, the rift is more like a conduit. A doorway to other places, other times, other realms.*

"I don't understand. Why?"

*That is not the correct question.*

"What is the right question?"

*You know what it is. Ask.* Eleanor turns away from the Other and considers the thousand questions that flood her mind. Which of them is the right one? What happens if she asks the wrong one? She doesn't want to disappoint the Other.

Behind her, the Other waits.

She thinks about all she has seen, all that is yet to be revealed. The question comes to her at last, and she turns slowly to face the invisible Other.

"Why are you here?" Eleanor asks. Then, before the Other can reply, she blurts, "Wait! Before you answer."

The Other remains still.

"You know my name. What is yours?"

She can feel the Other's hesitation.

*I am called Mea.*

"Mea."

*It is the name I was . . .* A pause, then: *It is the name I chose for myself.*

"What does it mean?"

*I do not know,* the Other confesses.

"Should *I* choose a new name?"

*You are but a flickering candle in the rift,* Mea says. *No. Only the permanent—the dead—are made to take a name.*

"Okay," Eleanor says at last. "You can answer my question now."

*The rift is vast. It contains the whole of time itself.* At this, Mea caresses the membrane, and light sputters across its milky surface. *I am here now, and so I have been from the beginning of all things. Yet I have also only just arrived, and I have already left. Do you understand?*

Eleanor doesn't.

*You come from a place where time moves only forward,* Mea says. *But in the rift, time is a boundless sky. I can visit the very moment that you ceased to exist in your world, the moment when you entered the rift. I can also return to the instant when your world was formed in the darkness. I can visit your world at the moment of its death, when it is consumed by your sun. Do you understand?*

"Sort of," Eleanor says.

*You will understand this when your body dies, but for now you may think of me as a spirit, or a soul, or a consciousness—whatever word you prefer. It is not urgent that you understand all of this, Eleanor. It is enough that you have been told.*

Eleanor says, "But why are *you* here? Can't you leave?"

Mea seems to laugh. A pink rush of color explodes outward, and Eleanor almost laughs herself.

*It is not an original story,* Mea says. *Your storytellers have long understood my dilemma: I must remain in the rift until a wrong is put right again.*

"You're a ghost," Eleanor says. "You have to resolve your affairs!"

*Perhaps the storytellers were like you, Eleanor,* Mea says. *Travelers between your world and the rift. Perhaps that is how they have always known.*

"What wrong do you have to correct?" Eleanor asks.

*The same which you long to solve,* Mea says.

"What?"

*My family,* Mea says. *I wish to bring them peace.*


"My family is . . . We make the best of things," Eleanor says. "We do the best we can."

*That is naïve,* Mea says. *But that is not your fault. You believe that your family moves only forward in time; therefore, their affairs can only be addressed reactively. But you are incorrect.*

"I don't—," Eleanor says. "I—what?"

*You are temporarily absent from time. Like me, you exist outside of it. Imagine that time is a river, and you are a bird. A bird is not bound to follow the river. You may fly upriver, downriver, higher, or lower, or in any other direction you—*

"You can alter the past," Eleanor says suddenly.

Mea is pleased. *Yes.*

"My family—they—*we*—haven't been fine for a long time."

*I am aware.*

"But how?"

*Eleanor,* Mea says. *I must ask you a question now.*

Eleanor says, "Okay."

*If you could heal your family, would you?*

"Of course," Eleanor answers immediately.

*What if there were conditions?*

"I wouldn't care."

*If, for instance, healing your family meant that you had to relive a part of your life—would you do it?*

Eleanor thinks of the terrible morning all those years ago, of her mother bleeding behind the wheel, of her sister draped in a sheet.

"I would do anything," she says softly. "Even for just a single day, I'd do anything."

*That is what I hoped to hear,* Mea says.

"How do you know about my family?" Eleanor asks, her colors urgent and bright in the darkness.

*Ask the proper question,* Mea says.

Eleanor struggles with this. "I don't know the right question!" she says, almost shouting.

*Slowly, Eleanor,* Mea says. *Still yourself. Agitation will only expel you from the rift, as before. Be calm. Think.*

Eleanor counts slowly to fifty. In that time, it seems as if a billion years flicker by. But she rests in the darkness, feeling her body grow still.

"I don't know the question," she says finally. "Tell me what to ask."

*You asked my name,* Mea says.

"Yes," Eleanor says.

And then the correct question comes to her, quite suddenly, and she is afraid to ask.

*Do not be frightened. It is only a question. It changes nothing that is not already true.*

Before she even asks the question, she knows the answer, and she wants to weep.

*Ask.*

Eleanor does. "Who—who *were* you?"

And Mea answers.

# the keeper

She mourns her valley.

The bowl shape of it is gone, entire slopes of the mountains crushed like fireplace embers. A sluggish river of melted rock has begun to cool, steaming like a doused campfire. The quakes since the orb's last appearance have been violent, shaking what's left into rubble, shaking the rubble into pebbles. For the first time, the keeper can see beyond the mountains that have embraced her for so many years.

There's nothing there at all.

The clouds seem to tumble to the earth, swirling into a fog so dense it might be solid. She would expect the fog to spill through the shattered mountain range, but it doesn't. It is an unnatural boundary; it frightens her.

Her shadow returns to her.

"It's all gone," the keeper croaks.

Her shadow has heard this before.

The keeper has become fragile, more than before. Each aftershock threatens to dash her bones on the rocks. The black stain gnaws at her, eating her alive.

She senses her shadow tugging at her. It strains away from her, like a puppy on a leash.

The beasts are moving.

No—not both. The largest takes a thunderous step, then another. In the blackness of its shadow, its smaller companion struggles and fails to stand.

"What's wrong with you?" the keeper rasps. "Where are you going?"

The large beast stares down upon her, as if it has understood. Then it dips its head and entwines its neck with the smaller beast's crooked one. It grunts, then steps backward, tugging its companion upright. For a moment the smaller beast sways uncertainly, and the keeper is afraid it will pitch over and die before her. With halting steps, it follows the larger beast.

"Wait," the keeper whispers.

She tries to run after the animals, but she is weak herself and falls.

"Wait," she cries, her voice cracking. "Don't go! Don't leave me!"

But the beasts have spotted the same hole in the mountains that the keeper saw, and they turn slowly toward it.

They are leaving the valley.

# eleanor

Eleanor can hear him hit the water.

Mea *has* learned much since Eleanor's previous visit to the rift. She returned Eleanor to her world at the precise moment of her departure—but has deposited her, naked, on the island shore.

"Jack!" Eleanor shouts.

She doesn't think he can hear her over the waves, which heave in large shelves, higher than before. She worries for him. The water is frigid and moves in such broad swells that she wonders if he will be able to swim around the hook of the island and back to the boat.

But he does, dragging himself onto the shore. He doesn't see her. She can see even from this distance that he is shaking.

The sky turns dark, and Jack comes ashore like a ghost, pale and chattering. He staggers and almost falls, and Eleanor could strangle herself for the danger she's put him in. What would have happened to him if she hadn't returned to this same *when*? She pushes the image of a hypothermic, shuddering Jack out of her mind and runs to him.

His eyes widen at the sight of her.

"Don't try to talk," she says.

He quivers like a sapling in a stiff wind. She takes his windbreaker from the boat, not caring that she is unclothed herself, and wraps it around Jack's shoulders. She rubs him down vigorously. He shakes so hard that he can barely stand. His eyes flutter shut, then snap open.

"Into the boat," she says.

She helps him in, and he sinks to the bottom and curls into a ball. Eleanor leans against the boat with all her might, and somehow, miraculously, shoves it into the sea, then leaps inside.

"I'll get you home," she says to Jack.

She takes up the oars and hopes she can row them back.

\* \* \*

SHE SLAPS HIM awake on the mainland shore. He doesn't respond, so she slaps him again, and he twitches a little. She hits him harder, with the flat of her hand, and he starts awake. His eyes are shot through with red, his lips the color of frozen plums.

"I'm sorry," she says. "It was the only way to wake you up."

He blinks and tries to look around.

"D-don't g-go," he stammers. His voice is small and reedy.

"We're on the mainland," Eleanor says. "I can't get you onto the bicycle by myself."

"Bi-bi-bi—," he tries to say.

"Can you hang on while I pedal?" she asks.

Jack can only nod, and she wraps him up in her own cold arms while he shakes and shakes.


SHE PUTS HIM into the bathtub and runs water over him. The house is quiet except for the rush of the faucet and the knock of Jack's knees against the tub. She makes sure the water is lukewarm, and she watches as his submerged body slowly turns pink.

Jack takes long, unsteady breaths, and she says, "Can you sit up on your own?"

He nods uncertainly.

"I'll make you some warm milk," Eleanor says. "Stay here. Don't drown."

He almost laughs.

She finds one of Jack's T-shirts in his bedroom and also pulls on a pair of his shorts. They're too big, so she rolls the waistband down until it's thick enough to hang on her hips.

The kitchen looks the same as it did hours before, when they sat at the table, poring over Jack's box of memories, drinking cocoa. Eleanor pours milk into a coffee mug and warms it in the microwave, and while it turns and turns inside the humming box, she studies the room more carefully. Every object she sees has a maker, has a life span, has a history. Someone put it together or pulled levers on a machine that assembled it. Someone even assembled the machine that assembled the objects, probably someone who was long dead by now.

*Time is a river,* Mea told her. *You exist outside of it.*

That was how it felt, too, inside the rift. But here, on the outside again—for this is how Eleanor thinks of the world around her now—she is all too aware of the passage of time. The glowing red numbers that jitter and change on the microwave readout. The faint tick of a clock somewhere in the house. The dining table and its chairs aren't expensive pieces of furniture and probably won't last that long, but they will change hands at a yard sale someday, or follow Jack to college, or gather dust when Jack's father passes away.

She looks around the house and thinks, *Time is a gift.*

The microwave chimes.

"How do you feel?" she asks.

"You rowed us b-back," he says. "How did you do that?"

Eleanor shrugs. *"You* did it," she says. "Can't be all that hard."

He tries to smile, but it comes off as a grimace.

She lifts his hands and wraps his fingers around the mug of milk. "Drink," she says. "Just be still, and warm up."

"Hypo—," he begins.

"I don't think you have hypothermia," she says. "You *should.* But your fingers and toes looked okay to me."

"Where did you g-g-go?" he asks. "Did it—"

Eleanor leans close to him. "It *worked.* I know what it all means now. Everything is going to be okay."

\*   \*   \*

SHE SITS ON the edge of his bed after tucking him in. He's wearing sweatpants, a sweatshirt, a wool hat, socks, a fleece jacket. His trembling hasn't gone away entirely, but it has diminished. He yawns, at sleep's doorstep.

"I have to go away again," she says. "But I told Mea to let me come back and make sure you were safe first."

He is confused.

"It's a long story, Jack. I can't tell you all of it right now, but I'll tell you when I come back."

"From wh-where?"

"There's something I have to do," Eleanor says. "I can't explain it. It'll sound crazy, but it's all going to be just fine."

She touches his cheek softly. Jack leans into her hand.

"You did a very important thing for me," Eleanor says. "You're the only person who could have. You might not ever know how important it was. So I want to tell you before I leave that—that you—that what you did means everything to me." She hesitates, fighting the urge to cry. "And it could have killed you. I'm so sorry."

"I don't underst-st-stand."

"I know." She kisses his cold lips, then his forehead, then goes to the door.

"Wait," he says. "Can I—can I s-say something?"

She shakes her head.

"It's all going to be okay," she says, pausing in the doorway. "Every single thing is going to be okay."

And she leaves, knowing what Jack did not say. There is far more at stake than his feelings, and she meant what she told him on the cliff: She might not leave if she heard him say it. So she leaves.

She doesn't see him reach for the phone beside his bed.


SHE COASTS DOWN the hill on Jack's bicycle, past darkened shops and blinking neon signs. The rain has stopped, but the road is still slick. She follows it to her mother's neighborhood, past squishy, puddled lawns and dripping mailboxes.

She stops at the end of Cove Street and leans on one foot.

Her father's Buick is parked in the driveway. She doesn't know how much that means now, or if it means anything at all.

But it's . . . nice.

Inside the house, one light is already on, and another window lights up as she straddles the bicycle, watching. They're awake, at least one of them. Probably her father. Her heart aches to imagine him puttering around the house in the wee hours, unable to sleep, sick to death over his lost daughter.

She wants to go to him. She wants to wake them both up, throw her arms around them, and tell them that everything is going to be fine. But leaving them again would be impossible. They wouldn't understand. They wouldn't let her go.

She points the bicycle toward the shore road, toward Huffnagle.

# paul

Paul stares at the phone in disbelief.

*Eleanor is alive.*

He drops the handset and dashes upstairs. Agnes is in bed, surrounded by the detritus of hospice care. The chemo has taken most of her hair. She sleeps most of the time.

Paul gently shakes her bony shoulder. When she doesn't wake, he turns on the bedside lamp. She flinches and grunts unhappily.

"Aggie," he says, his voice shaky. His eyes well up. "Aggie, the boy just called. Jack. He saw Ellie. He saw her. She's alive, Aggie. She's not dead. *She's not dead.*"

Agnes rubs her eyes.

"No," she croaks. "Both of my girls are dead."

"He said she went to the beach. He said we should—" He looks around and spies Agnes's housecoat draped across the rocking chair. He snatches it up. "Here. Let me put this on you. We can still get there if we leave now."

Agnes's eyes threaten to roll backward into her skull.

"Ags," Paul says, holding out the housecoat. "Come on. Get up! I'll help you. We can—"

"No," Agnes whispers.

Paul drops his arms to his sides. "No, you don't—you don't understand, Aggie. She's alive. We have to—"

"No," Agnes repeats. She closes her eyes.

Paul takes her hand and pulls. "Aggie, come on. You don't know what you're—"

Agnes's eyes fly open, dark and startlingly clear. "You go."

He is taken aback. "You don't *want* to see her. How could you not want to see her? Our Ellie is alive."

Agnes closes her eyes again and, with some effort, turns over. "And our other one isn't," she says, her voice like sandpaper.

THE STORM LANDS as he swings the car out of the neighborhood and down the hill. His heart pounds against his ribs as hard as the rain on the Buick's roof. The wipers swish in vain against the downpour, and the car slides a bit with every turn. The town's streets are empty at this hour, and most of the traffic lights blink yellow, not red. He roars through them all.

*Ellie's alive. She's g-going to the beach. You have t-t-to go, Mr. Witt. You have to see for yourself.*

Paul sees her from the hillside road, a lithe, tall ghost running along the old pier.

"Wait!" he shouts. The car fishtails as he spins the wheel, and he slides to a jittery stop in the empty parking lot. He almost crushes Jack's discarded bicycle. He throws open the door and shouts again, but Eleanor doesn't hear him, doesn't see him.

She drops to her knees at the end of the pier and wrestles with the rowboat's mooring.

The sight of her is like a hallucinogen, and it all rushes back: the first time she spit up on his shirt, the first time she clambered up onto the stool at his attic workbench, the first time she let him hold her after a nightmare. The first time she called for him, not Agnes; the first time she ate his Sunday waffles instead of shoving them away. With the rush of memories comes a future sense of those un-created: her graduation, her first date, her first beer with her father. So much lost, and yet there she was, right there.

*"Ellie, wait!"* Paul yells again, but the storm carries his words away.

He breaks into a run, his feet bare. There hadn't been time to put shoes on. The asphalt gives way to the black beach pebbles; he stumbles and sprawls headlong. He scrambles up again as quickly as he can, but already Eleanor is in the boat, and the ocean is startlingly powerful, dragging her away from the beach.

The pier is slick, and he falls again, almost tumbling over the edge. His knee protests this time as he gets to his feet, and he limps madly down the pier, desperately shouting. Without thinking, like a fool, he crashes awkwardly into the water. He rights himself, then strokes hard with the outgoing tide. But the currents are strange so close to the rocks; he goes under, claws his way to the surface, then is swallowed again. He loses Eleanor and the boat in the dark.

When he comes ashore, he falls upon the beach, sobbing. He stares helplessly into the mist, but there is no sign of her. When the storm breaks, Paul is still there, the lurching gray sea between him and the hazy shape of Huffnagle.

He can't form a coherent thought.

He's lost her again.

# *eleanor*

E leanor crosses the sea that her grandmother so often swam, to the island that haunted her mother's childhood, and she climbs it in the dark. She doesn't bother to shed Jack's clothes this time. She wonders if they will come with her or flutter down to the ocean, empty.

Without hesitating, she walks to the sharp edge of the cliff and leaps. She cannot imagine how it ever frightened her before.

She plunges through the sky, then tears through it, and the pleasant dark welcomes her in.

Mea has been waiting.

*Hello, Eleanor,* Mea says.

"Hello, Esmerelda," Eleanor answers.

*part three*

*the rift*

# eleanor

Eleanor turns over in the black tide. Mea is close to her, much nearer than before. Eleanor can feel her sister's presence, as if a magnetic field around her own body is slightly disturbed by another. She and Esmerelda, two disembodied minds, two magnets of identical poles somehow drawn together.

*We have a great task ahead of us,* Mea says. *We should begin.*

"Tell me what it was like," Eleanor says.

*What do you mean?*

"Were you looking down on us? Did you see yourself?"

*I don't understand.*

"When—when you died," Eleanor says. "It's ghoulish to ask, I know. But I'm so curious!"

Mea stares accusingly at Efah's shadow, faint on the opposite side of the membrane. He stares back, unflinching.

*We have work to do,* Mea says.

"But we could talk for a million years and not lose a second," Eleanor says. "You said you can go anywhere in time. So we have time. Don't we?"

Mea hesitates.

"I want to know what you felt," Eleanor says. "Don't you want to know what I felt?"

*I saw you,* Mea answers reluctantly. *You were sad.*

"That's all?"

*What else is there?*

"It was the worst thing that ever happened in my life," Eleanor says. "And now I'm here, and we're—you're right here in front of me! After all these years!"

She pauses, waiting for Mea to say something, anything.

But Mea is quiet.

"I missed you," Eleanor says. "You must have missed me. Or Mom, or Dad."

*It is not the same for me,* Mea says. *I do not feel these things as you do.*

"But—" Eleanor can hardly imagine this. "Then why did you bring me here?"

*So we can set things right,* Mea says. *So all will be right again.*

"You didn't miss me, even a little?"

*It would hurt your feelings if I answered truthfully.*

"You didn't miss me," Eleanor says. "I don't know what to think about that."

*I am not Esmerelda,* Mea says. *I was, but now I am not.*

The darkness suddenly feels bleak, empty. Eleanor turns away.

*You are upset.*

"I'm heartbroken," Eleanor says. "It isn't the same."

*We have a task, Eleanor.*

"It's all about what's best for you, then."

*What is best for me is also infinitely better for you.*

Eleanor drifts slowly in the dark.

"I am so happy to see you," she mutters softly. "I just want to remember one happy moment. Just one, before we do this."

Mea says nothing.

"Just one."

# mea

**M**ea has witnessed her own death, has even memorized the tiny events that contributed to it, has studied each of the threads that tangled up in that knotted, violent second of human history: Her father travels to the real estate convention because a man named Richard breaks his ankle. Richard was to attend the convention, but, upon his injury, Paul transfers the flight into his own name. This is the single event that creates the accident in the timeline. A broken ankle.

Logistics dictate almost everything else. The Witts have only one car. Had Paul driven it himself, the car would have remained in airport parking for days, useless to Agnes and the girls. A taxi is too expensive, so the whole family drives to Portland to see Paul off. Agnes and the twins return a few days later to retrieve Paul from the airport. This puts them on Highway 26, speeding through the rain and fog to meet Esmerelda's—*Mea's*—fate.

*Just one happy moment,* Eleanor had said.

For Eleanor's sake, Mea tries to remember life before she died. She knows her death well but little of the days and years that preceded it.

So, for a time, she is quiet, searching the membrane, observing. She spends time watching herself, as she has watched Eleanor. The Esmerelda she sees feels at once alien and familiar to her.

Finally she turns back to Eleanor.

*Let me show you something.*

In all of history, *there are very few people like you,* Mea says. *Like us.*

Eleanor listens quietly.

*Human beings live in one direction—forward. They are born, expe-*

*rience the events of their lifetime, and die. But a few are different,* Mea explains. *A few may live in* many *directions. You and I, we are different together. We share a connection that most do not have.*

"Because we're twins?"

*Perhaps,* Mea says. *I do not know why, only that it is true. We're different, Eleanor. We can do things that others cannot.*

"What do you mean?" Eleanor asks.

*Time. Events. Consequences.*

"What does that mean?"

Mea says, *It means that we could start over.*

"Start over," Eleanor says. She floats closer to Mea, the gauzy wisps of their forms tangling like kelp.

*I have seen our past. Were we ever truly happy?*

"Of course we were."

*No, Eleanor. We were children. We were ignorant, as children are. It isn't the same.*

"I don't understand," Eleanor says.

Mea gestures at the membrane, vast and deep and wide. *This is time,* she says. *Time is a river.*

She parts the river to isolate a single memory. In it, both girls are sitting up in their shared bed. The bedroom is pale, lit by the moon. They're arguing, and Eleanor pinches Esmerelda's arm. Esmerelda shrieks. A thin scratch of light appears beneath their bedroom door, and a moment later the door opens to reveal Agnes, harsh even in shadow.

"I told you to lie down and go to sleep," Agnes snaps.

Eleanor lies down, but Esmerelda remains upright, rubbing her arm, her face contorted.

"You're so pissed," Eleanor whispers to Mea now, almost laughing.

Agnes waggles a finger at Esmerelda. "No more fighting, no more crying. Go to sleep. Lie down."

Esmerelda huffs in frustration, but she lies down.

Eleanor springs upright.

"Eleanor!" Agnes barks. "Lie down!"

Eleanor does, but Esmerelda sits up at the same time. This repeats itself until Agnes, practically glowing with anger, slams the
bedroom door and yells for Paul.

"I remember this. They got another bed after this," Eleanor says
to Mea. "I remember. Mom was so angry. We played all sorts of
games like that with her. I always thought she didn't understand
because she didn't have a sister of her own. Do you remember our
secret word?"

Mea says, *Secret word?*

"Bubbles," Eleanor says. "If one of us said it, we traded places.
Just to mess with people."

In the memory, Paul opens the bedroom door and says, "Girls.
Sleep. Now." Agnes stands just behind him, her eyes hard black
marbles.

"I wish I remembered her smile," Eleanor says wistfully. Then
she turns to Mea. "Can we go back?"

*Further?* Mea asks. *Of course.*

"I just want to see her smile. I barely remember it."

Mea wheels through memory after memory, but Eleanor quickly
grows doubtful. None of the memories is quite how Eleanor remembers them herself. In the joyful days, before Esmerelda's death,
she and her sister and father are often squealing and rolling about
like hedgehogs, but when Agnes is there, she's never quite *there*.

Before too long they arrive at their own birth and have found
nothing.

"More," Eleanor says. "Go back more."

Mea expertly navigates through the time stream, and they pause
now and again to witness Agnes in the years before they knew her.
They see her courtship with Paul; quiet moments alone, writing in a
journal; lonely holidays spent with Grandpa Hob.

*Perhaps she was never happy,* Mea says.

In the memory that is open now, Agnes is a teenager, older than
her years. She sits at a table, arguing with Grandpa Hob, who is
setting places. He puts a plate and silverware in front of Agnes and

another at his own chair. Then he puts a third place setting on the table, and Agnes scoots away from the table in a rage. The chair topples over behind her. Her father stares sadly after her as she storms out of the room; then he sits down before the third place setting and weeps.

Mea remains quiet.

"It wasn't our fault," Eleanor says softly. "She's always been unhappy."

Mea closes the memory. *I'm sorry to have shown you any of this.*

"Wait," Eleanor says. "One more. But not Mom."

IN THE FINAL memory, a woman wades nude through strong waves, moving deeper and deeper. Eleanor and Mea watch in silence as the woman dives forward and begins to stroke through the incoming tide. The sky above her is nearly black, and rain turns the surface of the water around her into a battlefield. She makes precious little progress; the sea pushes her backward until she finally breaks through the waves and into the lurching plains of open water. She is exhausted long before she can reach the island, and her strokes weaken. She stops, at last, and floats in the shifting sea, staring at the still-distant outline of Huffnagle.

She turns her face up to the rain and closes her eyes.

She is there, and then, without a word, she isn't.

*Your namesake?* Mea says.

"Our grandmother," Eleanor says. "She was pregnant. I didn't know that."

Mea tries to close this last memory, but the membrane, strangely, resists. It ripples like a curtain stirred by rising floodwaters. Something unseen rushes through, past Mea, and she gasps.

"Do you feel that?" Eleanor asks.

*I cannot seem to—*, Mea says, still wrestling with the bubble of the memory, which remains stubbornly open against her will.

Efah appears on the other side of the membrane and speaks urgently, privately, to Mea. *Close it. It is not permitted.*

"It feels like . . . water," Eleanor says.

*It will not allow me,* Mea says.

"It's warm," Eleanor says, not hearing either of them. "It's like waves over my toes."

*Close it!* Efah demands, his voice thunderous within Mea's mind, where Eleanor cannot hear him. *You shouldn't have opened this one!*

Mea cannot, and Efah surges forward and collapses the memory, and it winks shut.

*There are rules,* he hisses to Mea. *This is not a game!*

Eleanor feels the strange sensation of water recede. "It's gone."

*What have you done?* Efah demands of Mea.

Mea ignores him and turns away from the membrane, to Eleanor, who seems dazed.

*Come, Eleanor,* Mea says. *We have work to do.*

# *eleanor*

So we can go back," Eleanor says. "How far? To *that* day?"

*Yes.*

"And you'll be—"

*Alive.*

"What happens then?"

Mea says, *I do not know.*

"But—then what? The crash, all over again? I feel that hurt all over again? Watch you—watch you—"

She cannot finish the thought.

*Time will begin to move forward for us,* Mea says. *But I do not think that it will be predestined.*

"So we can prevent the—what happened," Eleanor says.

*I am not certain. But I think so.*

"We'll be six years old again."

*Yes.*

"How do little girls stop something like that? How do we stop a car crash?"

*I do not know. Perhaps we will devise a plan.*

Eleanor is filled with fear and wonder. "We'll have to relive everything. All those years of school, of—"

*Yes. Is that undesirable?*

Eleanor laughs. "Are you kidding? I won't be alone this time!" Then she pauses. "Wait. Will—will we remember?"

*I do not know.*

Eleanor turns in a circle and laughs again. "Esme," she says, "you'll be alive! We'll grow up together! Can you imagine? All the things we'll share?" Eleanor faces Mea in the darkness. "Maybe this time you won't be such a little shit," she says pointedly.

Mea does not answer.

"Hey," Eleanor says. "I was only kidding. I'm sorry, it—"

*There are other things you must know.*

Eleanor feels that strange swell again, as if the sea has licked at her ankles.

"Did you feel—" She pauses, looks around in the dark. "Someone else is here. Is there?"

Mea is silent.

"Mea," Eleanor says. "Are we alone here?"

*The rift holds all the souls of people who wait,* Mea says. *But we are mostly alone.*

"Mostly?"

*Efah is here.*

"Who is Efah?"

*Efah has been here for a very long time.*

Eleanor feels a tingle of coldness, of fear.

*Do not be afraid,* Efah says. *Fear will send you back. I wish for you to stay.*

*This is Efah,* Mea says to Eleanor.

*Mea has not told you the most important thing,* Efah says. *I will tell you, and then I will leave you.*

Behind the membrane, Efah swirls like a cloud of blackbirds.

"Mea, I'm scared."

Mea has diminished in size, cowed by Efah's appearance. *Efah is good. Efah is—*

Efah says, *Do not be afraid. The rift belongs to me. You are my guest. You are both my guests, after a fashion.*

Eleanor presses close to Mea. To her surprise—and to Mea's, she senses—their amorphous selves begin to bleed into each other. The sensation is electric, a sustained, wavering hum. For a moment, they mingle and become one shape, one form, startling them both. But then it feels . . . natural. Mea understands what has happened first and speaks.

*Can you hear me, Eleanor?*

"Yes."

Beyond the membrane, Efah continues talking, unaware of their private conversation.

*He can't hear us, I think,* Mea says. *He is a snake. Do not trust him. He is wise and old, but he is duplicitous.*

Mea pulls away, and Eleanor stares at Mea, worried.

*You are human,* Efah continues, oblivious to what has just happened between the sisters. *You can exist in only your world, your Earth, but you are special: because of Mea, you may visit this one. But there are infinite worlds. My rift is a window to all of them.* Efah pauses. *All save one, that is.*

*You have been to that one,* Mea says to Eleanor.

"What?" Eleanor asks, incredulous. "I haven't been any—"

*You have seen dreams, nightmares,* Efah says, silencing them both. *Mea has shown these worlds to you, though she did not intend to.*

*You slipped out of my hands,* Mea says, ashamed. *I dropped you.*

*Between the rift and your own world,* Efah continues, *are dreams. You have been there. We have seen you enter, though we cannot follow. But I have seen the mark you left. It bleeds like an open wound.*

Eleanor feels as if her head might burst. "I'm—I don't understand," she says. "I haven't been to any dream worlds."

*Think,* Mea urges. *Remember.*

Memories of strange skies, of venomous rain, take shape in Eleanor's mind.

*What did you see?*

"Farms," Eleanor says. "I saw farms . . . and corn . . . and—children. I saw myself. I saw—I saw Jack." She remembers the words cut into the trees: J LOVES E 4EVER.

*Before you were there, you were near the boy,* Efah says. *Yes?*

"Yes."

*This is how the chasm of the dream world works,* Efah explains. *You fall into the dream world of someone near you, or someone of great importance to you.*

"It was Jack's dream," Eleanor says. "You're saying that I—I went into his—"

*Yes,* Mea confirms.

"Then—the other one—Aunt Gerry," Eleanor gasps. "When you tried to take me from my father's office."

*The woman in the doorway?* Mea asks.

"She's our aunt," Eleanor says. "When you lost me, I fell into her dream. I saw our cousins. I saw—I saw them *die.* Her awful dreams, poor Aunt—"

*That was the third time,* Efah interrupts. *What of the second time? What do you remember?*

Eleanor recalls the scorched woods, remembers being naked and slick with mud. "I was in a forest," she says. "I was—I was—"

*Home,* Mea finishes. *You were at home.*

"That's right," Eleanor says. "I was at home, and then I was in the woods."

*Were you alone?* Efah asks. At home?

Mea understands and answers for Eleanor. *She was not.*

Eleanor's heart seems to stop beating.

"My *mother* was there," she says. "Oh, *god.*"

YOUR MOTHER, EFAH says. *I have watched her.*

Eleanor looks at Mea worriedly. "What does he mean?"

*Every life leaves a tiny trail as it passes through time,* Efah answers. *A wake. Your own trail has grown weaker since you were small.*

"I was *grieving,*" Eleanor protests.

Mea says, *But your mother's trail—*

"She's *your* mother, too," Eleanor interjects, suddenly angry.

*Your mother's trail is withered,* Efah says. *Frail. It will snap soon, I am sorry to say.*

"What happens when they snap?"

*Death,* Efah answers simply. *Your task will be more difficult than we had imagined.*

"What do you know about it?" Eleanor asks.

*I know all things,* Efah says. After a pause, during which time Eleanor feels, somehow, *probed,* Efah adds: *I know you both desire to leave this place.*

*Will you stop us?* Mea asks.

*Stop you? On the contrary. I will help you, children.*

"Couldn't we just—go back in time?" Eleanor asks. "Like Mea said?"

*When time resets,* Efah says, *a person carries their being back with them. They won't remember the future—but they will harbor all the things that future made them feel. If they had a joyful life and then returned to the beginning, they would be full of happiness.*

"My mother is depressed," Eleanor says. "She has liver cancer."

*Her cancer would unwind,* Efah explains. *Her body would be healed—but it would harbor the memory of her grief. Your mother would still suffer enormously, although in her reality, Esmerelda would not have died. Worse, it would be senseless pain; she wouldn't understand it. It would swallow her like a beast.*

"Why would you tell me that it can all be undone if it really can't?"

*Because it* can *be,* Efah says.

"How?" Eleanor asks. "How am I supposed to—"

*Heal her.*

*And your father, too,* Mea says. She looks from Eleanor to Efah. *He also grieves.*

"Their daughter is still dead! How am I supposed to fix that?"

*Isn't it obvious?* Efah asks.

"No," Eleanor retorts, frustrated. "No, it's not obvious to me!"

*Through their dreams,* Efah says. *You must restore them. Mea will send you.*

*We should start with her mother,* Mea suggests. *Her trail is the most fragile.*

*I agree,* Efah says. To Eleanor, he says, *Are you ready, child?*

Mea moves closer, merges once more with Eleanor. Efah watches from the other side of the membrane but does not speak.

When they are joined and share each other's thoughts, Mea says, *You are worried.*

"Is it safe?" Eleanor asks.

*I don't know.*

"Is it going to work?"

*I don't know.*

"Come with me," Eleanor says. "Please come with me."

*Child,* Efah repeats. *Are you ready?*

*I cannot leave,* Mea says. *Efah won't permit it. I don't trust him— but there's no other way.*

Eleanor peels herself away from Mea. Efah has pushed against the membrane, peering in at the two of them.

*Decide,* he says.

Eleanor looks first at Mea, then at Efah.

"I'm ready."

*dreams*

# *eleanor*

The house looms before her. There are no lights in the windows. Clouds drift in front of a fat moon, throwing marbled shadows upon the lawn.

"How close do I need to be?" Eleanor had asked.

*There are no rules. But closer to your mother than to your father,* Mea had explained. *So that you will enter her dreams and not his.*

Her father's car is parked in the driveway. Naked once again, she crosses the yard and peers into the car. Her father's briefcase is on the passenger seat, still open. An unwrapped, barely-eaten sandwich rests on a pile of papers.

She goes around the house, her skin as pale as death in the thin moonlight, her red hair turned the color of dark wine. The spare key to the garage is still there, forgotten beneath the terra-cotta flowerpot. The flowers are dead and crackle like paper beneath her touch.

Eleanor slips into the garage and steps around the old, gummy oil stain on the concrete floor. She pauses for a moment, staring at the boxes that her father never took with him when he moved out. They are marked ATTIC JUNK in her mother's angry, hasty hand. A strap of old tape holds the flaps loosely together. Eleanor peels it away and opens the box.

Staring up at her from the depths of the first box is the toothless gaze of a broken model house. The cellophane windows have been punctured by tiny tree trunks. The walls of the house are buckled;

fake grass has crumbled free of its glue and is scattered everywhere like mossy tobacco dust.

She sighs and feels her eyes fill up with tears, remembering the mailbox that she broke years ago, on that awful day. She had fretted about it as her mother drove the Subaru to the airport. Her mother had noticed her concern—Eleanor barely remembers what it felt like for her mother to notice her—and had plucked at Eleanor's mood. "What's going on with you, kiddo?" she had asked.

Eleanor never told her, and then the accident rose up and demanded everyone's attention, and she had forgotten about the broken mailbox. Until now.

She carefully closes the box, presses the tape back into place, and turns away.

The inner garage door is closed. She lifts the knob slightly as she turns it, so the door won't squeak, then silently closes it behind her. For a long moment she stands still, letting her eyes adjust to the shadows, listening to the quiet of the house: the soft tick of the water heater, the subtle groan of the foundation settling.

She pauses beside the laundry room door. It is ajar, and she sees a pile of clean laundry in a basket atop the dryer. Her father's doing, she thinks. Her mother hasn't done laundry in years. She rummages through the pile and finds her father's Glacier Pilots T-shirt, and she remembers his story of watching Mark McGwire, all of nineteen years old, hit three home runs in a game. She pulls the shirt on. It smells like dryer sheets and her father and hangs almost to her knees.

Eleanor creeps into the kitchen. Beneath the sink, the red plastic glass-recycling bin is empty. She breathes a sigh of relief. Her father must be doing something right if her mother isn't drinking.

Or maybe her father just isn't finding the bottles.

The living room is empty, dusky. Her mother's chair is unoccupied. The blanket Eleanor used to drape over Agnes is folded carefully on the footstool. The side table is free of bottles.

She carefully crosses the room, then stops dead.

Her father is sitting upright on the couch in the dark.

Eleanor's breath catches.

Then her father snores—faintly, but enough that she can hear it. She exhales softly and heads for the stairs. The floor creaks beneath her feet, and her father starts awake. She can hear the thin click of his lips parting, and her skin prickles when he says her name.

MEA TAKES HER then.

The space between the world and the rift is uneven, and Eleanor feels the air spark and shimmer around her. Her father's voice wavers, stretches, her name on his lips turned to taffy.

"*Elllllllllllllllaaaaaaaaaaaaannnnnnnnnnnnahhhhhhh—*"

It is the first time she is aware of her passage between worlds, and she is determined to understand it, to remember it. For a moment, as the air glimmers, she sees a cloud of black tar. It begins as a tiny jet, a crystal of ink, and then unfolds like a crackling flower. She can *hear* it, and she reaches her arms forward. The rift is blacker than black, its edges spreading wide to take her in.

It sings to her.

She had imagined it differently. She had thought of the rift as a perfect, rectangular door, a black window that she could step through, or a tiny, traversable chasm between her world and the rift itself—the chasm that would lead to the world of dreams, into the ash forest and the farm on another planet.

But that isn't how it happens at all.

She feels a coldness in the space before her—not from the rift, but from something *in front of it*—and as she is drawn in, the cold grips her like a thousand desperate, clawing hands. She is crushed in between, by the weight of a million possible Earths that squeeze upon her from all sides, and the reality that she belongs to—the living room of her mother's house, the smoky soap bubble of the rift—folds up like a box, and Eleanor becomes nothing at all.

## mea

**M**ea presses herself against the membrane.

Efah looms ominously before her, wordless.

*She is gone,* Mea says.

Eleanor falls like a tiny ember into that ocean, and they watch her as she is carried far, far away.

Something tugs at Mea's form, and she trembles.

*What is it?* Efah asks.

*I felt—I felt something.*

*What did you feel?*

*Water,* Mea says.

It is different than the black tide she has grown accustomed to within her fishbowl. This water, invisible to her sight, seems to crowd out the blackness, to buoy her. It threads through her, encloses her.

*Did you feel it? Are we alone? Efah?*

Efah does not answer.

Which is an answer all its own.

## eleanor

**T**he first thing she notices is that she is not naked.

Her body is wrapped in some sort of animal hide. The clothing is the color of death, a peculiar and lifeless blue, unlike the hide of any animal she has ever seen before. Her feet are wrapped in the same hide. Taut, sinewy cords wind around it, transforming the hide into makeshift boots.

The second thing she notices is the fire, and the fire shows her everything else.

It flickers in a small round pit circled by stones. Its light reveals cold black soil, smoothed of life. A floor. There are bits of furniture; a chair made of cut tree limbs is held together with thin ropes, maybe the same as what binds the hide to her feet.

She can make out the walls of a structure around her. They flap and billow softly: they're made from animal hide, as well, tanned and tethered to slim poles and lashed to the ground to keep out the . . .

Snow.

Some of it has crept into the tent structure, anyway. She sees it collecting around the base of the animal-skin walls, mixed with dirt, as if it has been kicked back by someone's foot.

There's little else in the tent with her. Some rudimentary utensils on a stump beside the fire. A metal cup, some flint.

She tries to sit up but pitches over. Her body throbs painfully, as if she has been thrown from a car. She's colder than she has ever felt.

"Hello?" she says to the empty tent.

The tent walls flap angrily, and snow rushes in beneath one end. It melts quickly, warmed by the fire, and sinks into the dark soil.

She puts her feet on the ground and stands up. Her legs are numb and heavy, and her first step closer to the fire is a wobbly one, and she falls like a titan, crashing into the tree-branch chair.

WHEN SHE WAKES up, her legs are made of concrete; there is dirt in her mouth. An ancient cold swims up from the permafrost and fills her lungs with ice. The fire—so close to her face, she notices, realizing how close she must have come to burning herself to death—has dwindled, a small orange blanket that chews on ash-crusted wood.

A flap opens in the tent, and stinging snow whips in. She puts an arm over her eyes. The whiteness beyond the tent flap blinds her.

A dark figure stomps its feet and drops a bundle of cut wood upon the cold dirt. Eleanor is afraid, suddenly, and drags herself away from the fire with her feeble arms.

The figure stands still, bundled in heavy furs, watching her. The fire is too weak to light the stranger's face.

Eleanor's body feels like lead. After dragging herself only a few inches, she collapses to the ground.

"Leave me alone," Eleanor whispers. Her lips are cracked, cold. Speaking hurts.

The figure bends and scoops up a few pieces of wood, then lumbers close to the pit. The stranger brushes back the charred bits of used-up trees, then carefully arranges the fresh pieces in the center. It takes time, but the fire warms the icy chunks of new wood, and tiny veins of the stuff flare and smolder and smoke, and then the wood begins to glow orange. Eleanor rolls onto her back and stares up at the ceiling of the tent, and she notices for the first time the hole above her. Smoke twists up like licorice and passes through the hole and into the bright, cold sky.

The stranger goes down on one knee. Eleanor is too exhausted and cold and defeated to protest. The stranger's face is wrapped in dark cloth. Eleanor wishes she could fall again, fall straight through the Earth and come out again someplace else. She is afraid of her mother's dream world and of what her mother might do to her in it.

"Mea," she moans. "I want out."

The stranger peels the mask away, and her father smiles down at her.

Eleanor begins to cry, and her father says, "Oh, honey," and lifts her into his arms. She buries her face in the wet fur of his strange cloak, grateful that he exists in her mother's dreams. Maybe her father can help her save her mother. Maybe she won't have to do this alone.

His voice is crisp and joyous in her ear.

"My Esmerelda," he whispers. "You've come back to me."

And Eleanor realizes that this isn't her mother's dream at all.

\*    \*    \*

PAUL IS HUNCHED over the fire when Eleanor wakes many hours later. She watches him from her pallet of skins and furs. He stirs something in a pot that hangs from a tripod over the flames. She sniffs the air.

"Awake?" he says.

She nods.

"I've made something for you," he says, nodding at the pot.

It smells strange and delicious.

"What is it?"

He turns back to it, dips a ladle into the broth, and lifts it to his lips and slurps loudly.

"Not ready yet," he apologizes.

She remains beneath the heavy furs and flexes her toes. Unlike the day before, she can feel them, though they tingle painfully. She can feel the muscles in her calves tense, too. A good sign, she thinks.

"Dad," she says. "What happened to my legs?"

He settles back into the wooden chair and surprises her by lighting a long, slim pipe. Her father has never smoked.

"Found you," he says.

"Found me?"

"In the crick," he answers.

"I don't remember," Eleanor says.

"You were on the bank in the snow," he says. "Legs broke through the ice."

This isn't her father at all, she thinks. Her father doesn't talk this way. Her father doesn't smoke or wear fur.

"Blue as the old skies," he says. "Your legs were."

"The old skies?" she asks, confused.

"The old blues," he says. "Before the grays."

She stares at him.

"Long time ago," he says, seeing her confusion, "the skies were blue as birds."

"And now they aren't?"

"Then you went away from me," he explains. "And so did the blue."

He leans forward and sniffs the pot, then settles back into the chair again. He puffs on the pipe. A sweet smell fills the tent, mingling with the scent of food.

"They'll return now," he says. "Now that you're home again."

"Where are we?" she asks. "What is this place? Why are you dressed that way?"

Now her father looks confused. "It's our home, love. Always has been."

He climbs out of the chair and comes to her side. His palm is rough on her forehead, nothing like her father's skin should feel. Her father's touch is softer than this. Her father has the hands of a realtor. This person before her—this person is a mountain man, with hands like a bear's.

"You're addled," he says. "The cold-bite does it. It'll ease."

He rocks back onto his knees and sniffs the air.

"Food'll be a while yet," he says. "Sleep more, if you like."

The newness, the strangeness of it all overwhelms her. Sleep, she thinks. Yes, okay. Sleep.


WHEN SHE WAKES again, the tent is bright, the fire extinguished. She squints, adjusting to the light. The roof of the tent has been rolled back, and high above her she can see slate-blue skies, thin clouds disintegrating like cotton candy. The door to the tent is pinned open, and the white snowbound world has been replaced by a green one. There are distant hills, and she sees a thin wire of blue strung below them—"the crick," of course.

Directly before her, a green shoot has pushed up through the dirt.

As she watches, it unfolds a pair of damp new leaves, and a tiny white flower pushes open.

"This is a dream," she says aloud. "A dream, don't forget. Just a dream."

She lingers on the flower, then looks around for a bee. As if she has conjured it from nothing, a rotund yellow bee swoops past her ear and circles the flower before landing gingerly upon its ivory petals. To her amazement, it has wide, delicate dragonfly wings.

"Pink," she says.

The flower blushes pastel pink. The bee flits into the air, then settles back upon its petals.

Her father appears in the doorway. "Awake!"

Eleanor points at the flower. She starts to tell him what just happened—then she sees him more fully and forgets. His furs are gone, replaced by what looks like an animal-skin poncho. His heavy beard is half-gone, too, and in his hand is a sharp rock. The smooth side of his face is flecked with tiny cuts and beads of blood.

He waves his free hand at her. "Come," he says. "Come see the new world!"

Eleanor can only stare.

He laughs—*hoots*—and prances out of sight again. She can hear water splashing, can hear him gasp as he cuts his face again with the shaving rock.

Her fur blanket has been replaced with a single animal-hide sheet. She pulls it back and is surprised to see that her father has removed the hide leggings and boots from her body. She's wearing a poncho just like his. Her legs are pink and alive, and she wiggles her feet. Nothing hurts. Everything is fine.

"This is so bizarre," she says quietly.

Her belly rumbles, but she ignores it. Whatever her father eats, she no longer wants any part of it.

She gets up and walks slowly to the door of the tent, just as one entire wall falls away. Her father, bare-faced and alive, releases another set of lashes and begins to roll up the wide swath of sewn hides.

"What are you doing?"

"Sun," he says, pointing up. "Don't need this now."

Eleanor steps out into the grass—there is grass everywhere, as if there weren't just a field of snow here hours ago—and squints in the bright light, watching her father work. He happily deconstructs the tent, folding up the hides and gathering the tent poles.

"Told you the blue would return," her father sings out as he works.

Eleanor shields her eyes from the new sun and surveys her father's dreamscape. Even in the warm light, a chill knifes through her belly at what she sees.

THERE ARE THOUSANDS of them.

The crosses spread out in all directions from the tent site, each made from the branches of a tree or from ashen firewood remnants, their crossbeams held together by more of that twine she saw before. The sight of the graves crawling away from the tent is unlike anything she has ever seen. It is as if her father has set up camp in the middle of an old battlefield.

He puts his hand on her shoulder, and she jumps and shouts.

He ignores this and says, "What do you see?"

She looks up at him. Every nick from his primitive shave-job has been pasted over with a damp bit of soil.

Her father is insane.

"What do you see?" he asks again, sweeping his hand wide.

She shakes her head to clear it.

"I see . . . graves," she says. She is afraid to ask what is buried beneath each marker.

"No," he says. "Not graves. Memories." He shakes his head. "*Memorials.*"

She doesn't say anything to that.

"Every day that you were gone," he explains, "I made one."

Thousands of markers. Seven thousand, maybe eight. Eleanor cannot remember how old she is now, but she, too, has counted the days since Esmerelda died. A memory rushes back of a notebook she kept under her pillow, hidden from her mother. She had tried to write Esmerelda's name once for every day her sister had been gone. She filled the notebook quickly and lost count of how many days she had recorded. By the end, after she had filled the pages and the cardboard covers of the notebook, she had lost the ability to make any sense of Esmerelda's name. It transformed into something alien and unfamiliar, something without meaning.

"But now my Esmerelda is home," her father says. "And we must work."

He turns and produces a wooden bucket filled with sticky black tar. He puts it on the ground and then hands Eleanor a stick. He shows her how to dip it into the tar and stir it around, folding the black stuff over the stick in a thick paste.

"Not too close to your hand," he says. "Bad."

He snaps flint against a knife blade, and a spark falls from his hands.

"Put your stick here," he says.

She holds it out, and he makes more sparks. One settles on the tar, and it whooshes to life. Eleanor shouts and drops the stick, but her father catches it before it falls to the ground.

"Hold here," he says. "Do what I do."

He makes another torch for himself, then walks into the field and touches it to the first cross. After a moment, the cross is wrapped in flame. Her father smiles happily and gestures at her to do the same. She watches him set another on fire, then another.

He waits.

Heat radiates from her torch like an oven. Eleanor carries it into the field and stops before one of the untouched crosses. She imagines her father kneeling in the snow, teeth chattering, lashing two sticks together, then hammering them into the hard ground. She thinks of her notebook, of the empty bed that occupied the room she once shared with her sister—the bed she had to haul to the curb on her own, because her parents were too broken to help her. She remembers boxing up her sister's things and carrying them to the attic. Esmerelda's absence was only one of many holes in the world now: the gutted side of the room Eleanor couldn't bear to fill; the hole in the attic where she had jammed Esmerelda's things, hoping she might forget where she'd put them; the hole her sister's tiny body had punched in the windshield of their mother's car.

Like her father, she tips the torch to a cross, and they work side by side, burning the fields clean of memories.

SHE STAYS WITH her father for weeks. The crosses crumble into small black piles of charred wood, and then one morning they are simply gone. The skies are blue all day. She asks about the tent—what if it rains? But this land knows no rain. Her father's dream world seems to exist in a binary state: everything is wonderful, or everything is painful. Mistaking her arrival for the return of his perished daughter has inverted his world. Sunflower groves push up overnight from the green earth. The creek deepens into a river, and they swim and splash in the sunlight.

At night she tells him stories of where she has been, building a history for Esmerelda. She tells him of the lands beyond the mountains, of shining cities filled with beautiful people who make exciting things and share them. He asks her where her favorite place was, and she tells him about Anchor Bend, about the town and its history, about the people who have built homes and made lives there.

She does not know if she is fooling herself, but she thinks she sees a spark of recognition in his eyes when she talks about the tide wall, about the shops and businesses on the main street.

"I met a woman there," she says one evening.

"Where?"

"In Anchor Bend, the town beside the sea."

She has begun to speak like her father, slipping into his cadence and the sense of history that swells in his clipped sentences. He, in return, has met her halfway, saying more than a few words at a time, his speech becoming ever so much more casual.

"What was her name?"

Eleanor says, "Agnes."

Her father tips his head, considering this. "Agnes. A sturdy name."

"Yes, and a pretty one," Eleanor says. "She grew up there. Her father was a warrior. Her mother was a goddess of the sea."

Paul listens intently, lying on his back, staring up at the ocean of stars.

"She lives there with a girl," Eleanor says. She's frightened of saying the wrong thing, or too much, but she must try.

"What girl?"

"She has a daughter."

Her father grunts approval. "Daughters are life."

"Her daughter looks just like me," Eleanor says.

Paul turns onto his side. Their bedrolls are a few feet apart. He plucks at the grass. "Just like you?"

Eleanor nods, not looking at him. She watches the moon and wonders if it is the same moon that hangs over the real Anchor Bend.

"Her name—" Eleanor stops.

Her father waits.

"Her name is Eleanor."

She turns over and looks at her father, searching his face for any sign of recognition.

Nothing.

"I want you to meet them," Eleanor says.

"Bring them," her father answers. "They are welcome here."

"No," Eleanor says. "They are very happy there. But we could go to them."

Her father looks around. "This is home."

"No. Home is you and me."

"We don't need them."

"I want to be with them. Don't you want me to be happy?"

Her father looks pained. "Yes. But—"

She waits, but he doesn't finish.

"Think about it," she says. "That's all."

He rolls onto his back wordlessly, and Eleanor goes to sleep.

HER FATHER'S BEDROLL is gone when she wakes up. The grass, matted flat beneath him during the night, is already beginning to rise. She calls his name, but he doesn't answer.

She sits where she is for hours. There is nowhere for her to go. She thinks that she could walk to the horizon in any direction, and then the world might simply fall away into nothingness. What would have happened if she and her father had begun walking toward Anchor Bend? It's his world. Would it have borders for him? Would his sleeping brain fill in the blanks? Would it even matter in which direction they walked?

He comes over the hill when the sun is high above.

"We go," he says.

He has fashioned a tall pack from animal hide and filled it with things they will need. Bladders of water hang from his hips. The metal cook pot dangles from a looped string, bouncing against the pack as he walks. He leans on a gnarled walking stick.

Eleanor sits up. "Anchor Bend?"

"What my Esmerelda asks, my Esmerelda shall have," he answers.

He begins to walk, and Eleanor follows.

THEY WALK FOR miles and miles, and the horizon only recedes. The world does not crumble into the void, as Eleanor had feared it might. She sees no steaming craters, no oceans of dark matter. There are only more green hills, more spreading forests, more branching rivers and clouds and lush mountains. There are animals, too. Though most of her father's possessions seem to have been made from the husks of dead creatures, Eleanor had, before now, seen none herself. But now there are flocks of great-winged birds, with wingspans dozens of feet wide, rising from the treetops as she and her father pass by. As they crest a field speckled with wildflowers, Eleanor can see a herd of something—elk? buffalo? she can't tell—lazily milling about, the big dark shadows of idle clouds drifting over them.

She and her father do not talk much. He seems content with this, as if it hasn't occurred to him to ask why she went away or how she came back. As they walk, Eleanor glances at him surreptitiously, his face golden in the sun, his hair turned the color of pale yellow silk. He stares happily ahead, often closing his eyes and turning his head toward the warmth above. He looks younger, and Eleanor realizes that he *is* younger: the nicks on his face have disappeared, his beard has faded, and his skin has flushed with color. The crow's-feet around his eyes have softened, and a few hours later they are gone altogether.

Before long he looks the way she remembers him from her childhood, in the months before Esmerelda died.

"Dad," Eleanor ventures, wanting to call his attention to the change that has overtaken him. But when he looks down at her, so young and alive, not much more than a kid himself, her breath catches, and she can't say a thing.

He just smiles, and they continue walking.

"Look," he says as they emerge from a grove of tall oaks. Before them is a new sea, one made of flowers that have grown impossibly tall. There are rose-colored flowers, rich, plum-tinted blooms.

Eleanor has no words.

Her father's dreamscape is a beautiful fantasyland.

THEY SLEEP FOR many weeks beneath a perfect hooked moon, listening to the calls of night birds and the symphonies of crickets and frogs. They sleep at the bottom of a small mountain one night, and in the morning they climb it, her father's hands looped in the straps of his animal-hide pack, Eleanor walking with his sturdy stick. The mountain is soft beneath her feet, the ground spongy and inviting like spring tundra. They climb for hours and hours, and when they reach the top, a flat shelf of rock, they sit and eat bits of dried meat that her father has carried along.

Far below them a valley spreads wide like a bowl. It is carpeted with tall, waving grasses, and a stream winds through it like a shoelace.

Eleanor feels a tingle at the base of her neck.

"It's beautiful," her father says, happily munching on a handful of nuts.

But Eleanor is not so sure. He's right, of course, and the valley is quite stunning to look at, but Eleanor feels as if she's looking backward in time. The view below chews at her. She knows this place.

"That's quite nice," her father says, pointing.

Far away—miles, perhaps—is a structure in the middle of the valley. She recognizes it, too. It's a cabin, one that her father built long ago in his workshop in the attic. If they walk far enough, Eleanor thinks, maybe they will stumble upon the other houses that her father created. Maybe one of them will have a broken mailbox.

But this cabin worries her. It is too perfect, too lovely.

A tuft of clouds passes overhead, throwing tiny pale shadows onto the meadows below. Eleanor jerks as a memory returns to her: an ash forest, poisonous and tumultuous. She stares down at the valley, and the sense of something looming in the paradise below only grows.

She turns to her father, and she knows what she has to do.


"Anchor Bend is not far away," she tells him. She points at the far rim of the valley, where the grasses give way to dense forests and

march up into the mountains again. "Over there, past those mountains."

"We should go!" he chirps, gathering the remnants of their lunch.
But Eleanor puts her hand on his and shakes her head.

"They're very shy," she says, hoping he won't press her. "I think
I should go and tell them we're coming, so that they have time to
prepare for us. It would be the polite thing to do."

He considers this and then, to her surprise, acquiesces. "I'll sleep
here," he says, patting the rock. He sweeps his hand over the pan-
orama. "I'll wake to this."

She tells him she will return in a few days, and they'll go to Anchor Bend then, together. He offers his pack, but she doesn't want
the weight. He gives her a folded package and tells her to eat to keep
up her strength, and then Eleanor kisses his youthful cheek, and she
sets off down the mountainside alone.

He does not tell her to take care, for what harm can come to her
in this perfect world he has created?

Eleanor sidesteps down the mountain, her sense of dread growing, and when she finally comes to the trees and steps into their
thicket of shade and rich green smells, she falls through the world
and disappears.

# mea

*L*ook, Efah says.

Mea sees the tiny, sparking flame growing larger in the
distance.

*The child returns.*

# *eleanor*

E leanor wakes up on the floor of the garage. Her arm is stained black from the old oil spot. She is, unsurprisingly, naked. She crosses the concrete to the garage door and stands on tiptoe to peek outside. It's raining. Her father's car is not in the driveway. It's late morning, as best she can tell.

Her father must be at work.

She is as quiet as can be when she slips into the house. For a long time she stands in the hall, listening for the sound of her mother moving about.

A terrible thought occurs to her—what if her latest vacation from reality has lasted for years yet again? What if she has lost the opportunity to save her mother? What if the house is this quiet because Agnes has already died of her cancer?

She goes to the downstairs bathroom and turns on the light. There are fancy soaps in a dish, a bit dusty from disuse. A guest towel hangs on a bar. She looks at herself in the mirror and recognizes the shape of her face and body. If she has aged, it cannot be by more than a few days, maybe a few weeks.

She moves through the kitchen and dining room and into the living room, where her father had slept upright. The curtains are drawn, the room tidy. A pair of glasses rests on the side table, and she picks them up. They're reading glasses, masculine in form. She feels an ache inside—in this world, her father has aged. She had grown accustomed to his recaptured youth.

She wonders how he is coping now, a grieving father of two dead children, caring for a dying ex-wife who despises him.

She turns to the staircase and is stopped by the sight of her mother's chair.

Her father's Glacier Pilots T-shirt is folded neatly upon it.

Resting on the shirt is a folded piece of paper.

She stares at it for a long time, the silence of the house rising around her, the creak of old wood and the tick of the water heater gone for now.

At last she opens it.

She reads its contents once, twice, then again.

A tiny rustle comes from upstairs, from her mother's bedroom—an invitation, but a dark one. Eleanor turns to look at the staircase. The stairs seem to multiply and grow taller, farther apart, as she watches.

She unfolds the T-shirt and pulls it over her head, the soft scent of detergent filling her nose.

She returns the note to the chair, walks to the stairs, and begins to climb.

# *the keeper*

D on't go!"

The keeper's throat burns with the effort of shouting. Her body is little more than bones dressed in skin, her skin little more than paper. She sobs bitterly, broken at last. Her shadow has weakened, too, just a dusky smudge on the raw ground. She has her answer now, she thinks. When she goes, her shadow will pass, as well.

The beasts retreat, with each step cracking the charred crust beneath their feet. The small one leans against the other, hardly able to support its own weight. They stagger together through the broken landscape, searching for a new home.

"Don't go," she whispers again.

The large beast cranes its neck to look at her, and the keeper holds its beautiful gaze for a moment.

Then the sky ruptures in flames, and the moment ends.

\*    \*    \*

A BRIGHT ORANGE flower bulges in the black clouds, and the keeper forgets her woes immediately. The air turns electric and begins to twist, the rain turning to curved needles as a funnel forms. The keeper rises on spindly legs, fixated on the growing maelstrom. It is the same as before, the sky pregnant with her enemy, and she summons every bit of strength she has, and she screams at the sky.

Rage like a thousand suns boils within her.

She is a crushed and flightless bird. But she is not finished. Not while she can stand.

She puts her hands up, curls her fingers, and beckons the demon in the sky.

"*Come!*" she bellows, and her shadow flushes dark against the earth, suddenly strong.

## mea

*B*ring *her to us,* Efah says to Mea. *I must know if she has succeeded.*

Mea says, *I don't think I'm in control anymore.*

Eleanor treks up the stairs, each step tentative, deliberate. Mea peers through the membrane at the familiar staircase, the thready carpet on the landing. She remembers that carpet, suddenly. Remembers slipping her bare toes into the shag loops of the upstairs rug. Remembers snipping the loops with scissors one afternoon when no one was looking.

Eleanor knocks lightly on her mother's open bedroom door but doesn't enter. There, small on the bed her parents once shared, is Agnes. Her skin sags over her shriveled frame; what muscles she had are all but gone. Her auburn hair has grayed and fallen out in clumps, and the little that remains is wispy and sparse. Her sunken eyes are closed. She breathes weakly.

*She does not have much time,* Efah says.

Mea stares at the woman on the bed. *Tell me the rules,* she says.

*The rules?*

*You told me there are laws about the dream realm. Tell me.*

*I can only speculate, you understand.*

*Yes, yes.*

*Dream worlds are refuges from life,* Efah says. *The same way that the rift is full of lost, aching souls, the dream worlds are full of the living, seeking escape from their own deaths, their own pain and regrets. They use the dreams like a cloak, to protect them.*

*But there's a way in.*

*The dream world is not impenetrable,* Efah agrees. *There is still a seam where it closes, and the child has found a way through.*

*What will happen?* Mea asks. *When Eleanor enters?*

*The world that her mother has so carefully shut out will rush in. The cancer. The pain. The regret, the fear, the memories. Eleanor will release all of it, like a flood. It will frighten her mother. It will overwhelm them both.*

*Why are you helping her? Why do you help me? Why now, after all this time?*

Efah is quiet for a long time. Then: *I cannot say.*

Agnes stirs ever so slightly on the bed.

Eleanor takes a step forward, into the doorway.

*It will be a mistake, won't it?* Mea asks.

*It is time. Take her,* Efah commands.

Mea does.

# *eleanor*

Her parents' bedroom, once so bright and cheerful, has become a dour, odorous cave. The curtains are drawn, the room gloomy. The air is heavy and still, as if it hasn't stirred in weeks. It is pungent, dense with the smell of unwashed skin, of sickness.

For a long time Eleanor stands in the doorway, her heart caught in her throat, staring at her mother.

At what *used* to be her mother.

The thing on the bed is hardly human anymore. It is spindly and compact, its branch-thin limbs pulled close to its body. It doesn't resemble Agnes Witt any more than a crushed dog on a highway resembles a lion.

"Mom," Eleanor whispers.

A breathing apparatus hisses portentously beside the bed. A thin, clear cord slinks across the sheets, connected to a plastic mask strapped over Agnes's mouth and nose. A green-and-silver oxygen tank stands on a cart below the machine, pumping rich air through the cord.

Eleanor is afraid. She forgets about her mission, forgets the rift, forgets her sister. The only thing she can think of is her mother's funeral. It looms over the scene before her like a thunderhead. Her mother cannot be more than a few hours from death. She cannot help but wonder where her father is, where the hospice nurse is. Will no one be here with her mother when the end comes?

She wonders what it will do to her father to have lost them all. First Esmerelda, in a violent car crash. Then, a decade later, Eleanor, who, for all he knows, has simply disappeared into thin air, never to return. And finally Agnes, who in her final years has turned into a pile of twigs beneath a blanket.

Agnes stirs, and Eleanor steps forward, her eyes damp.

"Mom?"

Mea takes her—

—AND ELEANOR BECOMES a missile.

Around her the air burns hot. Her hair is almost torn from her scalp. Her breath is stolen away; her eyes dry out. She can barely see—the sky flickers like a forest fire, turning her skin a hundred million shades of orange. Through the acrid haze she sees—what? Shapes, blurry shapes. She fights the urge to scream.

There is ground down there—that much she can see. It is charred and smoking, some of it burning, some of it weeping magma.

*Magma?*

Where is she?

And then the sky clears, and Eleanor punches through the atmosphere and the roiling black cloud cover, and she understands, suddenly. She knows *exactly* where she is. The upheaval far below her is the wreckage of the lush green valley she saw from her father's mountain. The mountains have been transformed into vast fields of steaming rock. She can see cinders and ashen splinters scattered about, the only remaining evidence of entire forests.

*Ash forests.*

*I've been here before.*

This is her mother's dream.

Her mother's valley.

IT IS HER mother's nightmare.

The black clouds smell like gasoline. They are thick, sludgy, and seem to slow her fall, tugging at her like oatmeal. The air is dense and oppressive and utterly hot. Eleanor breaks free of the clouds altogether, and the ruined world spreads out before her. She cannot reconcile the pretty valley of her father's dream with this perverse vision.

When she was here before, long ago, the forests stood tall, albeit blackened by fire and stripped of their leaves and needles. She remembers the toxic downpour, remembers hiding naked in the mud, sheltering herself from the rains.

Three things catch her eye:

The first is the gaping crater—no, not a crater: a fissure, a bottomless pit—that hisses darkly. It must be a mile across, and she cannot see its bottom, even from this high. It plunges into the earth so far that it might very well have opened the entire planet straight through.

The second is a pair of dinosaurs. *Dinosaurs?* What else could they be? They are immense, like blue whales trudging about on land, except—bigger. Much, much bigger. The larger of the two beasts stares placidly at her, tracking Eleanor's fall, and then it turns away.

But the third thing—

The third thing is her mother.

Agnes is a scarecrow silhouetted against the flaming earth, naked and grimy. Skeletal. And she is looking straight at Eleanor.

Shouting something Eleanor can't understand.

The ground rushes up at Eleanor, and Eleanor wonders for the first time if she will survive this fall. She remembers a story Jack told her once, about a woman who fell out of a plane at twenty thousand feet and survived. "She was okay?" Eleanor had asked him. And Jack had shrugged and said, "Well—she broke, like, forty bones. But she was *alive*."

But this isn't reality, Eleanor cautions herself. This is a dream. There are no rules.

Except there *are* rules.

There are most certainly rules, and Eleanor does not write them.

Below her, the scarecrow who is Agnes Witt waves her open hand at the sky, and Eleanor feels her descent slow, then stop. She hangs suspended in the thick air, breathing hard, her lungs aching, and for one brief moment she thinks that her mother has just saved her.

"Mom!" she calls.

But Agnes doesn't seem to hear her or recognize her. She raises her hand, palm open, turning it this way and that. With a cold stare she holds Eleanor's gaze. Then her eyes flash darkly, and her fingers curl shut, forming a hard, bony fist.

Eleanor gasps as an invisible hand closes around her, tight as a vise.

*The pain, oh, my god, oh, my god—*

Eleanor screams.

# *the keeper*

I t feels so *good*.

The keeper clenches her fist. She can see her enemy clearly now—pink and naked, with fire-red hair and emerald-green eyes that sparkle with pain—suspended high above the valley.

"I expected . . . more," she says. She looks down at her shadow. "How could someone so small cause so much destruction?"

The keeper's nails dig into her palm until threads of blood stream down her wrist. A piercing scream splits the sky above. The girl twists and struggles in the keeper's invisible grip. Her scream crumbles the rocks around the keeper's feet, sets the earth vibrating like a tuning fork.

"*You are not welcome here!*" the keeper bellows.

She squeezes tighter, and one of the girl's legs snaps in half. Squeezes again, and more bones break, the dry, awful sound echoing across the dead land like gunshots. The girl's tormented scream is horrific—but the keeper's next squeeze chokes the child into silence.

Then the keeper opens her hand, and the red-haired girl plummets from the sky, gurgling, and strikes the earth like a sack of blood.

\*   \*   \*

THE KEEPER SITS down on a rock and stares at the heap of bones and flesh and red hair.

She can feel purpose return to her, like a sun that blooms deep in her chest. She swallows air, expels it; this time she doesn't cough. She spits on the earth. Her saliva is almost clear, not black.

Where her spittle lands, a single blade of grass wriggles through the ash and charred dirt. An inch, then two, then six, and then it stops. The keeper bends over and gently caresses the shoot with one dirty fingertip.

"Welcome back," she says.

A few feet away, the crumpled girl clicks and moans.

She isn't dead.

Not yet.


THE KEEPER STRIDES over the broken earth, her shadow firmly re-affixed to her heels. In her wake, little crumpled clovers fight their way through the soil, filling her empty footprints. Tiny, curious green tendrils reach out, rousing the life still buried beneath the destruction, and in response, a thousand blades of grass rise like beautiful ghosts.

The girl's body is hardly recognizable; her legs are shattered, her torso pulped. Pale white bone splits her skin. Parts of her have burst open like fruit; her blood has turned the ground into a sticky pond. Bits of dirt and debris and ash settle onto its surface.

The girl groans and sucks in a breath, then coughs from the mashed-up cavern that once was her mouth. A froth of pink bubbles coats her ruined tongue.

The keeper crouches beside the girl. Warm blood squelches be-tween her toes.

The girl's face is wrecked, her eye sockets collapsed, her nose crushed into an unrecognizable mess. It is hard to tell if she even knows that the keeper is there. The keeper cups what she thinks is the girl's chin in her hand and lifts it. One eye is smashed in its socket, weeping viscous fluid. The other eye is filled with blood, but it flicks in the keeper's direction, staring blindly.

"Only a child," the keeper says.

The dying girl says nothing. She coughs. Blood spills from her mouth in a rush, like gouts of water from a hand pump.

"What were you doing here?" the keeper asks. "Why destroy my home?"

With every beat of the girl's heart, blood jets from cuts and gashes all over her body. The red pond widens around her. The girl's jaw, broken into pieces, slides this way and that, and a thin click comes from within.

"Did you say something?" the keeper asks.

Another click.

The girl groans, the sound horrid and unintelligible. "*Aaaaa-naaa.*"

"I don't understand," the keeper says.

She grabs the girl's jaw-pieces and holds them together, grinding the bones, trying to shape them back into something familiar. The girl's blood-red eye wheels about wildly, in pain.

The keeper holds the girl's jaw in place and breathes softly on the broken skin and bone. In her hand, the broken jaw stitches itself together beneath the girl's skin. The girl's mouth still doesn't move right—too many other bones are destroyed—but it is close enough.

"Say again," the keeper orders.

The girl gags, coughs. She moves her jaw like a rusted mailbox.

"*Maaaaa—,*" she moans.

The keeper frowns. "*Maaaaa,*" she mimics. "That's all you have to say for yourself?" She stands up and turns to her shadow. "Take her to the pit. Put this . . . *infant* out of its misery."

"—*mmmmm,*" the girl finishes. "*Maahmmm.*"

"Enough," the keeper says. "Quiet, now."

The keeper's shadow peels free of her feet, fastens itself to the girl's own broken limbs, and begins to pull.

The girl screams again, and the keeper turns away, bored.

"*Mamm*," the girl cries. "*Mom!*"

The keeper pauses and looks over her shoulder at the dying child. The girl's eye flits to the left, to the right, then seems to focus intently on the keeper, twitching all the while. The keeper holds the girl's stare until the girl herself cannot do so any longer. The girl's pupil expands rapidly, then contracts to a fine point, then abruptly, as though an optic nerve has been severed, her eye sags in its fractured socket and stares dumbly at nothing. The life goes out of her, and her crushed body relaxes and is still.

"To work," the keeper says to her shadow, turning her back on the girl.

There is green everywhere, bursting up from the rubble. High above, the keeper sees a hint of blue through the fading clouds. Something flies into her face, and she bats it away—then realizes that it is a strand of hair, waving in a soft breeze. She touches her head and feels the brush of new growth there, winding through her fingers even now.

"To work," the keeper repeats, her lungs and heart full.

While her shadow drags away what remains of the girl, the keeper lifts her hands gracefully, like a conductor, and great boulders rise from the ground, as light as feathers.

## *mea*

I don't see her.

*She is there*, Efah says. *Barely*.

*Where?* Mea asks.

Then she sees a faint, sputtering red cinder, far away in the blackness.

*What's wrong with her?* Mea asks. *Why is she so dim?*

*I feared this could happen.*

Mea feels a hard stone of panic form within her. There is a faint note of pleasure in Efah's words.

*What do you mean?*

Efah says, *Her thread. It is torn.*

Mea bristles. *You knew this would happen! You let me send her there, knowing that she—*

The strange water within Mea's fishbowl gathers itself and rushes away from her, past her, moving desperately toward the faint ember in the distance.

Efah senses it, too, and is made uneasy. Without a word, he backs away from the membrane and disappears into the greater dark of the rift.

*Did you feel—*, Mea begins, then stops, aghast.

In the distance, the tiny spark that is Eleanor flares briefly and goes dark.

*part four*

*1978*

# *agnes*

**R**ain.

Agnes carefully saws through the baguette. Flakes of crust flutter onto the cutting board. The radio plays a Marvin Gaye song quietly, one she doesn't know. She hums along anyway, feeling the music in her hips. She sets aside the knife and reaches for the butter, then gasps softly and stops. She puts a hand on her round belly, turns, and leans against the counter. She can feel the baby kicking, almost in time with the music.

"You like that?" Agnes asks.

Six weeks from her due date, and all she can think about is food. Her appetite had fled her during the first few months, worrying her. She and Paul had stayed up late one evening after an appointment with Agnes's doctor. Paul wanted her to eat anyway, and he'd prepared chicken and dumplings—"My great-grandmother's Texas recipe," he said—but Agnes couldn't manage a bite. Even the smell of food made her want to throw up.

But now she wants everything. She slathers butter and pickle relish on the baguette, craving the weird combination in some primal way that doesn't even make sense to her. Paul wrinkles his nose at her unusual food pairings. She thinks that Paul would be less critical of them if they didn't seem like something a four-year-old would make herself for dinner: peanut-butter-and-maple-syrup sandwiches, pizza with ketchup on top.

The baby kicks again, harder.

Paul is confident that it will be a drummer. They often lie awake at night, Paul's cheek resting on the slope of Agnes's belly, laughing at the rhythm of the baby's kicks. The thumps come so quickly that they form a staccato beat, as if the baby is a tiny boxer trapped inside a punching bag.

"Except it's learned to punch with its feet, too," Paul says.

Agnes carries her plate into the dining room and sits down with a magazine. She narrates her actions so the baby will know her voice when it is born. "Your father says this magazine is trash," she says, laying a copy of *Cosmopolitan* on the table, "but I like it. You'll get to know that about us. Your father takes everything way too seriously. Me, I like the stories on TV and the gossip pages."

Outside, the rain comes down harder.

THEY PUT OFF choosing a name for as long as they can.

"We should wait until it's born," Paul says.

Agnes disagrees, if only because she hates calling the baby "it."

"We'll pick tonight," she announces one evening when Paul comes home from work, and that's what they do. No television, no board games, no yard work. They sit together in the bathtub, pink bubbles covering all but their knees and the crown of Agnes's belly. She rests with her back against Paul's chest, their skin slick and soapy, and Paul puts his arms around her.

"Henry," she says. "If it's a boy."

She can feel his frown.

"What's wrong with Henry?" she asks.

"I knew a kid named Henry when I was little," Paul says. "We called him Slimesucker."

"I don't want to know why," Agnes says. "Fine. No Henry."

"No Henry," Paul agrees.

"What about Robert? It's a good, solid name."

"Robert's fine," Paul says. "Boring, maybe, but I guess that's not necessarily a bad thing. You can surprise people when you're a Robert. They don't expect anything from you, and then—*wham*—you write a best seller, and they ask each other where in the world *that* came from."

"It's not a boring name. Maybe Stephen?"

"Gerald."

"Ugh. No."

Paul says, "What about if it's a girl?"

Agnes says, "I don't know. I haven't thought about that."

"Maybe we could name her after—"

"Don't say it," Agnes warns.

But Paul finishes: "—after your mother."

Agnes tries to get up but struggles against the wet porcelain.

"Honey," Paul says.

"I told you," Agnes says, floundering around, trying to stand up. "I don't want to do that."

She slips and splashes back into the water, and a wave of suds cascades onto the floor.

"God *damn* it," she says, then stops struggling and slumps against Paul. "God damn *you*."

"Sorry," Paul says. "I just thought—"

"*Fuck* what you just thought."

"It would be a nice tribute."

"Yes, let's name our child after a terrible, hateful woman who abandoned her family," Agnes says. She starts to cry.

"Hey," Paul says.

Agnes waves him off and covers her face.

"It isn't as if she ran away," he says quietly. "She disappeared. Something might have happened to her. It isn't like she ran off with a movie star or—"

"I know what you think," she says. She sighs. "And, shit. I get it. I appreciate that you want to think the best of her. But—"

Agnes sits up, water streaming down her sides. She labors to turn sideways, then faces Paul. She parts her knees to make room for her belly and leans forward.

"It doesn't matter if she ran away or if she drowned at sea or if she was—it doesn't matter," she says. "I was a child, Paul. I was a goddamn child, and my mother fucking vanished when I needed her most. What do you think it was like, growing up with Dad without her? I spent all my childhood making sure he was okay while he got worse and worse and worse." She looks away and shakes her head bitterly. "Childhood. *Hardly.* So I don't want to name our child after the person who took everything away from me. Including herself."

Paul says, "But she was still your mother."

Agnes just glares at him.

BUT IT ISN'T a boy, and it isn't a girl.

It's two girls.

Agnes wakes up from an afternoon nap, three weeks before her due date, to find the bed drenched. Paul comes home from work when she calls, grabs the bags that they packed, and drives her to the hospital. It's a Thursday. The labor is prolonged, painful; the girls don't come until early Sunday morning. Agnes is only semiconscious when the first cries sound in the crowded hospital room, and she doesn't hear the nurse exclaim, "There's another!" She only grips Paul's hand and pulls him close and whispers, "You name it," and passes out.

When she wakes up, the girls have been washed and tagged and swaddled and are sleeping in a rolling bassinet beside the hospital bed. Paul is standing over them, enraptured—she can see on his face that he will be a better father than she will be a mother. She sees the two babies—each with a thicket of red hair, swaddled in pink blankets, one a little larger than the other—and then looks back at Paul.

He hasn't noticed that she's awake.

"I'm going to be the worst mother," Agnes says quietly.

He shakes his head and opens his mouth, but she puts a finger to her lips.

"My mother *left* me," Agnes whispers to him. "I don't know what a mother *is*."

Paul puts his hand on Agnes's. "We'll do it together," he says.

But he has missed the point. Agnes is not afraid of being a parent. She's afraid of being a mother.

She's afraid of those little girls.

"There are two of them," she says.

Paul nods. "Two beautiful girls. I'm so proud of you."

"What are their names?" she asks.

Paul hesitates, then puts his hand on the first bassinet.

"This is Esmerelda."

He looks at Agnes for a reaction, then puts his hand on the next bassinet.

"And this . . . is Eleanor," he says.

Agnes studies the girls without looking at Paul.

"I love you," he says hurriedly. "Are you mad?"

"No," Agnes says. She doesn't meet his eyes, but after a long while, she says again, "No, I'm not mad."

He takes her hand and squeezes. She makes no room for him on the hospital bed. Paul smiles and stretches out in a vinyl chair. When sometime later the girls wake—first Esmerelda, then Eleanor—Paul shoots up from his chair, but Agnes doesn't stir.

WEEKS LATER, WHEN the girls are finally asleep at four a.m., Paul returns to their bedroom. He stubs his toe on the cedar chest at the end of their bed, and the jolt stirs Agnes from sleep. She blinks sleepily at him in the pale light.

"It's snowing," he says, voice hushed. "I rocked them by the window and watched it. It's really coming down."

Agnes says, "It's so early."

"It's a little past four," Paul says.

"I mean, it's early for snow."

"Oh," he says. "Yes. It is."

He opens the curtains before he joins Agnes in the bed. He turns on his side, then scoots backward until he bumps into her.

"No," she says reflexively. "I'm not ready yet."

"Just be close," he says. "Watch the snow with me."

Agnes sighs and turns over and rests her arm over Paul's chest.

"I bet there's six inches by morning," he speculates.

"It's already morning."

"You know what I mean."

The snow drifts down like feathers, glittering like crisp diamonds in the glow of the back porch light. The house is still, the girls slumbering. Agnes can hear Paul's breath slow, and when he is asleep, she lifts her arm away, turns her back to him, and pulls a pillow close to her breast. This isn't what she expected—none of it. Her insides are knotted, her chest hollowed out. There should be room in there for her family, she knows. There should be room for herself. But the space is thunderously empty.

She lies awake for a long time, the silence around her so complete that she can almost hear the snowflakes crushing each other on the lawn below. Sleep finally overtakes her as the sun begins to rise, turning the room to rose and taffeta. Before long, Paul will wake her to tell her that it's time to feed the twins, and Agnes will sleepwalk through her day, as she has begun to sleepwalk through every one of them.

She doesn't know what she expected from motherhood. She feels like a toddler thrown into college, completely inexperienced in the language of mothers and daughters. Beside her Paul begins to snore lightly. She envies him his contented rest. She feels as if they are unevenly matched: he is ecstatic to be a father and cannot understand why Agnes is not similarly excited.

She tries to think of the last time and place that she and Paul were perfectly in step, perfectly happy. It occurs to her as she slowly drifts to sleep that the last time she felt that way was during their vacation in the woods, when they'd hiked miles from any town and stayed in the most remote of cabins. She'd chopped wood; he'd fished in the stream. They'd made love while rain pounded against the roof and stirred the evening mists, then rocked in chairs on the porch while a pond formed on the valley floor. When they returned, Paul worked for months in the attic, building a replica of the cabin, settled in a painted plywood valley, and presented it to her as a birthday gift.

Now, in the ghostly stillness of the house, she lowers herself into sleep, descending through wispy clouds into the tall, waving grasses of that isolated, familiar valley. She stands barefoot, naked, beside a creek and marvels at the warm breeze on her skin, in her hair, at the quietude that envelops her.

She kneels beside the water and drags her fingers over its surface. The water beads on her skin. She looks for fish and sees a few, and she plunges her hand into the water to startle them, her heart suddenly alive like a child's. Her hand disappears into the inches-deep creek up to her wrist, then her forearm, then her elbow, and Agnes wiggles her fingers, feeling the faintest brush of wind in a gaping void that yawns beneath the earth. She removes her hand from the stream and inspects it. It isn't wet at all.

She knows that she is dreaming. She looks up at the clouds and wonders if the same void exists above them, out of sight. And around her, past the mountains that seem to cup the valley in their palm. What lies beyond that craggy range?

Birds flutter overhead, sailing low over the meadow and skidding down upon the water. They flap and paddle about, dipping their beaks into the stream, and Agnes smiles. She feels a bit like Eve, permitted reentry into the garden.

A tiny mewling sound comes from the sheaves of grass on the opposite side of the creek. Agnes cocks her head and stares. The grass moves, but nothing emerges. So Agnes steps over the water, the soft valley floor spongy beneath her bare toes, and cautiously kneels before the tall grass. She leans forward and parts it and finds, to her surprise, a pair of lizard-like creatures, tiny and tangled together in the undergrowth. Broken bits of red shell are scattered around their damp bodies.

They look like dinosaurs, almost, like the pictures in the books Agnes read as a little girl.

One is a little larger than the other. It looks up at Agnes, its dark eyes gleaming.

Then it recoils, as if it senses something wrong, and before Agnes can react, the little thing urges the smaller creature to its feet and leans into it, and the two strange little beasts flee, damp and clumsy, into the grass. Agnes stands up, the wind whipping urgently through her auburn hair, and watches the grass ripple as the small creatures run like hell, putting as much ground between her and them as they can.

She turns and surveys the valley that unfolds behind her, around her, and is not surprised one bit to see that the sun has been chewed up by the lumbering clouds, to see the distant trees bending under the sudden winds. A single drop of water spatters on her shoulder, and she holds out her hand, and the rain fills her cupped palm in minutes. There is nowhere to shelter herself—the woods are easily a mile or more away.

She looks down at her body. Rain drips between her breasts, slides down her belly. That her body is changed is only a mild curiosity— the marks on her abdomen are gone; her breasts are smaller, her hips narrower. Her skin is pink and alive and—

She stops. There, against her thigh, is the strangest thing.

She reaches down, nervously, and takes the thing in her finger-tips, holding it up to the dim sky to inspect it.

A damp sliver of reddish shell, brittle and cracked.

Agnes drops it and reaches between her legs.

Her hand comes away red with blood, speckled with shell fragments.

She wakes up.

Paul is shaking her. Her head pounds, her breasts throb.

"I'm sorry," Paul says. "They're hungry."

The girls are bawling in their cribs. Paul gently lifts Esmerelda into his arms and begins to sway. Almost immediately the little girl calms and drifts into a momentary sleep against his chest.

Agnes scoops Eleanor into her hands and settles into the rocking chair beside the window, loosening the flap on her nightgown. Eleanor fastens to Agnes's nipple and begins to suck, and Agnes weeps.

*the rift*

## mea

There is no trace of her.

Mea scours Eleanor's world: Paul and Agnes's house, Jack's house, the island, the sea, the forests. But Eleanor has disappeared like a spark from a guttering match.

*She's gone,* Mea says. *Where did she go?*

But Efah is absent. Mea turns and sweeps angrily through her fishbowl until she finds him, small and distant beyond her cage.

Efah is displeased at her interruption. *What do you want?*

*Something happened to her,* Mea says. *In her mother's dream.*

*Perhaps.*

*She's gone,* Mea says again. *Why don't you know where she is? Why don't you know what happened?*

*I can see many things,* Efah says. *But even I cannot see into the realm of dreams.*

*But she was just here! You saw her,* Mea accuses. *She could be hurt!*

*This is true.*

*She might be*—Mea chokes on the word—*dead.*

*Until she returns, I can do nothing for her.*

The fishbowl is wide and deep and black and empty around Mea. The unfamiliar sea that warmed her is entirely gone, leaving only the unsoothing black tide.

*This is what you wanted,* she says. *You were supposed to help her! You promised!*

*I promised nothing!* Efah thunders. He turns from Mea and vanishes into the dark, leaving her alone.

MEA FEELS AS if her own thread has snapped.

She slumps against the membrane. She feels Eleanor's absence from the world keenly, a ravenous hollow within her. She scans the river of time, visiting their shared past. There's Paul in the attic, painting tiny houses. There's Eleanor and Esmerelda in their infancy, asleep in side-by-side cribs. Agnes stands over them, the unease on her face strikingly clear to Mea now.

Eleanor can only be dead. Efah will not say so, but Mea feels it.

The river of time churns forward, less one precious soul, not at all concerned about such things.

Eleanor, pale like the moon, hair like a flickering campfire, eyes like dew-speckled spring leaves, is gone.

Mea's newest feeling in the dark rift: regret.

She winds time back, pausing to watch Esmerelda and Eleanor in the backyard, digging a hole beneath their father's watchful eye. He helps them turn the garden hose on their excavation, transforming it into a glorious, sludgy mud hole. They stomp happily, clapping fat little hands.

She can see Eleanor's thread, fat and bright like golden smoke, issuing into the sky, unseen by anyone but Mea. It is beautiful, full of life and promise. Esmerelda's own thread has not yet begun to darken. Behind the girls, Agnes sits on the porch, reading a magazine.

Her thread is already the color of charcoal, and it is fraying.

If any of them had known what was coming, would life have been different? Would her father have skipped the Florida seminar? Would her mother have tried harder to love her?

Mea prowls the time stream again, finding the moment of her own death. She watches it for the thousandth time, slowing it to watch her small body punch through the windshield, the glass shattering around her. She soars forward, blood trailing like ribbons from her skin, and falls unceremoniously to the wet shoulder of the road, already lifeless, her thread completely shredded.

She stares at her own broken body.

There is nothing left to change.

Eleanor is dead.

All is lost.

# *eleanor*

She is dead.

She knows she is.

The moment she saw her mother, a frail witch in a gutted wasteland, Eleanor knew that she was going to die. Even from such a height, she saw her mother's eyes burning. There was no question why. Her mother was furious with *her*.

In the dark calm of her death, she has plenty of time to consider this. She has known for years and years that her mother's grief was toxic. Each morning Eleanor would wake from sleep and stand in front of the mirror with her eyes closed, hoping that when she opened them, she would look like someone else. If she could only do that—if she could only strip Esmerelda's face from her own reflection—then maybe her mother would . . . What? Love her again?

Of course, that never happened. And each day that Eleanor grew older was another day that Esmerelda didn't. Eleanor at ten was a haunting reminder of a future that Esmerelda would never see.

Eleanor understood—had always understood—why her mother hated her so.

But she had never realized just how powerful that hatred really was.

Eleanor is dead, and her mother has killed her.

*  *  *

BEFORE, WHEN ELEANOR passed into the dream world, she left the fabric of her own world behind. Mea described it to her as like slipping into bed and hiding beneath a blanket—she exists, in a way, *beneath* the world. Between worlds.

*Dreams do not occupy any particular reality,* Efah had explained to Eleanor. *They are a fabricated world, wholly owned by their makers.*

The rules do not apply.

But Eleanor is dead. She has left no body in her own world. There are no remains for someone to stumble upon, rotting in the brush beside the highway. No bloodstains on the carpet to be investigated. Eleanor walked into her mother's bedroom and fell out of the world, a missing child, never to return.

The expression on her mother's face haunts her. She has never seen anger so raw, so unrestrained.

Eleanor has failed in her task.

Does Mea know? Neither Mea nor Efah can see into the dream worlds—they said as much when Eleanor was in the rift with them. How will they know she has failed, that she has been extinguished?

Eleanor considers this, then stops. She's clearly been evicted from her mother's strange valley of death.

So where is she?


IT MUST BE the rift.

She is surrounded by darkness and is formless, as she once was in the rift. She tests her theory and waves her hand—her hand which is not a hand at all, which is as shapeless as the dark itself—and gasps when a tendril of pink echoes into the dark.

It has to be the rift.

But if it is, where is Mea? Where is Efah?

Eleanor speaks into the great black.

*Hello?*

She waits uneasily for a reply, feeling that same dislocating sensation of millennia passing by while she lingers here, sightless, like a blind shrimp in an underground sea.

No Mea. No Efah.

Eleanor cannot even see the membrane of Mea's fishbowl. Either she's somewhere else, or she's so deep within the bowl that she can't see its glassy borders.

But she isn't entirely alone.

A black ocean rises around Eleanor in the rift, warm and dense and alive. It stirs around her, lifting her, bearing her up until she feels like a tiny ship bobbing atop a vast, fathomless sea.

*Hello?* Eleanor turns slowly on the invisible waters and says it again. *Who's there? Mea?*

Iridescent colors ripple like the aurora borealis upon the surface of the dark ocean. The sea is preternaturally calm.

*Hello?* Eleanor repeats.

Mea doesn't answer.

But the ocean does.

# mea

Mea is haunted by her failure.

Efah returns quietly.

*You feel because she is gone,* he says, attempting to explain her pain. His kindness is foreign to Mea.

*You are evil,* Mea accuses. *You did this to me, to us.*

But Efah isn't wrong. She is one half of two. This is how Eleanor must have felt when Esmerelda died. Mea spins time back and watches: Eleanor does not sleep for weeks after the accident. She hides, crying, under her bed, awake until exhaustion consumes her. Every morning she wakes and remembers that she is alone. Every morning, Esmerelda dies all over again.

Mea wishes she could breach the membrane and hold that little girl.

*You must let it go,* Efah says.

*I am not whole,* Mea laments. *Go away.*

Before Efah can respond, something happens: the rift begins to shimmer like the surface of a lake, as if dawn has come to the blackness.

Mea says, *What is this?*

Efah does not answer her, but she feels him tremble even through the membrane.

*You don't know,* Mea says in wonder. *Something is happening. You don't know what it is.*

*Silence!* Efah commands, but the colors that issue forth from him are wavery and full of static.

The brightness grows and grows, and the rift is consumed.


# *eleanor*

T he silence would be deafening, she thinks, if she had ears. Somewhere, Mea must be hiding. The ocean had put on quite a show when it returned Eleanor to Mea's cage.

Eleanor cannot blame her sister. The rift has lit up, as if a camera flash has imprinted upon her nonexistent eyes. Illuminated, the membrane of Mea's fishbowl is clearly visible, a milky, almost translucent egg that separates Mea from the greater void.

As Eleanor watches, the bright flash dwindles, slowly restoring the eternal night of this strange place. She feels as if she has just witnessed the universe before its birth.

Eleanor feels the hesitant ripple of Mea's voice cross the darkness.
*Hello?*

Eleanor says, *I'm back,* and then she is swallowed by Mea's embrace.


*WHERE WERE YOU?* Mea demands.

*I died,* Eleanor says.

*Impossible,* Efah interrupts, presenting himself.

Eleanor is startled to see that Efah is now within Mea's fishbowl, perhaps deposited here by the same ocean. This rattles Mea, who makes herself small and nestles into Eleanor's wispy form.

*I died,* Eleanor repeats.

*Not impossible that you died,* Efah says, confused. *Impossible that you are here.*

*Well, I am,* Eleanor says. *And so are you, Efah. In case you hadn't noticed.*

Efah ignores this.

*Dream worlds do not permit the passage of the dead,* he insists. *This has never happened.*

Eleanor would shrug if she had shoulders. *I'm here,* she says again. *Maybe you don't know everything. You don't frighten me.*

*Your mother,* Efah says. *Did you succeed?*

*I saw her,* Eleanor says. *She was a . . . sorceress. Her world was once the same as our father's world. When I arrived in his dream, it changed everything—his world was barren and covered in ice at first, but it . . . it was reborn. We walked and walked—*

*Where? Why?*

*We were walking home,* Eleanor says. *Back to our house in Anchor Bend. He wanted to go.*

*You did it,* Mea says. *You healed his wounds.*

Efah is confused. *He volunteered? He accompanied you willingly?*

*Yes,* Eleanor says.

*Then what happened?* Mea asks.

*We came upon a valley*, Eleanor continues. *It was familiar, and it took some time to figure out why, but I knew that place. I had been there before. But it looked different. My father's version of the valley was green and rich. It was beautiful. But the valley I had been to before was burning.*

*It cannot be*, Efah says.

*When you took me into my mother's dream, it was that same valley*, Eleanor says to Mea. *Except it had been . . . slaughtered. It was like a bomb had fallen right in the middle of it and destroyed everything, and she somehow survived it.*

*It is impossible*, Efah repeats. *Dream worlds cannot be shared.*

*Eleanor shares their dream worlds*, Mea argues. *You are wrong.*

*No. She pierces their dreams. She is an intruder.*

To Mea Eleanor says, *Dad thought I was you.*

Mea is delighted and unnerved. *Me?*

*What was your mother's response?* Efah interrupts.

Eleanor says, matter-of-factly, *My mother murdered me.*

*So you failed*, Efah says, and again there is a hint of pleasure in his tone.

Eleanor reluctantly agrees. *She didn't even seem to know who I was.*

*Now what do we do?* Mea asks Eleanor.

But Efah answers, resolute. *It is over. No more. You will not return.*

*It's not over*, Eleanor says firmly.

Efah is taken aback. *It is not for you to debate. You belong to the rift now. She belongs to me, too.*

*Like hell*, Eleanor says. *I'm going back to see her.*

*Impossible*, Efah declares. *Even if it were not, you could not return. You're no longer human, child. The rift is your home now. You and your dead sister, together for always. Mine.*

*No*, Mea protests. *No, you have to—*

*Quiet!* Efah erupts. *Remember, Mea child, that you have given up your human form. Do not weep for a life that you cannot return to.*

*Esmerelda can return*, Eleanor says. *With me.*

*Her name is Mea*, Efah says. *And what you say is impossible. Perhaps you do not understand.*

*I understand that you're a bully,* Eleanor says.

*It has never been done.*

*Maybe not,* Eleanor says, *but that doesn't mean it can never be done. I know the way back in.* She turns to Mea. *The path lies in the beasts of the field. I saw their eyes. I saw myself. I saw you. They aren't beasts at all—they're us. We may be dead here, but in Mom's nightmare, we live.*

Mea dances with light.

Eleanor turns back to Efah. *And in case you didn't notice, Efah, you're stuck in here with us now. You don't own anyone.*

Efah explodes into an immense, bulbous, tumorous shape, and hard spines of obsidian erupt from the bustle of his body, running Eleanor and Mea through. The spikes are terrifyingly hard, utterly cold, and Eleanor gasps. A red mist of panic surges from Mea.

*Mea!* Eleanor cries.

Mea gurgles and tries to form words, but the red mist only blooms wider around her.

*You have given up your body, Eleanor!* Efah thunders. *Take your death name!*

Eleanor stares up at Efah and his angry stalactites. The spike that pierces her has missed her center, but Mea has not been so fortunate. The red mist drifts across Eleanor's vision.

*Keep your fucking name!* she roars back. *We're going back, and Esmerelda is coming with us!*

*Us? We?* There is a hitch in Efah's question, and he throbs dangerously, each pulse stirring the beam that has impaled Mea. *You are not alone. Someone is there with you.*

Mea begins to shrivel, to disappear in the red cloud.

Eleanor says, *You aren't the only ancient soul in the rift, you son of a—*

*Give me your name!* Efah screams. *You must give it to me!*

*I will not!*

Beside Eleanor, Mea twitches and flails. The red mist deepens and becomes a sickly purple.

*How petulant you are,* a new voice answers, chidingly, motherly. *Who taught you to behave this way?*

Efah shudders. *Who are you? I do not see you!* he cries.

*A child's tantrum, thrown by a little dead child,* the new voice says. *I know you're afraid, little Patrick. Don't be.*

*Show yourself!* Efah rages in desperation.

The ocean, grand and blue and alive and steep, reveals itself, swelling up among them. Efah yelps in fear. They are all lifted in the black void, Mea's fishbowl filling to its highest height. Efah is dwarfed by the ocean's great power.

Eleanor goes to Mea, enfolding her sister's broken body in her own amorphous form.

Efah bellows in terror; as the ocean brushes against him, his cry weakens. To Eleanor it sounds like a newborn's wail.

The ocean's response is a melody of light and color, and Efah is subsumed by its waters.

*I am afraid!* Efah cries as he sinks. *Please!*

*Hush, my child.* The ocean takes Efah into itself, soothing him. To Eleanor and Mea it appears that Efah becomes a part of the sea. His shape dwindles, flaring orange within the ocean's depths, then fading away.

*Who are you?* Mea asks timidly.

*I am Eleanor, children,* the ocean sings. *And I will see my family restored.*

the valley

# the keeper

Trees stab into the sky, rushing out of the earth like the spines of a puffer fish, sprouting leaves and needles, forming forests. The keeper delights in her power. New birds are born among the branches, shaking themselves in the sun.

"Yes," the keeper says. Her shadow flits happily about her feet.

The restoration of her valley has been a long affair. She hardly remembers the fire that chewed through the woods, the black ash that fell from the sky. The mountains have been reassembled, pebble by pebble, and they stand glorious against the cloudless sky, smooth, fresh incisors planted in strong, earthy gums.

She filled the chasm with new rock that she formed in her palms from nothing, for the old rock had been melted away. She cooled the glowing magma with a breath, and the scent of death faded soon after. With her aid, the earth has closed up, a new foundation upon which the bright sky rests.

The keeper climbs to the top of the highest mountain. There she finds a shining, still puddle, a few inches deep. She kneels beside it and spies tiny minnows darting about within.

"Hello," she says.

Her shadow passes over the water, darkening it, and for the first time in centuries, she sees her reflection stare up at her. Her cheeks are pink, her hair long and rust-colored. Her eyes sparkle. She smiles, revealing orderly white teeth. She touches her tongue; it is smooth, clean, bearing no trace of the black sludge.

She stands up and lifts the hem of her new dress. When she is naked, she touches her small breasts, smooths her palms over her middle, and rests them on her belly, which is flat, unmarked.

The black stain is gone.

To her shadow she says, "Let's celebrate."

The keeper sits down on the edge of the flat cliff, points her slim finger at the far horizon, and begins to draw anew the creek that once ran through the meadow.

## eleanor

Now, the ocean commands. *She carves my path.*

Eleanor gathers Mea to herself. *Hold on,* she says, and Mea weakly clings to her. To the ocean: *We're ready, grandmother.*

The ocean illuminates the rift once more, revealing the great membrane that borders the fishbowl and the strange fissure that has opened within its borders. Then she rushes forward, sucking the girls along with her, and surges through.

Behind it, the fissure seals, leaving only the empty membrane and the dark of the rift behind.

## the keeper

The keeper pauses to appreciate the glittering new creek, then frowns as the valley falls dark. High above, black clouds appear from nowhere, blooming like dark roses.

"Where have you come from?" the keeper growls. "What is this?"

She lifts her hands to the sky and tries to wave the clouds aside. They do not move. They are as heavy as lead.

It begins to rain, instead, and a knot of dread forms in her throat.

"No," she says, steeling herself against the unwanted downpour. "No, no. No, this valley is *mine!*"

But the sun does not burn away the storm when she commands it.

She looks at her hands, then back up at the valley. A ferocious wind screams through the distant mountains, and her new trees tilt and snap. She can hear their trunks splitting even from here.

"*No!*" the keeper howls.

Her voice is drowned out by an ocean that sweeps over the mountain range, crumbling the newborn peaks to rubble. The keeper staggers back, falling to her knees.

Her shadow loops around her feet and climbs, dragging the keeper behind it, rushing to the summit of the nearest surviving mountain. The keeper stares in horror as the water rises steadily, frothy and dark, and finally abates only a few feet below the peak of the keeper's mountain, all that is left of her valley.

In minutes, everything she has rebuilt has been decimated.

Everything is gone.

FOR DAYS SHE remains cornered atop the mountain. For days she summons her strength and attempts to push the ocean away; again and again, she fails. The sun ignores her call. Inhospitable clouds meet the sea, dousing the keeper in fog. She cries, she roars, she collapses. Her valley is silent, drowned; it no longer calls out to her, no longer sings for her.

She can feel her lonely mountain rumble beneath her feet, threatened by the weight of the sea.

Soon, she thinks, it will crumble; soon she will sink beneath this black, alien ocean, and she will drown, and that will be the end of everything.

"Hopeless," she moans.

Her shadow does not respond, and when she looks down, she does not see it at all. She searches the summit of her mountain, but it is gone.

At last, the keeper has been abandoned.

She huddles naked in the rain and waits for the end.

Surely it comes.

IT DOES, MUCH sooner than she anticipated.

She hears a horrendous crack—feels it—and then the mountain calves beneath her, sliding violently into the ocean. The keeper wheels her arms against the sky, imagining the great crushing end that she will meet when she falls into the roiling sea, when the mountain grinds her bones into silt. She squeezes her eyes shut, crying out helplessly.

But she lands on something hard and strong, and the wind is knocked from her chest, and then she is climbing, *rising* high into the misty clouds. She fights for breath as the ocean falls away below her, and she looks down, surprised at her rescuers, who have borne her into the sky.

Her beasts have returned.

THE GREAT CREATURES wade ponderously through the gray sea. Their long necks crane high above the water, scraping the clouds, and the keeper, seasick, flattens herself upon the larger beast's crown, holding on for dear life. Below her, massive waves break over the beast's ridged back. The other beast, the smaller one, is submerged to the base of its neck.

Time seems to stretch. The sun never appears, though they climb higher and higher through the clouds. The world is dim and full of spray and salt.

"Am I in hell?" she asks.

The beast does not answer. She doesn't know if it hears her or understands.

It only keeps trudging through the sea.

SHE SLEEPS. THE beast's skull is wide and flat, almost as large as her mountaintop. Its skin is warm, pebbled. She does not know what has become of her shadow. She imagines it upon the sea, an oil slick of memories, lost forever.

The rain tastes like the sea, as though the sky is an ocean, strained through the dark clouds. She is thirsty.

"Where are we?" the keeper asks the beast. "Where are we going?"

The beast slows, then comes to a heavy stop. The smaller beast looks up at her, blinking its great dark eyes, tilting its head curiously at the keeper, who must seem like a parasite, a barnacle.

"Where are you taking me?" the keeper asks again.

The small beast only stares. Rain collects in a hollow on its head, and suddenly the keeper understands why the creature lumbers about, sickly and tired. One side of its head is caved in, the old skin scarred and thick where the wound has healed.

"What happened to you?" the keeper asks. "Who did that to you?"

The larger beast begins to sing, like a moon-size oboe. The keeper feels the song vibrate in her blood, the sound separating into pulses, into words she cannot understand.

And she remembers.

Rain.

A highway, a plane in the sky.

Remembers red hair.

Remembers every bit of glass that scissored through her own clothes and skin. The awful teeth of the windshield, the new mouth punched through it.

The cratered head of her own child upon the asphalt.

The keeper falls to her knees. A wail escapes from her throat.

The small beast blinks curiously at the keeper.

The large beast suddenly drops its head, quickly, and the keeper nearly slides into space. The wind rushes up about her as the creature's long neck sinks into the ocean, waves churning over its plated skin. It rests its head upon the sea. Gray water splashes up around the keeper's feet, and she retreats to the highest, boniest point of the beast's skull.

She huddles there, shaking. The wind is a saw blade, keening in her ears. Its cold teeth scrape against her bones.

"You'll kill me," the keeper moans. "Just kill me. You must hate me so."

But the beast only hums deeply, urgently, and the keeper forgets her words.

Before her, a woman emerges from the sea.

SHE IS LIKE a forgotten ship hauled to the surface. Great gushes of saltwater stream from her skin. She wears a simple black swimsuit and removes a tight black swimmer's cap to reveal short, dark hair. Her belly is round and full beneath the black suit. She removes clouded goggles; her eyes beneath are intensely green, flecked with orange. Her exposed skin is dotted with bits of kelp and debris.

The keeper retreats, scuttling backward on the beast's crown like a crab without a shell.

"Go away," she says. "Go away! Get out of here! Go!"

The strange woman stands at the water's edge, her bare toes flexing against the beast's knobby skin.

"Go away," the keeper repeats. She pounds her fist against the beast's skull, pleading with it. "Take me away! Take me away!"

The woman says, "They hear you, but they will not listen."

The keeper falls silent. She pulls her knees tightly against her chest. Without her shadow, without her powers, she feels exposed beneath the stranger's firm gaze.

The woman squints up at the rain and rests a hand on her belly.

"Rough out here," she says casually.

The keeper feels a pang of familiarity. She stares at the stranger, then says, hopefully, "I used to be able to fix it."

"No longer?" the woman asks.

The keeper shakes her head. "It has gone from me."

"May I sit?"

The keeper shrugs and looks away.

The woman in the swimsuit lowers herself with some difficulty, cradling her belly, splaying her legs wide for balance.

"Thank you," she says. She rubs her belly gently. "Someone's heavy today."

The keeper's hair has fallen over her eyes, and she leaves it there. The curtain it creates is calming. They sit quietly for a long time, the beasts swaying in place.

"What is the baby's name?" the keeper asks, hesitantly.

The woman laughs. "He wants to be called Efah."

The keeper pulls back her hair. "That is a bad name. A dark name."

"Yes," the woman agrees. "He does not know the difference yet. I think . . . Patrick. It was his sister's idea."

"Patrick," the keeper repeats. "It's nice."

For a time they are silent again. It is cold, and wind howls over the surface of the sea, kicking up a sharp mist.

The stranger says, "I miss the sun."

The keeper picks at her fingernails. "I miss it, too. I made it."

"You made the sun?" the woman asks.

The keeper nods.

"Well done," the woman says. "It was beautiful. I wish it would come back. It's cold today."

The keeper doesn't answer. She lets her hair fall over her eyes again.

"What can I call you?" the woman asks. "Do you have a name?"

The keeper ducks her head.

"Do you know your name?" the woman asks.

The keeper is ashamed. Only a short time ago she was a goddess, with the powers of life and death sizzling in her veins. She cast her enemy from the sky to the earth. But now she is small.

"I am good at names," the stranger says. "Perhaps I could give you one. You could use it, if you wanted to."

The keeper says, "I don't need a name."

"Everyone needs a name. What will I call you if you don't have a name?"

"You could go away," the keeper says. "You could leave me be."

The woman waves her hands at the sea that surrounds them both. "Where would I go?"

The keeper stands up suddenly and looks desperately around. She sees a narrow scrawl of dark land on the horizon, a beach that was not there before.

"There," she says. "Go there."


THE BEAST LIFTS its great neck into the sky. The clouds fall over its head, draping the two women in gauzy shadow. The keeper fixes her gaze on the woman's indistinct shape opposite her, ready to leap to her death if the woman should so much as scoot an inch in her direction.

The beasts crash through the sea like drifting continents. In their wake, the parted sea collapses together again in a storm of feather-white foam. Before them, the beach is a half-moon of fine black pebbles, yellow saw grass at its edges. The fog is deep and heavy, obscuring the land behind it. The keeper can see the hint of trees in the fog, trapped as if in great, dense spiderwebs. She notices a rickety pier stretching out from the land into the water, something tiny bobbing beside it.

The beasts stop in the deep water off the shoreline, and the large one dips its head. The pier is only a few feet away, just below the two women.

"We'll have to jump," the stranger says.

# *eleanor*

She does not know what she expected, but her new body is a comfortable fit. Her legs are skyscrapers, her body a small moon, her neck a graceful ribbon. The clouds are a fine mist against her broad face and hardened skin. When she dips her head into the sea, she is unperturbed by the salt that stings her eyes. She sees the sea floor, disturbed by her mass, clouds of dirt and mulch clotting her view.

She watches the two women climb down to the pier. The woman in the swimsuit struggles, and, miraculously, the keeper helps her.

Eleanor raises her head high into the sky and turns to her sister.

*How do you feel?* she asks.

Esmerelda leans against Eleanor and closes her eyes.

*Free,* she says, her voice heavy with relief. *Oh, free.*

*Let's leave them,* Eleanor says.

*Where should we go?*

Eleanor looks around. The beach—Splinter Beach, she realizes, recognizing it easily—appears to be the only part of Anchor Bend that exists here. A smoky haze of fog, like a fist of clouds, holds the beach like a knife blade. Beyond the mass of clouds, though, the sea stretches forever in every direction.

*To sea,* she says. *Come.*

Eleanor and Esmerelda slowly turn their giant bodies and head for the horizon. Eleanor thinks of the inflatable swimming pool her father bought, the one that she and Esmerelda splashed in, pretending they were great beasts who crossed oceans as if they were but puddles. Now the sea itself is a child's pool at their feet, and together they move slowly away from the shore.

*What if they need us?* Esmerelda asks.

Eleanor says, *I think our part is done.*


# the keeper

Tiny pebbles have settled into the cracks between the pier's heavy planks. The wood is black, old, saturated.

The larger of the beasts lifts its head into the clouds. A powerful wave surges over the keeper's feet, almost toppling her. The beast sings out as it ascends, and the keeper is startled when the smaller, wounded beast sings back. The beasts lean against each other as if conferring and then turn away from the beach.

Her heart aches as she watches them go.

"I'm glad you came with me," the stranger says. "I thought you were going to desert me."

The keeper had almost forgotten the woman was there. "I should have," she answers regretfully. "Where are we? I don't—"

"You know where we are."

Something twists inside the keeper's mind.

"Do I know you?" she asks.

The woman smiles. It's a lovely smile, very kind. "You know me."

"What is your name?"

Quietly, the woman says, "You know my name. But you knew me by some other name."

The keeper turns away. "Don't play games with me!"

She walks a few feet but does not hear the woman follow. When she looks back, the stranger is no longer there.

The keeper wheels about, then spots her. The woman is on

the beach. She is wearing a flannel housecoat now. As the keeper watches, the woman releases the sash and steps out of her clothing and walks naked and pregnant into the water.

THE WOMAN WADES for a bit, the water rising to the bottom of her curved belly, then her heavy breasts. She dives forward and begins to swim, slicing through the water with sure, powerful strokes. The keeper grips the railing and watches as the stranger swims right past her, as if she is following the beasts into open water. The creatures are too far away already, their long necks lost among the clouds, their bodies like islands in motion, crawling slowly across the horizon.

The keeper doesn't think the woman can catch up to them. Their wake is violent, and huge ocean swells lift the woman up and throw her backward, undoing her slow progress.

Something knocks loudly against the pier.

The keeper leans over the rail and sees the bobbing thing she had spied from the sky.

A rowboat.

SHE DRAWS THE oars, pushes them forward, draws them back again. The vessel bucks on the waves, but she fights. The boat is as old as the pier, its shallow bottom full of water, its oarlocks rotted and soft. When she pulls again on the oars, the locks come apart like damp bread, and the oars fall out of her hands. Water gushes into the rowboat.

The stranger swims farther away, a tiny speck now between the enormous swells.

Without thinking, the keeper abandons the boat and swims after her.

*    *    *

"I HOPED YOU would come," the woman says, surfacing in the trough of a wave.

A new wave slams down upon them both. When the keeper comes up, sputtering, the stranger is there, laughing through the pounding rain.

The keeper says, "You're a crazy person! You're with child!"

The woman laughs again, and another wave folds over them, pushing them under. When they come up again, the stranger says, "Are you ready for your name?"

The keeper spits salt water and shouts, "I don't need a name!"

A blue dash of lightning illuminates the sea around them. The beach is gone. The beasts are nowhere to be found. The women are alone in the hungry sea. It bats them around like toy boats.

"Everyone needs a name!" the stranger shouts.

Another wave thunders down, more violent than the others, and forces the two women below the surface, into the cold, dark veil of the sea. The keeper kicks against the current, and her body exhausts itself quickly. She could stop, she thinks. She could stop kicking, could let the sea have her. Farewell to her valley, her only home; to the beasts, her only family. Farewell to this fragile, nameless body.

*Everyone needs a name.*

The keeper fights, and though her muscles burn and her lungs threaten to cave in, she breaks the surface. Lightning skitters through the clouds above, illuminating the tossing waves. She looks around for the other woman, but she is alone. The world is nothing but water: tumbling from the sky, rising up from beneath. In the next flicker of lightning the keeper sees a towering wave, green-black and rushing furiously toward her. As it crests and begins to fold upon itself, the other woman appears in the distance, shaking the water out of her eyes and coughing mightily.

The keeper shouts, "Fine! What is my name, then? Tell me!"

The other woman smiles despite the storm that threatens them both, her face a beacon bobbing on the distant waves. With a thunderous roar the immense wave collapses upon them both. Faintly, the keeper hears the woman's shouted reply.

*"Agnes! Your name is Agnes."*

The water falls upon them both and swallows them up.


*I've made up my mind.*

*Oh? What about?*

*I'm going swimming with you today.*

*Is that so?*

*Yes, that's so. I'm going swimming in the ocean with you.*

*Look outside, dear. What about that?*

*Oh. It's raining.*

*That's right. What does that mean?*

*It means I'm not allowed.*

*That's right.*

*I have an idea!*

*What's your idea?*

*I'll just swim under the water instead.*

*There you go. It's all just water.*

*It's all just water.*


The memories threaten to drown her.

The breakfast nook her father built. Cinnamon toast. Rain beating against the windows.

Watching from the neighbor's porch as her parents left together for the beach. The expression of contentment on her mother's face when they returned.

Memories give rise to other memories, ones that would blind her if the dark sea had not already stolen her sight.

The ringing telephone.

Her father's frightened voice.

The crowd that gathered on the lawn to listen to the sheriff give them directions.

Her father, a wrecked ship upon the porch.

The misguided sense that her mother had only gone out for groceries and stayed away too long.

The horrible certainty that her mother was forever lost.

The television news, the interview with the man from the beach.

*She just walked right into the ocean and started swimming. I couldn't stop her. Was she pregnant? She looked pregnant.*

The lifeless house.

Her father's tormented sobs every night.

His stunned, slowed movements every day.

The memorial service, people in black, standing on the hateful beach.

Her mother, gone, forever gone.

Her mother.

*Eleanor.*


SOMETHING GRIPS AGNES'S hand in the depths. Her eyes fly open, the salt like knives. She can see a shadow in the water: the woman, pulling Agnes close. Though the light is almost entirely absent, Agnes recognizes the glint of the woman's eyes all the same.

Eleanor's eyes.

Her *mother's* eyes.

She is hurled into the past: She isn't allowed in the ocean. Only the hated city pool, never the vicious sea, never the—

But her mother squeezes Agnes's hand fiercely, and though her words are distorted, her voice thick with bubbles, she speaks.

*Come swimming with me!*

And it's as if all the years between then and now never happened, as if her mother never left her. Her grief, her anger, all of it falls away in the depths. If the sea that swallowed them both did not exist, Agnes would weep and invent it.

Eleanor pulls her daughter close, pressing her lips to her ear.

*Leaving you was my greatest mistake.*

*Mama!* Agnes cries, and the sea rushes into her mouth and throat and nose. Her eyes fly open, bright with panic.

*Don't be afraid,* Eleanor says. She wraps her arms around Agnes, forcing her words through the water, shouting them with her last breath. *I love you!*

Agnes wants to say it back, but her lungs are full. Her arms spasm at the sensation, locking around Eleanor, and together they sink, mother and daughter, clutching each other tightly, into the deep, silent, dark sea.

# *eleanor*

The end of the world sounds like rain.

Eleanor and Esmerelda stop trudging through the sea. The horizon, so far away for so long, seems to have drawn closer.

*It's the end, isn't it?* Esmerelda asks.

Eleanor cranes her enormous neck. Already the ocean spills over the edge of their mother's dream world. There is only darkness beyond, starless and black.

*I think it's more than that,* Eleanor says. *Look.*

Together the twins watch as the darkness presses forward, chewing at the boundaries of the world. The sea churns and boils. They turn and look around them and see the darkness marching inward from all directions. Far behind them, the beach of Anchor Bend crumples in gouts of sand and rock and spray.

*It's happening,* Esmerelda says. *The reset.*

Eleanor searches for her mother and grandmother but does not see them.

*They're gone,* she says. *Where did they go?*

Esmerelda looks at her sister. *Swimming. Together.*

*And Efah?*

*I feel sorry for him,* Esmerelda says. *To have been alone for so long in the dark, without his mother. He didn't know what happened to him.*

*This feels . . . right. Doesn't it?*

Esmerelda nods her dented head and says nothing.

They watch the dark walls of nothing as they squeeze like a hand around the sea. Geysers of water shoot into the sky, punching through the dark clouds, and for a faint moment the absent sun can be seen once more, gray and ghostlike, before the darkness collapses upon it from above.

*What will happen?* Eleanor asks.

*I don't know.*

*Will we wake up?*

*I don't know. Maybe.*

*When will it be? Will we remember?*

Esmerelda just looks at Eleanor. *I missed you,* she says. *I'm so sorry.*

Eleanor stretches her neck out, winding it around Esmerelda's. She presses her scaly head against her sister's.

*I missed you forever,* Eleanor says.

The sound of the disintegrating world fills their ears, thrums in their chests and hearts and necks. It is deafening. Eleanor feels as if her heart will explode from the drumbeat. The sea around her warms, and she closes her eyes and imagines their inflatable pool. Two giant monsters, stomping about.

*Bubbles,* Esmerelda says, and Eleanor laughs.

*I love you, Esmerelda.*

Esmerelda's dark, reptilian eyes shine.

*Will it hurt?* Eleanor asks.

*I don't know. Maybe.*

*I don't care if it does,* Eleanor says.

*Me, neither.*

The darkness falls upon them like a blanket, conjuring memories of the forts the sisters once built between their bedposts in the middle of the night, where they huddled with flashlights and laughed.

Eleanor draws close to Esmerelda now.

*Tell me it will be okay,* Eleanor whispers.

*It will,* Esmerelda answers.

Eleanor closes her eyes.

*It* will *be okay,* she thinks.

And for the first time in a very long time, it is.

*reset*

# gerry

Geraldine shakes the rain from her umbrella, coughing, then goes into the office, dropping the umbrella into a bucket and letting the glass door fall shut behind her.

"It's a mess out there," she says loudly.

She turns and looks through the door at the street. Water has gathered in the gutters and sweeps over the sidewalk. A green Oldsmobile glides by, sending up a gray fan of water.

"My, it's a mess out there," Gerry says again. Then, a little louder, "Paul?"

The light is on in Paul's office, but he isn't there. The desk is covered with paperwork and file folders grown dusty.

Gerry eyes the light switch. "Why are you on?"

She turns Paul's light off, then makes coffee, enough for two people, though she is no longer certain she'll see Paul today. He comes to the office less often now, and when he does, he calls home every hour to ask the hospice nurse how Agnes is doing. Gerry has told him to go home many times, to be close to his wife, who needs him more than the town's few home buyers.

"I'm almost done with the licensing exams," she told him the last time. "In a month you can just turn the keys over to me."

Paul hadn't laughed at her joke. Instead, he had wrapped her up in the tightest hug and thanked her and swept out the door.

The coffee pot beeps, and Gerry pours a cup, mixes in cream and a little sugar, and then stands in the middle of the room, watching the rain. It seems to fall harder now than it did just a few minutes before. She crosses to the window and tilts her head at the sky, which can only be described as utterly black. A wrinkle of lightning ricochets about without leaving the clouds, and a moment later the thunderclap rattles the windows so violently that she jumps and spills her coffee.

"Oh, darn it, darn it."

She goes for napkins. Another clap of thunder roars, angry enough to take the lights out, and Gerry stops where she is. The air is electric; it fairly hums. The hairs on her arms stand up.

"What the—," she says.

She turns around and looks at the windows, and her lips part. Across the street, beyond the storefronts, the sky seems to be falling upon the earth, a heavy soot curtain. She can feel the ground trembling beneath her, and everything on her desk begins to vibrate. The beige telephone clatters to the floor, its bell ringing out at the impact. A cup full of pencils.

In a rush, she *knows*.

"Ellie," Gerry whispers.

Something topples onto the floor and skids to a stop at her feet. Even in the darkness she knows what it is. She keeps only one photograph on her desk. Gerry lets the coffee cup fall out of her hand and bends over to pick up the frame. The loose glass pricks her finger, but she doesn't feel it.

The air is so charged with electricity that tiny blue sparks pop around her, all over the office.

In the flashes of blue, she sees her two uniformed boys staring up at her through the shattered glass. She feels her heart swell, feels a tingle of anticipation that she does not understand.

"My boys," Gerry whispers. "My sweet boys, I'm—"
*Reset.*

# *paul*

The box is marked ATTIC JUNK.

Paul sighs and shakes his head. "Aggie."

He sinks to the garage floor, crosses his legs, and pulls the box into his lap. It is dusty, the corners crumpled, the cardboard softened with age. It is long and wide, and the tape across its mouth has lost its tack. Some of the dust on the flaps has been smudged away, as though the box was opened recently.

Paul turns the flaps back and peers inside. He exhales softly.

The little model house is fractured on its foundation, thrown carelessly into the box. Some of the trees sprinkled on the fake grass have snapped. The mailbox at the end of the sidewalk is broken in half. He expected as much when he saw Agnes's scrawl on the box flaps. She had never truly understood his passion for the models. But she'd never resented it. The houses are broken because she resented *him*.

She still does, as far as he knows.

He stares at the broken house, and the memories swim up like dust motes. He closes his eyes and lets himself remember, something he doesn't allow often. Rainy afternoons; the cool, musty attic smell. Eleanor sitting on the stool beside him, kicking her small feet. Esmerelda somewhere else in the house, singing. Agnes—somewhere.

A knot rises in his throat, and he tries to swallow it.

How different his life has turned out than he expected. He is still a relatively young man, he knows. If he opened the garage door now and walked out into the street and never looked back—if he walked away, as Aggie's mother had done, except up the street instead of into the sea—he could start over. He could buy a small house in a small town, disappear into the world, stop picking at the scabs, wait for his scars to fade.

Would they? Would they fade?

His daughters are gone, one long in the ground, the other—the other—

He fumbles in his pocket and takes out a piece of paper. It is the same one he found on the chair in the living room. The one he had folded carefully.

The one that was unfolded when he came back to the house later.

Outside, a gust of wind batters the garage door, slinging rain against it in a wave. He stares at the windows in the garage door, startled by how dark it is. The wind is strong—how had he failed to notice it before?—and the garage door seems to bend inward the tiniest bit.

He gets up and presses a button on the wall, and the door starts to slide upward. He can see it clearly now—the door *is* bending, bending so much that it slips the chain and jams. There are now two or three feet of space between the door and the concrete floor, and rain whips through the gap like ocean spray, surprising him. He presses the button again, but the door groans and doesn't budge.

Wind roars through the gap, and the box of house parts inches backward, just a little. The paper note catches the gust and lifts into the air, and Paul reaches for it. He misses, and for a moment the paper seems to hang in the air, and his heart nearly stops.

The words on the paper are not his own.

The words are Eleanor's, penned in her careful, precise hand.

*I love you both.*

Tears spring to his eyes, and he flails about, snatching at the note, and then by some miracle he grabs it out of the air, and he turns it over and holds it up, and Eleanor's words are not there at all; the writing is his, and all it says is *Don't go.*

But she did go.

"Where?" he cries, and he kicks the cardboard box. It splits open like a sack of groceries, spilling tiny broken balsa twigs and green-capped tree trunks onto the floor. "Where did you go?"

The wind sweeps through the model parts, scattering building materials and hardened glue and pipe cleaners and cellophane. There are four tiny figures in the box that he had forgotten about—a grown man and woman and two smaller figures whose hair he had delicately painted red—and the wind lifts them from the pile and into the air, and he stares at them as they seem to hover, just like the note.

And he hears it then, in the strange quiet of that moment.

*Eeeeeeeeeeeeeeeeeeeeeee*—

"Aggie," he whispers, and he runs.

She is dead when he enters the room. The hospice nurse is not here today, and the respirator beside the bed is still, and the little machine on the wheeled cart blinks red lights and beeps in a single, unwavering pitch.

Paul stands at the foot of the bed, the bed he once slept in, the same bed where his daughters were conceived a thousand lifetimes ago, and stares at the small, frail body of his wife. Agnes is curled into a ball, and her arms are wrapped around her pillow, and, to his amazement, her lips are curled up in the slightest smile.

He forgets the years in that moment. The accusations and the blame and the bottles and the fights. He forgets the torment of it all, forgets even about his daughters, just for a second, and steps out of his shoes and climbs onto the bed. He lies down beside Agnes, not touching her, and just looks at her, taking her in. Her eyes are open but unfocused, her cheeks rose-colored, the way they haven't been in so long. Her hair is splayed across the pillow in a cloud, like a mermaid's in a gentle current.

He puts his palm on her cheek, the first time he has touched her tenderly in years. The warmth is fading from her skin. He can feel it going. He thinks that some of it might enter him, that she will carry on, a part of him.

He traces his fingertips over her skin and moves a wisp of hair away from her eyes. She stares through him. He can see himself in the dark of her eyes. He gently touches her eyes closed, and it is as if she is sleeping beside him, the way she once did. For the briefest moment he remembers his wife the way she was, the memories swimming up from the deep, turning colors in the air, uncovered for the first time in a decade. He remembers when she smiled at him, when she whispered with him in this very room as the light faded, her voice growing thick with sleep, but the words still coming.

*I wish I could hear your voice again,* Paul thinks. *I wish we could go back.*

The room grows dim, and outside the wind swells and roars like a dragon curling around the house, and as the world pulls itself apart around them, Paul dips his head forward and softly kisses Agnes's forehead. He rests his head against hers and breathes in, her scent alive and fresh for the first time in so very long.

He doesn't wonder what he will do next.

He lies there, in the dark, as her heat dissipates.

He is the last of his family. He has lost them all. He has been losing them for fifteen years.

A weight rises from him, and he feels as if he might float away. The blanket lifts into the air soundlessly, and blackness seeps into the room as the window breaks, and the curtains billow up to the ceiling, and the great storm consumes the Witt house.

*Reset.*

# jack

The rowboat is lashed to the pier beside the beach. By all rights it should not be—as best Jack can imagine, Eleanor must have left it on the shore of the island. He thinks back to the last time he saw her. She'd saved his life, somehow brought him home. And then she had left him again, left him forever. He remembers the last thing he said to her and wishes he had been thinking clearly enough to say so much more.

*Wait,* he had said.

*I love you,* he would have said. Should have said.

But she had taken his bicycle and disappeared.

Maybe not forever.

He has dreamed of her since her last disappearance. Dreamed that she has climbed into his room through the window, the rain at her heels, spattering his face and waking him. Dreamed that she slides into his bed and turns her back to him, dreams that he holds her and tells her he won't ever let go.

Dreams are all he has now.

He unties the bristly rope and climbs down into the boat. The old oars are gone, replaced with new ones. Plastic ones, or some kind of polycarbonate thing. Maybe someone found the boat on the island and brought it back. Maybe Eleanor didn't pull it far enough ashore, and it slipped out with the rising sea, and some fisherman recognized it and towed it home.

He never told a soul that Eleanor had taken it out that last day. Never told them that she'd rescued him from the cold sea. The news headlines had tapered off, and now only the occasional reminder appeared in the form of a new MISSING poster tacked to a street post. The red-haired girl was yesterday's news now.

He does not know what he expects to find on the island. The rational voice in his skull warns him off. *You'll only find a body, if anything,* that voice says to him. *She'll be washed up and decaying on the rocks. Do you really want to remember her that way?*

But part of him believes everything that she told him, crazy as it may have sounded. Part of him knows he will find only the abandoned shore of the island, the lonely cliff, the empty waters below.

And that is what he finds.

He pulls the boat ashore, tugging it as far up the rocks as he can. The rain falls harder now, and the ocean is gray and hard, and the sky is falling black against the horizon. He doesn't want to lose the boat.

*You won't need it again.*

The skeptical voice inside him is silent. The other voice—the one that believes everything Eleanor said—whispers to him gently.

*It can wash away. You won't need it.*

He climbs the path, the last mortal earth that Eleanor's feet would have touched. He takes his shoes off, clenches his toes against the grit and sand. He wants to feel every last thing that she did. He pulls his shirt over his head. The rain comes down hard, creating faint red welts where it hits his bare skin.

When he crests the last rise, he stops and exhales in awe.

The sky is a void. Utterly black, with misty, cottony edges that twist against the dying daylight.

*She was here,* the quiet voice says inside. *Whatever she left to do, it's done.*

"I know," Jack whispers back.

He sits on the edge of the cliff, bare feet and shoulders, and watches the black storm consume the sea. He is not afraid.

Jack takes a long, deep, slow breath and closes his eyes. When he opens them again, the storm is at his feet, the sea below resisting and thrashing against the relentless black.

Jack stares into its depths, wondering if Eleanor is on the other side, looking back at him.

"I never got to say it," he says to the storm as it advances. "I always loved you, Ellie. I always, always—"

*Reset.*

*epilogue*

*1963*

# eleanor

Eleanor sits in the breakfast nook and watches the rain fall.

The tree that her husband and daughter planted two summers ago bends sideways in the wind. If the storm gets much worse, the little tree will be uprooted by the stiff gale. The house is buffeted by it, rain lashing against the windows. The glass in the back door rattles. The attic groans like a ghost.

She imagines what Hob will say when he comes downstairs.

*Rough out there.*

It isn't that he wants to talk her out of the excursion, she knows. It's that he wishes she would concede defeat and agree to swim competitively again, to propel herself through the lanes of a regulation pool. He had been drawn to her winner's instinct, she thinks. He wanted to be responsible for awakening that part of her again. But that isn't the part of her she wishes to arouse from its slumber. She only wants to summon the other Eleanor, the one she discovers when the sea takes her into its quiet dark, embracing her.

Eleanor gently rubs her belly, thinking of the child inside—Patricia, Patrick. She imagines the day, only months away, when their house will not rest, day or night, when the cries of the new child will keep them from sleep.

"Seize the moment," she says to herself, almost startled by the sound of her voice in the quiet kitchen. She stares out at the rain, imagining how lovely it would feel to lie on her back in the mud of the softening yard while the rain patters on the earth, forming a rising lake around her body, overtaking her.

Having a child is a form of drowning, she thinks. Then she banishes the terrible thought, and, while her family sleeps, she gathers her housecoat around herself, takes Hob's keys, goes outside into the storm, and climbs into his old Ford.

THE SKY IS dim, the sun tucked away behind a curtain of clouds. Eleanor sits behind the wheel of the pickup, one hand resting on her small pregnant belly, one arm resting on the window. She pushes her fingers idly through the short hair at her temple, again and again.

Before her the ocean is wide and gray. Far beyond Huffnagle a black curtain moves away over the water, flickers of lightning echoing deep within its heavy mass. Behind it the ocean steams and hisses and sparks.

The rain hammers the old truck like a thousand thrown stones. She closes her eyes and listens.

SHE FALLS ASLEEP.

Not for long, only a few minutes.

When she opens her eyes again, the rain is thunderous, vicious.

Impulsively, she opens the door. The keys dangle in the ignition. She steps into the rain, tugging her housecoat more tightly around her swollen middle. The coat is drenched in only a moment and turns to lead.

Another pickup truck is parked at the far end of the beach lot. She doesn't recognize it, can barely make out the shape of a person behind the glass. The person lifts an arm. She raises her hand tentatively, then walks across the beach.

The beach stones are wet and black and almost sparkle in the pale dawn. She walks carefully, her feet bare. A tiny crab shuffles away from her, and two sandpipers pace by the water's edge, exploring. Hunting.

Eleanor walks close enough that the rising tide laps at her toes, the water slate-gray, grainy, depositing tongues of foam on the rocks. She stands there, feeling the sea tug at her, the rain like needles on her skin.

Hob means well. He only wants to see her happy, she knows. But she doesn't know what will make her happy. She only knows that she isn't.

The pier juts into the water, the rowboat tossed about on its lashing. If Hob were here, he would, of course, take them home. The waves pressed upon the beach, and Eleanor is, for only a moment, afraid of the water.

She thinks of the child in her belly, this strange new being who has imprisoned her, who has taken her away from her beloved sea. But she can't bring herself to resent the little one, who didn't ask to be here, imprisoned itself within Eleanor's middle.

And she thinks of Agnes: her knotted hair, soft, plump cheeks, dark eyes. Those dark, sad eyes. Too sad. That's Eleanor's fault; she is a lead weight, strung to the ankles of those who love her.

Behind her, she hears the stranger's truck door shut, and a voice calls down to her. She can't understand it and doesn't try.

Something gnaws at her, the same pain she feels when she hides in the closet, and Eleanor falls to her knees on the rough sand. Not the same pain, exactly, but a similar one, infinitely stronger than she is. A cry rises in her throat, and she is bewildered when it emerges from her mouth, unselfconscious and loud and animal-like. She presses her hands to her belly, as if trying to hold her body together, and then a wave strikes her like a beast, taking her down and sweeping over her and into her nose and mouth. The salt stings her eyes. The sea pulls at her, cold and heartless, and drags her over the sand, under the wave, toward its depths. The ocean she loves so dearly attacks, savagely, like the wild thing it has always been. Eleanor panics and cannot find her feet, and then she is be-neath the surface, staring up at concentric circles, raindrops upon the waves. It is oddly peaceful, she notices, and that's what scares her the most. She hadn't taken a breath before the ocean dragged her away, and she stupidly takes one now, and her lungs invite the sea into her body. She thinks of Agnes, those dark eyes, and she wishes more than anything she could scoop the little girl into her arms and—

Someone is there, then, a strong hand grasping hers.

## *agnes*

The carpet is soft beneath her feet.

She takes the stairs slowly, one at a time, planting each heel against the back of the previous riser, pretending she is a tiny child robot.

"Meep," she says, once for each stair. "Meep. Meep. Meep."

All the lights in the house are out, which is unusual. Normally when Agnes comes downstairs in the morning, the kitchen glows orange, and her father makes breakfast, and she asks for a sip of coffee, which her father always allows. She doesn't know why she asks. The coffee tastes like dirt. She knows the taste of dirt because of the time she fell in the garden and bit her tongue and cried, and some dirt got into her mouth, between her teeth, and she tasted it for hours.

She walks through the dining room, through the den. The house is still, as if she is the only person alive in the entire world. Agnes thinks that such a thing might scare any other child, but she's proud that she is not afraid. She sometimes thinks about what she might do if everybody else in the world disappeared. She would go to the grocery store, the one that her father takes her to on Saturday mornings, and she would get two pieces of candy from the bin, and she would have a Coca-Cola, and then she would take a loaf of bread and go to the pond behind the school and feed the mallards.

But this is not that day.

Her father sits quietly in the breakfast nook, a cup of coffee steaming between his palms.

She doesn't say anything for a moment, just watches him. He stares out the window at the falling rain, his shoulders slumped, his posture bowed. Her father has always seemed older to her than her mother, as if he had somehow seen more of the world, had more stories to tell. But if he did, they were bottled up inside him. Now and then one leaked out, and he told her wonderful tales of knights and wizards and sometimes about a queen named Agnes.

He looks over and sees her then. "Well, hello there," he says.

"Why is it dark?" Agnes asks.

"Power's out," he says.

"Can you turn it on?"

Her father shakes his head. "Whole block, at least. Maybe the town."

"Good," Agnes says.

"You like it dark like this?"

She climbs up into her mother's seat, opposite him. "I like the way it feels," she says.

"How does it feel?" he asks.

"Private," she says.

"Private, huh?" he says, and he sips his coffee. "I can see that."

Agnes swings her feet, too short to touch the floor.

"I'm in Mama's seat," she says.

"It's a good seat. Probably the best one."

"I like sitting here. I wish she was here, too. Where is she?"

"Truck's gone," her father says. "She probably had to go to the store. Power's probably out there, too."

Agnes considers this, then shifts her attention to her father's cup.

"May I have a sip?" she asks.

Her father shakes his head. "Maybe not," he says. "Coffee's kind of a grown-up drink."

"You always let me before."

"You sure you're big enough?"

She nods vigorously, and he pushes the cup across the table. She slurps noisily without lifting it, and Hob laughs when her nose wrinkles up.

"When do you think she'll be home?" Agnes asks.

"When do *you* think she'll be home?"

Agnes sticks her tongue out and thinks. "In one minute," she says. "When do *you* think?"

Her father sips his coffee again, then screws up his face in thought. Finally he says, "Now."

The power returns abruptly. The kitchen glows golden and warm like a painting. The back door swings open. Agnes gasps, and both she and Hob turn to look at the open door.

"Mama!" Agnes chirps brightly. "Come sit with me."

"Come inside!" Hob says, laughing. "You'll let the rain in!"

Eleanor stands dripping in the doorway, her eyes stung red, sand fixed in the crevices of her nose and ears. She holds her round belly with one hand. Behind her the cloudless sky blooms pink and gold, setting the watery lawn and trees afire.

"Don't worry, Hob," Eleanor says. She smiles at her little Agnes, and her voice breaks. "It stopped."

# ACKNOWLEDGMENTS

I began writing *Eleanor* in the fall of 2001, and completed it in the spring of 2015. It was composed in many different places, among them Reno, Nevada (where it began), and Portland, Oregon (where it came to an end). Over the course of those fourteen years, many people have, in one way or another, contributed to this novel. I am certain to forget as many here as I remember, and for that I apologize in advance.

Thanks to my editors at Crown, Zachary Wagman and Hilary Rubin Teeman, for seeing *Eleanor*'s potential, and for making it an even better novel; I'm grateful to have worked with these two great talents on this book. Thanks as well to Lindsay Sagnette and the many others at Crown who were involved in *Eleanor*'s publication: Sarah Bedingfield, Aislinn Belton, Terry Deal, Lauren Dong, Rose Fox, Kayleigh George, Leslie Kazanjian, Lauren Kuhn, Michael Morris, and Heather Williamson. Thank you all! I am also thrilled and very moved by the enthusiasm of Kate Elton and Natasha Bardon at HarperCollins UK, Vivian Wyler at Editora Rocco, and everyone at Heyne Verlag.

I am extraordinarily grateful to Seth Fishman for all of his hard work—and magic—on behalf of this novel; also to Rebecca Gardner, Will Roberts, Andy Kifer, and everyone else at the Gernert Company. Additionally, I owe a tremendous debt to John Joseph Adams and Hugh Howey for their advice, mentorship, kindnesses, and friendship; they are both, in their ways, responsible for paving much of my own path.

*Eleanor* was originally self-published in the summer of 2014. I am grateful for the support of many people who helped make that initial publication possible: David Gatewood, the novel's first editor, whose sure hand and keen eye saved *Eleanor* from a doorstop's fate; and Krista Slavin, who proofread the novel and rescued it from an especially cataclysmic error. I'm further grateful to my friends at Amazon and CreateSpace for their championing of this novel: Christopher Carlin, Caroline Carr, Genevieve Cushing, Serra Hagedorn, Todd Hollenbeck, Lauren McCullough, Brian Mitchell, Philip Patrick, and Russell Douglas Powell. While I designed *Eleanor*'s original book cover myself, the very talented Ian Koviak and Alan Hebel of the Book Designers were responsible for its beautiful interior, which stood head and shoulders above anything I could have done. I'm also thankful for the support of my friends at Powell's City of Books, who went out of their way to make this independent author feel welcome on their shelves; special gratitude to Shannon Bowman-Sarkisian, Peter Honigstock, and Renee James. My deepest thanks to the many readers who gave their time to the novel's early drafts and offered their valuable insights, and who have enthusiastically championed this story: David Adams, Eamon Ambrose, Alan Bester, Rita Bodiford, Robert Box, David Bruns, Idella Burmester, Nancy Butler, John Capps, Terry Chase, Joshua Cooper, Carlos Correa, Shanna Cushing, Kathy Czarnecki, W. J. Davies, Diego de los Santos, Glen Dickinson, Ron Dillon, Annette Drake, Michael Engard, Patrice Fitzgerald, Jason Fuhrman, Heidi Garrett, Hollie Gerk, Sheryl Ginsberg, Max Handelman, Tim Harding, John Hindmarsh, Tyler Hiteshew, Kevin Hopper, CeeCee James, Elizabeth Kay, Kari Kilgore, Samantha Kluth, Helen Kuhnsman, Jen Leigh, Richard Leslie, Jason Lockwood, Candy Lowd, Linda Maepa, Roxanne Masters, Marla Mazalan, Gretchen McNeely, Anthony Meek, Sarah Mensinga, Jordan Murphy, Dian Napier, Angela Neff, Elizabeth Phillips, Christine Reyes, Thomas Robins,

Cynthia Rose, Mr. and Mrs. Josh Rosen, Stefano Scaglione, Terry Schulze, Jachin Sheehy, Elizabeth Shelton, Andy Sherwood, Keith Skillin, Amelia Smith, Jeremy Smith, Lesley Smith, Janet Stanley, Jed Sutter, Will Swardstrom, Matt Thyer, Birdie Tracy, Scott Tracy, Nicole Tuttle, David Uebel, Sarana VerLin-Myers, Don Walker, Charles Wertz, Joanna Wilbur, Terry Wilson, Eve Wittenmeyer, Brian Zinnbauer, Ken Zufall, and a gentleman named Paul who never told me his last name.

In the many years preceding any publication of this novel, and including its brief stint as an independent webcomic, many friends shared encouragement, feedback, and support, among them Brian Amey, Katherine Arline, Garrett Braun, Lisa Braun, Bryan Chaffe, Mark Chester, Tony D'Amato, Jason Fuhrman, Lila Guzman, Michelle Herrera, Tyler Hiteshew, Michael Howard, Alexander Mahernia, Lindsay Manetta, Sarah Mensinga, Mark Nguyen, Pam Nguyen, Jacques Nyemb, Gabriel Rodriguez, Robert James Russell, Carrie Sundra, Hank Wethington, and Jesse Young. Very special thanks to Cat Bordhi, whose knitting retreat in the San Juan Islands served as one of my most creative homes-away-from-home. I am also thankful for the warmth of the Portland writing community and the generosity and knowledge of the Codex Writers' Group. I have found many friends and mentors among both.

I am likewise obliged to pay my respects to the late Carl Sagan, whose Eleanor deeply inspired my own.

My parents, Mike and Brenda Gurley, bought into a resort time-share program years ago, and thus enabled me to take many writing retreats over the years. More important, they taught me to love books when I was very young; they are voracious, lifelong readers, and I hope they know that all of this is their fault. (Happy birthday, Dad!) My sister, Elizabeth, was one of this novel's earliest readers and is a fine writer herself. My grandmother, Barbara Gurley, a lifelong educator, and my great-uncle, Henry Gurley, a poet and novelist, also read early drafts of this story and provided encouragement. Very special thanks to my mother-in-law, Akiko Sakai, who is perhaps one of the most positive and supportive people I know. And my heartfelt gratitude to Janice Gruhn, who shaped my love for storytelling when I was a student in her high school writing class, just beginning to dream.

Finally, and by far most important, I owe my greatest debt to my wife, Felicia—who knew, even when I did not, that I would complete this novel one day and that it would not be the last meaningful thing I would ever write—and to my daughter, Emma, who I hope someday will be even a fraction as proud of her father as I am of her. I love you both.